SON OF MAN

Yi Mun-yol

Son of Man

A NOVEL

TRANSLATED BY
BROTHER ANTHONY

 DALKEY ARCHIVE PRESS

Originally published in Korean as *Saramui adeul* by Mineusma in 1979.
Copyright ©1979, Yi Mun-yol
Translation copyright ©2015, Brother Anthony

First edition, 2015

Library of Congress Cataloging-in-Publication Data
Yi, Mun-yol, 1948-
  [Saram ui adul. English]
  Son of man : a novel / by Yi Mun-yol ; translated by
Brother Anthony of Taize. -- First edition.
      pages cm
  ISBN 978-1-62897-119-4 (pbk. : alk. paper)
  1. Seminarians--Fiction. 2. Spiritual life--Fiction. 3.
Murder--Investigation--Fiction. I. Title.
  PL992.9.M83S2813 2015
  895.73'4--dc23

                              2015030141

            LIBRARY OF KOREAN LITERATURE

ILLINOIS ARTS COUNCIL AGENCY   ○ **LTI Korea**
Literature Translation Institute of Korea

Partially funded by the Illinois Arts Council, a state agency
The translation of this novel was supported by a grant from the Daesan
Foundation Published in collaboration with the Literature Translation
Institute of Korea
Dalkey Archive Press publications are, in part, made possible through the
support of the University of Houston-Victoria and its program in creative
writing, publishing, and translation. www.uhv.edu/asa/

Dalkey Archive Press
Victoria, TX / Dublin / London
www.dalkeyarchive.com

Cover: design and composition by Mikhail Iliatov
Printed on permanent/durable acid-free paper

Introduction

Brother Anthony

Readers outside of Korea may well find certain aspects of this novel difficult and a few brief introductory remarks should be made. In 1945, with the end of the Pacific War, the Korean peninsula was abruptly freed from the Japanese yoke under which it had suffered humiliation since 1910, when it was forcibly annexed by Japan. The country was not prepared for this sudden change, and Korean society found itself deeply divided over the directions in which the newly independent land should develop. Moreover, the wartime allies had agreed that during a transition period, the move to independent nationhood should be overseen by the Soviet Union in the portion of Korea lying north of the 38th parallel, while the United States would take similar responsibility for the regions to the south of it. Almost at once, North Korea began to be controlled by anti-Japanese and pro-socialist (or communist) forces; many people who had collaborated with the Japanese fled south, as did many of the Protestant Christians. In what was to become South Korea, violence flared as Syngman Rhee, supported by the US, moved to take control and establish a society that would allow capitalism to flourish freely. This division caused intense conflicts that led finally to the Korean War.

Yi Mun-yol was born in May 1948. His father, like many Korean intellectuals of the time, was an idealist who inclined to favor socialism, if not outright communism. The writer's life was deeply affected by his father's decision to support the North Korean regime, and move north soon after the start of the Korean War in late June, 1950, leaving his wife and young children in Seoul. He had no idea, of course, of the absolute division that would soon be established between North and South. Yi Mun-yol therefore grew up not only in great poverty, but also stigmatized and penalized as the son of a "traitor." Unable even to complete regular university studies, he was very largely an "autodidact" who studied the things that interested him on his own. He soon turned to writing fiction. In 1979 his novella *Saehagok* (Song under a Border Fortress) won the prestigious *Dong-A Ilbo* Literary Award, and this marked the beginning of his career as an established writer. In the same year, his *Saram eui adeul* (Son of Man) was published and received the Today's Writer Award. The novel was the young author's first full-length work of fiction, and Yi Mun-yol was only 31 years old at the time. It was considerably revised and expanded in the years that followed, and became such an iconic work among Korean students that it has sold some two million copies.

The secret of its appeal, which will probably not be obvious to readers from other countries and cultures, should mainly be sought in the way it embodies criticism of the particular forms and directions taken by Protestant Christianity in South Korea after the Korean War. There were years when many pastors declared that the country was about to become entirely Christian, causing deep anxiety among those who saw the corruption of so many undereducated churchmen who used their spiritual authority to demand more and more money from their often impoverished flocks. Yi Mun-yol, in particular, had grown up in a family that cherished the Confucian culture of old Korea—a culture mainly concerned with social values, hostile to supernatural religion and clericalism of all kinds.

The resulting personal quest, in which he tried to understand the value of the different great religions of the world and the place of Christianity among them, resulted in the novel *Son of Man*. It is a double novel. On a primary level, it tells the story of a police officer, Sergeant Nam, trying to find out who murdered Min Yoseop, a former student at a small theological seminary who had quit the church and set off in strange directions years before. As he reconstructs Min's career, visiting those who knew him, Sergeant Nam is given the handwritten text of a long novel Min wrote years before. Sections of this novel are inserted into the account of Sergeant Nam's travels, as he slowly reads through it in quest of clues to help him find the killer and also the reason for the crime.

It is this second novel that forms the true core and essential "message" of *Son of Man*. Yi Mun-yol starts by using the European legend of the Wandering Jew, in which a Jew named Ahasuerus refuses to allow Jesus to rest as he is on his way to be crucified, and as a result finds himself condemned to endless wandering, never aging, unable to die. Yi Mun-yol (or in the fiction, Min Yoseop) develops this figure, making him a contemporary of Jesus and a radical critic of the way the Jewish God (Yahweh) is represented in the Old Testament. The narrative has two main parts; first, the young Ahasuerus travels across the ancient world with its many cults and myths in search of a true understanding of the divine, from Judea to Egypt, to Mesopotamia and India, finally returning to Judea by way of Rome and ancient Greek philosophy. He then returns to his homeland, where he encounters a Great Spirit who reveals himself to him in the desert. In this same desert he then meets the fasting Jesus, with whom he begins a series of hostile discussions centered on human freedom and divine injustice; the debate between Ahasuerus and Jesus only ends with the death of Jesus on the cross, after which Ahasuerus finds himself free to pursue his eternal quest for the truth about God.

At the end of the detective novel, Sergeant Nam finds the home of the former disciple of Min, and in pages he finds there he is able at last to read the "revelation" given to Ahasuerus by the Great Spirit. This text represents the climax of the "spiritual" quest of Min Yoseop and his disciple, and (presumably) the central thesis of the story of Ahasuerus. In the final pages we discover the reasons that led Min Yoseop's only follower and disciple to kill his master.

The main question facing the reader of *Son of Man* will probably be what Yi Mun-yol was trying to show by writing it. Obviously the novel-in-the-novel is the result of extensive research into comparative mythology and religion. It is at times overloaded with lists of gods and their attributes, all of which are finally rejected by Ahasuerus and the fictional narrator (Min Yoseop). For Sergeant

Nam, the main question is the extent to which Ahasuerus represents Min Yoseop; for us, the main question is where Yi Mun-yol stands in relation to Ahasuerus and Min Yoseop. Of course, the more important question must surely be where the individual reader stands in relation to all the figures in all the stories making up this complex narrative. There is no satisfactory answer provided by the novel to the questions it raises about gods and humans. And that is as it should be. Immensely thoughtful, *Son of Man* is certainly a masterly construction, but it refuses absolutely to provide answers to questions that each individual has to think about alone, over a whole lifetime.

Translator's Note

The translation of this novel presented considerable difficulties, and I was assisted throughout the preparation of the first draft by the late Professor Chung Chong-hwa (1934-2009), emeritus professor of Korea University, with whom I previously translated Yi Mun-yol's much acclaimed novel *The Poet*. I am grateful for all his help. The text published here has been extensively revised since his death. The text translated is that of the 4th edition, which was first published on June 15, 2004. The author has made many small changes—deletions, modifications and additions—to the text of the 3rd (1993) edition.

After consulting with the author, it was decided to eliminate the 335 footnotes. Such an apparatus is not a usual feature of works of fiction published in English. In many cases, the information has been inserted into the body of the text, especially in the lists of gods and brief accounts of polytheistic mythology and other religious details. In many other cases, the information offered seemed not to be needed for a full understanding of the novel.

With the author's agreement, the text contained on pages 211–219 of the Korean, which presents a series of notes on the life of Zoroaster and the main teachings of Zoroastrianism, has been omitted. This section interrupts the flow of the narrative unnecessarily, and gives an over-detailed account of a religion that is not destined to play any particularly significant role in the novel as a whole. The same decision was taken by the translators of the French version.

About the Author

The writer YI MUN-YOL was born in Seoul in 1948 and given the name Yi Yeol. Early in the Korean War, the writer's father, a firm supporter of the communist cause, left his family in Seoul and went to North Korea. Fleeing war-torn Seoul, the mother first took her five children back to her own home in North Gyeongsang Province, before moving to the home of her husband's family in Yeongyang-gun in the same province. The writer's childhood was marked by a number of moves to different localities. He began primary school in Andong in 1953, but in 1965 poverty obliged him to drop out of high school. He moved to Busan and spent three years in hardship there before falling seriously ill in 1967. After this, in 1968 he was admitted to study Korean in the College of Education in Seoul National University and resolved to become a writer. In 1970 he was forced to quit university for financial reasons.

He began to write stories and in 1977, his short story *Najarei reul asimnikka?* (*Do you know Najarei?*) received an honorable mention in the literary awards given by the Daegu Maeil Sinmun; he now began to use the name Yi Mun-yol. In 1979 his novella *Saehagok* (*Song Under a Border Fortress*) won the prestigious Donga Ilbo Literary Award, and this marks the beginning of his career as an established writer. In the same year, his first major full-length work, *Saram eui adeul* (*Son of Man*) received the Today's Writer Award.

His next published work, *Cheolmeun nal eui chosang* (*Portrait of Youthful Days*), was composed of three novellas forming an extended narrative of a youthful search for identity and value in an almost meaningless world. In 1982, the novella *Geumsijo* (*Bird with Golden Wings*) received the Dongin Literary Award. In 1983, the novel *Hwangje reul uihayeo* (*For the Emperor*) received a Republic of Korea Literary Award. Returning from a visit to Taiwan, he brought with him a Chinese text of the classic *Tale of the Three Kingdoms* which served as the basis for his own version of the story in Korean. In the following years this became enormously popular and still remains one of the author's best-selling works.

In late 1984, he moved to Seoul and his novel *Yeongungsidae* (*Heroic Age*) received the main prize in the Jungang munhwa daesang awards. In 1986, he moved into a house in the countryside outside of Seoul and in 1987 his *Urideul eui ilgeureojin yeongung* (*Our Twisted Hero*) received the Isang Literary Award. In 1991, he published his much acclaimed novel *Si-in* (*The Poet*) based on the life of the 19th-century poet popularly known as Kim Sakkat. In 1992 his novella *Siin gwa doduk* (*Poet and thief*, integrated into *The Poet soon after*) was awarded the Hyeondae Munhaksang and in the same year he received the Republic of Korea Cultural Award. His novel *Seontaek* (*Choice*), published in 1997, provoked a strong controversy in which he was accused of antifeminist attitudes, on account of the way he portrayed the life of women in Joseon Korea. He received the 1998 21st Century Literary Award for *Jeonya hogeun sidaeeuŭi majimak bam* (*The Night Before or the Last Night of This Era*) and the 1999 the Ho-am Arts Prize for *Byeon-gyeong* (*Borderline*). Since 1999 has been running the Buak Literary Center, a creative writing school he established. He published *Aga* (*Song of Songs*) in 2000.

Son of Man

1

Rain falling onto thick layers of accumulated dust had left the windows of the criminal investigations office so mottled that they were virtually opaque. Beyond them, the dim outlines of roofs could be seen, huddled grimly beneath a lowering city sky. When the Dongbu Police Station had first moved here, some two years before, the location had been nothing more than a hill on the city outskirts, in an area recently zoned for development. Then houses had begun to spring up, and now the area was completely built over. As he contemplated the brightly colored roofs, aligned in a variety of shapes that seemed to hint at their owners' pretentiousness, or their vain fondness for western things, Sergeant Nam fell into the state of melancholy that had recently become habitual for him. The fact that he owned no home of his own among all those houses stretching before his eyes, where his wife and children might live at ease, kindled in him a deep sense of inadequacy.

As he recalled the two little rented rooms he would return to after work, unless something unexpected occurred, Sergeant Nam glumly reviewed his career, over which the sense of impending failure darkly loomed. Nam Gyeongho was his name, born in 1945. His parents had been ordinary, run-of-the-mill folk; however, they too had experienced the almost universal poverty of the 1950s, and his childhood had been subject to the same degree of misery that other children of his age had had to endure. His middle and high school years, spent in a small country town, had left no memories, sad or happy. As he neared the end of his high school education, his parents' enthusiasm for furthering his education was growing out of proportion to their limited financial resources. This took him away from their small town and turned him into a student enrolled in evening classes at a second-rate university in this city, following a course of study that he would eventually give up, halfway through.

Even after dropping out of university, he still kept trying to better himself, during the early years at least. The university he attended was so mediocre that it was even hard for him to get a part-time tutoring job; but still, he had been studying law. At one point he shut himself up in a room in a rural temple for several months with the intention of preparing for the civil service exam. Another time, he suddenly became fascinated by writing, burying himself under reams of manuscripts. Not one of his works ever got beyond the preliminary selection process, but he wrote enough in the course of six months to submit something to every newspaper that ran any kind of New Year literary contest. That intense passion for literature was perhaps only a perverse way of dealing with the frustration he had felt when he gave up all hope of ever passing the civil service exam.

Poverty had never allowed him to complete anything he undertook, as with his university studies. All the while, his elderly parents and his younger siblings, who had no one else to look to for support, were waiting. But they were all gone now. His parents had died, one after the other, before he had even managed to escape from the single room they all shared. His older sister had left home suddenly, fed up with being poor, and had given no news for the last nine years. Supporting his younger sister had made the start of his own married life difficult; after graduating from commercial high school, she married a colleague who had worked at the same bank as her some two years before. Nam's younger brother had studied at a technical college, and as soon as he finished his military service, the previous year, he went to the Middle East to work as a technician for construction equipment. It was for their sake that he had joined the ranks of the job seekers, who were having a hard time of it in those days. Taking the easiest path, he joined the police, where he had settled down. Promotion was neither rapid nor slow compared to the hard work he put in; the job afforded neither satisfaction nor regret, but his eight years in the criminal investigations unit had passed by quickly, the years speeding by like days.

"So why did you kick the young lady on the backside as she passed, eh? Why?"

Sergeant Nam came to himself at the abrupt sound of someone shouting in a shrill voice, which penetrated his mind as if it
had ruptured his eardrums. It was Detective Kim, who was sitting
at the desk next to his. He was three or four years younger than
Sergeant Nam, but he had joined the police earlier and had a few
years' seniority on Nam in the crime squad. Judging by what he
had just overheard, it seemed that he was taking down a statement
for some kind of assault case, but on closer examination he was
looking thoroughly rattled.

"Because of those damned leather boots . . ."

The suspect replied imperturbably, as if to show that Detective Kim's shouting did not impress him. He was a youngish man,
about twenty-four or -five perhaps, with a completely shaved head.
If he hadn't attracted Sergeant Nam's attention before, it must have
been because he had been brought in much too quietly for someone guilty of an assault.

"What about her leather boots?" Detective Kim asked, as if
lost for words, after glancing in the direction the young man had
indicated, pursing his lips. The long, slender legs of the victim,
who was still crying to herself, were sheathed in brown boots high
enough to hide her knees.

"Because they're too tall."

"Are you drunk?"

Detective Kim burst out so loudly, as if unable to put up with the
insolent way the young man was addressing him, that everyone in
the office turned to look. But the youth did not so much as flinch.

"Not in the least."

"This guy must be completely mad."

At that, someone sniggered in a corner. Detective Kim turned and
threw a furious glance in that direction, then went back to questioning the young man, seemingly trying to provoke a quarrel.

"So you kick some girl on the backside because you reckon her
boots are a bit too tall?"

It was rather obscene, but from time to time, when Sergeant
Nam encountered a woman wearing high leather boots, he felt a
powerful desire to strip off all her clothing, leaving only her boots,

and have his way with her. The fantasy arose less from the generally perverted desires of a man in his mid-thirties than from a particular pornographic movie that had been confiscated the previous autumn. Under the pretext of making an investigation, one of the staff who knew how to use a video machine had played it in a corner of the office, and in it the women never removed their boots or stockings while things were being done to them. Oddly, he had found that much more titillating than sex with a completely naked woman.

"So you just felt like kicking her?"

Sensing something slightly strange, Sergeant Nam began to scrutinize the accused youth more closely. At first glance, he looked to be a dim, stubborn kind of fellow, but the deep furrows between his eyebrows and the dark shadows around his eyes suggested intelligence. He sensed a kind of detachment in his eyes, which were directed vacantly at a spot of bare plaster in a corner of the room. That was not something you found in professional criminals, with all their bluff and bluster. Then, going on to examine his clothes, it was different again. A military jacket of a kind no one now wore, at least not for fashion, dyed black and with sleeves shiny at the cuffs from use and accumulated dirt, accompanied by trousers made of coarse tan corduroy, and plastic shoes so covered in dust it was impossible to distinguish their color. His dress was so completely at odds with his face, it was almost as if he had deliberately disguised himself.

"One pair of boots like that . . . could keep several pairs . . . of frozen feet warm. Just beside the road where that woman was passing . . . a kid was begging, wearing nothing but rubber slippers on her bare feet, lying on the ground, shivering . . ."

The young man began to speak haltingly, as if unsure of himself. Still crying, the girl was losing her patience and fired back a reply: "Is it my fault if a kid's begging?"

"Of course, it might not be you personally. It might be your rotten dad who bought you such expensive leather boots but never gave so much as a penny to someone starving right beside him, or it could be your old boyfriend, crazy about your pussy. Anyway, it makes no difference. The fact remains that a kid was shivering with bare feet because you were using up all that leather."

The young man spoke without once raising his eyes to look at the girl, as if to show that it annoyed him to reply but he was doing it as a special favor. To Sergeant Nam, he seemed like someone who had committed a crime of conviction, but more than that, he thought he must be either crazy or deliberately trying to irritate the person he was addressing. Growing increasingly angry, Detective Kim rebuked him on her behalf.

"Shut up! You idiot! I can't believe what I'm hearing. Who asked you to interfere in things like that?"

"I did it because nobody else was interfering."

"You! The more you go on, the worse it gets. Here, do you want a taste of the national hotel?"

"I've already been there several times."

"How many times? How many stars have you got, then?"

"As many as the Milky Way in the night sky. I only came out the day before yesterday, after a full year."

Detective Kim, whose quick temper and irascibility were well known in the office, seemed to just want to argue with the accused, rather than take a statement. Along with Sergeant Nam, a few detectives who had relatively less work had been observing the scene for some time with amusement. However, Sergeant Nam found himself unable to go on watching for long. The sudden ringing of a phone attracted his attention. Lieutenant Lee, the head of the third division to which he belonged and who was sitting two desks away, could be seen picking up the receiver, turning away from the document he had been reading.

"Looks like a robbery—two or three wounded," Sergeant Nam thought to himself as he watched him answer the phone. Because he had been working closely with him for the past two years, Sergeant Nam was usually able to tell the seriousness of an incident simply by the expression and tone of voice Lee adopted while taking a phone call.

That day, too, his guess wasn't too far off. When he finally finished speaking, Lieutenant Lee called Sergeant Nam over; his expression was grave, as always when it concerned a violent crime.

"Sergeant Nam, follow me, with Detectives Im and Park."

"What's up?"

"Looks like a murder."

"Where?"

"Over in Yeongji county."

In terms of administration, Yeongji belonged to the neighboring district, but the local police came under their responsibility. A well-known mountain rose nearby; the valleys were beautiful, the streams pure. Halfway up the mountain stood a large temple called Donggak-sa. It was a popular picnic spot for the people of Daegu in three seasons out of four—spring, summer, and autumn.

As far as the police were concerned, the area was a constant nuisance, one that inspired a strong sense of grievance among them. Since the place attracted large numbers of people, it was the site of a correspondingly large number of crimes of all kinds. The fact that it was far away and they didn't have enough men made their work that much harder. Especially during the high season, in the spring and autumn, they were obliged to send extra officers from the main station in addition to the regular staff stationed there.

Now it was winter, when the men at the small local station had time to breathe, and for a violent crime, a murder, to happen there was totally unexpected.

The body lay at the side of a mountain path a little way outside the village. When the head of the investigation team removed the sheet that covered the corpse, the long, pale face of a man who looked to be in his early thirties appeared. The face was unharmed, the eyes were closed in a natural manner, there was almost nothing to awaken the sense of shock or repulsion that a dead body usually provokes. However, even a brief glimpse of the rest of the uncovered body indicated plainly that this was a murder. Blood lay thickly clotted over the chest, seemingly from repeated stabbings with a sharp weapon.

The scene was relatively well preserved. The head of the investigation team questioned the officer in charge of the local station, who was already there.

"Nothing new, apart from what's already been reported?"

"I found this lying on an oak stump down there." The man showed him a pair of bloodstained gloves wrapped in newspaper, as if he had been anticipating the question. They were ordinary gloves, made of white cotton. He then went on to repeat what he had already said on the telephone, with additional details.

The body had been found about one hour earlier, by someone from a neighboring village going into town. The fact that the body had been moved a little way from the scene of the crime to a place more secluded suggested that the criminal had tried to hide it. The time of death, which would only be known precisely after the autopsy, was probably sometime very early in the morning. A fruit knife had been left lying beside the body, and given the sharpness of the blade the crime appeared to have been premeditated. Since the scene of the crime was some way from any houses, it seemed that the criminal had persuaded the victim to come there and, judging by the location of the wounds and the posture of the body, there was virtually no sign of any struggle.

"The victim's identity?" The lieutenant's question cut short the station head's flow of words, which seemed likely to go on for some time. He replied with an apologetic air, as if to say he knew everything but that: "Impossible to tell. He's not got a single paper left on him. That could be the work of the killer, of course."

"No name inside the jacket?"

"I looked, but there's nothing there."

"Couldn't any of the local people identify him?"

"I called some of those who live in the nearest village, but they all said they'd never seen his face before." The patrolman in charge of preserving the crime scene, who was standing nearby, began to speak hesitatingly: "A while ago, after you'd gone somewhere, one of the villagers told me he was sure he'd seen him in a prayer house."

"A prayer house?" The lieutenant repeated the words, staring at the man.

The local station head answered the lieutenant, glaring at the patrolman as if to ask why he hadn't mentioned this earlier: "There are several prayer houses and hermitages around here. So which one did he mean?"

"The one called the House of Eternal Life."

"I know the place; it's just over this hill. It's a clean enough place, never any problems."

The head of the investigation turned to his team: "Is that so? In that case, Lieutenant Lee, you'd better send one of your men over there to inquire about the identity of the victim; the others can make inquiries in all the villages around here. I'll set up a headquarters in the local station and that's where I'll be."

He was looking utterly worn out. He had not been able to sleep properly for several nights on account of a series of violent crimes that had followed one after another recently, waiting as he was for promotion.

The forensic unit had been as quick as it could, but it was a little after two in the afternoon when Sergeant Nam arrived at the Eternal Life prayer house, carrying a still-damp photo of the victim. The prayer house was built out of cement blocks at the entrance to a valley, on the far side of the hill from the spot where the body had been found. Everything was quiet, probably because it was winter, and the sound Sergeant Nam made when he knocked on the door seemed to echo loudly in the stillness. A middle-aged man who might have been a handyman opened the door with an unwarrantedly cautious air. Sergeant Nam, unsure of the hierarchies of a place like this, decided to ask to see the director.

He found the director, whom he soon learned to be an elder at a church in the city, sitting by a stove with a youngster who seemed to be serving as an errand boy. He read the police identity card that Sergeant Nam held out to him with a look of surprise.

"Is there anyone from here who went out between yesterday and today and hasn't come back?"

"I can't be sure. We have very few people at present. And we don't really keep track of comings and goings here. Why do you ask?" The director turned the question back on him. Sergeant Nam took out the photo of the victim.

"Have you ever seen this person, by any chance?"

After looking at the picture for a long while, the director murmured, almost to himself, "I have a feeling I've seen him somewhere.

Is it that fellow who came for a bit last autumn?"

He turned abruptly to the young man who was standing beside him.

"Look at this. Who is this?"

"What, him? Why, isn't that Preacher Hwang's friend?" Glancing at the photo, the boy replied in a flash. The director nodded.

"That's right. Now you mention him, I'm sure that's who it is. I only met him in passing, so I didn't recognize him at once, but . . ." He turned to Sergeant Nam. "But why does he look like that?"

"He's dead," Sergeant Nam replied in a toneless voice. By now such deaths inspired no special reaction in him, whereas the director raised his voice in surprise.

"What? How did it happen?"

"He was murdered. What's this man's name?"

"Let me see, now. Min something I think. Anyway, Preacher Hwang knows him well. He was the one who brought him here a short time ago, saying he was an old friend. I only spoke to him once, when we exchanged greetings that first day."

Intuition derived from long years of police experience told Sergeant Nam that the man was not simply making excuses to avoid further inconvenience.

"This Preacher Hwang—where is he now?"

"He ought to be in the house somewhere. He didn't tell me he was going out today. I'll have this young man go and fetch him."

At those words, Sergeant Nam felt vaguely troubled. He suddenly wondered if this preacher was deeply implicated in what had happened, in which case he might already have disappeared. But before the boy could even leave the room, the preacher in question came in. He looked about thirty-one or -two. His face had a fragile, vulnerable look to it, but somehow the overall impression he made was very similar to the dead man.

"Why, here you are. Mr. Hwang, let me introduce you to this gentleman, from the police." The director spoke in a deliberately calm voice, as if it would be a great help in the investigation. But Sergeant Nam, seeing traces of tears on the man's cheeks, questioned him without bothering with formal greetings.

"So you went to look before you came. Did you go because

you'd heard rumors?"

The preacher nodded, saying nothing.

"You must be very upset; you were friends." Sergeant Nam spoke words of comfort, but at the same time he slyly observed the man's expression. But he took the words at their face value.

"Everything is God's will. But I felt so sorry for him . . ."

Once again, his eyes began to fill with tears. If pushed any further, the tears would turn into sobs, so Sergeant Nam deliberately adopted an official tone, drawing out his notebook with a rather exaggerated gesture.

"First I am just going to ask for a few pieces of information. His full name?"

"Min Yoseop."

"His age?"

"He must have been thirty-two."

"His profession?"

"I don't know."

"His address?"

"I don't know that, either."

"Weren't you friends?" Sergeant Nam spoke in a somewhat harsher voice. Something didn't seem to make sense. The preacher seemed startled by the change but the tone of his voice did not vary.

"Yes, a long while back. After nearly ten years without any news of him, I only just met him again about a month ago."

"What was your relationship before?"

"We were classmates in our school days. He dropped out halfway through, but we were pretty close for a while when we were both students. To tell you the truth, he was more than a mere friend; I used to respect him deeply."

Up to this point the preacher's voice had sounded like that of a schoolboy answering his teacher's questions, but it suddenly grew emotional. Vague memories from the old days seemed to be welling up. Pretending not to notice, Sergeant Nam continued with his questions.

"So you know nothing of what he's been doing recently?"

"Almost nothing. He didn't tell me, and I didn't ask."

"But you say he's been here a month. You must have been curious after not seeing him for such a long time?"

"It was for his sake; I thought I might only rub salt in his wounds to no purpose."

"Then how did he happen to come here?"

"I met him by chance in the street. He was dressed so shabbily that I asked what he'd been doing. He made no reply, only smiled sadly. Then he asked me what church I was in charge of. I told him that I didn't feel I was ready to serve as a minister yet, and that I was thus spending time here in prayer, and he suddenly said he'd like to spend some time here too. Obviously, although I'm only a guest here, I accepted with pleasure. More than that, I was delighted."

"Delighted? Why?"

"It was like a lost sheep was coming home. In the old days, he had a deeper faith than anyone else and was a first-class theology student. He made such sincere efforts to put the teachings of our Lord into practice that it would have been hard for any of us ordinary folk to imitate him. He never had so much as an extra pair of socks or underclothes for himself. During the holidays he used to do volunteer service in an orphanage or help in a lepers' village. Only he went a bit strange, in the fall of his second year I think it was. It wasn't just that he distanced himself from us; he seemed to distance himself from God and the church. Then, after a big row with the teachers, we never found out what it was about, he quit the seminary. I heard that he hadn't only given up studying then, but had left the church and God behind as well."

"Right. Enough about the past. Did he have any money?"

"So far as I know, he was practically penniless."

"What about his relations with women—his wife, or other women?"

"I've never heard anything at all about that. If I were to guess, he seemed to have been wandering about completely alone before arriving here."

Sergeant Nam found the reply deeply disheartening. In his experience, nine times out of ten incidents that were not connected with money or women turned into cases where he made no progress but only developed a headache. Sergeant Nam's next question seemed to just be seeking confirmation of his fears.

"In short, you're saying you know nothing about his present life?"

"That's about it. If I'd known something like this would happen, I'd have questioned him, even against his will." The preacher muttered his reply, adopting an apologetic expression for no apparent reason.

"What did he do while he was here?"

"He prayed endlessly, and read the Bible to the point where he forgot about sleep, that was all. Even the monks in the Middle Ages would never have mortified themselves as he did."

"He never went out?"

"Well, yes; the day before yesterday he went out, saying he was going into town, and he spent the night out."

"He didn't say where he'd been?"

"I asked him, but he didn't answer, only smiled sadly. He seemed to be counting the days recently, so I reckoned he had an appointment with someone."

"When was the last time you saw him?"

"Yesterday evening. We went to bed at the same time. But he didn't read the Bible or say any prayers, and he seemed unable to sleep. That was about as odd a thing as could be, you know. At any rate, I opened my eyes from time to time almost until daybreak and could see him curled up on his bedding, but when I woke up in the morning he was gone. He often used to go for an early morning stroll in the nearby hills, so I didn't bother to go looking for him, but . . ."

After that, Sergeant Nam tried asking a few more questions, but none of the replies were of any real help to his investigation. There being nothing more he could do, he jotted down the necessary details in his notebook, then finally asked, "Could I see his room?"

"He shared my room. Follow me."

Preacher Hwang led the way without the least hesitation.

He was brought to a room with wood floors, simple and clean, away from daily routine and suitable for solitary prayer. Some books were lying on a low wooden desk and on the opposite wall hung what seemed to be a charcoal drawing of the head of Jesus in a simple frame. Nothing else could be seen, no bedding, clothes, or other objects used in daily life. Everything must be in the large closet that was built into the left-hand side of the room.

After looking around, Sergeant Nam set about searching for things belonging to Min Yoseop. As he had expected, the preacher opened the closet door and produced a small, worn suitcase. Looking through the open door, he saw some folded up bedding and another, larger suitcase. That apparently belonged to the preacher, as did the clothes that were hanging on the wall. Sergeant Nam opened the case that he had pulled out. Except for a few neatly folded items of clothing, which almost seemed to have been prepared in advance, there was no clue to reveal anything about the owner. The absence of any personal traces was so total that it almost prompted a suspicion that he had deliberately set about concealing his identity in order to help the criminal.

"Is this all?" Sergeant Nam asked, looking rather disappointed. The preacher picked up a Bible lying among the other books on the desk. The book was new, apparently purchased recently, but portions were already darkly stained by frequent fingering. Sergeant Nam flipped through the Bible. There was no sign of the address he had hoped to find; but on the inside of the back cover he noticed a scribbled phrase in a foreign tongue that he could not decipher.

"*Desperatus, credere potes. Mortuus, vivere potes.* Now that you have despaired, you can believe. Now that you have died, you can live."

Such was the content of the phrase the preacher said was Latin and translated for him. Sergeant Nam found the phrase hard to understand, even in translation.

"Despair here seems to signify despair concerning one's self and the essence of one's being. It is a compelling situation, one in which we cannot help but turn to the Absolute Being, God. Death, too, suggests here something spiritual rather than physical death. Intellectual pride, self-righteousness, prejudice, vanity, all the poisons that have to be banished from the heart in order to attain true faith. I can't quite recall where, but I think you'll find something like those words in the epistles of Saint Paul. In them, it looks as though Min Yoseop is confessing a sincere conversion and expressing a decision."

To Sergeant Nam, who was still scrutinizing the Bible closely, the explanation sounded like a sermon. For him, whose life had long been spent among statements written in a clichéd style full of Chinese characters, the words were barely comprehensible. But even if he had understood them fully, they hardly seemed likely to be of very much help in his investigation. Finally, Sergeant Nam left the prayer house feeling discouraged.

Returning to his unit, he found that the head of the investigation had been called to the main station and none of the others were to be seen, with the exception of Lieutenant Lee, who was going through a list of petty criminals from the neighborhood with the second-in-command of the local station. A few of those had already been called in for questioning and were quarreling with the patrolmen over their alibis. The continuing inquiries of Detectives Im and Park in the nearby villages seemed not to have produced any clues.

Lieutenant Lee looked extremely disappointed on hearing Sergeant Nam's report. He had intended to speak at length but the lieutenant hurried him up; after getting the main points, he muttered more or less to himself, "So we've got his identity, but there's no knowing what he's been doing for the past eight years . . ."

He remained sunk in thought for a brief moment, then gave Sergeant Nam orders in a manner befitting an experienced investigator with more than twenty years of service.

"Sergeant Nam, go back to the main station and prepare to take a trip."

"Sir?"

"Report to the chief, then go up to Seoul. To that seminary. If you search their academic records, you should find his old address at least. Try that first."

It felt like a very vague lead, but Sergeant Nam agreed that there seemed to be no other way.

2

The seminary Sergeant Nam visited on arriving in Seoul the following day was a small building in an antiquated style, located incongruously in the very center of the city. Initially built on a modest scale on a hill outside the city limits formerly marked by the four gates, the expansion of Seoul had resulted in its present appearance. The building could only have held about thirty classrooms at most and the front yard seemed no bigger than a large primary school playground. Still, the red brick walls of the main building, covered in leafless creepers, and the girth of the old trees scattered here and there suggested a particular weight of tradition and an antiquity demanding devotion and reverence.

It being the winter vacation, the place was deserted and provoked a melancholy feeling. Passing the empty janitor's room, Sergeant Nam crossed the yard and encountered a student near a gnarled old tree in front of the main building, whether an undergraduate or a graduate assistant he could not tell, whom he asked to show him the office of student affairs. The student kindly led him to a room where a few clerks were chatting around a large oil stove. The office was so poorly furnished that, as he came in, Sergeant Nam wondered for a moment what on earth he could hope to find there. Yet the records on Min Yoseop that he found with the help of one of the clerks were not only better preserved than he had expected, they also yielded some interesting information.

Judging by his age, Min Yoseop must have been left an orphan while still a child, during the Korean War. He had been adopted by a foreign missionary called Thomas D. Allen. He had graduated from what had been in those days prestigious middle and high schools, the names of which were immediately familiar, and for almost two years had studied philosophy at a university as distinguished as his secondary schools, before moving to the seminary. His grades there were equally outstanding. Those in the first year, in particular, amazed the clerk who had fetched the dossier. He was nearly certain that no one had done as well since then. Yet his grades dropped in the second semester of the second year, and soon after beginning the third year he took a leave of absence, then left the seminary for good.

Sergeant Nam noted down everything that might be relevant to his inquiries in his notebook, then asked if he could meet any of the faculty who had been teaching at the school when Min Yoseop was a student there. There were several, it seemed, but not many had come in that day. Sergeant Nam decided to visit the professor whose room was nearest, and left the student affairs office.

It was in the same building, but in so secluded a corner that he momentarily lost his way trying to find it; he knocked on the door and was received rather reluctantly by a middle-aged professor. He barely recalled Min Yoseop and could remember nothing that might be of use in the inquiry. If there was anything strange, it wasn't so much that he had no memories, but rather that there was something suggesting he had deliberately eliminated them, as people often do with unpleasant or painful recollections. Apparently feeling sorry at Sergeant Nam's disappointed air, he added, "If it's that student, Professor Bae will know much more. He was very fond of him."

"Where could I meet Professor Bae?"

"He's probably in his office now. If you follow this corridor all the way back, his office is the second room from the end."

Following his directions, Sergeant Nam arrived at Professor Bae's room. The door was opened quietly by an elderly professor with completely white hair, who must have been well past retirement age. He gave the impression of having long been a pastor as well as a professor, perhaps because of the aura emanating from his old but respectable black suit, his voice that tended to grow increasingly soft, and his posture that manifested such modesty that it might be thought exaggerated.

"Yoseop is dead?" On hearing the news, Professor Bae fell into a heavy silence that lasted for a while. After Sergeant Nam repeated a number of questions, however, the professor gradually began to speak. His voice was oddly tremulous, possibly on account of the shock caused by the news of Min Yoseop's death.

"Yes, certainly I prized him; there's no doubt about it. His adoptive father was someone I had respected deeply, ever since I was young; in fact we were graduates, many years apart, from the same American university. Besides, he was the brightest student I ever taught in the ten or more years I've been here. But I don't think that I have the kind of information about him that the police would need."

"Still, tell me just one thing. Why did Min Yoseop leave the seminary?"

The professor looked at the police officer, who seemed to be hanging on his every word. He seemed to be weighing something up, probably his interlocutor's intellectual capacity. He finally made up his mind and replied in a voice filled with sorrow.

"Faith does not always go well with knowledge, you see. He was more interested in the pursuit of knowledge than in faith, and inevitably he ran out of energy. He went out with Kagawa and came back on the tail of the Ophites. We could not accept him under those conditions. Even if he was intellectually brilliant, we could not allow him to shake the foundations of belief. That angered him and he left, never to return."

Sergeant Nam could only understand about half of what he said. More from his own interest in Min Yoseop as a person than in the needs of the investigation, he asked, "What's Kagawa? Ophites?"

"To put it more simply, shall I say radicalism and heterodoxy — or something like that."

"It would be better if you could explain simply, so that I can understand."

"Kagawa Toyohiko was a Japanese practical theologian, a social reformer, a member of the workers' movement, an evangelist and a writer, too, the scion of an aristocratic family that disowned him when he became a Christian. Yet he did not yield, but kept his faith. He graduated from Kobe Theological Seminary and went to study at Princeton Theological College. After his return from Princeton, still only twenty, he went to live in the Shinkawa slum in Kobe and began to organize the workers, playing a leading role in the Kobe docks strike, as well as leading the farmworkers' union movement and the cooperative movement. During the war he was imprisoned by the military police for having apologized to the Chinese for the Japanese invasion, and became widely known as a writer for his novel *Across the Death Line*. He was an extraordinary person in many ways. Min Yoseop appeared to have been fascinated by his practical theology."

He closed his eyes wearily, then slowly continued: "The Ophites were heretics in ancient times who did not consider the serpent in the Bible as a messenger of Satan charged with humanity's fall, but instead venerated it as an apostle of wisdom. The ideas of Min Yoseop did not correspond to theirs exactly, but his way of viewing Satan as a spirit of wisdom or as an alternative attribute of God was something we could never approve. Do you see now?"

"Yes, a bit . . ." Sergeant Nam replied in some confusion, having listened to every word with intense concentration. It had been better than the explanation he had heard a little before, but his long years in the police constituted a considerable handicap to understanding Professor Bae's words fully. Professor Bae stopped talking, as if to say that was enough.

"I think you'd better go now. I am very tired. I do not think I have anything more to add."

As words designed to dismiss a visitor without upsetting him, they could not have been clearer. Sergeant Nam still had points that were unclear, but he had no choice. After speaking, Professor Bae had closed his eyes gently and fallen into a deep silence such that it seemed no word could break it, no matter how strong. Just as Sergeant Nam was going out of the door, he heard him murmur, "Dr. Allen, it's truly a great pity. But at least, he said he was on his way back."

After a simple lunch near the seminary, Sergeant Nam went to the address where Min Yoseop had lived eight years before. It too was now in the center of the city, but the area must have been a remote suburb in those days. The single-story, flat-roofed house, scarcely more than a hovel, stood wretchedly amidst recently constructed, luxurious dwellings. Luckily, a person connected to Min Yoseop was still living there: a woman in her sixties who said she had spent more than half her life as housekeeper for Doctor Allen. It turned out that it was she who had mostly raised Min Yoseop, after his adoption while he was still an infant.

On hearing the name Min Yoseop, she immediately burst into tears, although she knew nothing of his death. She clearly felt for him as if he were her own son.

"And where is he now?" Her voice was filled with the tender affection of an elderly mother longing for her faraway son. Even without knowing how much contact there had been between them during the past eight years, it was easy to imagine the profound shock and grief his death would cause her.

Wishing to spare her, Sergeant Nam prevaricated: "He's in Daegu now."

"What's he doing? Is he well?"

"Yes. But where is Dr. Allen nowadays?"

A gleam of doubt showed in the old woman's tear-filled eyes.

"Why, he went back home more than ten years ago, a year after Mrs. Allen died. At the time, he asked me and Yoseop to go with him, but when the boy refused, I stayed here too. But who are you?"

"A friend of his. How are you nowadays?"

Again Sergeant Nam avoided telling the truth, glad that he had not revealed his police identity. This time it was less for her sake than in order to do his job. He had only exchanged a few words with her so far, but he had a feeling that her strong attachment to Min Yoseop might end up hindering his inquiries. If she decided to stay silent, thinking she might harm him if she spoke, his visit would be useless.

Apparently reassured by Sergeant Nam's relaxed attitude, she replied with a slightly less suspicious expression: "Not too bad, thanks to the boy. Though things are not as they were before, of course."

"Before what?"

"You call yourself his friend, and he hasn't told you about it? But of course, he was always obedient to the Lord's words: 'Do not let your left hand know what your right hand is doing.'"

"I haven't known him all that long, you see. And he doesn't talk very much, either. What happened?"

Recalling what he had heard from Preacher Hwang and Professor Bae, Sergeant Nam paid careful attention to her words. He seemed to have somehow overcome her doubts and she began to tell him everything, with an expression that showed she was quite glad to be able to talk about it.

"Doctor Allen left him well provided for when he went back, all he had accumulated in the more than thirty years he had lived here. But once Yoseop moved to the seminary, he began to share it with others. Later, he even went so far as to sell the big house up in Seongbuk-dong. We wouldn't even have kept this shabby little house, if it hadn't been for me."

"Why, who did he give it all to?"

"To those with nothing, of course. Isn't that what there's most of in the world—cold, hungry folk? In lepers' villages, orphanages, and rehabilitation centers. You wouldn't believe how many places there are to give money to! Once you start, it's all gone pretty soon. In less than two years he had to work to pay his tuition. At first, I tried to stop him. But after all, it had been given to him, hadn't it? I thought about letting Doctor Allen know, back in his country, but I might as well be blind as far as writing goes."

"Then what happened?"

"When there was nothing more to give away, he left. He said that once you have nothing to give, you have to serve with your own body. Still, he never forgot me. During the past seven years he's always sent me enough to buy food."

"Still, did he really give away all that money just to the poor? Might he not have spent it in other ways?"

Sergeant Nam's question was a sincere one. He simply could not believe that such an act of charity, unlike anything he had ever read about in the social pages of newspapers, could happen in reality.

"Don't say such things! God might punish you. That kind boy . . . As soon as he was old enough, he went through winters without ever putting on a pair of socks. It was from thinking about his poor neighbors who didn't have warm clothes to wear. Once he came home shivering in his shirtsleeves, on a day when it was snowing hard, because he had given his jacket to a beggar huddled on the roadside. He went so far that even moderately tolerant pastors used to scold him. It's true. Such a kind boy . . ."

The old lady looked thoroughly upset. Sergeant Nam felt a deep emotion surging up from his heart for no apparent reason. He suddenly recalled the long-forgotten Sunday school he had attended for years as a child for the sake of the maize flour and the powdered milk distributed there, and the noisy festivities on Christmas Eve. Later, after he had stopped going to church, and up until he began to approach manhood, he would still look up from time to time at the white cross on the pointed spire with a vague sense of longing. But at some point he began to think that the world those things symbolized was not part of life here, where the only things left were rituals and systems corrupted and debased by human greed and hypocrisy. As a result, Min Yoseop's past life that the old woman was describing filled him with a strange sense of loss.

"Ah! I knew he was good, but I couldn't believe he went that far. Have you not heard from him lately?"

"Some money came about a month and a half ago, from Daegu."

"But no letter?"

"No. He rarely writes letters."

"You've got his address, though?"

"No, I don't have that. The boy never writes his address."

"Will you let me see the envelopes?"

"I know I kept them, but everything's in a jumble here, I wonder if I can find them."

She burrowed into the drawer of an old dresser and pulled out a bundle of envelopes. They bore postmarks from almost all the main cities, beginning with Seoul, then Gwangju, Busan, Daejeon, Incheon. Only three were postmarked from Daegu, including the one she had mentioned from the post office near the Dongbu Police Station. Sergeant Nam noted down the names of all the post offices from which Min Yoseop had mailed four money orders or more.

Feeling that this was still not enough, he examined the letters inserted in some of the envelopes. There was one letter for every five or six envelopes, written, it appeared, each time that he was preparing to move from one city to another, although he hardly ever indicated any reason or purpose. In the letters he would ask how she was, specify how much he was sending, and indicate approximately when he was going to send the next one. Sergeant Nam felt that if he had made any new discovery, it was that, corresponding to the maternal affection the old lady harbored toward him, Min Yoseop considered himself indebted to her, more or less duty-bound to support her.

"Isn't there anything left that belonged to Yoseop—books or notes, for example?"

After he had done with the letters, Sergeant Nam asked again. It might prove important for the investigation to understand what kind of a person Min Yoseop was. This thought occurred to him from his intuition as a detective, not merely from personal curiosity.

"As far as books go, Doctor Allen left a lot, but Yoseop got rid of them all. He sold them to secondhand bookstores for the money, I suppose. He took a few of his own books with him in a bag when he left. There ought to be quite a few notebooks somewhere, though."

"That would do. Can I see them?"

"The box over there is full of his notebooks, but you won't have time to go through them all."

Seeming to sense something out of the ordinary, she asked more doubtfully, "Why are you asking all this? Has something happened to our Yoseop? Who are you, anyway?"

She seemed to have become suspicious when Sergeant Nam began noting down the postmarks on the envelopes and scanning the letters. For a moment he thought about disclosing who he was, but instead he made something up again, in the hope of hearing more.

"Actually, Yoseop asked me to find him a job several months ago and yesterday I got good news about it. But there's been no sign of him for a month now. I figured he must have gone to work somewhere else, but I just wondered if he hadn't come back here by any chance, and that's why I came. I examined the envelopes and letters because I thought I might be able to find him if only I knew what town he was in. As for the books and notebooks, Yoseop told me about them some time ago. He said that one day he would come and fetch them. I thought I could take them, since I'm here. I'm sure to meet him soon, one way or another." Sergeant Nam was amazed at how naturally he was able to relieve the old lady's doubts. The story didn't hold together very well when he thought about it afterwards, but it seemed to work. The old woman's expression, which had suddenly hardened in doubt, gradually softened again. Noting this with a sideways glance, Sergeant Nam felt quietly pleased and set it aside for future reference.

"But if Yoseop takes this job, he'll have to travel a long way away. It's a country called Saudi Arabia and it takes months to get there and back. It's going to be hard for him to send news for quite a long time."

"I somehow guessed he might be leaving for some far-off place, from a letter I received about two months back. But why should he go abroad? He resisted so stubbornly when Dr. Allen asked him to go with him."

"Still, that's the way it is now. Look, I'll just take what's needed."

"Do as you like, if he asked you to. There's nothing I need."

She finally agreed, still looking rather reluctant despite her suspicions having lifted. Sergeant Nam opened the box and set about examining the notebooks. It was a jumble of lecture notes, documents in files, a personal diary, and manuscript pages. Among all the rest, Sergeant Nam picked out the volumes of his diary that corresponded to the time when he left home, and a pile of manuscripts in a separate bundle.

"I heard about what happened from some neighbors while I was looking for this house. Do you know if he's kept in touch with that woman?"

As he was about to leave, he allowed himself to be greedy. He spoke in a low, natural voice, as if he knew all about something that was in fact blind guesswork. He invented a woman because, in light of all he had heard, he felt sure that Min's death had nothing to do with money. Sergeant Nam was no different from any other detective in reckoning that every crime was invariably connected to either money or a woman.

The effect exceeded his expectations. Before he had even finished talking, the old lady's eyes narrowed, and her face hardened more than ever.

"Who dared repeat those worn-out old tales? I swear to you that Yoseop is not like that at all. Trying to expose people's stinking backsides, they're so wicked they'll make up any kind of story. Besides, Elder Mun and his wife left the neighborhood years ago. Don't talk to me about that again. And don't say you're any kind of friend of his, if you believe stories like that."

Her reaction convinced Sergeant Nam that he had just discovered a definite clue that might shed some light on the cause of Min Yoseop's death. Cowering before the old lady's stubbornness, as she stood there staring into the distance with her arms crossed and her lips compressed, he left without asking anything more. After all, apart from her there were other old acquaintances of Min Yoseop he had yet to meet.

3

With the help of the local ward office, and after a few inquiries, Sergeant Nam succeeded in finding a man who had known Min Yoseop quite well some eight years earlier. This man described a very different side of Min Yoseop's character from what he had just heard. Needless to say, in the course of an investigation he often ended up bringing to light the ugliness and baseness hidden behind someone's gentle, noble appearances, but the case of Min Yoseop was proving to be rather unusual. The man Sergeant Nam tracked down was a deacon at the local church, an older man who had been living there for twenty years, and who had no hesitation in calling Min Yoseop "that breed of Satan."

"He came into our church wearing a sheep's mask. He committed adultery with someone's wife within the sacred confines of the church building, and he struck God's faithful minister on the cheek. Worse than that, he tempted the simpleminded faithful with the cunning wisdom of the Sons of Darkness, sowing division among them, setting people at each other's throats, turning the church upside down . . ."

Once he had started there was no end to his tirade. The woman with whom he had committed adultery was no less than the young second wife of one of the church's elders; he had slapped the cheek of the minister, an outrage committed after he had surrendered to "heretical doctrines," when he dragged the minister down from the pulpit while he was preaching. He divided the flock by intervening in the church's financial affairs, making accusations against the minister and the elders so that some of the church members began to demand an inquiry into certain irregularities in the construction of their new church, leading to a fight for control against those who supported the minister.

"As a result of all that, our church was devastated. The shepherd left, abandoning the sheep, who scattered. Elder Mun was unable to show his face on account of what was said about his wife, and he eventually left the area, a broken man. Later, fortunately, shepherd and sheep finally came together again and the church was restored to life. But God will never forgive that man, that cunning child of Satan. I don't know what brings you here, but since you say you're a policeman perhaps something bad has befallen him. That would be a sign that God's judgment is upon him."

In the deacon's voice he heard faint echoes of a curse.

Whenever he discovered these traces of ugliness and baseness behind gentle, noble appearances, Sergeant Nam usually experienced a feeling of pleasure on finding what he had been expecting, and an inexplicable sense of relief. In the case of Min Yoseop, however, it was different; he felt instead a kind of bitterness, as if he had been betrayed by someone he trusted. He even found himself wondering if Min Yoseop hadn't not fallen victim to some kind of trap.

If Sergeant Nam set off to meet another of Min Yoseop's former acquaintances, it was entirely on account of a personal feeling he had, almost unconnected with the investigation itself. This time, having deliberately searched in that direction, he met a former member of the church, whose memories were different from those of the deacon.

"I remember that student quite well. He had a radical streak to him, but he was a good churchman and a devoted Sunday school teacher. As for his alleged adultery, I really don't know . . . Everyone was talking about it at the time, but there were aspects that were very hard to understand. He was, I suppose, barely twenty then—certainly not the age to know much about that kind of thing. Even if he had been so depraved at such an early age, why would he have seduced a married woman approaching thirty, with two children to boot? There were plenty of pretty girls his own age that he could easily have associated with if he'd wanted to. If there was someone untrustworthy in the whole affair, it was her. She was supposed to be the daughter of the elder at another church, but she didn't seem to have much real faith. Besides, to marry a man over forty who had already been married once when she was only twenty-four, that was enough to make you wonder. Her behavior after her marriage with Elder Mun was far from perfect. She had two children, but it wasn't sure they were both his—at least, that's what some people were saying. If something did happen between the student and that woman, he's not the one who should be blamed. The people who sympathized with him claimed he was the victim.

"The fight in the church? I don't know about other things, but as far as the minister goes, frankly I'm on the side of the student. I'm not sure what people will think of me talking like this to a stranger. To all appearances, the minister seemed an extraordinary man. In those days, that neighborhood was a shantytown outside the city limits. The minister arrived with just an army tent that could hold thirty people, but within five years he'd succeeded in building the present church. I've been told that he'd already built two other churches in the same way. If building big, elaborate churches is the only way for someone to be a faithful servant of God, then he was certainly the most faithful servant of all. The problem was that the new building and the land it stood on had been registered in his own name. He had bribed some of the leading members of the church in order to do that. Later we learned that he had registered the other two churches, those he had built before, either under his own name or that of his wife. Once he had built those churches, he had employed ministers to serve in them, then moved to our area with his rolled-up tent and started a new church here.

"In other words, erecting a church offered him a fully legal way of making a fortune. He would take all the money offered by the believers in the first two churches, claiming to be using it for the costs of the new building, leaving only enough to pay minimal living expenses to the minister in charge, and to cover basic maintenance costs. But at the same time he was demanding the maximum in offerings from the faithful of our church. Just think! When it comes to building a church, the house of God, what believer wouldn't consider it important?

"In a poor shantytown like ours, the faithful were mostly ignorant, uneducated folk who did all they could to contribute to the construction of the church. People living from hand to mouth would labor without pay at least once a week to cut into the hill and level the ground for the new building. Since it was being done for God, there was no question of taking a break, even on Sundays. The minister urged them to make the work go faster, even reducing the length of the services. And do you know how much he demanded in offerings? People who had just enough for that day's evening meal gave the money for their next day's breakfast to the church. Obviously, some people did that out of a deep faith, but most of them did it on account of the minister's threatening descriptions of the wrath of God, with the fire and brimstone of hell. Most of his sermons would begin with 'Do not lay up for yourselves treasures on earth' and 'Man does not live by bread alone, but by the Word of God,' and end with descriptions of the Last Judgment and the terrible punishments God had in store for those who did not obey those commands.

"By the time that student moved into the neighborhood, the church had already taken shape. At first, he was extremely polite to the minister, as docile as could be. But as time passed he became increasingly critical; in the end, once he realized what was going on, he began to demand that he repent and that corrections be made. The minister probably viewed this as youthful rashness, and did not take his demands seriously. Once the young man had denounced the minister's behavior publicly to the faithful and begun to gather support, the minister reacted with every means at his disposal. He tried to control the faithful by asserting his pastoral authority; he tried to threaten them in God's name, coaxed them with small advantages, anything to keep them on his side. In response to the situation, the minister's supporters accused him of sowing discord among the faithful, and leading them into temptation.

"It was then that the incident occurred that I feel ashamed to talk about, since it involves our church. It happened one Sunday, shortly before the student disappeared from our neighborhood. That day, as usual, the minister was preaching in such a way as to put himself in an advantageous situation, repeating 'Man does not live by bread alone.' The student, who had been sitting in the front row, rushed toward the pulpit, pointed his finger at the minister and shouted, 'Shut up! What can the Word give us? Misused by someone like you, the very bread is being snatched out of our mouths!' Up in the pulpit, the minister cried, 'Get thee hence, Satan!' and the student, unable to take any more, climbed up to the pulpit, grabbed the minister by the neck, and forced him down while denouncing all his corruptions. The minister responded with equal vigor, accusing the student of adultery—which was the first anyone had heard of it. Then those who supported the minister rushed up and tried to throw the student out, while those who believed him and thought he was right rallied round him. The church fell into utter turmoil.

"Because of the fight, the police were brought in; since his illicit actions were about to be exposed, the minister abruptly transferred ownership of the church and land to the church members, and resigned. Many, disgusted by the ugly fight, left to join other churches, far away but peaceful. I was one of them. The situation in our church at that time was absolutely appalling. It took four or five years to bring it back to the state you can see today. The church was devastated, so you could say that that student did not act in the best possible way. But it wouldn't be fair to blindly take the minister's side and blame it all on the student."

He had spent nearly an hour listening to the man, and the short winter's day was already drawing to a close. Sergeant Nam still hoped to meet Elder Mun and catch the night train back to Daegu. He had spent a long time listening to a story that didn't seem directly helpful to the investigation, but he was feeling much relieved.

It made sense for him to meet Elder Mun, since he was now included among the suspects. Elder Mun had moved to the city of Seongnam, where he had become a grain merchant. Sergeant Nam felt rather disappointed as he pushed open the door of a run-down shop that might be more accurately termed a rice store, having imagined him to be quite rich. It took over two hours for him to make the journey from Seoul and then have supper, and it had already been dark for some time when he arrived at the store. There was nobody inside, and it seemed like the owner had gone in for a late-evening meal.

He called in a loud voice toward the door at the back of the shop. He was obliged to call several times before an old man with a gloomy face emerged. It was Elder Mun. The moment Sergeant Nam saw him, he realized how foolish his suspicions had been and smiled bitterly to himself. Still, he had to be cautious because of the way crime often refused to follow the dictates of common sense.

Sergeant Nam asked him immediately about his second wife. Elder Mun replied calmly, "She left me long ago."

"Did you get a divorce?" Sergeant Nam felt slightly tense as he asked. If she had lived with Min Yoseop after leaving him, it might not have been so foolish to suspect Elder Mun.

"No. How can men separate those whom God has joined together? I even moved here for her sake, but she still ended up leaving. But what do all these questions mean? Why are you looking for her?"

His voice was full of sadness. After a moment's hesitation, Sergeant Nam told him about the death of Min Yoseop. Elder Mun's face hardened for a second.

"I hate to say it, but he was already a dead man." Sergeant Nam offered the hint casually, without taking his eyes off Elder Mun, whose face quickly returned to its normal calm expression.

"No, I don't hate him. Looking back, I reckon he too was merely a victim. I forgave him long ago, and forgot him."

"What do you mean, he too?"

"She was Satan's agent in all that happened. I did everything for her, but less than a year after we moved here there was already another man . . ."

His voice died away and his face creased with lines of deep anguish.

"Another man?"

"The man working in this shop. But God forgive me, I'm sure it would take more than the fingers of one hand to count the people she had been with in this street alone."

It was the same story that Sergeant Nam had heard in Seoul. There was no reason why Elder Mun should have directed his resentment against Min Yoseop in particular. Besides, even if he had possessed such animosity, it hardly seemed possible that he would have been able to use a knife to kill young Min Yoseop, with his body like a withered, old tree trunk. But on the basis of what he said, he couldn't draw any definite conclusions regarding the young wife. He felt he had to meet her in person to confirm for sure that the unfortunate couple had had nothing to do with Min Yoseop's death.

"Do you know where your wife is now?"

"I have no idea. I haven't had any news of her for the past five years."

"How many children do you have?"

"Two—a girl who's just started middle school and a boy in the fifth year of primary school."

"Are they both her children?"

"Yes, my first wife died without having any children. Why are you asking about them?"

"No particular reason. You must have had a very hard time."

"Please, I beg you, don't let the children hear anything about their mother. They still think of her as a good mother. I told them she died in an accident. Last autumn I took them to visit her grave; of course, it was actually that of my first wife . . ."

Elder Mun's request sounded sincere. Yet the more he listened to him, the more Sergeant Nam felt that it would be important for him to meet this woman, even if she turned out to have had nothing to do with Min Yoseop's death. That was why he had asked about the children. He knew that when separated parents break off all contact with each other, the children usually stay in touch with both. Especially if the older child was already in middle school. No matter how carefully Elder Mun tried to hide everything, the girl was bound to have at least a vague idea of what had become of her mother, and might even have some kind of contact with her. Sergeant Nam nodded his acceptance of Elder Mun's request as he went out, but he felt that he had to find the children and see if they had their mother's address.

Sergeant Nam's guess proved correct. He spent the night at a nearby inn, then got up early in the morning and went to wait at the corner of a cold alley near Elder Mun's shop. At around eight, he saw his daughter leaving for school, and he was able to obtain the address of the girl's mother without much difficulty. She was living in Seoul.

Returning quickly to Seoul, Sergeant Nam found the house, which turned out to be a neat, traditional-style house in the Insadong area. From the outside it looked like an ordinary private home, but once inside it seemed to be an unlicensed "house of pleasure." On the branches of the well-kept trees in the yard a number of sea fish—cod and pollack—were hanging to dry, destined to be served as snacks. Flounders and squid were swimming in a large aquarium in the wood-floored hall, and they certainly weren't there for decoration. However, the clearest indication of the nature of the place came from the women. Although it was past ten in the morning, young women of a particular type were bustling around in their nightdresses with puffy faces.

Sergeant Nam asked for Elder Mun's wife, giving her name to a girl who was filing her nails at one end of the veranda, her hair wrapped in a towel, as though she had just finished bathing. Without any special caution, she called toward the inner room, "Madam Jin, a visitor!"

Without any reply, a door slid back and a woman emerged. The wife of Elder Mun looked less than thirty, although he knew she was actually approaching forty. Perhaps because she had already applied makeup, Sergeant Nam thought she looked younger and more sensual than the other girls. But at her age she couldn't be an ordinary employee, she had to be the manageress.

To Sergeant Nam's surprise, at first she had no recollection of Min Yoseop. He reminded her of certain events and showed her his photo, at which she finally recognized him. "Oh, that student!" She registered no more feeling than if she had been shown the photo of a casual acquaintance from primary school. It was the same when she heard of Min Yoseop's death. Not only did she not display any surprise or sorrow, she didn't even utter a single word of regret.

As she later explained, Min Yoseop had not been the only man with whom she was having illicit relations at that time. It had been the same when she left Elder Mun, and judging by the overall atmosphere of her current situation, Sergeant Nam had the impression that she was still involved in a giddy tour of the available men. Her relationship with Min Yoseop had been so scandalous for the members of the church because he was a seminary student and a Sunday school teacher in the church where her husband was an elder, and because their secret meetings had mainly taken place during church activities.

Sergeant Nam, although no churchgoer, was taken aback to hear her relate what had happened one evening during a revival meeting. She spared no detail. When everyone was in the church engaged in all-night prayers, they had slipped out surreptitiously and made love in a shed behind the minister's house, making so much noise that a neighboring dog had begun to bark in surprise. Due to the commotion, they had been discovered by the minister's cook, who must have told the minister.

Sergeant Nam was stunned to hear her tell him not only that, but a lot of other things women do not usually discuss, without any hint of embarrassment. She struck him as being a mindless doll, the very incarnation of carnal desire. But strangely enough, despite all her promiscuous deeds, he could not sense any indecency or depravity in her conduct or her manner of speaking. It all suited her so well, like a well-fitting dress, and even served to highlight her almost bewitching impertinence.

As time went by, Sergeant Nam increasingly felt that he was on the wrong track. Yet in one corner of his mind he stubbornly believed that something would come out. Although knowing the obvious answer, he asked her, "Have you heard from him recently, by any chance?"

She looked incredulous and laughed to herself as she replied, "You really don't believe me? Even now, I don't leave anything behind with men. Once our bodies separate, I take my heart back. Why drag things on, once you're apart? And in any case, with that student, it only got physical a few times. One evening there was a power outage, and the sight of him praying under the oil lamp tickled my appetite, like a fresh fish, so I just took him. He was a novice; his talents were not so wonderful as to leave any memories . . ."

She pulled out a cigarette from inside her dress and lit it. The way she sat there with her legs crossed, carelessly exhaling the smoke, made her look like an arrogant queen. As he watched her, Sergeant Nam felt the hope he had harbored of finding another clue for his investigation die away. His intuition, resulting from the last ten years' experience as a detective, told him that she had no direct relationship with the death of Min Yoseop. Sergeant Nam hurriedly parted from her. If he was to get to the police station before office hours were over, he would have to catch the midday train for Daegu at the latest.

4

Sergeant Nam just barely caught the train, and once he was seated he closed his eyes for a moment, feeling dispirited. Then he set about examining the notebooks he had taken from Min Yoseop's house, one by one. As things stood now, they were the only hope he had. The personal notes and diaries of culprits and victims could sometimes provide significant information. But apart from that, he was beginning to develop a personal interest in Min Yoseop.

The first thing he opened was the bundle of diaries. The one he

picked up happened to begin just after Min had entered the seminary. The first parts were full of expressions of the ardent faith and
ambition to attain true goodness that had motivated his decision
to quit university and enter the seminary. Soon, though, his interest shifted to the material conditions of human life and to social
problems, and he began to doubt the Christian religion itself. Particularly after returning from a lepers' village, his days became filled
with religious doubt.

"How can misfortune befall humanity, irrespective of consider-
ations of good or evil?" "The words of Jesus declare that those who
are rich, strong, and powerful are nothing. Then why are they everything in this world? According to the words of Jesus, the poor,
the sick, and the rejected are everything. Why then are they nothing in this world?" "The world is full of superstitions designed to
foster belief. Religion is perhaps in some way nothing more than
the most artful form of superstition." Although the contents of the
diary were mostly abstract and conceptual, Sergeant Nam was able
to keep on reading thanks to these kind of poignant questions inserted here and there.

The train was passing Yeongdong Station by the time he had
finished looking over the whole diary. Although Sergeant Nam
scanned quickly through the abstract parts, he paid close attention
to the sections dealing with his daily life; but the diary ended on
the day of his expulsion from the seminary, without providing any
definite clues that could shed light on events that followed.

Sergeant Nam opened the remaining bundles of paper next. It
was a manuscript for a novel, but to Sergeant Nam, whose rusty
brain was dulled by the daily routine of his profession, it was just as
hard to read as the diary. As the train approached Daegu, he would
have probably given up before the end of the second page, had it
not been for his sense of frustration at bringing so little back from
his trip, combined with the fact that he had nothing else to do except go on reading.

In the days of Octavius Augustus, in the early years of the Roman
Empire, the Three Wise Men from the East must have been an im-

mense disappointment to Yahweh, who had until then only been the God of Jacob and his descendants. Later generations invariably considered Caspar, Melchior, and Balthazar to have been wise men, but it seems extremely doubtful whether they were truly wise and whether their actions really contributed to "Glory in the Highest" and "Peace on Earth."

No matter how faithfully Yahweh may have been fulfilling the prophecies made by the servants he had sent previously, he must have been deeply embarrassed when they arrived so noisily, seeking the birthplace of his son, bearing extraordinary gifts of gold, frankincense, and myrrh. For Yahweh, the occasion was destined to be one he would regret for ages on end. Because Mary was another man's wedded wife, her son was later mocked as a god who "demolished the gates of the prescriptive law he himself had erected" and had "come in by a shortcut," and because she was a human being, controversies about the status of her son drove the early Church into conflicts so terrible that Arius, that lofty ascetic, was condemned to the humiliation of being expelled from the Church, while Nestorius, austere and faithful servant though he was, died in exile. It would have been preferable if those irresponsible prophecies of Isaiah—"Behold, a virgin will conceive and bear a son," and "the Messiah will be born of David's line," and the rest—had been ignored. It would have been far better if the Son of God had come down in a flash of lightning or sprung from a rock. Or he could have fulfilled Daniel's prophecy and arrived borne on a cloud.

Further doubts as to the wisdom of those men from the East arise from the immaturity of their words and deeds prior to Yahweh's arrival in the humble stable that served as a delivery room for his son. They kept asking everywhere they passed where the King of the Jews was going to be born, causing Jerusalem to be stirred up, and betraying Yahweh's intention to keep the birth of his son secret until the proper moment. That was presumably why he sent down angels, when the birth of his son was imminent, who announced it in haste to shepherds, who were as lowly as tax collectors or tanners.

The foolishness and indiscretion of the three men from the East did not stop there, for news of the amazing birth finally reached the ears of the tyrant himself. While his dearest son was making the dangerous journey to the unfamiliar, faraway land of Egypt, passing through a forest of swords, Yahweh must have felt deep anxiety as he watched over him. How vexed he must have been on seeing Limbo suddenly crowded with the souls of all those Jewish babies massacred by Herod's troops, and what regret he must have felt at all those reproaches throughout the ages, that he had brought about his son's birth on the basis of the sacrifice of innumerable innocent lives.

Blessed be the Evangelist who, ignorant of all this, discretely praised the three for their simplicity. Likewise whoever it was who later created the legend that they were kings from some oriental lands, finding no better way of glorifying them. To say nothing of the apostle Thomas, reputed to have traveled far to visit the three men in their old age; and Saint Helena, who made such efforts to recover their remains; and Fredrick Barbarossa, who did all he could to transfer those relics to the great cathedral of Cologne, uncertain though it is if they were authentic or not. *Sancta simplicitas!*

Moreover, the story of the three men from the East did not end with their controversial veneration of the baby. Yahweh, fearful that on their way home they might drop in on Herod and tell him truthfully where his son was, belatedly intervened by sending angels. That very night, avoiding Herod and following a different road as instructed by the angels, the three men arrived in the Plain of Esdraelon, where they beheld another star that inspired them, a great dark-red star, possessing all the attributes of the star known to astrologers as the Star of Disaster.

At the sight of a star so utterly different from the one they had been following eagerly all those months, they stopped in their tracks, at first only vaguely intrigued. But then they found themselves seized with an inexplicable fear and trembling. It was above all on account of the strange light emanating from it, rather than any preconception inspired by their knowledge of oriental mysteries. Ill-boding yet darkly tempting, the light seemed to be directed at their hearts like a shower of black arrows, and at the same time it soothed their souls like a warm blessing.

Their beliefs led them to see everything only in terms of good or evil, darkness or light, and therefore they trembled all the more in fear before the unfamiliar ambivalence and complexity of the light from this star. Caspar in particular, with his weak heart, shocked by his own conclusion that it was a trick of Satan directed at them, would have fallen from his camel if Melchior had not held him up. Even Balthazar, the eldest of the three, with the widest experience of the world, broke out in a cold sweat and set about reciting all the prayers people of those times reckoned effective in such cases.

But impervious to every kind of threat—be it an eternally burning pillar of fire, or a blazing lake of molten rock, or the frozen ocean that extinguishes the sun, or the hell of a flogging more agonizing than all the whips of the Assyrian tyrant Ashurbanipal, the heavenly warrior of lightning and thunder, the swords of the Zoroastrian divinity Spenta Armaiti, sharper than all the weapons of the Hittites, or the chains of adamant that bind for a thousand years— the star shone brightly until the rising of the morning sun. As a result of their prejudices, equaled by their blindness and ignorance, the three men from the East took the star for a sign of calamity, whereas in fact it shone for another great providential event. At that very hour, in a house near Bethel belonging to a teacher of the school of Shammai, a true Son of Man had been born, Ahasuerus.

No surviving record recounts how Ahasuerus avoided wicked Herod's swords. One malicious legend claims that he was easily able to deceive the soldiers of Herod, who were only looking for infants younger than two years old, because an evil spirit allowed him to walk and talk from the moment of his birth. However, rather than believe such nonsense, it seems more reasonable to conjecture that it was his father's skills of social survival that allowed him to escape death. According to the known facts, while his father was publicly a member of the party of the Pharisees, from an early age he had secretly been linked to the Sadducees and the supporters of Herod.

At any rate, while the son of Yahweh was growing up in wretched poverty in Heliopolis, Ahasuerus was able to enjoy a peaceful childhood in his father's small but charming house. Apart from that detail, most of his childhood, like that of the son of Yahweh, is buried in the darkness of history. As a result, in order to reconstitute his youth we are obliged to rely on fragmentary, uncertain legends, just as people rely entirely on apocryphal gospels for stories about the childhood of the son of Yahweh.

According to them, Ahasuerus was already extremely thoughtful and intelligent as an infant. The malicious claim that he was able to walk and speak from birth was probably an embellishment based on these remarkable talents. He had such an exceptional memory that by the age of ten he could virtually recite the Torah by heart. His father, although he considered himself a master of the Law, had spent his whole life carefully repeating the words of others, and dreamed of raising his impressive son to become the greatest rabbi in Judea. Indeed, his dream might have been realized, if it had not been for the call of a greater destiny.

The first sign of providence revealed itself when Ahasuerus was twelve. For the Passover that year, he set out with his parents to worship at Jerusalem. They entered the city after a long journey; the sun was setting and people were already slaughtering sacrificial lambs and anointing their thresholds with branches of hyssop dipped in the blood.

They made their way through streets bustling with preparations for the Feast of Unleavened Bread and headed for the house of an uncle of Ahasuerus, who lived in the eastern section of the city. Unlike his scholarly brother, his uncle had gone up to Jerusalem early on and begun life as a merchant, going into leather trading, a vocation that most were loath to take up, and was currently doing very well in shoemaking.

After initial greetings, the grown-ups set about preparing things for the festival. Taking advantage of this, Ahasuerus went outside, where suddenly an odd sight attracted his attention. A crowd of neighborhood children was following a man, mocking him and shouting:

"Thedos, Thedos, Thedos the Braggart!
Thedos, Thedos, Thedos, fake Messiah!"

Some naughty children threw handfuls of sand at the man, or poked him with long sticks. The man walked on, not scolding them and showing no anger. He did not look mad, or possessed, but his unsteady gait, his projecting cheekbones, and the pallor of his face all indicated how exhausted and hungry he was. For some reason Ahasuerus felt sorry for him, and ran back to his uncle's house to fetch some leavened bread and unclean meat that was going to be thrown away.

When Ahasuerus came running back to the man, he was resting with his back against a wall in the open space at the end of the village. Slumped on the paving stone he had carefully chosen, he quickly glanced round at the children who had been following him. His expression was one of slight annoyance, not of anger, yet it somehow intimidated the crowd of children, so that they ran away in all directions.

The man, noticing Ahasuerus, who was still lingering there when all the other children had left, asked him, "Child, what do you want?"

"There's some bread and meat here . . ."

Ahasuerus replied cautiously, showing him the basket he was carrying.

"Really? That's very kind of you. Did you bring it for me?"

"Yes, but it's leavened bread."

"That doesn't matter. The Feast of Unleavened Bread hasn't begun yet."

The man took the basket and hungrily ate the bread and meat. Then he drank from a nearby well before slowly examining Ahasuerus. Finally he asked him, "Do you live near here?"

"No, I'm visiting my uncle."

"I suppose you came with your parents to worship in the Temple?"

"Yes."

"Thank you, anyway. I feel stronger now, thanks to you."

Ahasuerus could see nothing particular about him that might have made the children follow him, mocking. He plucked up his courage to ask the question that had been preoccupying him.

"Say . . . what did you do?"

"What? Oh, you mean the children . . . ?"

"Yes. Why were they following behind you and teasing you?"

"It was because . . ."

He paused and smiled sourly.

"It was because I commanded the walls of Jerusalem to collapse."

"Why?" Unable to understand, Ahasuerus repeated his question. Again the man smiled sourly and replied as if he were talking about someone else.

"In order to manifest my power to all the Jews; I made out that I was the Messiah."

Hearing that, Ahasuerus felt he somehow understood what the man meant. Although only a child, he had already heard, through the whispers and sniggers of grown-ups, rumors of the false messiahs who were causing such a stir. One false messiah had assembled a crowd beside the Jordan, claiming to be able to walk on water like Moses, but then he sank. Another self-proclaimed messiah had summoned people to gather in the plain where he would reveal to them the face of God, but only ended up covered in sand. Ahasuerus thought he had heard something about what the man before him had done. But on meeting him, instead of finding it amusing as most grown-ups had, Ahasuerus was intrigued and wanted to know more.

"So what happened?"

"Well, not a stone moved, of course."

The man continued to speak as if it had happened to someone else. Ahasuerus found his way of talking very strange.

"So you're not the Messiah and you did what you did knowing that the walls were not going to fall down?"

"Right. And I did it after gathering tens of thousands of people on the Mount of Olives."

Once again, the man smiled strangely.

Bewildered, Ahasuerus asked again, "But why did you do it?"

"More importantly, you're listening to what I say and not laughing. Why don't you laugh like the rest?"

Suddenly looking serious as he spoke, the man stared intently into Ahasuerus's face. Then he looked more sternly and asked another question: "Child, how old are you?"

"I'm twelve."

"What do you want to become in the future?"

"I would like to become the most respected rabbi in the country."

Ahasuerus gave the reply he had learned from his parents and the teachers in the synagogue.

"In that case, you must already have learned many things."

"I can recite the entire Torah by heart, almost without missing a line. I have also learned the *Nevi'im*, the Prophets, and the *Kethuvim*, the other writings, as well as the commentaries of the *Midrash*, the *Halakha,* and the *Mishneh.*"

With childish pride, Ahasuerus reeled off everything he had ever studied. But unlike the teachers of the law and the scribes, the *Sophrim*, who had been his instructors, the man did not seem surprised, nor did he show any interest in testing his knowledge. Ahasuerus had wanted to boast that he also knew the Talmudic *Aggadah* and the apocryphal books, that he could speak Aramaic fluently, and that he had begun to read and write Greek, but he said nothing more, rather disappointed.

"You have certainly studied some difficult texts, hard even for grown men to master. I believe you. But tell me, what can all those words give us?"

The man, who had been observing the boy for a while in silence, questioned him with a watchful look. Ahasuerus hesitated, unsure of what the man was asking, then finally repeated the reply he usually gave to his parents and teachers.

"Why, everything—blessings and peace, and the strength capable of awakening the love and compassion of God."

"Really . . . ?"

On hearing Ahasuerus's reply, the sad smile returned to the man's face. He murmured disapprovingly: "Your father seems to have entrusted the formation of your wisdom to the priests and rabbis too soon."

What he said was too hard for a child in his twelfth year to reply to. The man remained silent, apparently absorbed in his own deep thoughts. An awkward silence settled between them.

"Child . . ."

The man finally addressed the boy in a firmer voice, as if he had just come to a difficult decision. His look was no longer that of the starving, exhausted vagrant he had been only a short time before. "Will you meet me again tomorrow?"

"Why?" the boy asked, feeling apprehension mingled with a strange sense of expectancy.

"I've not answered the question you were curious about yet. I'll give you an answer. But first, there's something I want to show you."

"What is it?"

"Something that will teach you what the Word and the Law are. Anyhow, will you come to me tomorrow?"

His eyes seemed to be burning bright with a host of small flames. That, together with his low, powerful voice, was more than enough to overwhelm the soul of young Ahasuerus.

"Yes. I'll ask my parents."

"No, you must say nothing to them. You can go with them to the Temple, then steal away secretly while they are busy worshipping. I'll be waiting for you out front, where the money changers sit."

The man rose abruptly and hobbled away. The words he had spoken were like an order that Ahasuerus could not disobey.

The next day, drawn by an unknown power, he duly went to the appointed place to meet the false messiah Thedos, who took him to a slum on the outskirts of the city. There, naked children without so much as a stitch of clothing were weeping for hunger, while beside them women were rolling on the ground, tearing at each other's hair, hurling coarse insults at one another over a scrap of bread, in a scene that showed to what extent material penury causes misery and pain. Next, they visited a workshop manned by slaves. There, men were treating other men in a way no animal, no matter how fierce and brutal a beast, ever treated another of its own species, harnessing them and thrashing them with whips. Reduced to slavery after being defeated in war, or for not paying debts, yet prisoners of a superstition known as hope, they endured an existence worse than death, and would only escape from the bonds of misery and pain on the day their souls finally left their bodies. Thedos and the boy then went to an underground prison. It was not clear how they managed to enter into a place so strictly guarded, but Ahasuerus was deeply shocked by what he saw in that dark, dank jail. Theft, robbery, murder, rape . . . People guilty of such crimes, which sounded dreadful from a distance, were simply wretched men who had lost the battle with their own flesh; the scales had been turned against them by their culture and their social situation. In addition, ever since the miserable end of the Hasmonaeans over thirty years before, some prisoners had been awaiting a Messiah from the family of David, one who would establish a political regime; others thought he would come from among the descendants of Levi, the priestly caste, with their otherworldly religious vision. As for the Zealots who had fought and been taken prisoner in the resistance against Rome, there might be concern over their fanaticism, but not the least shadow of evil could be found in them.

Thedos did not stop there, but led Ahasuerus outside the city walls. He wanted to show him the Hill of Crosses, which was the main place of execution, and then the Valley of Lepers. On the Hill of Crosses, several Galileans were being executed; they had killed a Roman centurion and a tax collector. The man most recently crucified was screaming in pain, while others, having already spent long hours there, were slowly dying, calling on the name of God or Elijah. Inside a cave in the Valley of Lepers, filthier than any pig sty, lepers, whose only crime was to have been born with a body capable of being infected with such a terrible disease, addressed unending prayers to Heaven, lifting up disfigured faces and truncated limbs.

It is hard to believe that a boy of twelve, no matter how intelligent and thoughtful, would be able to fully comprehend the true implications of such scenes. But it seems clear that he was being led by some kind of power, going far beyond mere curiosity, for he continued to follow Thedos to the very end of that strange pilgrimage without turning away, although at such an age he was bound to be disturbed and frightened. Indeed, more than that; for at the very moment Ahasuerus was plumbing every recess of misery and misfortune that can befall the physical body of a human being, the son of Yahweh was in the Temple discussing the Word with famous priests and teachers, in which we cannot help but sense an intervention of Providence.

The day was drawing to a close by the time Thedos and Ahasuerus had finished their visits and returned to the city. Thedos had walked ahead of the boy from beginning to end, not speaking, merely guiding, and it was only when they reached the vacant lot where they had met on the previous day that he looked at Ahasuerus and spoke, as if resuming their previous conversation:

"Child, you are intelligent, so you will remember what I say, even if you do not yet understand fully the meaning of what you have seen today. Listen, and then think about it all for yourself, when your mind and intelligence are fully grown. Yesterday, you said that the Word can give us everything. But today you have seen for yourself that the Word can give us nothing. Were not people suffering and dying at the very moment when the priests and teachers were proclaiming at the top of their voices the Word in all its beauty and hope? The Word was unable to fill the bellies of the hungry or clothe the naked. It was unable to protect people from crime and from disease; it was powerless against misery and misfortune. At this very moment, many thousand times the number of people you have seen today are dying pointlessly in pain, believing in the superstition of the Word."

Although Ahasuerus could understand almost nothing, the words penetrated deep into his soul, like rain soaking into parched ground. Thedos looked at the boy with piercing eyes, as if checking how deeply his words were engraving themselves on his soul, then went on, his tone growing more passionate.

"Listen well. I feel that a critical moment is approaching. Someone is coming. But he must not simply be an incarnation of the Word. The one who comes must be able to give us everything we desire.

"For that, he must bring three keys with him: first, bread, to save our wretched bodies from starvation; second, a miracle, to protect our feeble minds from evil; and third, worldly power, to impose the order of justice and love and banish blindness and cruelty. If any of those three are lacking, that person cannot be our Messiah.

"What I did on the Mount of Olives was designed to teach people that. I initially promised to give bread to my followers, but I could not keep my word. Then I declared that I would drive out the Romans, establish the kingdom of God in this land, and defend righteousness with the royal scepter and the sword, but that too I was unable to achieve. Finally, I revealed to the people on the Mount of Olives, through the memory of their disappointment, that the last of the signs a Messiah must bring with him is a miracle. Be sure to remember: bread, a miracle, and power. The mere incarnation of the Word, just like the Word itself, can give us nothing."

After speaking, Thedos returned his piercing stare to Ahasuerus, who was moved for a reason he could not fathom. At last Thedos smiled in satisfaction, as if confirming that his words were safely lodged deep in the boy's memory, then rose determinedly. "Night has fallen, child. Go home now. I must be on my way, too."

Thedos hastily bade Ahasuerus farewell, and left him standing there with a dazed expression. He disappeared down an already darkening alley without once looking back. His words of farewell were spoken in the tired, weak voice of their first meeting, perhaps because he felt that he had finally done what he had to do in life, but there was a mysterious aura about him as he walked away.

Ahasuerus only came to himself long after Thedos had parted. He suddenly thought of the anxious expressions of his parents, who would be searching everywhere for him, and his heart filled with anguish as he wondered what excuse he could find to explain where he had been all day, for they would never understand if he told them the truth. He began to run as fast as he could toward his uncle's house, and the world of a twelve-year-old awaiting him there, forgetting Thedos and the rest. The memory of that strange day, engraved forever upon his mind, would come rising up again in later days, steering his life in uncommon directions; but as it stood, this youth was utterly powerless to deal with the problem of God or of spiritual experience.

5

Time passed: time that was recorded nowhere, remembered by no one, known only to the soul of legend. Now Ahasuerus was in his eighteenth year, in the full springtime of his youth.

Physically, his body had fully matured. He was nearly a foot taller than his father and as broad-shouldered as the laborers engaged in felling the cedars of Lebanon. His face, where blond side locks had begun to grow, was so handsome that girls would lie dreaming of him for several nights after a single glance; his brown eyes had lost their boyish twinkle and had taken on a dark, glistening sheen.

Like his body, his mind had matured. No other youth had studied and memorized as much as he had about the Word of Yahweh and his Law, the teachings of the prophets and their prophecies, the faith and exploits of kings and judges, the exegesis and commentaries of all the doctors of the Law, all the hymns of faith and the various apocalypses, the rituals and services of the Temple and the synagogues, all the rules and customs that determined the life of his people, and much more. His skill in mastering languages was exceptional; besides the written Hebrew inherited from his forefathers, he could speak Aramaic with the merchants arriving with caravans from exotic eastern lands as though he were speaking with hometown friends. He had learned Greek by studying the translation of the Septuagint, and if it weren't for the Pharisees' restrictions, he would have been able to undertake a thorough study of Greek culture.

Legends even claim that he could speak every tongue from the land where the sun rises to the land where the sun sets. That rumor probably arose from exaggerations, intending to prove that he had been assisted by Satan; but in view of the fact that Judea was situated at a crossroads of trade, where caravans arrived from all directions, it is quite possible that he might have known other languages in addition to Aramaic and Greek. All of Ahasuerus's knowledge of language, inherited from his ancestors, or borne in from other regions, filled his mind and overflowed, giving his face a unique expression. It was an expression of serenity and depth, resulting from the addition of intellectual charm to an already handsome man. But in years when he should have been whispering words of love to girls his own age, the call of manhood sought him out in an unusual form.

One night in late summer, during the month of Elul, Ahasuerus was prowling the dew-soaked garden surrounding the house of Asaph, a local merchant. Asaph was extremely rich, owning several caravans and a wharf of his own, as well as a warehouse in the nearby port of Jaffa. Ahasuerus was waiting for the huge house's inhabitants to go to sleep. The lamps in the windows soon went out, one after another, and the servants, who had been bustling about until late in the night, coming and going as they finished washing the last dishes, finally seemed ready to retire. Ahasuerus continued to wait in the shadow of the trees in the well-tended garden; only when a deep silence had fallen over the entire house did he finally move toward it. Approaching the single window from which a bright and peculiarly voluptuous light still shone, he knocked lightly several times at regular intervals, as if tapping a signal.

Without any other sign, the curtain lifted and the window opened silently. Ahasuerus climbed skillfully over the marble sill and into the room.

"Oh, Ahasuerus!"

He was welcomed joyfully by Asaph's young wife, wrapped in a silk robe, eager to embrace his dew-soaked body. After Asaph's first wife died, his immense wealth had enabled him to take a new wife, a beautiful young woman from an illustrious family. That was several years ago; since then she had become the mother of a boy and a girl, and her beauty was still dazzling as she approached thirty.

She kissed Ahasuerus passionately, then held him in her arms and whispered to him: "I don't know how I could have endured such a long and dreary night if you hadn't come. It's been five days since he's been gone—he went to Parthia to open up a new caravan route. I was waiting for you yesterday and the day before, with the blue veil hanging at the window." The blue veil at the window of her room was a signal they had adopted to indicate that her husband was absent.

"I knew, Sarah, of course I knew."

Ahasuerus stammered, giddy with the fragrance of the woman's flesh, a fragrance he had been deprived of for some time. He had actually spent several days in agonies of indecision, ever since he learned that Asaph was away. The remorse and guilt he felt at having broken Yahweh's commandment and committed adultery with another man's wife had grown stronger than his reckless passion. He had already sworn to himself on several occasions, as he staggered from the deep shadows of Asaph's garden in the early morning light, that he would not come to her again.

Yet it had only taken a glimpse of the blue veil at her window for him to be swept away by an uncontrollable desire. No dreadful warning as to the wages of sin, no verse from any of the books of Wisdom teaching the vanity of carnal desire had been of the slightest help to him. This time he had spent three whole days in an intense struggle with himself. After those wide-eyed, sleepless nights, in which each moment had been like a cruel whiplash, he found himself brought to his knees before her, or rather before his own immense desire, finally defeated, shuddering with a greater ardor and excitement than on any of the previous nights he had spent with her.

"My beauty, my love! Why did the Lord not send you into the world a little later? Why did he not place you among our neighborhood girls so that I might take you for my lawful wedded wife? Why did he deliver you into the arms of that ugly old merchant? Why does he not allow us to spend every day and night in love together?"

Ahasuerus stammered out his words, in the throes of deep sorrow, lying like a child in the woman's arms with his head pressed between her warm breasts. The torment and agony he had experienced over the course of those nights now turned into uncontrollable tears that flowed down his haggard cheeks.

"My poor dear! You're crying like a fool. Here we are together, and we can feel our love for each other like this."

"That's not what I meant, Sarah. Why has God . . ."

Sarah loosened her embrace and placed her soft white hand over Ahasuerus's mouth.

"That nonsense again! Now, take me in your arms. Hold me tightly, passionately. The morning star and the cock that will crow at dawn are jealous of us as they await their hour. Stop hurting yourself with pointless regrets. We should simply enjoy the cup that is set before us. All we have to do is drink and enjoy it when we can. Come, quickly."

With those words, she warmly embraced Ahasuerus, who was caught in a strange vortex of passion and torment, and drew him toward the bed. The luxuriously adorned bed and the memories of the pleasures they had shared there soothed his body and soul, igniting a fire of intense carnal desire that burned away every other thought.

As on previous occasions, they rolled across the bed in a tight embrace. They were a boat rocking to the movement of fierce waves; a mighty waterfall, an inextricable swamp, wild stallions, tenacious serpents. They gave themselves unsparingly and at the same time took greedily from each other, tormenting and enduring torments. It was a simultaneous focusing and releasing, a suffocating act of coming together, then pulling away.

The bed creaked despite the skilled carpenter's boasts of how solid it was; strange groans that might be shouts or sobs burst out in spite of every caution and effort to restrain them, and a storm of passion swept over them amidst a rustling of bedding. Finally, bathed in sweat, Ahasuerus lay as if dead on top of the woman, without the least movement. She gently pulled him down to lie at her side and whispered as she snuggled against his breast, "Could Heaven be more delightful, more blissful than the place we have just passed through together? Could Heaven be more beautiful or more resplendent? Oh, beloved Ahasuerus, when I saw you for the very first time in the olive grove at Shekhem on the feast day of Purim, I recognized that you bore heaven within you. In your red, warm lips, your profound stare, in your soft hands, and above all in your body, so well-proportioned and strong, like a Greek statue, I saw . . ."

Her voice was moist, thick with the pleasure still thrilling and flowing through every vein of her body. For Ahasuerus it was otherwise. He was staring up at the ceiling with a vacant expression. He tried to stifle the voice of guilt and repentance rising from deep in his heart by the memory of the rapture of the previous moments, but to no avail. Rather, as the fire of desire subsided and the palpitations of his body slowed, the voices grew louder.

"Why has the Lord not allowed us to enjoy our bodies freely, after giving them to us? Why did he belatedly send his Word to name this joy a sin? Why is it that as soon as I've finished making love to you, so many helpless tears flow like this?"

Ahasuerus spoke sadly, unable to endure the tormenting voices in his heart. His words vexed Sarah, who was intent on savoring her pleasure for as long as possible, regretting only that it was already fading; but she spoke with a gentle, caressing voice to soothe him:

"Ahasuerus, you should forget all that. Those commandments are for old men and for priests, not for us. They were handed down to Moses by the cantankerous spirit of Horeb, intent on forbidding for no reason at all anything that might give us joy or pleasure; it's not something demanded by the almighty El Shaddai, God of Abraham."

"They're one and the same God, not two. Besides, ever since the Word was received by our forefathers and placed in the Ark of the Covenant, it has been the object of our faith and worship, equivalent to God's presence. Sarah, we mustn't deny the Word and the Law in our attempt to deny our sin."

At that, she finally revealed her displeasure. She drew Ahasuerus's head toward her, and gazed into his eyes as she spoke sharply:

"You're afraid. What you really fear isn't the Word of God, or his Law; it's being dragged into the street and struck with stones, isn't it? But I'm not afraid. If I am to be rewarded with the moments of ecstasy I have just experienced, no flying stone, however sharp, could ever hurt me."

"I fear the stone that is flying toward my conscience."

"A stone flying toward your conscience? My mother's a daughter of the tribe of Levi and my brother's a well-known rabbi, but I don't believe in all that. Did you know what sin was at the moment you were born? Isn't it because people have told you that things are sins that now you regard them as sins? Nothing in this world is a sin from the beginning. It's the same with adultery ... Turning it into a sin is a mean trick invented by men uncertain of being able to keep control of their wives by the power of love alone, as a way of binding them to themselves. Just think for a moment! What harm have we done, except to the vanity of an ugly old merchant and his warped self-esteem? We've simply been happily enjoying the bodies that the Lord gave us.

"Besides, even if it is a sin, I don't regret or fear anything. Because between knowing nothing of this pleasure or of the pangs of conscience, or knowing it and suffering, there's almost no difference. It's better to eat both sweet figs and bitter figs than not to eat the sweet fig for fear of the bitter one that may follow it."

To Ahasuerus, who had only known the celebrated masters and only heard orthodox forms of teaching, Sarah's reasoning was new and cunning, and it therefore felt strange to him. Still, one thing he could not comprehend was the light that seemed to be shining from her flushed face. It wasn't the gloom of sin and death, but the fullness of beauty and life. It was a light he had never before seen emanating from her or from anyone else.

Ahasuerus looked at her in astonishment, but soon turned his eyes away. Flowing through his people's veins, faith in the Word and the Law had accumulated like perpetual snows in their souls as generation followed generation: his astonishment turned suddenly into a strong sense of guilt. Instead of contradicting her, he slowly rose, feeling even grimmer than before, and went to where his clothes lay strewn.

"Ahasuerus, wait. Will you leave before you drain the cup poured out for you? There are still many hours before the cock's first crow."

Presumably she was acting on her still unfulfilled desires, for Sarah now moved toward him on her knees, trying to prevent him from getting dressed. Her beauty, radiating in a bewitching manner from her naked body, served to stimulate Ahasuerus afresh. He stopped briefly, then pushed her hand away. He struggled to control his mindless desire by imagining the vulgar coquetry of the prostitutes in the streets.

"Sarah, you must let me go. I need to reflect on things, alone. If I find enough self-confidence, I will come back."

He stuttered as he spoke. Yet he knew full well that this was the end. Sarah, awakened now from her dizzy passion by the humiliation of rejection, seemed to have realized this as well. Her renunciation of him was so swift and so final that Ahasuerus was puzzled when he later recalled the moment. Rising with a little sigh, Sarah put on the silk nightdress that Ahasuerus had so hastily torn from her. Going to a mirror, she straightened her clothing and arranged her disheveled hair, then she calmly addressed Ahasuerus as he was about to climb out the window:

"Good-bye, Ahasuerus. What was nothing special for me was highly painful for you. But now I am giving you your freedom. Don't yearn for me. What I loved was a healthy man in the fresh flush of youth, not some particular person with your name and your mind."

Her words might have seemed to be exacting revenge, but nothing in her face suggested that she was lying or exaggerating.

So Ahasuerus found himself back in his own world, which he had paid no heed to for some time. Yet it was no longer the world of the Temple or the synagogues where his former teachers were still to be found; nor that of his father's library with its smell of parchment; nor was it still the world of the Word. Ridding himself of all the preconceptions and prejudices he had acquired over his years of learning, he focused now on an aspect of human life that he had come to discover for himself through Sarah. He had previously only detected a vague trace of it here and there, in a few verses of the Psalms and the Song of Songs; but there were no texts he had read, no words he had heard, that explained the strange light, so full of beauty and life, that he had glimpsed during the last night he had spent with her. Yet despite the many sleepless nights he spent thinking about the problem, the true nature of that light remained unfathomable to him. No matter how hard he tried to suppress it, his carnal desire came surging back whenever his vigilance lapsed, and his longing for her grew ever stronger.

A few months passed. One day Ahasuerus went for a walk through the streets to clear his mind, exhausted by his sorrowful musings, and noticed a strange commotion in a crowd gathered on some open ground in front of a synagogue. As he approached the throng, he realized from their threatening eyes and the stones they were carrying that it had to be one of the impromptu street-side trials that occasionally happened. He had no desire to see the cruel spectacle, and was about to leave when he saw the woman who was being dragged into the center of the crowd. It was Sarah. Although she was surrounded by a furious mob, she had the appearance of a noblewoman. Instead of a sinner trembling before her imminent death, she resembled someone who had been awakened from slumber by the noise of the crowd and come out to see what vulgar activities they were up to.

"What has that woman done?"

Ahasuerus questioned an unknown bystander in a shaken voice. The man spat out a reply, his face expressing an insidious mixture of instinctive disgust and incomprehensible jealousy:

"She has broken the Law, committing the sin of adultery."

"Who was her partner?"

Quailing inwardly, Ahasuerus questioned him again urgently. The man's face twisted with reinforced viciousness as he replied:

"A young groom in the service of Asaph. He's already been killed by his master."

"Where is Asaph?"

"He's over there beside the priests. Since she's not a slave, he's handed her over to the Law and to us."

The judgment must have been pronounced as they were speaking, for someone shouted and stones began to fly from all sides. Paralyzed by a sudden dread and an awareness of his own helplessness, Ahasuerus stared dumbly at Sarah. At that very moment, her eyes seemed to be drawn toward him by some force; Sarah saw Ahasuerus in the crowd. Their eyes met for a second. Despite the distance separating them, he felt she was standing just in front of him. Blood was flowing from her forehead, but still she remained erect as the stones flew at her; strangely, there was the hint of a smile in her eyes. It was a frightening, mysterious smile, suggesting mockery or compassion. But that was all. Then a sharp stone thrown from close range slammed into her back and brought her down, without so much as a single cry, and she lay crumpled on the ground. Then stones rained down and her bloodied body was soon covered.

Ahasuerus remained standing there, unaware of anything, his body and mind frozen. When he came to his senses, the crowd had already scattered. All that remained were the stifled sobs and lamentations of relatives who had come to take away the body and the insoluble question posed by that corpse buried under the stones of the Word.

In the time that followed, Ahasuerus devoted himself to an arduous investigation into the essence of human existence, which originated in the riddle posed by Sarah's death, and the misery and misfortunes of every person endowed with a body and desires. Legends report that at this period he was "a friend to thieves and beggars; a brother to prostitutes, slaves, the possessed, and lepers." That might seem to have little connection with the shock caused by Sarah's death, but at least one thing can be asserted definitely: he had rid himself of the traditional view that sees the misery and misfortunes of all who suffer as merely the wages of sin. And there is no doubt that at some level he was being driven by his memory of the vagabond Thedos, whom he had met in Jerusalem as a child.

One evening in his nineteenth year, having returned home after a lengthy absence, Ahasuerus went to see his father in his study, and without any preliminaries abruptly asked him, "Father, do you really believe in the sin of Cain?"

His father considered him with a look of deep solicitude and carefully rolled up the *megillah* scroll he had been reading. Six months had passed since his son had left the family home to follow his own unknown path, with considerable difficulty. He had been worried about his perilous wanderings and wildness, but all young people have to experience that at least once, and since he had full confidence in his son's unique intelligence and good character, he had never allowed himself to scold him. However, the rumors that had recently come to his ears were such that he could not remain indifferent. He was deeply anxious and at a loss as to where to begin. Now here was his son, breezing in and asking preposterous questions.

Ahasuerus asked a different question, perhaps unaware of his father's inner perplexity: "Father, who would you punish more severely, the perpetrator of a crime or the instigator?" Unable to sense the intention behind his son's first question, he had hesitated to reply; he now only reluctantly replied to the second, more obvious question.

"The instigator, of course."

"Then is the perpetrator always innocent?"

"Not necessarily. Even a mere perpetrator should be punished if he knows the evil of the action or the wrongness of the outcome."

The father answered his son's question warily, but with all the sincerity he could muster. His son pursued his questioning, as if he had expected that answer.

"What if all the feelings and the will of the perpetrator were entirely under the control of the instigator, or if he had been compelled to act by the irresistible power of the instigator?"

"In such a case, no. Are you suggesting that Cain was a perpetrator of that kind?"

"Exactly. He was the Lord's perpetrator. Just a poor agent, betrayed by the instigator, who cursed him instead of rewarding him."

At that point, his father began to vaguely sense the drift of his son's words. He had no wish to enter into a lengthy discussion. It wasn't that the complexity of the topic troubled him, but that he feared his son's knowledge and cleverness, of which he had not yet tested the limits. He pretended not to understand his words, though this was not the case. He made him go on talking alone in order to avoid the risk of a conflict of opinions between them.

"I don't understand what you mean."

The son was not prepared to let his father off so easily. Instead of resolving his father's doubts, he tried to draw him into the argument he was formulating by asking a new question.

"Father, do you think that the will of a creature can ever transcend that of the Creator?"

"Of course not. Every hair on our bodies, our every breath, all without exception derive from him, and likewise our minds too are all under the will of the Lord our God."

"From whom, then, did Cain's murderous intent originate?"

"This is rather sudden . . . The Lord who is the Origin of everything must have given it to him, of course. But that went together with a prohibition."

"Then what about a will that ignores the prohibition and proceeds to kill?"

"What a tough exegesis! But I never considered it significant, so I haven't thought about it very deeply."

Again his father tried to escape from the discussion that he was being drawn into unprepared. As he had hoped, Ahasuerus continued to present his own ideas, but he did not let his father off the hook.

"There's no need to think so deeply. There can only be two solutions. The first is to say that it did not come from God. In which case, like the Persians, we are bound to acknowledge an aspect of humanity that escapes his control, with some other Mighty Being controlling that part. If this is so, then God's Word and the Law represent an abuse of power, an excessive self-confidence, or a misunderstanding about human nature. But you cannot accept that, since you believe that God is omniscient, absolutely perfect, and unique."

"Naturally. And what is the other?"

"The conclusion that every aspect of human nature comes from the Lord. The result remains the same, even if you invent a shield called Satan. In that case, Cain is not responsible for any sin. He merely carried out the Lord's prearranged plan with the instrument of the will he received from him. The all-knowing Lord allowed Abel to be struck down before his very eyes because he had an intention higher than forgiving Cain's homicide. We might say that he instigated Cain's act for a certain purpose. For example, to show through Cain a type of crime, murder, and its wickedness, and through his punishment impose a psychological constraint and threat on everyone, on all potential criminals.

"In that case Cain, having fulfilled his task to the letter, ought to have been rewarded rather than punished. Besides, what the Torah implies is God's hidden good will toward Cain. Though Cain is reported to have appealed to him, the Lord promised anyone who persecuted him a retaliation seven times as great. So why does everyone always consider Cain to have been simply a wicked sinner?"

When Ahasuerus reached this point, his father felt he needed to take a stand. The discussion was growing increasingly serious.

"My son, you are seeing the matter too one-sidedly. Questions about God and Heaven cannot be clarified by petty human wisdom. There is something in what you are saying, but it somehow reminds me of those Sophists who used to go wandering across Greece. You are deliberately confusing the nature of the law that forbids and the law that commands. Your defense of Cain would be correct if he had fulfilled God's command. Why do you only stress the evil hidden in human nature, and ignore the existence of the good will that is capable of opposing and conquering it? Has the Lord not given us strength enough to resist all the temptations of evil? Between those two wills, we are free to choose one as the motivation of our actions. That is why Cain should be blamed, because he paid no attention to the good side and dared to take a forbidden course."

"You talk like a Roman judge. So, Father, you believe in that freedom of the will that we're supposed to have been given in the days of Adam? Do you truly believe that any aspect of our actions or our thoughts is free of the Creator's all-inclusive providence?"

"I believe that to be the testimony of all the scriptures and the prophets."

"Knowing that everything was made according to the Creator's plan and that we therefore can never in any case be his equals?"

"Yes indeed. Insofar as he has foretold the Last Judgment; insofar as he has promised to reward good and punish evil . . ."

"That's not freedom; it's irresponsible *laissez-faire* on his part. Do you really believe that a being who stays silent while people struggle and bleed—caught between two contradictory wills, losing the internal battle and pursuing a course of depravity and ruin— do you believe such a being has the right to judge and punish the sins of people that result from that? Can you truly call such a being not a heartless jailer but a God of Love and Mercy?"

"But the Lord did not remain silent all the time. He has given us many Words and many Laws, while many prophets and righteous men have been sent to fortify our good will."

"But isn't the choice to believe them or not included within our freedom?"

"Any soul who believes in him and does his will is able to believe and follow his Word and those he has sent."

"It's a circular argument. Couldn't the choice whether or not to believe in him and obey him have been included in our freedom since the time of Adam?"

"But what do you understand by freedom?"

"I reckon it never existed from the very start. That freedom itself is part of his preordained plan, and likewise our salvation and our fall merely follows that plan."

"What about all the sincere intentions and endeavors we offer up to him in this world?"

"They are merely the mark of a small elect remnant whose destiny it is to be saved according to his plan. While the unchosen majority suffer and despair, without knowing when that curse will be revoked . . ."

Hearing Ahasuerus speaking in such terms, his father felt a nameless fear and an indistinct helplessness. It was an amplified form of the concern he experienced, simple and honest man that he was, every time he listened to the radical new exegeses of young rabbis obviously influenced by Persian dualism and eschatology, together with a sense of intellectual inferiority at being unable to challenge them in logical argument.

After a silence, his father stammered out a reply in which he slyly attempted to draw love and mercy from behind a traditional God of punishments and rewards:

"I do not think so. And even if I agreed with what you say of that plan, I cannot think that the plan of the One who loves us could be so narrow and capricious. He would rather wait thousands of years, tens of thousands of years, until we had all saved ourselves." But this only served to open up the floodgates of whatever dark passion had swept over his son. Suddenly bringing a new, malicious and aggressive energy to his sarcastic, mocking tone, Ahasuerus retorted:

"That's a foolish belief. If our God was so merciful, so full of love, he should never have given us that undefined freedom to start with. Then Adam would not have dared pluck the fruit of the Knowledge of Good and Evil and we could have avoided the yoke of original sin. Moreover, if freedom had to be given to us, he should never have established any proscriptive laws. If that were the case, even if Adam had picked the fruit it would not have been a sin.

"But God, loading our feeble wills with those two heavy burdens, is determined to make us responsible for the choices we make; we who are mere creatures, predisposed to irresponsibility. Worse still, while in Eden there had just been one forbidden thing, as time went on the number of proscriptions increased, including all the different edicts from before the time of Moses, the more than four thousand lessons in the Torah and the *Halakha*, and the countless rules hidden in the *Midrash*, the *Mishneh*, and goodness knows what else. I really cannot understand why they are needed, or what essential relation they have with our salvation or our eternal life. Why did such a long, meandering, and painful path have to be imposed on us, his 'dearly beloved children?'"

"My son, you must not try to attack the works of the immeasurably profound, almighty Lord with the puny simplifications of human logic. There is no light without darkness; a straight line would be meaningless if there were no curves. I don't know the ultimate answer, but if these proscriptions have made our path a long and painful one, and if for that reason the world has become wrapped in sin and darkness, there must be a sufficient explanation for it. It may be that through the sin and darkness of the world he intends to make his goodness and his light more clearly manifest . . ."

"That's precisely the point. What you are saying employs the logic used by the priests in the Temple and the teachers in the synagogues. According to them, Satan and sin exist by God's will. But if that is the case, why must they be cursed and condemned and why must those humans who follow them fall into Sheol or Gehenna? Why must they be hurled into the eternal flames of torment if they exist by permission of his will, and if they have fulfilled the role given them in order to contribute to his glory? If we go back to the problem I started with, the case of Cain provides us with an example. He earnestly carried out the will of God with the instrument he received from God, so at least the 'Mark of Cain' ought to have been a mark of trust, a mark of a promise showing that he had been chosen by God for a particular purpose, not a mark of forgiveness and mercy to a sinner."

"My son . . ."

His father suddenly stood up as if alarmed, recalling something.

"I've just remembered . . . when I was young, there was a group of blasphemers who used to make troubling assertions similar to yours. They were never able to form their own sect and eventually vanished, suffering under the curse of God and the wrath of the people; but I remember hearing that their origins were very ancient. Some said that they had first come about at the time of the division of the tribes after the death of Solomon, or during the Babylonian captivity, and that if they ever appeared again and received a name, it might well be 'the sect of Cain.' I think I also heard about a particular heretic belief that sees Satan as the Spirit of Wisdom and venerates the serpent that tempted Eve as the Apostle of Wisdom. The basis for what you are arguing seems to me to resemble the beliefs of those two groups. Where in heaven's name did you hear such ideas? Could that group of blasphemers still exist in the present day?"

Fear and anguish distorted his father's face as he questioned him. He was gripped by a disturbing premonition: rather than seeing his son respected as the finest rabbi in Judea, he might instead be obliged one day to drag his corpse from under a mound of stones. Fortunately, his son's reply was sufficient to alleviate, if not totally allay, his grim presentiment:

"It's not anything I've learned from anyone, or read anywhere. These are simply doubts that are bound to confront you as soon as you free yourself from the superficial exegeses of the scriptures and all the prejudices and fallacies that are so prevalent nowadays. Father, have you really lived your entire life with the faith and devotion you have now?"

The father detected in his son's tone a strong desire to be freed from an agonizing doubt, rather than a wish to impose his opinions.

"So much the better. I thought you'd been bewitched by some evil heretics. In my younger years, I too spent many a sleepless night reflecting on seemingly unresolvable doubts over what God's will might be."

"And did you overcome all those doubts?" Ahasuerus asked, his eyes suddenly filling with expectancy. Eager not to disappoint him, his father quickly replied:

"I think I can say so. And I even recall experiencing doubts similar to those you've been mentioning. But unfortunately I don't seem able to express things to you clearly in a few words."

His father was deeply perplexed. It was clear that the difficult questions regarding matters of faith from days gone by, long transformed into indifference and inertia, still remained within him, unspoken, a burden weighing on his shoulders. Despite his son's deeply disappointed expression, the best he could do was, after a long silence, imitate the discourse he once heard the high priest Annas use to scold some young atheists who had been corrupted by Hellenic thought.

"My child, you have too much trust in human knowledge and wisdom. Always remember: knowledge and wisdom, no matter how advanced, cannot solve the problem of God's Providence as if it were arithmetic; it is not by wisdom that we come to believe in God, it is by believing in him that we become wise; too much learning often harms our faith and devotion. Through ardent prayers delivered with a humble heart, and by our sincere efforts, reading his Word and putting it into practice, it is possible to perceive the true mind of God and, in that way, I feel sure you can finally take part in spiritual knowledge . . ."

The father was clearly aware that such vacuous arguments could never move his son. He, in turn, was still looking at his father's face, but his thoughts were elsewhere, as if he had lost interest in any further conversation. The father looked at his son with a new anxiety, and quickly concluded:

"Never let small doubts confuse you; always maintain a sense of the larger picture, and keep seeking true wisdom. I firmly believe you will become the finest rabbi in Judea. I am certain of it. Now I am tired. Kiss me. It's past my bedtime."

At that, Ahasuerus rose without a word, kissed his father's already wrinkled cheek, and went to his room. The serious talk they shared that evening was to be the last between the father and his son. In the time to come, the father found himself almost overwhelmed by a flood of letters and messages arriving from far and near—mostly they came from teachers of his acquaintance, from scribes in synagogues, old friends who had retired from the world or become priests—recounting his son's heretical opinions and blasphemous acts. He had left home and was wandering through Judea, having become Satan's hireling, trampling on everything sacred that came his way. Ahasuerus was sharp of mind and ready to employ his agile logic in intellectual battle, and when he denied original sin and defended Cain, many older priests and hermits withdrew from before him, shaking their heads muttering laments. Orthodox teachers and scribes exploded in fury on hearing his words. One day, Ahasuerus was driven out under a hail of stones for having dared to criticize the way Abraham had acquired wealth by selling his wife, and the trick by which Jacob had stolen the benediction destined for his elder brother; another day, he was denounced for having mocked the cruelness of Yahweh for provoking the massacre of the first-born in Egypt and inciting their Hebrew ancestors to slaughter every living creature in several cities. In addition, he was thrown out of a synagogue after accusing the sons of Korah, who had written a number of Psalms, and David himself of being sycophants; and he was beaten up by a mob in the street for having laughed about the cunning of Job, who had endured all those unjust torments because he believed he would be rewarded in the end, and also at the capriciousness of Yahweh, who sent calamity on Job without consideration of good or evil.

Though all of his negations were really a search for affirmation and acceptance, the world simply could not understand him. The cynical responses of the formalist scholars, who surrendered to higher authority, and the indiscriminate persecution he suffered at the hands of others made him more perverse and resolute.

"If all that the Scriptures say about God is true, it was he who received favors from us, not we who received favors from him. No other tribe paid any attention to a god of such jealousy, wrath, and capriciousness; our ancestors alone accepted him. More than that, it might even be said that we created him, not he us."

This was Ahasuerus's final conclusion at that time, according to legend, which also exaggerated his subsequent fall. It was presumed to be a result of the sense of desolation felt by a man who had finally lost the god he had firmly believed in, had yearned to believe in. He would stagger around drunk in broad daylight; he shamelessly consorted with the women of the back streets. He haunted gambling dens and took part completely naked in gladiator-style combat in the Roman arenas; sometimes he would be involved in bloody brawls with thugs in the streets. Then one day at last, Ahasuerus vanished completely from his native land. It happened just as his despairing parents, giving up all the hopes they had nourished for him, were considering sending him off as an apprentice to his uncle, a shoemaker in Jerusalem.

Min Yoseop's manuscript broke off there. Despite its difficulty, the text provoked a strange emotion in Sergeant Nam. For him, the question of God had occupied him only briefly in days long past, and had then been forgotten amidst the complications of everyday life; now, however, it took hold of Sergeant Nam again in a nostalgic manner. At the same time, he was convinced that the story was no mere fabrication, but rather a reformulation of Min Yoseop's own personal experiences. Sergeant Nam was curious to know what developments followed, thinking that they might reveal Min Yoseop's inner journey. He was about to pick up the next section to continue reading when he noticed that the train was already entering Daegu. He reluctantly bundled together the notebooks and manuscript, resolving to read more later, and prepared to disembark.

All the way from the train station to his office, the strange impression produced by the text remained with Sergeant Nam, but it all evaporated the moment he began to make his report to Lieutenant Lee.

"So, you're writing a novel now, are you? Are you going to publish it in the *Police Gazette*?"

Carried away by his emotions, Sergeant Nam was evoking Min Yoseop's personal details at tedious length, when Lieutenant Lee, who had been listening patiently, interrupted him.

"You haven't discovered anything new about his last eight years? What are you going to do with a few letters postmarked several years back? Really! I don't know how someone like you has managed to stay a detective for so many years!"

He was flipping roughly through the notebooks and manuscript Sergeant Nam had brought. His expression suggested that he would have laid into him with his hands, if he let himself go. Suddenly coming to his senses, Sergeant Nam realized he was making his report in the wrong order and pulled his notebook out of his pocket.

"I forgot to tell you that I also made inquiries in the local ward office. Six months after he left, Min Yoseop transferred his official residence to this address in Busan."

Sergeant Nam had completely forgotten about the address the moment he had noted it down, as if bewitched in some way. The lieutenant's expression relaxed a little.

"Well that's the most important detail. Why didn't you tell me that first? Don't lose a minute: go to Busan straightaway. Detective Im is at the hardware store where the fruit knife was sold. And Detective Park will have to go to Seoul . . ."

"Why to Seoul?"

"We're going to have to question that wife of Elder Mun or whoever she is again, to find out if your fortune-telling was right or not."

Lieutenant Lee was obviously far from satisfied with the way Sergeant Nam had simply given credence to the woman's words and casually wrapped up his investigation. There was a general tendency among policemen to be obsessed with any woman connected with a crime. In addition, the lieutenant considered the distorted picture of the woman that Sergeant Nam had presented, somewhat carried away by his feelings, as insufficient for the investigation.

By nature Lieutenant Lee was incapable of harshness; feeling sorry for Sergeant Nam, who was looking thoroughly dejected as he turned to leave, he called him back before he had gone more than a few steps.

"Look, it's already past five now. Go home and get some rest tonight and leave early tomorrow. But don't waste your time digging into every pointless detail again. Be back here with your report tomorrow before we go off duty."

6

Sergeant Nam was completely exhausted after the two-day trip, and it was nearly eight in the morning when he woke, despite having gone to bed early the previous evening. Beside his pillow, Min Yoseop's manuscript lay scattered in disorder. He had taken it out to read but then put it aside, unable to finish even the first page, overwhelmed by sleep. He washed hastily, had a quick breakfast, then grabbed the section of the manuscript he had been reading the night before and hurried to the station.

In Busan, unseasonable winter rain was falling. The place he was looking for was near the port, close to Pier Two, and he found it easily with the help of directions given by an officer at the nearby police station. It turned out to be a small rooming house on a four-lane road that had been recently built as part of a redevelopment plan. Sergeant Nam pushed open the iron gate with its peeling paintwork and found two men who looked like dockworkers sitting drinking *soju*, perched on the edge of the veranda at the center of the old house, built in the Japanese style. He asked for the landlord and one of them shouted in a slurred voice toward a room inside. In response to the shout or because he had heard Sergeant Nam's voice, an older looking man who seemed to have never once smiled in his entire lifetime slid open the door, with an expression suggesting that everything was just too much bother.

Sergeant Nam identified himself and produced Min Yoseop's photo. The furrows in the man's grim face grew deeper still, indicating that he recognized him at once.

"That bastard . . ." The man spat out the word. His voice seemed to reflect a deep grievance.

"You remember him?" Indifferent to the man's feelings and pleased that he recognized Min Yoseop, Sergeant Nam began with his questions. With an expression suggesting that he was struggling to control his emotions, the man replied:

"Remember him? I'll never forget him, not even when I'm dead and buried."

"Why's that?"

The old man clamped his mouth shut, and his bloodshot eyes looked up at the leaden sky from which raindrops were still falling. He seemed to be trying to suppress violent feelings rising up within him.

"He took my son . . . my only son . . . and led him astray."

The reply was completely unexpected. Sergeant Nam found himself tensing up.

"When was that?"

"About six years ago."

"How old was your son at that time?"

"If he'd stayed on, he would have been in his last year of high school. He was eighteen."

Despite the man's anguished expression, Sergeant Nam felt himself relaxing; the man, however, grew increasingly distrustful. People whose son or daughter had left home at an early age sometimes deliberately made false reports or statements. For example, if a corpse was found that was so decomposed or disfigured as to be unidentifiable, they would swear that it was their child. As a general rule, a thorough check would show that the missing person was alive and well. In this way, people could take advantage of an intensive investigation to find their long-lost child. Strictly speaking, they could be charged with conspiring to obstruct the police in the course of their duties—and they caused no little confusion with such actions and wasted plenty of time. But at the sight of parents and children meeting again after years of separation, hugging and weeping, it was difficult to charge them with even a minor misdemeanor. What Sergeant Nam suspected now was just such a false report or statement.

"Look, it's very important that you tell me the truth. If you want to find your lost son, file a separate report. Then we'll look into it as carefully as we can."

"What are you talking about?"

"Just think about it. Your son was no longer a child. Don't you find it strange to say that someone in his nineteenth year was tricked and led astray?"

At that, the man's rage boiled over. It was no ordinary anger: he trembled as he screamed:

"What? You think I'm lying to you because I want to find that good-for-nothing son? That's going too far. I've worked with the police. At least I know you're not allowed to use tricks like that."

"Still, when a boy's eighteen he's an adult . . ."

"There's no doubt in my mind; it was that fellow who led him astray. My son left me the very next day after that bastard went away. And he blamed us for having driven him out. That's not all. Later on, someone saw my son in his company." Sergeant Nam's doubts vanished. In view of the man's unflinching attitude and firm, unhesitating tone, he could not believe he was lying.

"All right, I understand. I believe you. Now, about this man, can you show me some proof that he really lived here?"

Sergeant Nam brought the talk back to Min Yoseop, partly to calm the man down. He thought about it for a moment, then replied:

"Yes, actually, there is something. It's a bundle that he forgot when he left in the middle of the night. I felt like burning it but I didn't."

Since Min Yoseop had officially registered this house as his new address, it was unnecessary to look for further confirmation. Sergeant

Nam began to question the man regarding things he wanted to know, starting from the beginning.

"Tell me step-by-step what happened. How did this man come to stay with you, what were his relations with your son, why did your son leave home to follow him, and what happened after that . . . ?"

The man calmed down and seemed to be recollecting old memories. He drew from his pocket a cigarette holder made of artificial ivory with blackened cracks from which tar was seeping, inserted a cigarette stub and lit it.

"I hate even thinking about it all, but I'll tell you for my wife's sake. If you ever come across any news of our son, you really have to let her know; she never stops crying, day and night."

When the stub in the ivory cigarette holder had completely fallen into ash, he began his tale with a sigh that issued from the depths of his heart.

. . . Seven years previously, when the neighborhood had not yet been touched by redevelopment, it was full of cheap bars and brothels for dockworkers and sailors. In those years, the man, whose name was Cho, had been running an unlicensed rooming house with his wife. One day in late spring Min Yoseop arrived at their door, scruffily dressed and carrying a heavy suitcase. He claimed to be a stevedore and asked for a room.

Cho agreed at once to take him in because he was able to pay the rent in advance, but from the start there were all kinds of odd things about him. In an unlicensed rooming house like theirs, it wasn't normal for a dockworker to take a room of his own; the books he took from his case and piled in one corner of the room were also out of the ordinary for someone of his claimed profession. His regular features, untanned skin, and slender, almost feminine body were all very unlike the appearance of a normal dockworker. That first impression had made Cho somewhat apprehensive, almost as an inkling of what was to come later. At first he suspected Min Yoseop of being a spy on some special mission, but as time passed those suspicions faded away. Not only was Min Yoseop actually working as a stevedore, but his outward appearance began to resemble that of his fellow dockers. After three months, he was almost indistinguishable from the others, except that he would read until late at night and mingled on familiar terms with clerks in the port authority office, with whom he wouldn't normally have had a close relationship. Cho felt a kind of pride when he saw tough dockers become as docile and submissive as children before his boarder, or when university students who had briefly shared his room returned later and addressed him respectfully. An unlicensed pier-side rooming house is at best a place where drunken sailors spend a night giggling with cheap bar girls, or where unmarried dockers spend a few nights with passing whores who take their fancy. Min Yoseop was an exceptional customer, equal to the clerks from the port authority office who occasionally spent a few days there while looking for more respectable rooms.

At that time, Cho's son was in his junior year of high school. His two older daughters were already married, and his son was the only child left at home. At some point he had begun going to Min Yoseop's room, and then one day, out of the blue, he told his father that he wanted to stop attending the private institute where he was preparing to take the university entrance exam and learn instead from Min Yoseop; in return, his father should stop charging him rent.

It was his only son's wish, and the father was sure of Min Yoseop's ability to coach him; yet for some reason he could not bring himself to agree. It was hard to put it into words, but he had a premonition that the link between Min Yoseop and his son was somehow unsavory, and ought to be avoided if at all possible.

Min Yoseop's feelings seemed to be in line with those of the father. He was unable to coldly rebuff the boy who followed him with such respect, but was uncomfortable with the reckless zeal with which the boy pursued him. It was the same when the father, pestered by his son's requests, asked him to take charge of the boy and tutor him. Min Yoseop had not only replied that he was not qualified to do it, but had even given him to understand that it wouldn't be good for the boy to become close with him.

Yet in the end neither of them were able to prevent the boy from becoming more involved with Min Yoseop. He pestered his father and Min Yoseop by turns, like a person possessed, until he finally obtained permission from both of them and even managed to move his desk into Min Yoseop's room.

The matter having been thus settled, his father tried to see everything in the best possible light. At least his son seemed to be studying much harder now that he worked with Min Yoseop. The light invariably stayed on in the room until late, and sometimes Min Yoseop could be heard teaching the son in a low voice until the early hours of the morning. Knowing no better, his father even started to think that their meeting had been a stroke of good fortune, and that, thanks to Min Yoseop, his son might be able to enter a better university than they had previously expected.

It was late in the autumn, when there was a strike at the docks, that his doubts returned. He never knew what role Min Yoseop had played in the strike, which had been accompanied by unprecedented violence, but he had been arrested in connection with it and harshly interrogated for more than two weeks; he returned in a terrible shape. The head of the local police substation, with whom Cho had been on friendly terms, had said that Min Yoseop was not only one of the strike leaders, but was also ideologically suspect. All that he knew, from his experience of the years of social confusion and conflict after the 1945 Liberation, was that strikes and labor disputes were all the work of Reds; so for him, the information was deeply shocking.

From that moment on, unlike before, he resolved to observe his son and Min Yoseop more closely, on account of the suspicions awakened by the police officer's words. One after another, he began to notice strange things. Firstly, there were the books his son read. Though he himself was so poorly educated that he thought reading any book was a legitimate form of study, he could still see that the books his son was reading in Min Yoseop's room were not like ordinary textbooks or study aids. Then there was Min Yoseop's attitude and the contents of what he was teaching. The father had peeped through a crack in the door several times, and never found Min Yoseop sitting at his desk opposite his son in a posture of serious teaching. Instead, he would invariably be half-reclining or leaning against the wall, occupied with his own work, and only responding when the boy asked a question. If he actually was teaching the boy, he detected after a moment's listening that the things he was saying had no bearing on preparations for the university entrance exam. There were times when they seemed to be studying English, but when Min Yoseop translated, it seemed to be dealing with seditious materials that could never be part of a school textbook.

Cho's apprehension became stronger when his son entered his senior year of high school. Around that time, he stopped going to the church that he had always devoutly attended. As a younger boy, in his middle school years, he had been so enthusiastic about church that he said he wanted to study in a seminary, disappointing his parents greatly.

They vehemently tried to dissuade him from becoming a minister, but did not attempt to take him away from belief as such. Even though they were not believers themselves, they felt, like the simple folk they were, that there could be nothing wrong in following the teachings of a holy man like Jesus. Now this same son had not only stopped attending church, but had even turned the minister and the leader of the church's youth club out of the house, his face crimson with rage, when they visited him at home. As he did so, he cursed at them, calling them "you who have imprisoned God in churches" and "you who have separated Jesus from the poor and abandoned"—insults that his father could not understand.

The next change to reveal itself came in the son's grades at school. Previously, he had always received excellent grades, invariably among the top ten of his year in a high school that was considered to be one of the best in Busan. But at the start of his senior year, his teacher could not hide his disappointment when he summoned his father and informed him that his son had moved up, but with such poor grades that he had only narrowly escaped being held back a year.

Returning home shocked, he had closely questioned his son and Min Yoseop in turn. Min Yoseop, looking startled, had reminded him of his initial unwillingness to tutor the boy, and insisted that he was ready to stop at any time. His son's attitude was different.

He calmly reassured his father that it was simply because, for various reasons, he had missed exams in several subjects at the end of the previous term. When his father told him he was going to have to send Min Yoseop away, his son was alarmed and began to make violent threats. So long as he was allowed to work with him, he said, he would regain his good grades and go to a good university; but if Min Yoseop was sent away, he would give up everything, starting with school.

Cho realized that the situation was going from bad to worse, but he had no choice, given his son's response. The fact remained that this was his one and only son, and even if things were bad now his hope was that it was just a passing phase, and that he would eventually get over it. So far, although he had grown up in an environment where nothing was favorable to education, he had never once given his parents any grounds for worry, which helped them to remain optimistic.

Yet finally, disaster struck. Less than three months had passed when Cho received notice that his son had been expelled. He rushed over to the school, where they informed him that his son had been absent for seventy-six days since the start of the term. Cho became furious, thinking how even that very morning his son had left home saying innocently that he was off to school, wearing his uniform and carrying his bag. It goes without saying that the five or six messages and warnings sent by the school had disappeared before arriving in Cho's hands.

Looking back after careful thought, Cho realized that there had been signs that should have aroused his suspicion. First, his son's delicate face had recently become sunburned and swarthy, while his rather feminine hands had grown rough. That was not all; seen on his way home from school after dark, he looked exhausted, worn out like someone who has been engaged in hard labor. His father had assumed it was because he was working extra hard at his studies all day long; yet, feeling that something was strange, he had taken his son to task on several occasions. But in addition to the excuse provided by his studies, he always had some extra reasons—either a school foundation day sports event, extracurricular farming activities, or two successive periods of physical education—things that explained not only his fatigue but also the sunburned face and blistered hands.

Moreover, he had been struck at the same period by frequent conflicts of opinion between his son and Min Yoseop. He did not know what it was all about, but his son seemed to be engaged in things that Min Yoseop did not approve of, and that he angrily tried to stop him from doing. Sometimes, pretending to accidentally open the door of their room, he found Min Yoseop scolding his son in a subdued voice, but then stopping abruptly when he saw Cho, while his son protested quietly with a flushed face.

After careful consideration, Cho came to a final decision. Following a clamorous dispute that woke half the neighborhood, he succeeded in separating his son from Min Yoseop—but it was too late. After being cut off from Min Yoseop, the boy likewise broke with his father. He declared that he was an adult, although he had barely turned eighteen, and would live his own life. Refusing the transfer to a private high school that his father had managed to arrange—at the price of a significant donation—the son set about doing openly what he had already been doing in secret with Min Yoseop. He often stayed idle in his room, lost in his thoughts, or went looking for work as a stevedore on the docks where Min Yoseop had been blacklisted after the strike, or as a laborer on the building site for a new export-goods factory. The father regarded his son's conduct as sheer madness.

Reaching this point in his story, he let out a long, bitter sigh. His red eyes were growing moist. Sergeant Nam waited in silence, not wishing to distract him from what he was saying. With a trembling hand, he inserted another cigarette into his holder and inhaled several times; then he went on, exhaling a cloud of smoke.

"But . . . worse was to follow. Not content with that, at some point that wretched son of mine began demanding money, never explaining what it was for. He even asked for an advance payment of the inheritance he would receive later. To tell you the truth, in those days my wife and I had a fair amount of spare money. Business here was doing at least as well as it is now, and my wife was making a go of it, lending money to some of the girls in the neighborhood. If I'd cashed in all my assets, there would have been enough money to buy a big house in a classy neighborhood. Until then we'd assumed our son was too young to know anything about these affairs. But in fact, I don't know how, he knew everything right down to the smallest details—how much we'd lent and at what daily rate to such a girl in such a house. I suppose it was that goddamn Min who told him; I remember how he used to glare at my wife whenever she came in with some personal possession she'd taken in place of money.

"Of course, we refused his request. I can't disclose details, but the origin of that money was in some sense the price of my blood. It was capital I was able to obtain from a wartime comrade with whom I had risked life and limb. But my son had his own ways too. He used to go in secret to those who owed us money, write off half the debt and ask them to give him the rest; or else he stole the IOUs from us and gave them back to the people in exchange for a reduced amount. With his build, his strength, there was nothing I could do. My wife's tears and her threats of suicide were no use at all.

"So in a few months almost all our spare capital had vanished. When you're in moneylending, there are times when you borrow a little from others and lend that out on a daily basis; but with him chopping off half the capital, regardless of whether it was my money or what I'd borrowed, how could I go on? In the end my wife gave up lending altogether, considering herself lucky to have managed to pay back at least what she had borrowed . . ."

"What do you think your son did with all that money?" Sergeant Nam could not help asking, detecting the Min Yoseop of earlier years in the father's descriptions of his son's actions.

Trembling with hatred, he replied, "Whatever that goddamn fool told him to do, I suppose."

"You mean you let Min Yoseop stay on in the house?"

At that, his tone changed, filling with regret.

"Thinking of it now, I really should have had it out with him earlier. Being more afraid of my son than of him, I couldn't bring myself to put him out of the house, despite having separated them.

My son kept the promise he made, not to set foot in his room if I did not turn him out."

"So it's only your guess that Min Yoseop told him what to do?"

"He'd already spent several months sharing the same room, hadn't he? If he told him what to do, it must have been during that time. Besides, there's no knowing if they met secretly outside of the house after that."

"What do you think they were up to?" Sergeant Nam asked, looking to verify something he had already guessed.

"To tell you the truth, I'm curious, too. That goddamn Min always went about looking like a beggar, never drinking so much as a glass of *soju*, and my son too, although he squandered all that money, I never saw him going around with any girls."

"Can't you make a guess?"

"Oh, he must have spent it on some misguided cause, with his usual heroism. He went to a girl owing us money, who was sick in bed, and handed back the IOU without taking anything. Once I saw some student who came to visit looking up at my son like he was some kind of Buddha, so I guess . . ."

"Isn't that better than just squandering it?"

"I wouldn't have minded so much if he had made merry with drinking or girls. Think what kind of money it was . . . how could anyone take him for some kind of Buddha?"

"Ah, I understand. How did he finally leave the house?" Wishing to avoid pointless arguments, Sergeant Nam wanted to hear the end of the story. The father's voice again grew distorted with hatred.

"That was also the work of that goddamn bastard. Haven't I already told you? He led my son astray."

"You have to explain it to me. I don't understand . . ."

"Once there was no more money available, my son started stealing our belongings and finally pestered us to sell the house. But that was not possible, even if he was our only son. My wife still feels guilty that we didn't do it, but this house was our last resource. Day after day there were scenes about it between our son and the two of us. When things reached that point, even that idiot Min seemed at a loss. He tried to reason with my son, tried to calm him down; then one night I'm glad to say he left the house without saying a word. The two of us felt relieved. But then the next day my son disappeared as well. He'd probably gone off in search of the bastard. I suppose he might not have deliberately led him astray. But even if my son acted on his own, how would things be different for us if he'd actively misled him? And that's not all . . ."

Cho seemed to hesitate for a moment, but then he went on, as if determined to tell everything.

"A few days after my son left, someone broke into the house. He only took a small amount of money that we'd carefully hidden and the ring my wife had when we got married. That was really strange. When it happened, we were too confused to think straight, but the way he knew the house so well, and the way he disguised his voice, all seemed to suggest it was our son. My wife felt sure of it too. So we never reported it to the police, just in case . . ."

By this point, Sergeant Nam felt he could understand the son's psychological state. The eighteen-year-old had become bold in his desire to imitate. At least, the final burglary drama he had put on was certainly not a crime done for profit . . .

"Have you had any news of your son since then? You said that someone had seen him."

"Yes, someone I know said he'd seen him at Daejeon with that jerk. Then he visited the ward office here without telling me, in connection with military service. He hoped he'd be exempted as he's an only son. But when I followed up on the rumors and went there to see, he was already gone."

"What's your son's name?"

"He's called Dongpal."

"Can you please show me the bundle Min left behind?"

Sergeant Nam decided to bring the conversation to an end there with his request. Cho replied curtly, went inside and brought out a dust-covered bundle. At a quick glance, it seemed to only be some books. Just then, Dongpal's mother emerged from somewhere, her eyes full of tears.

While trying to calm her down, the sergeant untied the bundle her husband had brought out. Apart from a few books in Korean, with recognizable titles like *Comparative Religion* and *Mystical Theo-*

logy, most of the rest were foreign books. There were a few note-books but, despite his hopes, there was no diary, no personal writing, only vocabulary lists and passages copied from books. Sergeant Nam jotted down the titles and authors of the foreign books in case it might be of use. Since his grasp of even basic English was uncertain, he didn't really write the words, but rather identified the letters one by one and drew them. But still, there were a few familiar names among the authors. Fumblingly deciphering them, he recognized that some of the names had often appeared in Min Yoseop's diary in connection with that of Kagawa Toyohiko—Karl Barth and Moltmann, for example.

After finishing his inspection of these belongings, Sergeant Nam asked, "Apart from yourself, is there anyone else in the neighborhood who knew Min Yoseop back then?"

He felt that the father's lopsided account might be insufficient, and hoped to be able to find more information.

The man racked his brains for a while, counting off this person, then that, before replying as if he were doing him a big favor:

"There were quite a few who kept company with him in those days, but they were all migrant workers; there's no knowing where they've gone ... but there was that one white-collar worker ... Shin Hyeongsik, he was called; he worked in the port authority office. He boarded with us for two months when he was first assigned here. He often went around with him, though we never really knew why."

"Is he still working there? Which section?"

"I don't know which section he's in but I'm quite certain he's still there. I met him in the street only a few days ago and we exchanged greetings."

Judging from what Cho said, it seemed that Shin Hyeongsik had occasionally used his inn later when he was moving from one boarding house to another, or when he had several friends visiting at the same time.

Sergeant Nam went straight to the port authority office and had no difficulty in finding Shin Hyeongsik. He was over thirty, still unmarried, and looked good-natured. He readily recalled Min Yoseop.

"Min Yoseop? I know him very well. We spent barely two months under the same roof, but I reckon I'll never forget him as long as I live. He really knew so much! I've never met anyone who knew so much about so many different things. Of course, maybe it was nothing so special, but I felt that way about him because I haven't studied very much myself . . . and what was interesting was the way he was always drunk without ever drinking a drop. Sometimes I got worried about how drunk he was, although I was the one who'd drunk half a pint of cheap *soju*. Yet he hadn't drunk a drop, mind you. What sort of a person was he? Well . . . In those days, I was utterly fascinated by him, he was like a god in my eyes. But a few years later, putting two and two together to complete the picture, I reckoned he would either end up as some kind of revolutionary, in the good sense or the bad, or as the head of a religious sect.

"As for the details of his private life, there's not much I know. We met in the evenings, after we'd finished work and gone back to the boarding house. We mainly talked about abstract aspects of religion and philosophy concerning God, man, and salvation, and about history and politics.

"Mr. Cho's son? Ah, I remember that student. I don't recall his name clearly, but he was outrageously precocious and clever. He was only in his junior year of high school, but he made a better partner in discussion with Min Yoseop than I did. He used to ask hard questions, and listen hard, too. But soon after he joined us I moved to another rooming house and I don't know what happened after that. I wonder if he didn't become a mini Min Yoseop . . ."

But that was all. What he had said was of almost no help to the investigation, apart from serving as indirect evidence that what Cho had said was not groundless exaggeration. Remembering Lieutenant Lee's rebuff from the previous day, Nam hurried to the station after leaving Shin Hyeongsik, stopping only to obtain Cho Dongpal's new address from the records at the ward office. If he was not going to obtain any significant new information, he was anxious to get back by the time his boss had specified. The trains were overcrowded, however, and he ended up having to take an express bus, barely making it in time.

On his return, he found the investigation team full of excitement. Following Lieutenant Lee's orders, Detective Im had gone to a hardware store and managed to obtain a description of a young man who had bought a fruit knife. Detective Park, who had gone up to Seoul, was continuing his inquiries regarding the wife of Elder Mun, and reported that he had uncovered new grounds for suspicion. Apparently a young man resembling Min Yoseop had recently been seen in her company. Now that Sergeant Nam had succeeded in obtaining information about two of Min Yoseop's eight lost years and the address he had moved to, they seemed to be getting close to a solution. Yet Lieutenant Lee was unimpressed with the information about Min Yoseop that Sergeant Nam had brought back from Busan concerning his changes in personality and lifestyle. He listened to Sergeant Nam's words distractedly, refusing the suggestion to consult a specialist about the books whose titles and authors he had noted.

"Do you think the criminal's name may be written somewhere among all those crooked letters? If you have time to waste like that, you'd do better to just go home and get some sleep. You'll have to search Daejeon tomorrow."

That was where Min Yoseop and Cho Dongpal had moved after leaving Busan.

7

After his return from Busan, Sergeant Nam was convinced that the case could never be solved by pursuing motives of greed, jealousy, or ordinary personal animosity. He began to feel a strong enmity toward Lieutenant Lee, who was recklessly trying to steer the investigation in that direction. It was in reaction to Lee that he decided to continue reading Min Yoseop's manuscript that evening, prior to leaving for Daejeon.

After arriving home, he had a late supper and then looked for

Min Yoseop's notebooks. He had left them scattered randomly on the floor of his room that morning, but now he found them neatly arranged on the table according to the numbers written on each one. It must have been his wife's doing. Sergeant Nam had no need to search his memory; he picked up the bundle starting where he had left off reading the previous night.

Having left his parents' house and the streets of his hometown behind, it wasn't long before Ahasuerus also parted ways with his country and its god. It was the beginning of a long journey, lasting more than ten years, during which he wandered to every corner of the world. It was a quest for a new god and a new truth that might be able to console him for the despair he felt about the old god of his people. But it was also a search for solutions to questions about the world and life that had complicated his existence from the very beginning, finally transforming into a raw fury that led him to spend part of his precious youth sunk in swamps of falsehood and evil.

Ahasuerus first headed for Egypt, sometimes known as "the birthplace of the gods." Viewed casually, that would seem to be what drew him there. But what really attracted him was not that land's other name—inspired by its numerous gods and temples, its many mysterious doctrines and ceremonies—but rather something he heard from a hermit he met while traveling through Judea in the midst of a crisis of doubt. The hermit had been rejected by his family and neighbors on account of his heretical beliefs, and now lived alone in a hovel he had built in a desolate spot at the foot of a stony hill. As soon as he heard Ahasuerus's doubts and despair about god, he explained their cause without hesitation.

"It's natural. Since they made one god by combining the shepherds' god El Shaddai with Horeb's warrior god, it's hardly surprising that they don't fit together!"

What he meant was that the god of Abraham and the god of Moses were incompatible. Seeing Ahasuerus taken aback by such a remarkable statement, the hermit went on to explain his reasons with increasing passion:

"Not only was Moses himself not circumcised, he did not have his son circumcised either until he was visited by the wrath of god. He had no problem living among the Egyptians; his wife Sephora and his father-in-law took him for an Egyptian. From the very start there were many odd things about his encounter with our ancestors, who all belonged to the same race. He killed an Egyptian soldier who was mistreating some of them, but instead of thanking him they used that as a weak point to threaten him. And later, when he had become their leader, Moses performed a host of miracles and displayed great power in a short space of time, yet during the barely forty days he was away from them in the desert, our forefathers were already making the golden calf. That shows a fundamental distrust of him. Another suspicious point is how he is reported to have had a severe stutter. It suddenly became pronounced when he made an official appearance before our forefathers, whereupon his brother Aaron appeared from nowhere and spoke in his place.

"Putting all this together, the truth becomes obvious: Moses was not descended from Israel as our forefathers were; he was an Egyptian. He approached our forefathers with a particular purpose in mind and became their leader, but they always distrusted him because he was from another race. As for the problem of his stutter—he did not really stutter at all, he simply did not speak our language very well; Aaron was not his older brother, but an interpreter."

"I cannot believe that Moses, who gave us the Torah, was really an Egyptian. Why did the God of Abraham and of Isaac set aside their descendants and choose a foreigner as the recipient of His promise?" Ahasuerus asked, astounded and overcome by irrepressible doubts. The hermit replied quite readily, as if he had been expecting the question.

"You're right. When I first went down to Egypt and heard these things, I could not believe them either. But once I closely studied and compared their history and legends with our own, it all became clear. And it's on account of this that I have suffered so much, and experienced such solitude and hardship; but my conviction about all that is still unshaken."

The hermit went on with enthusiasm, recounting part of the

story he had put together using facts drawn from both Egyptian and Jewish histories and records.

. . . It was long ago, in the days when their forefathers were living in Egypt as slaves. The Egyptian pharaoh of the time, Amenhotep IV, set out to abolish polytheism and establish Aton, the god of the sun, as the one and only god, unifying the faith of his entire kingdom. He was so determined to carry out this new religious policy that he even changed his own name to Akhenaton; with his passion and the immense power he wielded, it seemed at first that he had succeeded, to a certain degree at least.

But beyond the supporting clique composed of courtiers who bowed and scraped before him and generals who depended on the salary he paid, there was an opposing force, stronger than the pharaoh, far from the court and out of sight. The heart of this opposing party was found among the priests in the temples scattered across the land, whose lives were dependent on the gods worshipped there, as well as the local nobility, whose interests were closely bound up with theirs.

They decided to initiate a violent resistance against the pharaoh's policies, in order to defend their old beliefs and their vested interests before this new religion could put down deep roots among the common people. Rebellions and uprisings broke out here and there, and bloody battles were fought between those intent on defending the old religious order and those who wanted to overturn it. In the end, victory went to the rebellious forces, fighting for the old beliefs. Defeated, Amenhotep IV was driven from the throne and executed; the organizations that had supported his religious reform were disbanded, and his followers were driven away.

However, there was a high priest of the religion of Aton, or perhaps a member of the family of Amenhotep IV, who escaped and went into hiding in the land of Midian. After the immediate threat to his life had passed and he had established a new, stable existence, having become the son-in-law of a local landowner, he began to nourish ambitions of reviving their suppressed religious vision. Before taking any action toward that goal, however, and feeling he needed to strengthen his faith, he began a program of ascetic mortification.

He wandered across harsh mountains swarming with deadly snakes and crossed deserts full of thorny bushes. Throughout these travels he would constantly invoke his god, and he seems to have experienced a revelation somewhere on Mount Horeb.

Having reassured himself in his faith, he quit his land of exile and returned to his own people in Egypt. Once again, he tried to bring about a reform of their primitive, irrational religion through the single god, the unseen yet supreme god he had encountered. But no one heeded his teachings, not the reactionary nobles and priests who had successfully opposed the reforms of Amenhotep IV, nor the simple people who had long been immersed in polytheism.

He then turned his attention toward a group of foreigners who at the time were living a wretched existence as slaves. There were two reasons for his choice of that tribe. The first was their tradition of monotheism, already deeply rooted in their minds. Having failed to displace the ingrained polytheistic system of his own people, he must have seen more potential in the monotheistic tradition of this foreign tribe. The other reason was the miserable condition into which these foreigners had fallen. Given that slaves desire freedom above all else, he must have thought he could gain their support and submission by promising freedom.

The man in question was none other than Moses, and the foreigners were the descendants of Israel who had been brought by Joseph to live in Egypt. It is understandable that Moses would pretend to have the same origins as them, for nothing is more effective than bonds of blood to bring people together. Likewise, the change of names from Aton to Yahweh was a necessary concession by Moses, for it helped to convince the Israelites to make a compromise regarding some aspects of their faith. In short, the ancient, promise-centered religious thought of the Hebrew people simply took on a more concrete expression in the form of the so-called covenant with an ambitious, heretical priest from Egypt . . .

Such was the gist of the hermit's story. He sat in silence for a long moment looking at Ahasuerus, who was shocked, still reluctant to believe him, and then went on:

"Naturally, it is hard to accept. But how else are we to see the passive, defensive god of Abraham—with his quest for comfort and plenty, even to the point of offering his wife to an enemy—as one and the same as the god of Moses, who urged our forefathers to destroy all the inhabitants of Canaan, leaving no stone on top of another? Indeed, those of our forefathers who remained in Canaan and those who came back from Egypt used different names for their god for a while. The ones used Yahweh, the others used Elohim.

"If you were to go down to Egypt and see for yourself, the true picture would emerge more clearly. The things that the scholarly priests learned and remembered, or the historical facts I've been telling you on the basis of ancient records written on papyrus, may have been preserved in a slightly distorted form. The myths of the Isis cult also reflect those events, though in a symbolic form. After Seth was defeated in a battle with Horus, he was obliged to flee for one whole week, day and night, before finding a safe hiding place; there he is said to have had two sons, who were Jerusalem and Judea. No categorical assertion can be made, but it is clear that aspects of the monotheism that was driven out by the polytheistic cults are concealed within our religious traditions; the way we followed that god out of Egypt, finally succeeding in settling in Canaan and establishing the kingdom of Jerusalem and Judea, undoubtedly underlies the myths they fabricated."

In those days Ahasuerus was still trying to find answers to all of his questions within the bounds of his people's traditional doctrines. The shock verging on horror that he experienced while listening to the hermit lasted only a moment—then finally he left him. He did not defend his god and attack him as a blasphemer, nor did he treat him like a madman; instead, he adopted the attitude of "Even if it were true, so what?" Even if he completely accepted what the hermit said, Ahasuerus's doubts about the world and life and his disappointment with Yahweh could find no fundamental solution there.

The months of intense emotion that followed made Ahasuerus utterly forget all that the hermit had said. Those days were given over entirely to human desires, rampaging through the streets or competing in violent contests held in the arenas that the tributary dynasties were building in order to encourage the hellenization of the Jews. Then one day, waking after a night of wanton intoxication, he resolved to leave both his land and his god; he remembered the hermit and finally decided to make Egypt his first destination. It was not that he wanted to find out if the hermit's words had been true or false; rather, he simply wished to encounter the gods of that country directly.

There is no way of knowing what route Ahasuerus took on his journey to Egypt, nor in what city he first set foot. With the *pax romana* in those years, traffic by sea and by land had developed quickly, and he wouldn't have experienced great difficulties, no matter which route he chose. If he did face hardships, they mainly arose after he had been traveling around Egypt for about two years.

Lack of money was the first thing that troubled him. He had left on an impulse, without consulting his parents and without being able to prepare any funds for his journey; even if he had been able to make preparations, he would not have been able to raise enough to last him. He wasn't able to find a job in Egypt since he did not stay in one place, but was constantly on the move. Just finding one would have been difficult in any case, since he had nothing to sell except his not very useful knowledge. As a result, during the time he spent in Egypt, despite assistance he occasionally received from Jews of the Diaspora, his life was little different from that of a tramp.

Communication was also difficult for him. The Latin and Greek that Ahasuerus spoke, thanks to the hellenizing policies which had reached their height in the days of Herod the Great, were of little help once he left Alexandria and the other major cities of Lower Egypt. Aramaic, a language close to the communal Semitic tongue, was of no use except among merchants and some of the privileged classes. Unless he really was able to speak every dialect "from the land where the sun rises to the land where the sun sets, with the assistance of the Evil Spirit," as the malicious legends claim, he must have had great difficulty communicating with people, even in Lower Egypt, to say nothing of the remote regions of Upper Egypt. Additionally, whenever he arrived in a new town he would want to explore the temple of the guardian deities, which were normally closed to foreigners. That created even greater difficulties.

The loneliness he felt while wandering through unknown lands among foreign faces, far from his home, family, and friends, certainly contributed to his sufferings. Despite the mysterious passion driving him on, he must have spent many nights weeping into the arm that served as his pillow; after all, he had just turned twenty, the age of intense emotions.

For nearly two years, Ahasuerus roamed the four corners of Egypt as if possessed, suffering countless hardships. All the way from Thebes, Coptos, and Hermonthis in Upper Egypt to Memphis, Sais, and Mendes in Lower Egypt, and on into the regions of Libya and Nubia, his feet never failed to linger wherever the gods had a shrine or a temple. A hope drove him onward, like a strong wind that couldn't be opposed; a hope that, among these gods and teachings, he might perhaps be able to discover a new god and a new teaching that could soothe painful disillusion with the god of the Jews.

There was a multitude of strange gods: Amun, Amentet, Montu, Tefnut, Naunet, Imset, Duamutef, Ra, Mut, Horakhty, Sekhmet, Amun-ra, Bast, Khonsu, Hapi, Ptah, Khnum, Satet, Bennu, Atet, Hershef, Aten, Mersekhnet, along with many other ancient gods, lost or surviving, to say nothing of Osiris with his nearly two hundred names, and Isis, Horus, Set, Nephthys, Her-hepes, Shu, Anubis, Usert, Seb or Geb, Nut, Tem, Heru-ur, Khent-Maati, Uatchet, and the other gods of the Great Company of the Gods of Heliopolis, in addition to foreign gods such as Neith, Anat, Baal, Baalath, Reshep, Sutekh, Bes, Aasith, as well as the various animals that had been deified and were worshipped. For Ahasuerus, who had only ever known and believed in one god, the multiplicity made him dizzy.

But Ahasuerus could never shake off the god of his people, even if he wished to, nor the teachings centered around that god that his forefathers had refined through thousands of years. All of that had settled like a sediment deep in his soul, preventing him from truly opening his heart to any of the new gods he encountered in Egypt. They all invariably seemed to him to be nothing more than mere idols, fashioned by people's pains and desires, their fear and their rancor, while the hymns and prayers addressed to them just sounded like cries of torment. The blessings or the miracles believed to proceed from these gods seemed to be nothing more than an echo of these human cries, bouncing off the walls of an empty universe. As the days passed, the list of obscure gods still to be encountered diminished, but Ahasuerus began to feel a strange impatience. His dissatisfaction with the god of his people, which had formerly caused him so much distress, began to fade away due to the impact of his repeated experiences of disillusionment with these foreign gods. This led him to wonder whether his dissatisfaction hadn't simply been a way of complaining, and whether his present wanderings might turn out to have been a waste of time. On the other hand, his innate drive to negate untruth and call things into question was growing more intense.

"If you have two ugly things, and one thing is more ugly than the other, that does not make the less ugly thing beautiful. In the same way, the existence of gods that are more irrational than the god of my people does not make my less irrational god perfect. Moreover, I am seeing these new gods with eyes that are accustomed to the god of my people; I am hearing teachings about these new gods with ears trained by the Word of my god. That's not how it should be. First, let me free myself completely from the god of my people and his Word. No—more than that, I must try to get closer to these new gods. So far, I have only been observing them from a distance, like a kind of spectacle; I was listening to their teachings as if they were mere human knowledge . . ."

This was the decision that Ahasuerus finally came to when he was visiting Heliopolis for the second time. He realized that in deciding to head in that direction he had been swayed by an unconscious desire to return home, even though there still remained a few places for him to visit; from that point on he resolved to keep himself under a tighter rein.

Whether by coincidence or not, Heliopolis was the perfect place for Ahasuerus to carry out his decision. It was the most religious city of Egypt, the site of the sycamore tree sacred to Nut, the home of Aten, and the place where the spine of Osiris was buried and where he first began to be venerated. It had once been the home of the cult of the sun god Amun-Ra, but it had recently become the base for the fast-growing cult of Isis.

For his final Egyptian passion, Ahasuerus joined the temple of Isis at Heliopolis, no longer as an onlooker, as he had previously done, but as a brother in the same faith, swearing a formal oath of conversion before a priest. If it were possible, he hoped to become a priest of the cult and so approach mysteries that were not as easily accessible to lay believers. Yet despite their solemn and grandiose appearances, their doctrines proved to be exceptionally feeble, with the exception of a few moving verses in the hymns. He longed to find what it was in them that sent crowds of people into ecstasy, driving them to such a rapture that they no longer feared death.

Though he exaggerated his faith and devotion and made desperate efforts to make up for being a foreigner, particularly as a Jew, Ahasuerus was only able to attain a position as an acolyte to an old priest after several months of intense effort. Even that was not because the hierarchy had been impressed by his efforts and his devotion, but because the venerable priest had intervened on his behalf. The old priest happened to see him sweeping the temple yard one day; he took an interest in Ahasuerus and observed him for a while, and it was presumably the impression made that day that led the priest to defy the hierarchy.

The tasks assigned to him were trivial: following the old priest, carrying the ritual vessels, bearing sacrificial offerings, or keeping the temple clean, nothing more. But at least there was something he could see, having become one of them.

What first impressed Ahasuerus was the maternal nature of Isis. The god of his people in whom he had believed until that point had a paternal nature; he weighed human good and evil on the scales of his strict Word, and issued punishments and rewards accordingly. But Isis was different. She was a woman who had known the cruel sorrow of losing her husband, and had gone to the ends of the world in search of his body, which had been cut into more than ten pieces and scattered in various places. As a loyal wife, she reassembled his body and gave it a proper burial, then as a car-ing mother she brought up her husband's son, whom she had conceived without physical contact, and shielded him from merciless enemies. She represents motherhood as suffering and sorrow but also motherhood as mercy, which even saves her husband's murderer from being killed by her son's spear. With her, it seemed, human weakness could be a sufficient excuse for sin, and moreover, unconditional love and forgiveness could be sought from her.

Formed by the model of a strict, paternal god, Ahasuerus's mind was deeply moved by the attributes of Isis, even if he insisted that she was only the deification of undisciplined, irrational maternal love. They were all strands knotted together in one myth; Isis was clearly below the paternal gods in power and rank, yet it was obvious why the cult was called by her name, not that of Osiris or of Horus. It was also easy to see why the religion had spread far beyond the Mediterranean. What a fulfilling sense of comfort and encouragement this maternal being could offer people, someone they could entreat, grumble to, presume upon, irrespective of good or bad. Whenever a priestess with a closely shaved head sang the "Lament of Isis" with tears flowing down her lovely cheeks, tears would also stream down Ahasuerus's cheeks, although he fully realized it was nothing more than an expression of human pain and sorrow.

Another thing that impressed Ahasuerus was the idea of the incarnation or human embodiment of the divine. In the teachings he had previously followed, God was always God and man was always man. Just as men could never transcend their own humanity, so too God as such never came down to the human level, except as the Word or a pillar of fire. Several prophets had alluded to the advent of a man vested with the power of God, whom they termed the Messiah, and Daniel had come particularly close to suggesting the possibility of an incarnation of the divine under the name "Son of Man." But no one had ever spoken of the incarnation of Yahweh as such; and even if they had, that would be something that lay in a future that his people had not yet experienced. Osiris and Horus were the first gods Ahasuerus had heard of that were born with human bodies. A mortal god, born as a man, suffering on account of evil, and dying powerless—such a touching image! After fully experiencing human pain and sorrow, weakness and want, he dies, then rises again and judges us—what a close and affectionate deity! Despite recognizing the immaturity of the imagination that brought Osiris back from the dead and set him above death, and despite the traces of primitive religion, Ahasuerus felt as if he had perceived a ray of dazzling light. He even came to think that the notion of "the Messiah's foreordained suffering," which had appeared in recent years and been cautiously discussed among rabbis in his native land, must be somehow related to the Osiris myth.

Equally new to Ahasuerus was the idea that parthenogenesis could be used to distinguish between the birth of a god from that of a human. He had always considered the phrase in his people's scriptures—"Behold, a virgin shall conceive, and bear a son"—as a kind of symbol or parable; but it had already happened in the myths of the Egyptians. A teaching that was more inclined toward death than life also provoked a strange feeling in Ahasuerus, for he had grown up in a religion that laid more emphasis on life. Since the wars of the Maccabees, his people had also begun to talk much about death, but that was still death in connection to life. The Word of Ptah, although it was not directly related to the cult of Isis, also amazed Ahasuerus, for he too was said to have created the heavens and the earth by his Word alone.

Still, the day of his departure from Egypt soon arrived. Although he still occasionally experienced a fresh realization at this or that point as he penetrated further into their religion, Ahasuerus began to discover the absurdity, immorality, and corruption at its base. The inferiority of the imagination and logic revealed by their entire mythic system, the lack of morality that undermined the foundations of their doctrine, the extravagant ceremonies and rituals that occurred too often, the vulgarization of the sacred that gave the impression that the gods existed for the sake of the priests, and not vice versa, the corruption of the priestly caste who took advantage of the hedonism of the common people, the absurd superstitions and the improper use of talismans—all these aspects soon destroyed the insights and emotions Ahasuerus had encountered in that religion.

Before the end of his first year in the temple, he realized that staying there any longer would be a waste of time. What had fascinated him and kept him close to their gods was merely the novelty of a few ideas produced by an antiquated religion on its last reserves of wisdom, fearful of being completely rejected by the masses, parasitically dependent on the powers that be, sharing even their corruption and degeneracy. He regretted the effort he had made to become part of that ingenious agglomeration of religious devices, for he realized they had no connection with his own quest. He could not understand the common people of that country: how could they not see the true state of things, which had become so clear to him after little more than two years of observations, when they had been living there for thousands of years? Not only were they wholly unsuspicious and accepting of the corruption and degeneracy that happened beyond the altars—which any sharp eye could see at a glance—they also averted their eyes from the undisguised immorality and wrongdoings practiced before the altars. They almost seemed to enjoy submitting to the priests' blatant threats, allowing themselves to be exploited without receiving anything in return.

When Ahasuerus decided to leave, he quietly sought out the old priest, hoping perhaps to address some of the doubts he harbored about the people as a whole. On this particular night, the Nile had begun its flood and the festival of Isis was at its height; he took advantage of a spare moment and went to speak to the old priest who was resting alone:

"Priest, the people believe that the flooding of the Nile is caused by the tears of Isis, and since they consider it a blessing, they celebrate ceremonies of thanksgiving and worship. But I know the truth. We cannot see it since we are a long way downstream, but it is the rainy season far upstream that causes the flood. It is not at all on account of Isis's tears, which could never be a blessing in any case."

"We know that, too," the old priest replied without any sign of being troubled. Ahasuerus had spoken hesitantly, not wanting to hurt this man who had shown particular kindness toward him, and his reply amazed him.

"You mean you consciously mislead the people? That this sacred, solemn festival is in fact nothing but a great deception?"

"No. They know, too."

"They know, too?"

Ahasuerus was even more bewildered by this reply, made in exactly the same tone as before. The priest looked at Ahasuerus silently for a moment, then calmly went on, without seeming to think he was revealing anything out of the ordinary.

"Of course. Or rather, they want us to deceive them. The flooding of the Nile, a blessing and a catastrophe at the same time, has long been explained in a variety of ways. In the distant past, it was attributed to the power of Nu or Hapi and at other times it was seen as a blessing from Serapis. Nowadays we consider it as the tears of Isis, but there are some who say it is caused by semen from the liaison between Nephthys and Osiris. Yet even in days when there were no roads like those we have today, and no one had heard of the rainy season in the region beyond the First Cataract of the Nile, very few people really gave credence to such explanations. It was just that people wanted to believe something like that. Just think about it: rather than believe that the world was entirely given over to the violence of a cruel and unpredictable nature, how much more consolation and hope it gives them to believe that such a fury could be appeased by offerings, and that it was an order governed by gods of whom they could ask blessings through worship and prayer.

"All we really did was allow them to follow the path of their faith. Even when we propagate and encourage their false beliefs, it's simply in order to prevent them from falling into despair, from fear and inertia. Some people say that we deceive them, either for our own sake or for the sake of the pharaoh and his courtiers; but in fact, the people who say this are themselves deceived by the masses."

The old priest's reply came as a greater shock to Ahasuerus than any he had previously received from their doctrine. The teachings of his forefathers always began with an Absolute Being, beyond human approval or perception. From this background, the idea of a "superstition for the sake of faith" was bound to seem strange.

But unlike the other astonishing things he encountered, this one only served to hasten Ahasuerus's departure. Even though he could understand the old priest by human logic, such a system of belief was far removed from the idea of a new, true God he had been resolutely seeking.

"What I hoped to find here was a real God, not some kind of illusory image produced by a coarse mixture of necessity and imagination. I have reached the end of my days in this land." Murmuring these words to himself, Ahasuerus left the old priest, who still seemed to have more that he wanted to say, and that very night he packed his bags.

The next morning, while day was just breaking, Ahasuerus was taking a last farewell look inside the temple to which he had briefly entrusted his body and heart, when he heard someone walking toward him out of the darkness inside, then a voice calling out to him in a solemn, ceremonial tone:

"Stay a moment, son of Judea and Jerusalem."

Turning in surprise, Ahasuerus saw that it was the old priest. He approached with his robes rustling, stopping when he was near enough for his features to be clearly visible, and looked closely at Ahasuerus as he had done before. He asked in a halting, uncertain voice:

"Did you not come to this city long ago, with your parents? If you cannot remember, have you never heard them mention it? You came as a newborn baby and left when you were four or five."

His attitude was no longer that of a priest addressing his acolyte.

Ahasuerus replied, "Until three years ago, I had never gone outside my own land. I have never heard anything different from my parents." Ahasuerus had been taken aback by such an odd question, and the old priest scrutinized him, then sighed as he murmured: "That is fortunate. Then the time has not yet come . . ."

"What do you mean by that?" Ahasuerus asked, unable to contain his curiosity. The old priest began to speak slowly, raising his eyes to the eastern sky where dawn was just breaking:

"You are not that child, but you seem somehow not unrelated to him, so I want to tell you the story. It happened fifteen or sixteen years ago. A young couple from your nation came into this city, bearing a newborn baby. For some reason, witnessing their arrival,

I had the impression they were fleeing from something. They settled among people of the Diaspora not far from this temple; the husband worked as a carpenter and the wife did odd jobs for their neighbors for about five or six years.

"Yet something seemed strange with the child, who had arrived as a newborn baby. Perhaps because his parents were busy working, he started to toddle around the courtyard of our temple when he could still barely walk. Until he left the city with his parents when he was five or six, he grew up constantly hanging about our temple. Sometimes he spent the whole day watching the ceremonies; on days when there were no ceremonies he would play in front of the altars and statues; he was particularly fond of the statue of Isis. Whenever there was no one around it, he would stare at it with an attentive look unlike that of a child; sometimes he would stretch out a hand and stroke the statue, unwilling to leave it.

"But my position at the time did not allow me to regard that as something charming. In those days I was still young, more like the temple's caretaker than a priest, and on several occasions I tried to drive him away. Even if he was only an innocent child, there was no forgiving the disrespect involved in touching the statue of Isis like that. But I never succeeded in driving that child out of the temple until the day he left the city. No matter how firmly I steeled my heart as I approached, I would completely forget what I had been intending to do as soon as I saw his clear eyes, feeling a strange chill. Rather, I would smile involuntarily and go off to some other task that I would suddenly remember.

"It was the same, though to a lesser degree, with his young mother who used to come in search of him as night was falling. Intending to give her the warning I could not manage to give the child, I would leave my preparations for the evening prayers and go running toward her, but it was no use. A kind of sacred aura surrounding her used to freeze my lips.

"One day, for some reason I was sitting with that child in the shade of the fig tree in the courtyard, exchanging a few words. After talking about this and that, I happened to ask him about his father; without the least hesitation, the child pointed at the sky, and said that his father was the One who dwelt there. Thinking that he had literally believed something his parents had said, I asked him about his mother. He replied that although he considered the young woman to be his mother, she had conceived him as a virgin after an annunciation from this god. According to his words, they were a living Isis and Horus. As you know, Isis bore Horus without having received the seed of Osiris.

"What I still cannot understand is the way I reacted to what he said. This was disrespect, the most extraordinary disrespect—blasphemy, utter blasphemy; yet there I was sitting listening without a word, as if bewitched. I felt as if some kind of inexpressible power was weighing down on my body and my heart, and I simply sat there paralyzed until he had gone; then eventually I was just about able to walk again, trembling for no reason . . ."

The agitation he had felt then seemed to come flooding back into the priest's face. Ahasuerus, likewise feeling a strange agitation, asked:

"But why did you think that I was somehow related to that child on seeing me?"

"On account of a dream. One night, I had a strange dream. This child was going somewhere, pulling the statue of Isis along by the wrist. I followed them, summoning up all the energy and courage I possessed. With great difficulty I managed to seize the statue of Isis by a piece of its clothing, and she turned her face toward me. To my great amazement, it was the face of the child's young mother. Moreover, this new image of Isis addressed me: "Henceforth, I am leaving this land; I am going to all the peoples of the world. The traces of my past that I leave behind here will be utterly overthrown, burned, and destroyed by my son when he comes again." Then she coldly shook off my hand and went on her way.

"Waking from my dream, I ran to the statue of Isis to calm my startled, trembling heart. Nothing about it had changed, but still I stayed awake all night, burning incense and praying. As dawn broke, I walked back and forth in the yard, waiting for the child to appear. Once I was somewhat calmer, I decided never again to allow him anywhere near the statue.

"For some reason the child did not come that day. After I had spent much of the day waiting for him, I went to the Jewish neighborhood where he lived. After asking around, I found their hut, but the young couple and child had already left. According to their neighbors, they had set out for their own land very early in the morning, just at the moment when I was having that strange dream . . .

"That incident caused me a great shock. For a time, I thought of laying aside my priestly robes and going to look for the mother and child in your country. In the end, I stayed here in this temple. The shock naturally lost its sharpness over the time I spent hesitating, but there was also a more important reason. Just as you were unable to accept our Isis in spite of all your exceptional devotion and efforts over the past year, I simply could not believe that there might be a god and a teaching transcending a particular race and territory.

"Then you arrived. The first time I saw you, I trembled, strangely disturbed. You were obviously not that child, yet the mysterious power that I felt with you was very like the one radiating from the child. When I realized that you were from the same country, I arranged for you to be accepted in our temple, filled with a mixture of fear and inexplicable curiosity. Somehow it seemed to me that you must somehow be related to that child; I even went so far as to wonder whether you were him, or had come as his representative. I wanted to see how the prophecy I had heard in my dream so long ago would be fulfilled, to see how you were going to overthrow, burn, and destroy the statues of our god.

"This explains my response when you came to see me yesterday evening. I interpreted what you said as meaning that you were finally going to destroy our statues. That was why I took the initiative and tried to break the idol first with my blasphemous words, which went contrary to the teaching of my forebears. I overturned all our teachings, leaving only humanity on this earth. In doing so, I was hoping to see you raise up a new god and a new teaching in their place . . .

"But you were only surprised and disappointed by what I said, making no attempt to establish anything new. It seemed rather that you were also seeking a new idol."

"It's true. I am simply the son of a man. Despairing of the god of our people, I have been seeking a new god and new teachings."

"I know this now. As soon as you left I felt sorry not to have enlightened you about our religion with more skill and sincerity. I finally came to realize that you had no relationship with that child, and I suffered from having so readily destroyed the image of our god in front of you.

"Do you know what dream I awoke from just now? I was dreaming that the statue of Isis was collapsing. No one was breaking or burning it; it was collapsing and crumbling on its own, like grains of sand, together with this temple, turning back into soil. Awakened from my dream by amazement and fear, just as I was ten years before, I ran toward the statue. I burned incense and began to pray, but before I had finished praying, I heard your steps as you were leaving. Who on earth are you? How could such a thing happen? What inspiration provoked such a dreadful dream?"

The old priest was becoming increasingly breathless and was trembling. But Ahasuerus could give him no answer. After a long, awkward silence, he could only repeat what he had said previously: "I was born, without the least doubt, the son of a man, inheriting my father's vital spirit and my mother's blood. I am simply seeking, never wanting to break down or destroy."

"To seek new things is to destroy the old. But oh, who are you really?"

The old priest murmured in a voice from which anxiety had still not been banished. His anxiety transferred itself to Ahasuerus in the form of a vague premonition as to the future destiny of his own people's god.

As a rule, gods willingly take on a martial role in times of growth or at periods of reform; and although some aspects of Yahweh were a transformation of Aton, such problems hardly constituted a serious response to his quest. Still, finding more about this past history of Yahweh was precisely what had first directed his attention toward Egypt. Yet after nearly three years of wandering, all he had gained in that country was a premonition of Yahweh's future history, although that came unexpectedly, and had almost nothing to do with what he was seeking at that moment. Not wishing to be detained any longer by the old priest's questions, Ahasuerus hastened to take his leave.

"In any case, I am not the child you say you once knew. So, farewell."

He set off, leaving the old man standing lost in thought in the darkness that precedes the dawn.

8

Leaving Egypt, Ahasuerus headed for his homeland, as if it was the natural thing to do. But as he approached his native soil, his thinking began to change. He dwelled on the fact that he had gained nothing during his journeys, and he decided that he was not willing to pass the remaining years of his life cowering before a god and a Word he could neither believe in nor respect—thus, he felt that he could not return home. Moreover, his experience of direct contact with strange gods and teachings had awakened in him a new interest in the various idols of the land of Canaan that had previously been the objects of his habitual contempt and ridicule. Designating them as pagan idols had surely been nothing more than a reflection of the self-righteousness and prejudices of his forefathers. For this reason he passed over his homeland, and traveled instead through the region of Canaan and the Phoenician coast. In those regions, in addition to the gods imposed by Rome, there were numerous gods living in the ruins of towns that had been destroyed, as well as in the memories and oral legends of the gentile tribes who still rejected Yahweh. Those gods had flourished in earlier days, before Yahweh became a merciless, martial god and carried out his cruel revenge by way of Ahasuerus's forefathers. Among all those gods it was Baal, whose name has become a synonym for every kind of idol, who first attracted his attention, together with his father El. Then there

was Dagon, god of harvests; Asherah and Anat, wives in turn to El
and Baal; Yam, the eldest son of El, a sea god represented as a dragon, who had been killed fighting against Baal while attempting to
take revenge on his father's enemy; and Mot, god of death, who finally took revenge on Baal. Around them were Athtart, the goddess
who assisted Baal in the battle with Yam together with Kothar-wa-
Khasis the blacksmith and Shapash; Athar, the goddess of the sun
who tried to sit on Baal's throne after his death but failed; as well
as the seventy gods born from the union of El and Asherah. Ahasuerus sought out descendants of the old priests, who stubbornly
kept guard over the ruined temples and the surviving fragmentary
records that transmitted their teachings and ceremonies. Through
these myths that were passed down orally through the generations,
which were no longer a religious system so much as a collection of
tales, he tried to understand how those who had once served these
gods had viewed life and the cosmos. However, at the end of the
months and years of painful, difficult searching, collecting materials
and deciphering them, all that Ahasuerus was able to gain from his
partial reconstitution of the teachings and ceremonies of Baal ended up being a disappointment greater than that which he had experienced in Egypt. All that he could see was the deification of fears
arising out of the simple hopes and ignorance of peasants, reflecting
the corrupt, chaotic morality of a stagnant, sedentary culture.

The battle between Baal and Yam, for example, was merely a
myth designed to explain how rain was more useful than seawa-
ter or springwater in farming; the revenge of Anat on Mot proved
to be nothing more than a description of agricultural technique:
when Anat caught Mot, who had killed her husband Baal, and
then "cut him into pieces, winnowed them, roasted them, ground
them in a mill, and sowed them in the fields," what else was it but
a dramatization of the process of harvesting the ripe grain at the
end of the year?

He was dumbfounded to discover the inverted morality of certain tales, such as when Baal, the chief god in their mythological system, drives out his old, weak father, El, and takes his two wives for
himself. No matter how much it was due to the skillful and lavish

embellishments of these stories, Ahasuerus could not understand how a cult based on such absurdity and immorality could have inspired such magnificent temples and solemn, sumptuous ceremonies, nor how its followers could have been driven to defend their faith against other gods and cults.

Yet all the efforts Ahasuerus had invested in this task were not completely wasted. Most importantly, it enabled him to understand how the god of his people came to be seen as an agricultural deity. Before the entry into Canaan, Yahweh was only considered to be a martial god and a god of shepherds; subsequently, he had become almighty by assimilating the power of an agricultural god on encountering Baal. Of course, even before that he could do as he wished with the rain, the wind, and the sun, but there was almost no sign of him using his power for the sake of agriculture until the victory of Elijah, when he finally manifested a power superior to Baal by bringing the rain, defeating four hundred and fifty of his priests.

It was also at that point that Ahasuerus discovered that his people's temple and their tradition of burnt offerings had developed through contact with Baal. It was only when they had settled in Canaan that the Sanctuary, which had originally taken the form of a tent that they carried on their wanderings, was transformed into a temple built of wood and stone, putting down roots. The irregular sacrifices of a nomadic tribe then became established as burnt offerings under the influence of the ceremonies of an agricultural people, which had grown sophisticated over a long course of regular repetition. As he explored the ruined temples of Baal and tried to imagine what they must have looked like at their height, he was surprised to find that the altar, the wooden pillars, and the vessels for the offerings were all very similar to those in the temple of his own people. Their word for priest and the word in his own tongue had a common origin, and he was bewildered to discover signs that the gods had been mixed and worshipped together.

As he listened to tales of the ancient prophets of Baal, who were said to have prophesied in a state of ecstasy, he recalled how, in the days evoked in the Torah, there had been none of the crazed prophets who filled the roads of present-day Judea, nor the inflamed prophets of the past such as Amos, Elijah, or Jeremiah. During this time he also learned that the cultic prostitution from the days of the Kings had its roots in Canaan, from the time when such practices were used to venerate Baal. He also wondered if the wife of Jael, who had killed Sisera in violation of the nomads' absolute law that required protection for those who came in search of shelter, had not been corrupted by the cunning of the farmers who worshipped Baal. The fact that his people had poured out fiercer denunciations and curses on Baal than on any other god might even be an expression of a corresponding fear of assimilation or fusion.

As he made his way along the Phoenician coast, then passing through Abilene and heading for Syria, Ahasuerus encountered many more gods beside Baal—Chemosh of Moab, Moloch of the Ammonites, the mother goddess Cybele and the shepherd god Attis from Asia Minor, Elagabalus the sun god of Emesa, Jove, who is identified with Zeus in the eastern regions, Hammon of Carthage, Mot and Anat of Phoenicia, Athena Aphaea, venerated in Aegina, Nergal of Cuth, Ashima of Hamath, Nibhaz and Tartak of the Avites, Adrammelech of Sepharvaim. Starting with the gods still worshipped in the various regions, as well as those mentioned in the Scriptures, or gods he heard about from the caravan travelers, Ahasuerus spared no effort to find out something about each of them. However, despite having broken free of the prejudices and dogmatism of his forefathers, none of these gods attracted so much as a second glance from him, to saying nothing of captivating him.

Ahasuerus continued his encounters with new mythic systems as he reached northern Syria and turned southward again after going as far as Asia Minor. As he was passing through the region of Karkemish, he came across a young man of his own age digging among the ruins of an ancient city and gathering certain objects. Finding it odd that anyone would be digging on the slopes of what seemed a barren hillside in a deserted region several miles from the nearest village, he went to investigate; it turned out that he was collecting dried clay tablets that were buried there. They were inscribed on both sides with small characters that looked like caterpillars and were presumably an ancient system of writing.

"What are you going to do with these things after you've dug them up?" Ahasuerus asked the young man, stopping in a sudden burst of curiosity. He had seen similar clay tablets before, but they received no attention because no one could read them. Their usual fate was to be left lying around until they finally crumbled back into dust. Seeing the effort he was making to dig them up, anyone would have asked the same question as Ahasuerus. The young man, who was not of the same race as Ahasuerus, stopped working and replied reluctantly:

"I have no idea. I've been doing this for several years now, simply because my father told me to."

Fortunately, he not only understood Ahasuerus's Aramaic but was able to speak it quite fluently. This delighted Ahasuerus, and he pursued his questions:

"You mean you don't know why your father is collecting these objects?"

"Well, he says he's trying to restore the glory of the gods of our ancient forefathers. He claims that the stories of their gods are written on these clay tablets." The young man's expression suggested that he found what he was doing disagreeable. Ahasuerus pricked up his ears at the mention of gods, and asked in a voice that quavered involuntarily:

"Those ancient forefathers . . . what kind of people were they?"

"Hittites, he said, or Hattians . . . anyway, my father insists that he's descended from their royal family." A slight sneer appeared at the corners of his lips as he replied. But Ahasuerus reacted differently. If he meant the people of Hatti, they were related to the Hurrians he had read about in the Scriptures. They had seemingly vanished from history long ago, after causing his own forefathers many difficulties with their sharp iron weapons and their strong, speedy chariots; but now, quite unexpectedly, he would be able to discover their gods.

Thrilled by this stroke of good fortune, Ahasuerus followed the young man, ignoring the looks he gave that suggested he thought Ahasuerus was crazy. They shared the load of undamaged tablets between them, which was more than one person could carry, and reached the young man's home after walking a good eight miles.

Contrary to Ahasuerus's worries that the father would be senile or ill-tempered, he turned out to be a sound-minded man, and not very old—not yet sixty by his looks. But his Aramaic was an even greater cause for rejoicing. Although he was now settled as a farmer with land and cattle, he had traveled far and wide in his youth, accompanying caravans to every corner of the earth, and as a result he had learned to speak and write Aramaic more fluently even than Ahasuerus.

Examining the clay tablets they had brought back, the old man scolded his son: "Why, you've picked out nothing but a load of useless stuff to bring back. All they deal with is soldiers' wages and methods of training horses. Didn't I tell you to hurry up and learn the letters?" He then looked up at Ahasuerus:

"You've come to learn about our gods, you say? A strange young man, indeed. Don't the people of your tribe refuse to acknowledge any god apart from your own?"

He seemed to have recognized Ahasuerus's origins at a glance. Ahasuerus responded curtly: "I have left my tribe and its god. It is in the hope of filling the empty place that I am traveling about like this in search of a new god."

"Nonetheless, the blood that flows in your veins is Jewish blood. Your god is one and the same as your blood. Still, you've come seeking our gods—something that no one ever seeks; no guest could be more welcome. Come in. I am heartily glad to have you here."

Having spoken thus, he led Ahasuerus into the house without further questions. However, after supper, when he began to talk of his past history, there was a trace of madness about him.

"I am Muwatallish. Have you ever heard of King Muwatallish? There's no reason why you should. Judging by the records I've seen, he could be considered to be the final glory of us Hattians. Well over a thousand years ago, he defeated the Egyptian army led by Pharaoh Rameses II near the Orontes River. My late father named me after such a great man as a sign of the hopes he nourished for me."

"What relation is there between you and King Muwatallish?" The air of incipient madness in the man's eyes made Ahasuerus apprehensive, but he could not help asking the question, unable to resist the curiosity that had taken hold of him. Old Muwatallish replied as though he had been expecting the question.

"Unless my father's recollections are mistaken, he was one of our distant ancestors. After the king's death, our Hittite kingdom was attacked by sea-borne peoples, coming from the Aegean Sea, and finally ceased to exist about a thousand years ago. The kingdom vanished, but some of the last king's descendants moved into this region of Karkemish, where they survived in a number of small kingdoms for several centuries. Some of those kingdoms are said to have survived until the arrival of Alexander, and my late father's forebears are said to have been the rulers of one such kingdom. In this case, it's much more likely that the blood flowing through my veins derives from that of Muwatallish than that yours comes from Abraham or Jacob."

"But why are you going to such pains to rediscover gods that have so completely disappeared?"

"It is natural for you to ask that. In fact, until I was forty that was what I thought, and I paid no attention to what my father said. Just the same as my own son now . . . It was only after Father had died and I was growing older that I gradually began to grasp what he had been saying while he was alive. Father used to say that when a nation perishes, it is not because its gods have abandoned it, but because it has abandoned its gods. Defeat in warfare or the rise to power of another, mightier nation are secondary problems, he would say, and in reality a nation that keeps faith with its gods has always survived. He even used to cite your people as an example. Since the day when you crossed the river and came into Canaan, any number of mighty nations have arisen and established empires; yet where are they now? The fact that you alone have resisted and survived through the centuries is due to the way you have never abandoned your god.

"Despite the fact that he gave me such a distinguished name, all that my father really wanted me to do was to restore our gods to life. That meant completing the work that he had begun, documenting the mysteries passed down from our forefathers. He firmly believed that the former glory of our clan could be restored if only our gods could be brought back to life, no matter how scattered they might now be, and irrespective of how few remained. So long as a pure Hittite pedigree was preserved, we would gather once again before those gods, drawn by the blood in our veins."

Despite the increasing folly and the logical incoherence of the man's words, Ahasuerus was certain that it was a good decision to learn about the man's gods. If gods were still capable of inspiring such a degree of passion in men even when they had vanished completely many centuries before, then they must be worth learning about at least briefly, even if he eventually continued on his way, leaving them behind.

Muwatallish welcomed Ahasuerus with a depth of feeling that went beyond words. There might have been an element of misdirected affection, made greater by his disappointment with a young son who did not understand him; there was also at times a sense of pride at being able to teach a young man from another tribe about his clan's gods and their religious system. As a result, Ahasuerus was able to study more comfortably and readily than at any time since leaving home, as he learned about the gods of the Hittites. According to Hittite mythology, Alalu was the original king of heaven, served by Anu, who later replaced him and was replaced in turn by the god Kumarbi. Teshub was the storm god, leader of the three gods born to Kumarbi. Hebat was the wife of Teshub, Sharruma was their son, as was Telipinu, a god whose wrathful withdrawal caused the earth to become a wasteland. Wurusema was the sun goddess of the city of Arinna. Shanshka was the equivalent of the Babylonian goddess Ishtar. The goddess Inara helped the storm god vanquish the dragon Illuyanka by following the advice of a human who was then allowed to sleep with her. Ullikummi was known as "the diorite giant," born of a rock, while Upelluri bore the world on his back . . . swept along by his passion, Muwatallish revealed those many gods one by one, explaining their genealogies and sometimes their tribal origins.

But as the days passed Ahasuerus grew increasingly frustrated. In spite of Muwatallish's enthusiasm, he soon felt that he was wasting his time without being fully convinced, learning about a mythical system that was far more crude than any he had previously encountered. Heavenly power seemed to function as a series of betrayals; Alalu, the pitiful high god was banished from heaven by his followers and condemned to live beneath the earth, and was eventually caught and devoured by one of them; the extraordinary virility of Kumarbi was such that he begot descendants by ejaculating semen onto a rock; occasional fights between dragons and gods seemed to happen at random. In a word, there was nowhere a trace of the sacred, or of anything solemn to be seen, certainly no mercy or love, without even the least concern for human beings. The symbolic role of Telipinu, the "god who disappeared," might have been of some interest. But the Hittites' understanding of the cosmos and humanity was extremely primitive, while their notions of ethics and codes of behavior were almost nonexistent. Ahasuerus's overall impression was of something similar to the debauched and noisy gods of the Greeks, mixed with the abruptness and violence typical of peoples that shine briefly by power of arms then vanish from history.

In other words, there was no other choice than to leave. It was not that the affection and care manifested by Muwatallish during his stay did not weigh with him, but one day, less than three months after his arrival, Ahasuerus expressed his intention of leaving. The disappointment and fury of Muwatallish were considerable; he had intended to transmit to Ahasuerus not only the oral traditions but even the secret of how to read the ancient writings. He tried to tempt Ahasuerus by offering to adopt him and bestow on him a share of his considerable wealth equal to that of his own son if he agreed to follow in his footsteps. Then he threatened to invoke the wrath of Kumarbi and Teshub, before finally letting Ahasuerus depart under a shower of curses he could not understand. Ahasuerus regretted having to part from Muwatallish in this way, but he felt he had no choice. Having already given up any expectations regarding these gods, learning the letters of what was already a dead language would have been a completely useless activity.

The section of the manuscript ended there; it was the second Sergeant Nam had read that night. Having read that far, he began to feel dejected. In the earlier part that he had read in the train, it had been easy to detect Min Yoseop behind the character of Ahasuerus, but this was no longer the case. The novel's protagonist now seemed to simply be playing intellectual games in antiquated spaces of history.

With a head dulled to literary things by his work as a detective, Sergeant Nam was unable to read the hidden meaning of Min Yoseop's religious wanderings expressed in the novel. The inclusion of certain interesting incidents and the overall exotic atmosphere kept the story moving, but more often the dialogue and stories demanded several rereadings before they made even a vague kind of sense. To make things worse, the proliferation of names of gods made his head ache, while explanatory notes scribbled in the margins of the pages in minute black letters left him even more confused. Had it not been for a heartfelt conviction that his investigation was going in the right direction, Sergeant Nam would have soon closed the book.

"The prize shall be harvested where you put your trust"—murmuring a proverb he had heard somewhere to himself, he pressed on, opening that night's third section.

9

On leaving Karkemish, Ahasuerus's next goal was Babylon. Whether it was because traveling had by now become a habit with him, or if he was simply being driven on by an increasing sense of emptiness, the desire to return home to his parents had faded from mind. He had now crossed Palestine, Phoenicia, Syria, and gone as far as remote Asia Minor; yet he had failed to discover the god he was seeking, and so it only seemed natural for him to travel along the Euphrates and then turn toward Babylon. Time had passed, and it was now spring in his fifth year since leaving home.

There were ample reasons for Ahasuerus to head to Babylon, and it shouldn't be surprising that he did not decide to abandon his travels. From the days when Seleucus I had first founded Seleucia on the banks of the Tigris, the political and economic significance of Babylon had diminished to the point where it was showing signs of collapse. Yet it was still known to many people as the place where the guardian divinities of the ancient Mesopotamian civilization, once so glorious, were still alive.

For Ahasuerus, this was the land where his forefathers had been forcibly taken in exile by King Nebuchadnezzar, and where they had suffered and wept, gazing toward faraway Zion. Going much further back in time, the land was also inscribed with memories of Abraham, father of the entire Jewish people. After having discovered how Baal's presence lingered within the traditions of his devout ancestors, it is understandable that Ahasuerus would nourish expectations regarding the gods of Babylon and Mesopotamia.

Moreover, his decision to head east had been helped by the peace that was already established between Parthia and Rome. Ever since Augustus had recaptured the Roman eagle lost at the defeat of Crassus, the two empires had ceased their ancient hostility, establishing a buffer state along a frontier marked by the Euphrates. As a result, it had become as safe to travel in Mesopotamia as in any of the other Roman provinces.

There is no doubt that one of the reasons Ahasuerus chose to go to Babylon, rather than Nineveh or Assur, was the report he had heard when he was still at home about Jews living there. Many of his countrymen, whose ancestors had not returned to Canaan when King Cyrus of Persia granted them permission at the end of the captivity, were still living and prospering in and around Babylon. The continuing hellenization of the city from the time of Alexander the Great may have been an additional attraction, in view of the need for communication. In those days Babylon had become the main center for Hellenism in Mesopotamia, and Ahasuerus would be able to speak and understand people there using only Greek.

Ahasuerus reached Babylon slightly less than six months after leaving Muwatallish, after a journey by land and by boat during which he visited several ancient cities along the Euphrates. But Babylon was no longer the Holy City of the gentiles he had dreamed of from afar. Along with the ambitions of emperors and the greed of merchants, the gods too had abandoned the city.

The great shrine Esagila, dedicated to Marduk, the city's main god, had fallen into disrepair, despite the six hundred thousand days' worth of wages Alexander had paid for its reconstruction, while the towering shrine to the north, which was said to have been modeled after the Tower of Babel, had burned and collapsed into a heap of stones. A few other temples had survived, but the gods no longer resided in them. They were barely worth a cursory glance from an idle passerby—or at best they provided a living for false priests who jabbered a syncretistic doctrine within their walls. The statue with its pedestal, worth eight hundred talents of gold, before which a thousand talents' worth of incense was burned at every festival; the days of former prosperity when countless animals large and small were sacrificed on the two golden altars—they were now nothing more than legends, even for those who still wore the ceremonial robes of those gods. Nevertheless, Ahasuerus went searching in every corner of the city with unprecedented passion. From the moment he decided to set off for Babylon, he had been seized by the idea that the Mesopotamian gods might prove to have a more fundamental relationship with the god of his people. As far as written records were concerned, this land was his ancestors' earliest place of residence.

Ahasuerus did not fail to explore anything that had once been a temple, no matter how ruined it was, nor did he neglect to listen to anyone, not necessarily priests, who knew any small detail about their ancient gods. He even went so far as to spend hours standing silently in the courtyard of a ruined temple, in the preposterous hope that a statue, now broken into fragments, might suddenly rise up and reassemble itself, providing him with some kind of answer to what he was seeking.

It was only three months after he began visiting the temples of Babylon that Ahasuerus recalled the method Muwatallish had employed. Like the old man, he knew that he would only be able to learn the truth about any god from someone who sincerely believed; but on discovering that it was impossible to find such people still living, he turned his attention to the records the ancients had left behind.

But here Ahasuerus encountered additional difficulties: while he set out to collect Babylonian clay tablets under the assumption that they would be written in the same script as those collected by old Muwatallish, he soon realized he had been mistaken. Despite some superficial similarities between the two writing systems, the scripts were different, and no matter how hard he tried to match them with the fragmentary knowledge he had acquired from Muwatallish, he could not make any sense of the Babylonian tablets.

Ahasuerus had no choice but to set off in search of someone who could read them. But the region around Babylon, like the rest of Mesopotamia, had been entirely taken over by either Greek or Aramaic; there were very few who still knew how to read cuneiform texts. Even after finding several people who could read the language, it was not enough for Ahasuerus. Though he was eager to learn, their writing system employed several hundred different complex signs, which drove Ahasuerus, who was accustomed to an alphabet of only a few dozen characters, to despair. Even when he asked these people to read the tablets and explain the meaning, the results were not satisfactory. There were several different ways of transcribing identical-looking characters, and no one was capable of reading all the clay tablets Ahasuerus had collected. Therefore, while all his efforts certainly added something to his knowledge about their ancient gods, it remained vague and fragmentary as before.

Ahasuerus was beginning to lose patience when an apostate Jew, who now considered himself a great Babylonian, gave him some welcome news. The man had established a close relationship with Ahasuerus soon after his arrival in the city, driven by some strange sense of kinship, and one day, as the Mesopotamian year was coming to an end, he whispered in his ear:

"Go to the ruins of the Summer Palace on the hill to the north of the city. I've heard that the surviving fanatical followers of the god Marduk are going to celebrate the New Year there. Perhaps you'll find some real priests among them, someone capable of reading those tablets you want to decipher."

Ahasuerus knew the Summer Palace. It was a large ruin some eight miles to the north in an uninhabited region, remote and forbidding.

It must have been an ancillary palace built on the outer defense wall, which had not been restored after the city's destruction by the Persians.

However, at that moment Ahasuerus was suffering from an unknown illness, possibly the same fever that had killed Alexander in that very city. Even apart from this bout of sickness, his health had reached its limits. He had rested quietly for several months in Muwatallish's house, but by this point the five years of traveling, with the accompanying poor diet and physical exertion, had almost completely exhausted his last reserves of youthful strength.

Instead of staying in bed and resting quietly in order to allow his body to recuperate, Ahasuerus quickly got up and headed for the Summer Palace as soon as he heard these words, carrying an armful of clay tablets. Among those he had collected, he chose the ones he guessed were records of something to do with gods or rituals.

He hastened along, clenching his teeth and looking as though he was about to collapse; but contrary to what he had been told, there was no sign of anyone in the ruins of the Summer Palace. Just as on a previous visit, an eerie silence reigned and nothing more. As he stood there, Ahasuerus suddenly felt all his energy beginning to drain away. Refusing to give up, he began to search among the ruins. Even disregarding the rumor he had heard, if there still existed a fanatical group dedicated to the ancient gods that no one now cared about, this ruin, some forty miles from the city, was an ideal place to celebrate elaborate ceremonies away from prying eyes. Furthermore, Ahasuerus felt intuitively that extraordinary things occurred around these ruins.

Soon it grew clear that this impression was not a mere hallucination produced by the alternations of burning fever and cold sweats racking his sick, exhausted body. As he returned to inspect a partially ruined chamber for a second time, he became aware of a muffled murmur of voices and a whiff of incense rising from the entrance to a subterranean, stone stairway concealed behind a fallen pillar.

"I've found them at last!" Ahasuerus exclaimed inwardly as he hastened over to these stairs that he had found with such difficulty.

But in taking the first step downward he used the very last drop of energy he had. His body wavered above the precipice; a moment later he was rolling on the floor of the underground room as if he had been hurled down by an awesome force.

How long did it last? When Ahasuerus opened his eyes, he was in a stone- walled room, burning with fever, not certain if it was day or night, nor if what he saw was a dream or hallucination. Peering through what seemed to be a fog, he perceived lamps fixed to the four walls. He could pick out the faint outlines of a carved relief of a monster that appeared to be a combination of a lion and a serpent, and another one of an ox; when he looked up, the ceiling appeared to be slightly slanted.

As the things in the room grew distinct one by one, Ahasuerus became aware that part of the sights he had taken for dream or hallucination were real. People in glittering costumes burning incense, a murmuring of invocations, what seemed like the meaty smell of burnt sacrifices, the juice of some bitter-tasting herb that someone had poured into his mouth ... but the most enchanting memory of all was the flickering image of a lovely, exotic girl, dressed in mysterious robes like a goddess, and her whisperings that sounded sweet, although he could not understand a word.

Ahasuerus tried to lift his head up to see more clearly. Suddenly he swooned, as if he had been struck hard on the back of the head, and he lost consciousness.

When he opened his eyes again, a considerable amount of time had passed. A middle-aged Babylonian was standing at his bedside, looking down at him with a ponderous, inscrutable gaze. The man was wearing one of the glittering robes he had seen in what he had thought was his hallucination. It appeared that he had come hurrying to the bedside shortly before, when Ahasuerus had first given signs of waking, and had been waiting for him to return to consciousness.

Seeing Ahasuerus open his eyes, he squeezed drops of wine between his lips with a sponge, murmuring a few incomprehensible words. Seeing that Ahasuerus could not understand him, the man changed language and questioned him in Greek.

"Who are you? Why did you come here?"

"I came seeking the gods of Babylon." Only with difficulty could Ahasuerus move his parched lips in reply. The man's face lit up with amazement.

"Our gods? Then are you the one Marduk has sent as his servant?"

"I do not know if the god Marduk summoned me here, but I am certainly not someone sent by him, for I do not know him yet."

Ahasuerus was troubled by the man's amazement, but he answered truthfully. The man questioned him again as if he didn't understand.

"Then what about this *Enuma Elish* containing our creation myth?"

He pointed toward a pile of clay tablets, which lay neatly arranged at Ahasuerus's feet. They looked like the tablets Ahasuerus had brought with him; the ones that had been broken when he fell seemed to have been put back together. Ahasuerus, guessing that the tablets contained something out of the ordinary, again replied frankly and simply:

"If by *Enuma Elish* you mean those tablets, I collected them at the sites of various temples within the city. Some I purchased from self-proclaimed priests. Those tablets I brought with me came from near Esagila."

"And why did you come? What induced you to come wandering around this deserted spot? How did you discover the entrance to this underground temple, when it is not easy even for us to find?"

"I was told by someone there was to be a New Year's celebration here. Naturally, there are celebrations in the city as well, but I have heard that those are merely noisy, unruly games, in which all kinds of old Babylonian gods, twisted beyond recognition, and foreign pseudo-deities are mixed together. What I wanted to see was Marduk and the other gods who accompany him in their original, unadulterated form."

After Ahasuerus's reply the man paused in his questioning. His initial surprise had vanished, but his expression seemed to show that he was still curious about many things.

At last he spoke again: "Too many things about you fulfill the predictions of the oracle for all this to be mere chance. But one thing is vital. Judging by your appearance, you are not of the same blood as us. Where have you come from? From what tribe and whose descendant are you?"

"I am from the land of Judea. I am descended from Abraham and Isaac; you may have heard of them?"

Hearing him reply in that manner, the man frowned briefly.

"Why, of all races, would a descendant of those who stole our myths . . ." He broke off and remained sunk in thought for a while before slowly rising and continuing to speak.

"Very well. You have come corresponding to our oracle, so I must discuss all of this with the elders. Take a good rest in the meanwhile. Your fever has fallen, but the sickness has not yet been eradicated, so you must not overexert yourself."

Once the man left his bedside, Ahasuerus felt the fever come sweeping heavily back over him and closed his eyes. A dazed sleepiness soon blurred his mind.

How long did that state last? Ahasuerus opened his eyes when he felt that something like a soft ray of sunlight was caressing his face. It proved to be not sunlight, but the eyes of a young girl, who had been standing beside his bed for some time, silently watching him. It was the girl he had seen in his fever and taken for a hallucination. Striving to control his pounding heart, Ahasuerus stared at her. Her dress was similar to those of a relief of a female figure he had seen in a small temple that was referred to as the temple of Ishtar, located in an outlying region of the city. This was what had made him recall her as being robed like a goddess.

Even more lovely than her dress was her face, which was beautiful and bright, endowed with uncanny dignity. Her complexion was of a light-brown hue commonly seen among Mesopotamian girls, manifesting to even the least attentive observers a purity like a glimpse of the fairest flesh. Above graceful red lips her lofty nose expressed a certain coldness, which the depth and tranquility of her dark eyes transformed into an air of the sacred. She possessed a strange beauty, different from that of the young wife of Asaph or the other girls of his native land who had occasionally made his heart beat faster when he was a youth.

Although she knew Ahasuerus was awake and was observing her, the girl stood without moving until their eyes met; then she bowed and silently held out to him the little jar she was holding. Judging by the smell, it seemed to be the same herbal juice that he recalled having drunk a number of times during his feverish delirium. He raised himself to take the jar she was offering. Seeming relieved that she no longer had to help him drink, the girl turned and silently withdrew. She vanished like a phantom.

Later, as Ahasuerus was waking from the sleep he had fallen into after drinking the juice, the middle-aged man who had first addressed him returned to his bedside. He spoke in a discontented tone, as if he were doing him a favor.

"We have decided to accept you as the one sent by Marduk. You should understand that the god Marduk has sent you to be our king."

His words were completely unexpected. Dumbfounded and unable to grasp at once what he meant, Ahasuerus simply looked up at him in silence, while the man suddenly became excited and began explaining things Ahasuerus had not asked him about.

"We are people who have joined together to seek the restoration of the god Marduk and the former glories of Babylon. Contrary to what is often said, we were not conquered by the Persians: we actually let them in, opening the gates ourselves. Once Belshazzar, our last king, began to venerate Shin, the moon god, and stopped serving Marduk, the people and the priests expelled him and welcomed Cyrus, who immediately celebrated the ritual known as "taking Bel's hand" in Esagila—for Marduk is also called Bel, not as conqueror but as protector of our faith. More than that, he retrieved the statues of gods that had been taken to other cities and returned them to Babylon and protected this city as a sacred center of faith.

"But his grandson Xerxes betrayed us. He used a series of revolts by Nebuchadnezzar III and others as an excuse, but in reality he had become a follower of Ahura Mazda, abandoning this city and its god Marduk. He destroyed the temple tower and carried off the statue of Marduk to his own country like a prisoner of war. That was when the true downfall of Babylon began.

"Yet Marduk is almighty and great. He brought Alexander from Greece to destroy sacrilegious Persia. Alexander offered sacrifice to Marduk and ordered the rebuilding of the ruined temples. If he had not died so unexpectedly while still very young, and if the Seleucid dynasty that succeeded him had not been so eager to be hellenized, Babylon would not have become what you see now.

"But Babylon will not remain in ruins like this forever. Marduk is everlasting and we Babylonians are still alive. We will not allow this sacred city to remain desolate; the great Marduk will not stand quietly by while his city becomes a spectacle for curious foreigners. In times past, we have repeatedly risen up from the midst of devastation and fought to restore the glory of Babylon and of Marduk; at present we are preparing another great battle. On the day when all Babylonians stand united in the name of Marduk, we will enter Babylon in triumph. We will restore the magnificent city gates of ancient times, made of white juniper clad in bronze, and return the Processional Way to its former splendor, paved with sandstone and limestone. We will rebuild Esagila and the ziggurats; we will raise up again the hundreds of outdoor shrines, the pedestals for the gods, the thousands of pulpits. Then, in this splendidly restored sacred city, we will sing the former glories of Babylon . . ."

It was downright madness, but of another order than that which he had sensed in Muwatallish. It was the madness he had glimpsed in the Zealots of his own land of Judea, a malignant madness, inspired by a passion that was more political than religious.

"But when you say I am king, what exactly do you mean?" Feeling his flesh crawl, Ahasuerus phrased his question carefully. The man acknowledged his question, but his tone indicated that he was simply continuing what he had been saying previously, rather than replying to him.

"As a means of uniting in Marduk, we have prepared the New Year's festival of Akitu in the coming month of Nisan. But although Marduk is in the heavens, we have had no king to guide us in his place here on earth. We prayed ardently to Marduk. Fortunately he answered our prayers, sending down an oracle through various elders and priests. It announced that in the Days of Chaos at the end of the year, before the month of Nisan begins, our king will appear bearing a token given him by Marduk. And on the first of the Days of Chaos, you arrived, carrying the *Enuma Elish* engraved with the story of the foundation of the world and the genealogy of the gods . . ."

Confronted with this account, Ahasuerus ventured a timid protest, for he felt that no matter how symbolic the role, it would be dangerous for him to become the head of a band in which nationalistic fervor combined with religious fanaticism, and it was also completely unrelated to his personal quest:

"I only came here to learn, guessing that those tablets were records about the gods; I did not know what they contained. Besides, I am nothing more than a wanderer from a foreign land."

The man's expression suddenly became fierce and his voice grew threatening:

"But we have no choice. It troubles me that you are from a foreign tribe, but at present we only have a few days left before Akitu and there is no other way. We need a king to preside over the ceremonies for the New Year's festival. For the sake of the many simple folk who believe in the oracle more firmly than I or the elders do, and who will be coming to witness the beginning of a new age of history, you have no choice but to become the king sent by Marduk. If you refuse, I'll simply hand you over to the people, who will be infuriated by disappointment, accusing you of profanity and blasphemy."

"Even if it becomes known that my blood is different in origin from theirs?"

"I have already given thought to that. It will be enough to say that you are not Judean, but a descendant of Nebuchadnezzar III— whose family fled to Phoenicia after his failed attempt to restore the Empire—who has now returned home. You will have to say that, not only to the common people but also to the priests."

Still, Ahasuerus could not understand why the man was so determined to assign this odd role to him. He could have made an equally convincing show by having someone from his own people appear with an appropriate sign on the appointed day in the underground temple. For some reason, Ahasuerus felt apprehensive at the crafty expression and the searching eyes of the man, who seemed to be constantly plotting wicked deeds and gauging people's reactions. He finally summoned up the courage to ask something that had been intriguing him for some time: "But who are you?"

"I am Himerus. I have sought out the scattered priests, restored the ceremonies of Marduk, convinced the most illustrious elders, and brought together the common people out of their desire to restore the glory of Babylon. Yet for the ordinary folk, I do not exist as yet. Only a name transmitted in legends . . ."

He smiled ambiguously as he replied, now employing a cajoling voice.

"If you accept, you will not merely receive the name of king; you will really be treated as a king. You will spend all your days in abundance and comfort, in the midst of our veneration and having a beautiful living goddess for queen. What do you say? Will you do it?"

When Himerus mentioned this living goddess, Ahasuerus recalled the exotic girl he had seen a little earlier. His heart started to pound. Yet the conspiratorial feeling that emanated from Himerus's bizarre proposition made him incapable of replying. Himerus rose, smiling in a sinister manner, as if he could read his every thought.

"I trust you are not going to refuse and choose to be thrown to the angry mob to be burned alive! I'll give you time to think. I'll come back after the evening meal."

With that he went out.

Left alone, Ahasuerus pondered his proposal. He seemed to have no other choice. In the course of the past five years, while drifting here and there, he had seen many examples of "superstition for the sake of belief" and numerous religious spectacles that priests had organized to their own advantage; and he had often witnessed people's need for living, breathing symbols, even to the point that a prostitute could be made into a goddess. He likewise knew the terror of a collective madness inspired by belief; he had heard enough of the atrocities priests committed in the name of a god.

Moreover, this group, which was forcing him to play a bizarre role, combined political fantasy with a violent, nationalistic fanaticism. Remembering the horror he had experienced on seeing how the nationalists of his own land were only too ready to take up the sword and shed blood, Ahasuerus realized that he could not possibly refuse Himerus's demand.

Ahasuerus, although he remained reluctant, had further reasons for taking on the role of their symbolic king. One was his hope of drawing closer to the Mesopotamian gods through this role; another was the assumption that the girl who attracted him with such power might prove to be the "living goddess" Himerus had mentioned.

"Very well. If you really need me, I will do as you wish. But you must order your priests to teach me everything I want to know about the gods of your land."

This was Ahasuerus's response to Himerus when he came to hear his reply after he had finished his supper of light gruel and had more or less recovered his strength. Himerus accepted readily.

"That's not difficult. In any case, you are the person who will have to come closest to our gods. I will select only learned, scholarly priests to instruct you."

He glanced at Ahasuerus and added: "But that will be after the festival of Akitu is over. The first thing you have to do is master the motions you will be obliged to perform for the people as king at the New Year's festival, and the ancient words you will have to speak for them. Tomorrow I will send the priest who speaks the best Greek; you must memorize all the motions and words he teaches you."

The words were spoken like an order, indicating to Ahasuerus that he had no choice.

From the next day onward, for several days, Ahasuerus studied the Babylonian New Year's ceremonies like an actor in a Greek theater, memorizing his text and role from a script. Physically he was still not well, but by the time he had recovered and was able to get up a few days later, his exceptional intelligence and memory enabled him to recite the larger part of the ceremonies.

Two days after he left his sickbed, when he was completely restored, the Akitu festival began. That was on the vernal equinox,
the first day of the month they called Nisan. The first three days
were celebrated among themselves. On the fourth day Ahasuerus,
robed according to ancient rules, was led by the priests before the
crowd that was beginning to enter a state of frenzy. With a hand
adorned by a ring of precious stones, he grasped a scepter that was
a symbol of royal power; on his head he wore a resplendent crown
modeled after ancient relics, and a crescent-shaped scimitar hung
at his side. His robes were woven of rare silk, and were decorated
with various ornaments.

Following the instructions he had received, Ahasuerus moved
toward the priests, who were standing in a row, and knelt before
them. Their leader stepped forward with an angry expression on his
face, scolded him, tore the scepter and the scimitar away from him,
and removed the crown. After he had ripped off all the ornaments
attached to his robes, he made as if to strike his face and spit on him.
This was the beginning of the ceremony of expiation the king had to
undergo, celebrating the suffering of Marduk. Ahasuerus carefully
recited the ceremonial words he had memorized so laboriously.

"Oh Master of all that is in this world, I have not sinned, I have
not neglected the worship of your holiness, nor have I been un-
generous in making offerings to you. I have done my best to guide
my people toward you, I have not been slow to protect your lands.
Greatest among the gods, forgive me . . ."

As Ahasuerus recited the words of the lengthy prayer of contri-
tion in the still unfamiliar Akkadian language, the angry expression of the head priest began to soften. It had all been determined
in advance. Still, Ahasuerus was obliged to repeat the words several times more before an expression of pity appeared on the priest's
face and confidence in the king was regained.

At last, the chief priest began to praise Marduk in a loud voice
with arms opened wide, then spoke to Ahasuerus in gentle tones.

"Fear not. Marduk will grant your prayers. He will increase
your lands and multiply your people . . ."

Following that, after benedictions and promises had been repeated at length, the day was filled with the frenzied festivities of the impassioned, jubilant crowd.

The next day's ceremony portrayed Marduk vanishing far away from the sun and light, then reappearing. On the following day, there was a ritual in which the various other gods came thronging round as the returning Marduk assigned to each of them a particular domain and destiny. In this ritual, Ahasuerus, acting as king on behalf of Marduk, carried each of the idols to its proper place. Like a smaller version of the ceremony celebrated in the days of ancient Babylon's prosperity, when the statues of the gods were enshrined in their respective temples around the outskirts of the city in the course of magnificent, festive processions, the statues of the lesser gods were re-enshrined in different corners of the underground temple.

The next day saw the ceremony representing the combat between Marduk and the evil gods. For this, Ahasuerus represented Marduk, leading a company of terrified gods in a violent battle against Tiamat, dragon goddess of the ocean. The solemn ritual ended with the scene in which, after killing and dismembering Tiamat, Marduk created the world.

The marriage rites that Ahasuerus had been anxiously awaiting were held on the final day of Akitu. On the afternoon of the day when the festival reached its climax, Ahasuerus took the living Ishtar as his wife in rites where he, as a human being, was king while attaining celestial holiness. The person playing the role of Ishtar was indeed the Babylonian girl he had seen at his bedside when he was sick. After he had accomplished the rites of sacred union with her, a series of benedictions for each month of the year marked the end of Ahasuerus's role in the celebration of Akitu. He himself considered it to have been a remarkably flawless performance.

The priests, who had initially manifested distrust, even enmity toward Ahasuerus on account of his unconcealed foreignness, showed a quite different attitude after the end of the festivities. They now seemed to consider him one of their own race, home after a long journey in foreign lands. Himerus and the elders likewise seemed satisfied. Apart from a trace of incomprehensible pity he occasionally perceived in their eyes, Ahasuerus's life there was no different from that of a real king.

His special delight was to have received the girl impersonating Ishtar as his wife. Because of a fiercer flame burning within him, he had not until then completely given himself over to desire; but he was, after all, a young man of twenty-four who was already experienced with women. As soon as he had the lovely girl in his arms, he gave himself over to the cravings of inflamed love, as if his youthful flesh was determined to make up in a single moment for all the time during which he had forgotten it. At certain moments he felt that he would be content to spend the rest of his life loving the girl, neglecting everything else and staying there with her.

However, Ahasuerus was unable to completely lose himself in these connubial pleasures. At times, in the midst of the fiery vortex of love, he felt his religious passion driving him to further his study of the Mesopotamian gods. Although there remained an uneasy feeling caused by his inability to understand why they had obliged him to play the not altogether unpleasant role of king, Himerus had been true to his promises. The priests instructed him readily about their gods and teachings whenever Ahasuerus wished, and in their attitudes they truly showed him the deference due to a king. He had already heard some of what they taught him in the various temples of Babylon in the form of legends or absurd myths, but frequently their interpretations and their commentaries, based as they were on devout belief, gave Ahasuerus the impression that he was encountering completely new gods. Among the priests there were several who had mastered the cuneiform writing that Ahasuerus had so eagerly wished to learn. There were also priests who could decipher not only old Babylonian but also Akkadian and Sumerian. Ahasuerus was already more or less familiar with the writing systems that had remained in use; that, together with his remarkable skill in languages and his intelligence, meant that in a few months he was capable of reading any kind of clay tablet no matter what writing system it employed. Despite the nights spent in fierce lovemaking with his young bride, by the time the seventh month of Tashritu arrived, he had learned not only about all the still-living gods of the Babylonian era but also about the gods of ancient Akkadia and Sumer, which had long since vanished.

An or Anu, the primal god of heaven; Nammu, the mother, the primal goddess of the sea; their offspring Enki, the god of the Earth, and Enlil, the god of the atmosphere; Ninhursag, mother-goddess and consort of Enki; Aruru, the goddess who in some tales created the first human beings; Inanna, the planet Venus and the goddess of love later known as Ishtar; Dumuzi or Tammuz, figuring in a fertility myth; Nidaba, goddess of learning; Utu, the sun god; Ereshkigal, goddess of the underworld and elder sister to Inanna; Ninshubur, the devoted friend of Inanna who helps rescue her from the underworld; Nanna-Suen, the moon god; Geshtinanna, sister of Dumuzi who rescues him from the underworld; Nergal, netherworld god of destruction; Ninkura, the daughter of Enki and Ninhursag; Ninlil, goddess of wind; Nuska, son of Enlil and god of light or fire; Ishullanu, Anu's gardener who falls in love with Ishtar; Sarpanitu, Marduk's consort; Namtar, god of diseases; Asushunamir, the god who saves Inanna from Ereshkigal; Apsu, the god of the fresh water from which everything was made; Tiamat, a female dragon representing the ocean; Lakhmu and Lakhamu, offspring of Tiamat and parents of Anshar; Mummu, the craftsman son of Tiamat and Apsu; Anshar and Kishar, the parents of Anu; Nudimmud, son of Anu also known as Ea, father of Marduk; Damkina, mother of Marduk; the nymph Siduri who offers Gilgamesh wine . . . In addition, among the clay tablets the priests had collected in various parts of Mesopotamia, such things as epic poems, proverbs, and moral treatises were of great help in giving him a better grasp of their gods and their cosmology.

As he had vaguely conjectured when he first traveled down the Euphrates, the region seemed to be not only the original homeland of his forefathers but also the birthplace of their god. The first thing that Ahasuerus found that hinted at this was a series of myths surrounding the creation of heaven and earth. The battle between Marduk and Tiamat could be seen as a remote archetype of the combat between Yahweh and Rahab or Leviathan before the creation of the world, while the manner in which the victorious Marduk created the world with the dead body of his enemy revealed to him the origin of his ancestors' division of the universe into three levels—heaven, earth, and sheol.

Concerning the creation of man and original sin, Babylonian myths gave him much food for thought. Although there were myths that said the first man had sprouted from the earth like a plant or had been made by the goddess Aruru, they mostly described him as being formed out of clay. On the other hand, human nature originally came to contain a sinful element by being contaminated with the blood of the Lagma gods. Moreover, the purpose of the gods in creating human beings was in order that they might be fed, clothed, and served by them, which Ahasuerus felt helped him understand the coldness and ruthlessness of Yahweh. These myths also contained the same repetitions of "He saw and it was good" after each act of creation. Ahasuerus's forefathers had declared in various places that the creation of humanity by Yahweh had been an expression of his mercy and love, but in what had happened in the past and what was now happening in the world, Ahasuerus was more inclined to see a Yahweh whose only concern was to be served and worshipped.

The Food of Life that Adapa did not eat during his visit to the heavens—and if he had eaten it he would have enjoyed eternal life—seemed not unrelated to the fruit of the Tree of Life that Adam was deprived of as a result of his sin. Adapa was not the first ancestor of humanity as Adam was, but like Adam he missed the chance to become immortal, though less on account of his sin than because of Ea's mistaken advice. Yet the coldhearted rejection of humanity's ardent desire to overcome its own limitations, as well as the firm division of the domain of the gods from that of humanity, was sufficient to recall the tragedy of Adam. The same theme was also repeated in the *Epic of Gilgamesh* in a similar form, when a snake steals the plant of perpetual youth from Gilgamesh.

The story of Noah's Ark was likewise mirrored by the Sumerian myth of Zisudra, referred to as Utnapishtim in the *Epic of Gilgamesh*. They were almost identical to the story of Noah, not only in their devotion and righteousness, but in the structure and size of the ark they were ordered to build by a god, the downpour lasting seven days and seven nights, and even the consecutive sending out of raven and dove to detect the subsiding of the waters.

The distinctive hostility toward serpents also seemed to derive from Babylon. Aside from the snake that steals the plant from Gilgamesh, the Sumerian myths also spoke of a great serpent that constantly disturbed the cosmic order. This attitude must have influenced his ancestors, who represented the serpent in Eden as an evil seducer.

It was clear that the Babylonian notions of sin and atonement must to some degree have influenced Abraham, who spent the earlier part of his life among them. These concepts, found only in later Babylonian ceremonies and not in ancient clay tablets, established a particularly strong link with his people, more than with any other. Ahasuerus also found that there were a number of points in the clay tablets related to the books of Wisdom and Proverbs that corresponded to his forefathers' records. This was the case with the assertions of futility that resembled the lamentations of the Preacher in the scriptures, and likewise the reproaches against Marduk in the "Poem of the Righteous Sufferer," so similar to the howls of Job. There even seemed to be a link with phrases such as "an eye for an eye, a tooth for a tooth." Having been forcibly brought here long ago, his forefathers had not simply spent seventy years gazing toward Zion and weeping; they must have learned a whole new style and grammar for their god.

Although it was somewhat removed from his original quest, Ahasuerus grew more fascinated than ever by the ancient gods and doctrines of Babylon, sensing that he was retracing the past history of Yahweh, whom he had given up and abandoned. And then, once night had fallen, another kind of passion awaited him in his bedroom, growing deeper and more intense as the days passed—this fiery love with his young wife, who seemed to also appreciate these private pleasures. All the gods he was learning about, just like other gods he had come across in his travels, were immersed in immorality, betrayal, and incest, and in such vices as cruelty, capriciousness, favoritism, and self-righteousness. Yet what made it possible for him to draw closer to them with curiosity and hope, rather than disappointment, might well have been the fact that the wife he loved belonged to them.

However, at some point an incomprehensible change occurred in her. Once the sweet moment of rapture had passed, her warm body would turn icy cold, and her eyes, full of passionate ardor a moment before, would grow dull with an unfathomable sorrow. What's more, there were moments when an inexplicable, almost undetectable pity shone in the elders' eyes, which would sometimes reflect deep anguish.

Finding this strange, Ahasuerus often asked his wife the reason for this behavior. Each time she would smile awkwardly and shake her head, or she would simply remain silent. But at last the riddle was solved by the woman herself, who gave in to the love she felt for Ahasuerus, and decided to bring his stay there to an end.

It was a night in the middle of the month of Tashritu, not long before the autumnal equinox. Returning home early because the priests were busy preparing for the autumn festival, Ahasuerus drew the woman with him toward the bedroom, eager to release all the passion that had accumulated during the day.

Yet on this occasion, her reaction was unusual. Usually, even though she only seemed to be fulfilling her duty, she would enter a passionate frenzy and wrap herself around him the moment his hand touched her; but on this day, for some reason, her body remained cold and rigid, unable to relax. Ahasuerus caressed her fervently, like someone trying to revive a dying ember, when suddenly he noticed the tears streaming down her cheeks.

"What's wrong? What's happened?" he asked her, surprised. Suddenly she began to sob. Bewildered, Ahasuerus tried to comfort her, but she continued weeping for some time, then swallowed her tears, let out a deep sigh, and asked him:

"Poor man! Can you still not guess what's awaiting you?"

"What do you mean?"

Ahasuerus was perplexed. She silently looked back at him with eyes still full of tears, then asked: "Don't you know who Himerus is?"

Indeed, that was something Ahasuerus had been curious about from the very beginning. Himerus ordered the elders and priests about as he pleased, yet almost none of the ordinary people seemed to know him.

"Who is he? I've been wondering about that."

She suddenly lowered her voice and whispered: "He is Himerus the Second."

"Himerus the Second?"

"Yes. Himerus the First, who he claims was his grandfather, is said to have liberated Babylon from the control of the Parthians with the help of the priests of Esagila. It's also said that he was King of Babylon for a time and even issued coins bearing his name; but he was soon driven out by the Parthians."

"So this Himerus has the same dream as his grandfather regarding those now ruling Babylon?" Ahasuerus asked, piecing things together. She nodded silently. Ahasuerus went on:

"But there's something I still don't understand. If that's his dream, shouldn't he become king himself and lead the people? Why has he forced a foreigner like me to play the king's role?"

"You've learned and read many things about our gods in all this time. Don't you know about Tammuz, or the substitute king?"

"This is the first time I've heard of a substitute king. I know a little about Tammuz, but what has he got to do with me?"

Again she sighed gently and replied in a low voice: "The substitute king is the sacrificial offering for the true king. Common people can offer a lamb or a calf in place of the disasters destined for them, but a king is different. A king can only avoid disaster by offering a man like himself in sacrifice. And that victim is the substitute king. I've heard it said that the Assyrian king Esarhaddon was only able to avoid calamity by selecting a substitute king and having him die instead of himself."

Her words filled him with a sickening terror. At last he was beginning to understand Himerus's sinister smile and the elders' pitying looks. But he still wanted to understand completely.

"Now I see. But what connection is there between Tammuz and me?"

"Tammuz is a god who spends six months above the ground and six months underground. The period he is permitted to spend above the ground lasts from the spring equinox until the autumn equinox. Tammuz is the husband of Ishtar. And since you are the husband of the living Ishtar, that is to say myself, that means you are the living Tammuz. Now when the autumn equinox comes, you have to disappear underground; you see what that means? You are to descend ceremonially as Tammuz into the underworld, and at the same time you will also die as Himerus's substitute king. Then Himerus intends to lead the people, who will be convinced of his immortality, and march against Babylon. He has not revealed himself directly to the people yet, but he is spreading news of his imminent coming through the prophecies of the priests and elders. Now do you understand?"

"But you are still young. How do you know all this?"

"Himerus is my adoptive father. After I lost my parents I was roaming the streets of Babylon begging; he took me in and raised me."

A dark shadow spread over her face, provoked by the inner pain of betraying the man who was at the same time her benefactor and her adoptive father. Quite forgetting the approaching danger, Ahasuerus embraced her with a sudden emotion and elation. For now he had felt her love for him, not just with ears and eyes but with his very heart—a love that surpassed an affection and gratitude formed over many years and was not even afraid to die for him.

"Is it really so? Really . . ." Ahasuerus murmured as he covered her tear-stained face with burning kisses. She briefly surrendered herself to him, then pushed him away gently, whispering: "There is no time to lose. You must leave at once. Tomorrow you will have to preside over the ceremony of purification for the autumn festival and it will be impossible for you to escape. Quick! Hurry!"

But Ahasuerus heard nothing of what she said. His heart, already strongly ablaze, craved for her body with a more heated passion than ever before, though it had almost nothing to do with carnal desire. She resisted him at first, then seemed to change her mind and began to respond to his advances with passionate abandon, as if she wanted to absorb him completely into herself, body and heart.

When Ahasuerus's mind returned to dark reality, he was lying beside her in a deep, lethargic torpor as intense as the violence of their lovemaking. He thought he heard someone calling him, knocking faintly on the door.

"It's Himerus," she whispered into Ahasuerus's ear as he was coming to his senses; then she quickly added: "Don't get dressed. Go and meet him without even wiping off the sweat; only cover the front of your body."

Still feeling dazed, Ahasuerus did as she told him. It was indeed Himerus at the door.

"What is it?" Ahasuerus asked, in a voice suggesting weariness and exasperation. Himerus examined Ahasuerus, then spoke with the treacherous smile that was characteristic of him:

"I have disturbed the bed of the king and the goddess. At the Persian court, I would have been beheaded. Excuse me. I will come again tomorrow morning."

Watching Himerus turn away with a strangely satisfied air, Ahasuerus realized that he was already being watched, and understood why she had told him to appear before Himerus in that state.

When Ahasuerus returned to the bed, she urged him on impatiently: "Quickly, make your preparations to leave now. Himerus will feel reassured until tomorrow morning at least." Yet Ahasuerus could not free himself from a lingering attachment to her, though she was pushing him toward the door.

"What about you? What will you do?"

"I have to stay in bed here until tomorrow morning. As if you were still asleep ... No matter which way you go over the course of one night, Himerus's people will easily catch up with you. Get as far away as you can, quickly; don't stop for two or three days."

"Will you be safe?" Ahasuerus asked, unable to move. Again a dark shadow crossed her face briefly, immediately replaced by an equally bright smile as she replied: "What harm could come to me? Himerus is my adoptive father; he's looked after me like his own daughter for more than ten years."

"No, it's not so. I want you to come with me."

He remembered the cruelty and heartlessness lurking in Hime-rus's insidious smile, and feared for her safety. She responded angrily: "Do you want to have your throat cut on the altar? Together, we would be stopped after a few steps. Do you still not know what kind of a man Himerus is?"

"I am asking because I know him. How do you expect me to believe he will leave you unharmed if he finds out that you helped me escape?"

"He wouldn't dare kill me for something like that. I know how things stand between him and me better than anyone; you must leave now, as quickly as possible," she replied with a more confident smile. It was not so much that he really believed her, but that he realized that they had no choice. Ahasuerus slowly dressed and prepared to leave.

Once he was ready, he asked her, as if struck by a new idea: "Why don't I just go to the authorities in Babylon, denounce Himerus, and save you?"

"You mustn't!" she replied suddenly in a piercing cry. Then, fixing him with an icy glare, she added, "If you did that, it would mean the death of my adoptive father; I would refuse to ever see you again. More than that, I would curse myself eternally for ever having become your wife."

"Then are we parting forever?"

"There may be another way. But in any case, I cannot love you if you kill Himerus." There was a kind of desolation echoing in her voice. Ahasuerus hesitated, then asked, "Couldn't you escape?"

"Yes, perhaps. I don't know when, but I'll try to get out of here and go looking for you."

"When you do, come to Jerusalem and ask for Zachiah of Shekhem. He's my uncle. Since he's the biggest shoemaker in Jerusalem, he won't be hard to find. I'll be waiting for you there."

"Very well. But you must not set out in the direction of Jerusalem straightaway. Himerus knows which country you are from; he'll pursue you all the way. Head east first instead, then go by boat, taking a roundabout way."

"Right. That's what I'll do. You must remember: Zachiah of

Shekhem in Jerusalem."

The promise being made, Ahasuerus made haste to leave. But the promise proved to be in vain. After escaping from the underground temple along a secret passage she told him about, Ahasuerus headed eastward and, less than three days later, heard the shocking news: the army and officials of Babylon had raided the ruins of the Summer Palace, killing or capturing several hundred followers of a certain Himerus, who had been plotting an insurrection using an underground chamber as his base. He heard the news from a traveler at a ferry station on the banks of the Tigris, where a road branched in the direction of Susa, then the capital of Persia. The traveler ended his account by adding these last details:

"The most shocking thing of the whole affair was the death of Himerus. He slashed his own throat before soldiers could capture him, and they say that beside him a beautiful girl, not yet twenty years old, was lying dead with her body full of stab wounds. I don't know the exact details, but they say she was his adopted daughter, and was somehow connected with the fellow who reported the rebellion."

It was well past midnight when Sergeant Nam finished reading this third section of the manuscript. It took him a long time, less on account of its length than because of the effort he was making to comprehend the contents.

The long-suffering sergeant was slightly discouraged to find Ahasuerus still wandering incomprehensibly in foreign lands. Considering the energy he expended reading and analyzing the novel, he was getting too little out of it, and there were still several sections left to read.

"Perhaps Lieutenant Lee is right after all, and all this really has nothing to do with the crime. Maybe they're just the clumsy scribbles of a failed theology student trying to write a novel . . ." With that thought, he pushed the pages aside and shut his eyes. Thinking of the urgent visit he was going to have to make to Daejeon the following day, he decided against staying up any later to read more of Min Yoseop's manuscript.

10

As he had expected, Sergeant Nam was able to discover more about Min Yoseop and Cho Dongpal in Daejeon. Several people remembered them as being together from the beginning, which seemed to suggest that Mr. Cho was not altogether wrong in suspecting Min Yoseop of having led his son astray. But toward lunchtime, Sergeant Nam happened to meet an elderly man who had known them well, from whom he heard a more precise account of their reunion.

"In those days construction work was going full swing in this neighborhood. The older of the two came first and found work on a construction site. Although he didn't look very robust, he did his share of work without complaining; then about a fortnight later a boy who looked like a high school student came searching for him on the building site. The older one seemed worried by the boy's arrival; I got the impression that he wanted to calm the boy down and make him go home. But it didn't work out as he hoped, I suppose, because a few days later he asked us to give the boy a job. Workers were in short supply in those times, so we got him carrying the sand used to make cement, and he did his work very well . . ." The old man had been foreman of a group of workers on the site of a government building, then had been employed as a guard in the building when the construction was finished. But as before, their story ended unhappily. After less than a month, the two of them set about denouncing every case of abuse by the supervisors, as well as all the ways the foremen cut corners on allowances for food and refreshments, break periods, and other little things that occur on any construction site; in the end they were beaten up and kicked out.

Next, Min Yoseop and Cho Dongpal had taken up residence in a poor neighborhood on the outskirts of the city, where there were still shantytowns. Apparently they had rented a site on a slope and built a wooden shack to live in. According to neighbors who were still living in the area, it had been barely more than a tent, and there had been from five or six up to ten or more people living in it, in addition to the two of them. Along with shoeshine boys and candy sellers, they took in homeless, old beggars who roamed the city, youths with mental disabilities, and crippled peddlers who could not earn a living for themselves, let alone for their families.

There was no trace of malice in the neighbors' tone when they related this, and what he knew of their past offered no basis for suspicions of unsavory activity; yet oddly enough, Sergeant Nam still sensed a faint whiff of something criminal going on. But any intimations of that kind were strongly rejected by the neighborhood people.

"A gang of exploited kids? Don't say such things. We've got eyes to see and ears to hear. What gang leader ever comforted troubled runaways, then sent them back home? Or provided boxes of chewing gum for homeless children to sell, and even paid for their evening classes? If anything, it looked more like the children were mooching off the young men, not the other way round."

"You're asking if they took money from the shoeshine boys or the peddlers? Sunni's mother, from the house down below, used to be employed to do the cooking and washing when there were too many of them living there, and she said they didn't. She told me that each of the boys who was old enough had a savings book. It was the two young men who provided food for the ones that couldn't earn anything."

"I know exactly how they earned a living. They did any work they could to earn money, it made no difference how menial or dangerous the job was. When there was no work, they would go begging at rich houses or in government offices, despite the unfriendly receptions they sometimes received. Sure, the younger one had a sharp temper and was good with his fists, but that usually happened elsewhere ..."

Still not fully convinced, Sergeant Nam searched the local police records. But there was not so much as a single minor misdemeanor involving Min Yoseop and Cho Dongpal. Rather, one senior detective who remembered them had formed such a favorable impression that he had even sent in a report recommending them for an official commendation. A journalist from a local paper had visited them, planning to write an article on their good work, but had not been able to do so on account of their stubborn refusal; the

City Hall even had a record of their having received food aid to distribute.

Yet before two years had passed, the two suddenly disappeared from Daejeon and transferred their official residence to the city of Incheon. If he were to go back to Daegu before heading for Incheon, that would pointlessly double or triple the length of the journey; so Sergeant Nam made a brief report to the investigation office by telephone, then boarded an express bus.

Min Yoseop's life in Incheon seemed to have been similar to that in Daejeon. Sergeant Nam was able to establish that a small band had once again formed around him and Cho Dongpal. He went to see a man who had rented an eight-square-foot shed on the roof of a building to Min Yoseop and Cho Dongpal; the man's son had been on friendly terms with them when he was a university student, and retained a good impression of their group:

"The kids those two had with them? What shall I say? You could call them deprived youths. They included street urchins who used to hang out around the docks ... some would go their own way, others would join, the numbers varied, but the total was usually somewhere around twenty. The two of them took them all in and helped them study. Those who were young enough were sent to school; for older ones without even a basic education they organized evening classes. I used to teach them math five hours a week." However the way the group was organized seemed to suggest that there was a hidden purpose, beyond a simple relief operation. Suddenly suspecting something, Sergeant Nam asked, "But they didn't only teach them school subjects, did they?"

"I don't know exactly, but at night I think they used to hold some kind of religion classes. That young Cho was mainly in charge ..."

"Weren't they associated with a church?"

"I thought so at first, but when I got to know them better, it seemed to be something quite different. I still remember the peculiar phrases they would always repeat: 'Do not offer me worship, do not build me altars, and do not waste your precious resources and efforts holding ceremonies and making offerings.' 'Save yourselves first.' 'Love your neighbors—not to please me, but to make your neighbors love you.' 'Do not seek to own too much—not because it's evil to own too much, but because it is evil for your neighbor to become poor on your account.' There was a whole set of phrases, more or less along those lines. But seeing as there was no sign of any cross or Bible, and they didn't sing hymns, it couldn't have been any kind of church."

Sergeant Nam could understand what he meant. Although they had given up the church and its teachings, it was quite clear that their group had some of the characteristics of a religious sect. Sergeant Nam was particularly curious to know how Min Yoseop and Cho Dongpal had managed to finance such a community. In Incheon, unlike in Daejeon, none of the boys were engaged in menial work, shining shoes or selling gum. According to the testimony of the landlord's son, there were some who had proper jobs as messenger boys in government offices and private companies, but more than half of the group had no steady employment.

"How do you think they covered their living expenses?" Sergeant Nam asked. "It must have cost a huge amount to feed, clothe, and educate at least ten boys."

"They both gave private lessons to a few groups of school children, but I think that was far from sufficient. Money seemed to be coming in from somewhere else."

"So they were receiving money from somewhere?"

"I think it was the younger one who provided it. At least, I heard he came from an enormously rich family. His people in Busan seemed to send him money from time to time."

The middle-aged house-owner hesitatingly added to what his son had said: "Since you're asking, there was one strange thing that happened. A few days before they left here, one of our neighbors who happened to be at the police station said he'd seen the younger one there in handcuffs. He was dressed like a beggar and seemed to be trying to pass himself off as someone else, but the neighbor was certain it was that young Cho fellow. I was surprised, and I went to tell Mr. Min about it, but his face instantly hardened and he flatly denied that it was true. He said Cho had gone home to Busan. And when I urged him to go to the police station to make sure, since you never could tell, he grew furious, which wasn't at all like him.

"But in the end Mr. Min left here before the younger fellow came back. And he left in a rush, like he was running away from something, without even bothering to claim the remaining few months of rent they had paid in advance." Sergeant Nam was puzzled by what he heard, but he rushed off to the police station, thinking he had found a clue in what he had heard. However, there was no trace of a record involving Cho Dongpal. During the month of August of the year the man had been talking about, there had been a total of five cases of assault in that precinct, but they were all unrelated to this case; it was the same with petty crimes, and his name didn't even figure among those who had been detained briefly.

Letting himself get carried away, Sergeant Nam requested a check of the list of repeat offenders at the National Police Headquarters. The result was the same. Despite the strong hints at something criminal in their activities, neither Cho Dongpal nor Min Yoseop had any connections with crime, at least not on the legal level.

The question of their officially registered residence was even stranger. Before Incheon, they had faithfully registered each time they moved, but from then onward they reported no new address. For precisely three years and six months their activities were impossible to follow, and their whereabouts became veiled in darkness. Sergeant Nam went rushing around Incheon in all directions, trying to find at least one of the boys who had lived with them, but to no avail. Finally, exhausted after spending most of the day on his feet, he loaded his weary body onto a train for Daegu and fell fast asleep.

Back at the office, Sergeant Nam's frustrations seemed to be representative of the overall state of the investigation. The person corresponding to the Identikit portrait produced by Detective Im had presented himself to the police and turned out to be a hiker with nothing in the least suspicious about him, and Detective Park came back shortly afterward, empty-handed, having investigated the wife of Elder Mun for almost a week. The investigation, which had been making progress in various directions, seemed suddenly to have come to a complete standstill.

Yet amidst all the rest, there was one thing that aroused Sergeant Nam's curiosity: Detective Park's attitude while he was making his report to Lieutenant Lee. Though he had only been with the detective squad for a short while, the inexplicably flustered and embarrassed way he replied to his chief's questions, which were nothing out of the ordinary, struck Sergeant Nam as unusual.

Leaving the office building, Sergeant Nam casually caught up with Park and questioned him in an offhand way, "So, what did you find out?"

Detective Park looked surprised as he muttered, "Wow . . . what a woman!"

"What do you mean?"

"Well, in five days I found eight men involved with her. They had all had or were still having regular physical relations with her."

Detective Park blushed slightly as he spoke. He was a bachelor, only twenty-six years old, and shy for his age. From the time he joined the police he had always worked in the general administration until the previous spring, when he had somehow gotten transferred to the crime squad; he had been a detective for less than a year.

Sergeant Nam nodded as if to encourage Detective Park and replied, "She's that kind of woman."

"At first, I felt there was something indecent about her, something blatantly criminal. Frankly speaking, I was convinced at first that she had something to do with Min Yoseop's death. But after getting to know her, I began to feel that she was innocent."

"Know her?"

At this, Detective Park's face went sufficiently red for it to be visible even under the streetlights. It seemed to have been as Sergeant Nam had guessed. "So something happened!"

"Well, if you must know—and you must promise to keep this to yourself—yesterday evening, I went to meet her one last time before giving up and returning to Daegu . . . she offered me a drink, and then . . ."

"It didn't end with just a drink?"

"You too, boss?"

Although they had an official boss in the detective squad, a man in his forties who was reputed to have spent his whole life in the police, the younger ones generally called Sergeant Nam "boss." It felt awkward to address him informally, but in the presence of outsiders they were reluctant to refer to his relatively low rank, so they had adopted that for convenience and it had become a habit.

"Heavens, no! Talk about accusing the innocent . . . Sex is equal to a bribe. That's not the reason you've given up the inquiry, is it?"

"Not at all! It happened after I'd already given up," Detective Park answered with a startled tone. Even without his denial, Sergeant Nam completely understood. If something had happened, it only meant that Elder Mun's wife had been playing with him. At the thought that Detective Park had been her victim, he could not avoid a bitter smile.

"It comes naturally to her . . . like eating . . . or like breathing. When I woke up the next morning I couldn't believe what had happened the night before," Detective Park stammered in embarrassment.

Trying to put him at ease, Sergeant Nam made a joke: "Such a pure heart—it won't do!"

Detective Park seemed reassured by that and smiled as he tugged at Sergeant Nam's sleeve: "Don't give me a hard time, boss. Let me buy you a strong drink."

"I don't know, I'm worn out . . . Well, all right then—just one."

As he replied, Sergeant Nam suddenly thought of Asaph's wife, the character from Min Yoseop's story.

One drink was followed by another, the second by a third . . . In the end Sergeant Nam returned home that evening quite drunk. Yet in his drunken state he felt inclined to take up Min Yoseop's notebooks again. Detective Park, who was easily affected by drink, had given unrestrained descriptions of Elder Mun's wife in ways that seemed to strengthen the resemblance to the wife of Asaph.

After his visits to Daejeon and Incheon, Sergeant Nam had already been reflecting with increased curiosity about the nature of the "god not of Christian origin" who had guided Min Yoseop and Cho Dongpal in their actions. The connections between Elder Mun's wife and Asaph's wife once again revived his conviction that Min Yoseop's story was not unrelated to his life. He decided to take up the manuscript again, for if at the end of his wanderings Ahasuerus had found a new god, then that might well be the god of the two young men, which would surely shed some light on their subsequent actions.

It remains unclear how Ahasuerus was able to recover from the shock and sorrow caused by the death of the Babylonian girl he had loved so much, or how he was able to so easily quit those Mesopotamian gods to which he had devoted so much effort, feeling that he had finally found the original home of his own god, whom he had abandoned. The legends simply state that Ahasuerus became a Zoroastrian monk after he left Mesopotamia, as if to portray him as a man possessed and led onwards by an evil spirit .

To see Ahasuerus burning sandalwood incense before the altar, a miter like that of a magician on his head, a mask over his nose and mouth to prevent his breath from defiling the sacred fire, holding golden tongs in hands sheathed in long gloves—it more readily brought to mind an evil-minded sorcerer rather than a monk. Even if not viewed with deliberate malice, his transformation is bound to seem not just abrupt but incongruous, even to those who have already grown accustomed to the unusual course Ahasuerus's life had been taking. However, if this transformation is seen in a more sympathetic light, it does not necessarily have to be seen as a deviation from his original goal. A longing to find a new god had originally driven him away from his home, family, and friends and sent him wandering to unknown lands—and the Zoroastrian gods were unquestionably new for him. In retrospect, his interest in the gods of Mesopotamia had largely been exaggerated because of his love for the exotic girl. The feeling that he might have found the hidden origin of Yahweh and the Scriptures was certainly interesting to him, but the Mesopotamian gods were essentially unable to satisfy his long quest.

As he recovered from the shock and sorrow provoked by the girl's death, he was also able to free himself from his obsession with those gods. So there is nothing particularly strange about the way he so quickly set off in quest of new gods. In any case, after a brief period of grief and mourning, during which Ahasuerus frequented groups of Magi, he soon quit their complex forms of syncretism and immersed himself in the teachings of Zoroaster, the cult of the fire worshippers. At this time the followers of this cult were elaborating their teachings and ceremonial rituals in secret, and it was only later that the cult experienced a revival, toward the beginning of the Sassanid dynasty.

It seems that what first attracted Ahasuerus's interest more than anything else was the dualism found in Zoroastrianism. "Why do disasters befall us irrespective of good or evil? How can the love and mercy of God be manifested as human pain and sorrow?" Ahasuerus felt that this perspective might allow him to find answers to the painful questions that had previously driven him away from the God of his forefathers. In addition, their eschatology and their notion of a savior inspired different feelings in him than when he had heard people speak of them back at home; they reawoke Ahasuerus's strange passion, which had remained alive through the repeated disappointments.

Driven by this passion, Ahasuerus once again prostrated himself before the altar of a new god. This conversion took place in an ancient Persian city that had survived like an isolated island amidst the wild waves of Hellenism that had swept over the land after Alexander the Great's eastward expedition. Generous toward foreigners, the religion accepted Ahasuerus as a priest without requiring a formative period of grueling ascesis; as a result, less than two years after he had left Mesopotamia he had transformed into a Zoroastrian priest.

Yet once again his priestly days did not last long. Only a few months after he had been invested with the miter and the long white robe, a high priest who had been living as a hermit in a historic temple in a distant town, and just happened to be passing through this city, made an unexpected visit to the altar where Ahasuerus was tending the sacred fire. When he arrived, Ahasuerus was reciting a long prayer, as one of the eight monks presiding over the ceremony.

Lord, I humbly ask you; I beg you, reply truthfully.
Who made the earth so firm that it cannot crumble?
Who holds the sky so steady that it is kept from falling?
Who created the streams and forests?
Who gave the winds their refreshing power and yoked the floating clouds?
Oh, Ahura Mazda, who brings good thoughts into this world? . . .

While Ahasuerus was reciting the prayer, he noticed that the fire on the altar was flickering out. He hurriedly brought his words to an end, for he was the one who was tasked to tend the fire that day. As he picked up the golden tongs and approached the altar to revive the flame, an angry cry suddenly rose behind him:

"Stop! Who permitted you to tend the sacred fire?"

Turning in surprise, Ahasuerus saw a stranger, an old man wearing a high priest's gown, staring angrily at him.

The old priest pressed Ahasuerus for an answer in an even louder voice: "I am Melchior, the high priest. Answer me. Who granted you that miter and robe?" The priest in charge of the temple, under whom Ahasuerus was serving, replied in an intimidated voice.

"I did. He belongs to Ormazd, not to Ahriman — to the god of good, not the god of evil. He is no evil spirit but a human being. I feel sure he is a creature of Ormazd."

"Not so. I know him. He does not belong to Ormazd but to Ahriman — to the god of evil, not the god of good. He is no human being but an evil spirit. He is a creature of Ahriman. He has not come to tend our sacred fire but to extinguish it."

Staring at Ahasuerus again, Melchior the high priest cried out, "Away with you! I do not know you, but I recognize the evil light surrounding you. It is the very same light that shone from the Star of Disaster that I saw with Caspar and Balthazar — who is dead now — more than twenty years ago, out in the desert on our way back from our journey to worship at the birth of a Jewish king."

It appeared as if the dread that Melchior had experienced twenty years before in the Plain of Esdraelon was returning to him. His voice and face strove to maintain their authority and express his anger, but his aged shoulders were trembling visibly. Ahasuerus could not understand.

Nonetheless, on account of Melchior's stubborn rage, Ahasuerus was banished from the altar. After Melchior had left, the head of the ceremonies summoned Ahasuerus furtively.

"I still believe that you belong to Ormazd. But the high priest Melchior is not only a respected elder of our religion but also a renowned scholar. There is no one who can oppose his will. I'm afraid you must now leave the sacred fire and its altar. But even if you are far away, Ormazd will not neglect to bestow the light of wisdom and goodness upon you."

The order left no room for appeal. Ahasuerus had no choice but to give up his robe and leave the sacred fire. Still, that did not mean that he had abandoned belief in the providence of Ahura Mazda and the teachings of Zoroaster as such. His still unsatisfied desire for knowledge about this new doctrine, together with his recently revived passion for knowledge of all the gods of the world, meant that he continued to look toward the altar of the sacred fire as an ordinary believer. It is unclear what he gained from his experiences with this religion, but given the link between his ancestors and the peoples who practiced this fire worship, one can guess that it may have involved the many analogies that could be drawn between the two doctrines. Indeed, the similarities are sometimes so great that one cannot help wondering if the land of Zoroaster was not also one of Yahweh's homes.

For example, the teachings Ahasuerus had inherited from his ancestors concerning angels and spirits, despite differences in details, undoubtedly had their roots in this eastern religion. The six archangels and the hierarchy of angels, the various roles of angels as intermediaries and companions of a god, elaborate notions about evil spirits, the existence of a supreme being controlling the power of evil—it could be argued that all of these themes arose through its influence. The notion of guardian angels had been unknown to his ancestors before the Babylonian captivity.

Likewise, the eschatological discourses that were being elaborated and refined in his own generation could hardly be unrelated to those of the Persians. It was true that there was no equivalent for their idea of the bridge of Chinwad, where the dead were judged, nor for the test for sin by means of molten iron. But there were far too many Persian features in his own people's eschatological model of a "Day of the Lord," based as it was on the immortality of the soul and the resurrection of the body, for it to have developed independent of Persian doctrine. The idea would have shocked the teachers and scribes of his native land, so deeply absorbed in their exegetic arguments, but their "Son of Man" could not easily be separated from Saoshyant, the archetypal savior announced from the earliest times by the fire worshippers. Although there were differences, in that the one had existed as a purely heavenly being even before the creation while the other would only be born on earth without previously existing, the similarity of their functions rendered those differences insignificant. The prophecies that the Son of Man would be born either to the family of David or, equally widespread, to the tribe of Levi, were not unconnected to the claim that Saoshyant would be born to the family of Zoroaster.

A notion like essentialism—the theological concept that god is one step further removed from man in consequence—and an eschatological model based on a fixed unit of time can be clearly traced back to their Persian origins. All these things made Ahasuerus linger there several months longer with a force of attraction no less powerful than that of the dualism that had first intrigued him. But in the end he had to leave the land and its gods. After nearly two years of immersion in the teachings of Zoroastrianism, the day came when he began to falter in his belief. He would shake his head thoughtfully and murmur to himself:

"The wisdom that was able to grasp the dualistic nature of god so early on is certainly impressive—and their use of dualism to explain the world's contradictions proves the religious genius these people possess. But there is nothing there that differs fundamentally from what is in Yahweh. If it is only opposition and struggle that forms the link between the two conflicting principles, then surely at some point the victory of one over the other will result in monism. Is not their dualism only a stage laying the foundations for a far stronger monism, a passing phenomenon making way for a far higher principal?

"Their treatment of the problem of free will is worse. The issue must have seemed quite astounding to our ancestors in their exile, which is why they borrowed those ideas and introduced them at the very beginning of Genesis. But isn't the imposition of this kind of subjective fantasy on humanity merely a way to excuse the capricious way God torments human beings?

"I have obviously been more dazzled by the glittering light of novelty and strangeness emanating from the wisdom of Ahura Mazda, rather than by any aura of truth. This is not the god and doctrine that I have been seeking in my wanderings through the world. Now that the novelty has worn off, all I can see here is a faint image of my old, irrational god."

So Ahasuerus finally packed his bags. It was a spring day almost seven years after he first left his native land. A malicious legend reports something that he is supposed to have said as he was leaving the ancient Persian capital:

"Yahweh was originally nothing but a shepherd god who lived secluded in the mountain of El Shaddai. It was only later, once the ravings of Moses had transformed the spirit of Mount Horeb into something fierce, that Yahweh became a merciless, martial god intent on taking control of Canaan. Subsequently Elijah and Hosea bestowed on him the powers of an agricultural god, and with the help of Amos and Isaiah he was transformed from a tribal god to the absolute, unique god of the cosmos. Finally, after plagiarizing Babylonian theories of creation and cosmology and introducing Persian notions of eschatology and Satan, our Yahweh was complete. This means that it was not Yahweh who made us but we who made Yahweh."

While to a devotee of Yahweh these words may seem to be blasphemy and sacrilege on the part of Ahasuerus, the legends have not portrayed it as such. In fact, if he had wished, Ahasuerus could have denounced Yahweh in far more violent terms:

"Bastard progeny of Mesopotamian gods! Abandoned early on in Canaan, carried off into Egypt and mated there with Aton, then returning to fornicate with Baal! Later hauled off to Babylon and inseminated there by both Marduk and Ahura Mazda! It is hard indeed to foresee what half-breed this whore will produce."

Since he was finally turning away from Ahura Mazda in disappointment, his way of looking at Yahweh might have been severer than before. Considering the direction that his religious beliefs had been moving in, such a stance was consistent with his overall progression.

11

Leaving Persia, Ahasuerus headed for India next in his quest for a new god. It had been almost eight years since he left his native Judea. Once more, instead of turning homeward, he headed off for a foreign land considered then to be the end of the world, driven by an unflagging passion more like possession by an evil spirit than mere madness.

Once he had come as far as Persia, it was clear that Ahasuerus had to continue on to India. Anyone hearing that the Indian gods and the ancient Persian gods shared a common origin—namely, the Aryan gods—was bound to wonder how those gods had been transformed after crossing the high plateau of Iran and the Ganges. Perhaps it was a last echo of the teachings of the fire worshippers, which had complicated his understanding of goodness, wisdom, and the divine, that led him to seek answers in India.

It appears that Ahasuerus followed the eastern route to enter India, which had been open since Alexander's expedition. Whether because of the remoteness of that land, in which he wandered for just over a year, or because the time he spent there was too brief to cover the entire land, the details of his Indian sojourn are lost, veiled by a particularly thick fog. No historical record has been passed down, and the legends only touch upon a few aspects of the land's gods and one of their hymns. The best that can be done is to attempt to reconstruct his time there based on these comments.

"There, too, the gods were born from human fear and ignorance. They grew out of helplessness and yearning. They developed by synthesis and reached maturity by personalization. But they grew old by logic and died by knowledge."

This is the first of Ahasuerus's recorded remarks on the Indian gods. Judging by these words, Ahasuerus must have begun again by studying the gods of ancient times. From mere deifications of the powers of nature—such as Dyaush, the Vedic sky god; Varuna, lord of cosmic order; Mitra, the Vedic deity of wisdom and light; Surya, the god of the sun; Ushas, goddess of the dawn; Savitr, another Vedic sun god; Indra, god of thunder and supreme defender of gods and men; the Maruts, storm deities; Agni, the god of fire; Yama, the god of death; Gauri, the goddess of purity; Rudra, a Vedic god of wild storms; or Bayu, god of the winds—he had gone on to the deification of abstract concepts or functions: Durgha, the goddess of truth; *Rta*, the embodiment of moral order; Vach, the god of eloquence; and Kubera, the god of wealth. Not one of the gods he examined, in all their stages of development, was capable of refuting Ahasuerus's basic assertion.

His comment about the synthesis and personalization of the gods can be seen as his summary of the origin and development of Brahmanism. Several different polytheistic deities would compete for position, almost in the manner sometimes designated as Kathenotheism, and eventually merge together through a synthetic process that united multiple functions under a single name. Such was the case with Indra, Agni, Mitra, and Varuna. In the end, they all became embodied as Vishnu, before leadership was transferred to the popular god Shiva, who was in turn synthesized into Brahma, source of prayer.

Naturally, there were periods of intermediate synthesis and role-sharing during the process—for example, when the two-headed Harihara, a combination of Shiva and Vishnu, united with Brahma to form the three-faced triad, Trimurti, or when the role of creation was assigned to Brahma, preservation to Vishnu, and destruction to Shiva. But the perfection of Brahma was achieved through the synthesis not only of the other two gods but of all beings and non-beings within his body.

Regarding Ahasuerus's remark that these gods "grew old by logic and died by knowledge," it seems to be a reference to one of the six main schools of Hindu belief, the one known as Sankhya.

"They set out in quest of god with the net of logic and knowledge, but they ended up strangling their own gods with that very same net."

Ahasuerus expounded upon this thought in detail elsewhere, mocking the school of Sankhya for its fascination with mathematical principles, which caused the gods to be lost. However, their atheism cannot be considered to represent Indian philosophy as a whole.

Some claim that Ahasuerus's statement was meant to refer to the teachings of Buddha. To his Hebraic eyes, Buddhism must have also seemed to be a disguised form of atheism—but Buddha did not strangle Brahma with logic and knowledge, at least. There exists a separate remark that appears to indicate what Ahasuerus said about Buddhism:

"The Buddha transformed those ancestors' faith from an abstract pantheism to a disguised atheism. If Brahman and Atman are one and the same, how does that differ from elevating the self to the place of the Absolute? Then again, consider the method of selective desire that he called emancipation. He rejected thousands of small desires but attained a desire greater than the sum total of all those. What can be made of such an intense craving for emancipation? He may have extinguished ten thousand anxieties, but what can be made of his all-consuming anxiety for emancipation, blazing more fiercely than all ten thousand, though it be only one?"

Ahasuerus may well have felt that Brahma, with a personalization far weaker than that of the gods he had encountered previously, represented an abstract pantheism. Since he was familiar with the teaching that God is God and man is man eternally, the Buddha's teaching that humans have a transcendental potential could have appeared to him as a form of disguised atheism. But to view emancipation as selective desire is an unusual way of interpreting it. To him, even a noble wish to attain Buddhahood could only be understood as one more human desire originating in selfishness.

Ahasuerus's questionings of Buddhism continued:

"Wise Vaccha! Was not what you guessed lay beyond Nirvana only the solitude and emptiness remaining after a fire has gone out? Malunkyaputra, was healing possible without knowing the nature and origin of the poisoned arrow that had struck you?"

Ahasuerus's allusions to Buddhism end with a song that seems to be the inversion of a hymn:

> The human body is no vortex,
> its sensations are not foam.
> Its appearance is no tongue of fire,
> its resolve does not resemble a plantain.
> How could its consciousness be mere illusion?

In addition to this, although no precise texts have survived, Ahasuerus is said to have spoken of belief in avatars and the future Buddha Maitreya, both of which can be understood in terms of metempsychosis, cyclical eschatology, and other transformations of the notion of rebirth.

What is problematic is that he seems to have spent far too short a period in these regions, given the quantity of learning he is said to have acquired there. Judging by the preceding comments on the gods of India, brief though they are, he appears to have been deeply versed not only in the teachings concerning all the gods of the region, but in the systems of thought that had developed from them. One year spent in India would not have been enough to attain such knowledge.

Even if he had joined a religious community or become a monk with direct access to important documents, the Buddhist scriptures together with the Vedas, the Brahmanas, and the Upanishads represent a huge body of texts, far more than one person can hope to read in an entire lifetime. Among the Vedas, the Rig Veda alone contains a thousand hymns with more than ten thousand verses, while the Buddhist scriptures of the Hinayana and Mahayana schools amount to several thousand volumes. Moreover, Ahasuerus had not learned Sanskrit, which was employed in the Vedas and Upanishads, let alone the Pali language, in which the earliest Buddhist scriptures were written. It is therefore difficult to claim that Ahasuerus gained access to the gods through religious texts when he could barely communicate; an alternative explanation will have to be found.

Here too the malicious legends have no qualms in citing the transcendent power of the evil spirit that guided and protected Ahasuerus throughout his life. They maintain that it was some kind of superhuman capability bestowed by this spirit that endowed him with such vast knowledge in so short a time. Moreover, as if that were not enough, they imply that while in India he worshipped innumerable spirits and received special favors from them.

However, under closer scrutiny it becomes possible to explain things without bringing in evil spirits. By this time, Ahasuerus had been traveling all over the world for almost ten years and had learned about thousands of gods and doctrines. He would have been able to recognize certain schemas or universal forms in the relationship between gods and men, and also see that there were rules governing the birth and death of the gods. That might have opened the way for him to more easily understand teachings and philosophies whenever he wished, without being distracted by superfluous features such as rituals and ceremonies.

Add to that his extraordinary linguistic skills, and the matter becomes simpler still: after studying their language for a few months, he would only have to seek out reputed sages and learned monks, ask coherent questions, listen to their sincere replies, and half a day would suffice for him to grasp the essential doctrines of any school. Even ordinary folk know how a few simple words can sometimes make some abstruse idea suddenly clear as day. Although he would have learned more had he stayed longer, one year was not too short a time for him to learn what he wished to know without relying on any supernatural power.

Ahasuerus's visit to Rome came as the last station in his long pilgrimage. But this was the only time he had not decided on his destination from the outset. While in India he had heard that there were other peoples beyond a range of great snow-covered mountains, each with their own gods. He still had unresolved questions and unquenched desires remaining within him, so he was tempted to go there and see; but this time he could not yield to the temptation. Over ten years of exhausting travel his body felt twenty years older, and his heart had grown heavy from the long years of loneliness and homesickness. Finally he chose to turn homeward, rather than cross those high, rugged mountain ranges.

Once he had made the decision to return home, Ahasuerus became impatient to arrive there. Feeling that the streets of his hometown and his parents were sorrowfully calling him, Ahasuerus left India with haste and headed back the way he had come. Crossing the Indus and the highlands of Iran, he arrived one day on the banks of the Euphrates, three months after leaving India. As he was waiting for a boat that would carry him across the river, an aging Roman appeared, singing some lines attributed to Virgil:

> If god let me choose the life I wished,
> I would choose a life in the saddle . . .

The verses he sang and the way he rocked on his horse seemed to suggest a leisurely journey. As he learned later, he was a lucky tourist who, thanks to the friendly relations currently reigning between Rome and Parthia, had gone to visit Babylon and was now on his way back to Rome.

Possibly on account of the long years he had spent traveling among foreign peoples, Ahasuerus felt a closeness to the man, as if he were a relative from back home, even though in earlier times he had not had a good opinion of Romans. The man, who had served as governor-general in a number of provinces, seemed to feel the same way. Taking a liking to Ahasuerus at first sight, he proposed that they should travel the rest of the way together, and Ahasuerus willingly consented. After a fortnight or so they reached Damascus, where they were to part ways—one heading southward and the other westward. The Roman was going to a port in the west, where he would board a boat taking him back to Rome. Ahasuerus was going to take the road leading south to his homeland. On the eve of the day they were to go their separate ways, the Roman suddenly suggested to Ahasuerus, who was feeling sad at the thought of their imminent separation, "Why don't you come to Rome with me? We have gods as well, you know."

Ahasuerus replied without much enthusiasm, "I've known all about those gods for a long time already. And if there's something I still don't know, I can learn about it in my own land." The other responded with a quiet smile: "What about the gods from Miletus? Are you fully acquainted with them?"

"Gods from Miletus? You mean the Greek gods?"

"No, I mean a new god, called the Love of Wisdom, Philosophy, nurtured in Miletus. I hear that nowadays large numbers of our young folk are becoming believers in that god."

Now Ahasuerus grasped his meaning. The man's invitation had already touched him considerably. On reflection, the last ten years had been spent on a quest that was more like a penance, from which he had gained nothing. He had not been able to discover any new god, nor had he succeeded in bringing back to life the god he had inherited. The Hebraic concept of god flowing in his veins had been too strong to allow him to accept any new deity, and he had found no solution to his doubts that would enable his former god to come back to life.

And although there was a hint of mockery in the Roman's words about a new god called Philosophy, they led him to reconsider his rejection of the Indian way of verifying divine nature by knowledge and logic. He belatedly realized that the risk of falling into pantheism or atheism might be preferable to blind faith.

In any case, the Greek philosophy that had taken up residence in a corner of Rome was by no means unfamiliar to Ahasuerus. Before he had abandoned his former god and his teachings, when he was devout in his studies, he had heard about Greek philosophy from a number of learned rabbis. But since they only brought it up to criticize and reject it, there was a considerable distance between what they said and what it was really like.

Indeed, why not visit Rome and draw on the wisdom of the

Greeks who had settled there. Before making his final decision, Ahasuerus asked with a worried expression, "But isn't Emperor Tiberius's order expelling our people from Rome still in force?"

"Yes, but so long as you are not absolutely determined to reveal that you're a Jew, I have enough power to protect you."

The Roman, who had grown fond of Ahasuerus, spoke confidently. With that, Ahasuerus had no further reason to hesitate. He no longer heard the lamenting cries of his hometown and his parents that had been calling him home. On the following day, instead of going their separate ways, he and the Roman headed for the Syrian port of Seleucia, where they boarded a boat for Rome.

Once in Rome, Ahasuerus drew on his last reserves of mental energy as he immersed himself in the study of Greek philosophy. The Roman proved as good as his word. He owned a large mansion in a suburb not far from the Via Appia, and he looked after Ahasuerus with the same kindness as when they had first met in that remote foreign land. He not only provided him with food and a room, he would also write letters of introduction allowing him to meet even the most conceited philosophers, and supplying without hesitation the required fee, no matter how outrageous.

Yet the day came when they were finally obliged to part. It came about one summer's day less than a year after Ahasuerus arrived in Rome. He was on his way to meet a philosopher who claimed to have inherited the true doctrine of the Greek materialists, and as he walked he was muttering his philosophical reflections to himself, to the effect that there may be no god other than an abstraction within our mind—perhaps a reflection of his inclination to Apollonian rationalism. He paused in the shade of a tree along the way. A group of lower-class citizens were engaged in heated discussion with serious expressions on their faces.

Drawing closer to listen, Ahasuerus understood that the disagreement had begun when a young cripple who had clearly never set foot outside the city affirmed that the sun rose from the roofs of the city. A blacksmith from a mountainous region who happened to be there declared that the sun rose from mountains and valleys, and a mortician who had previously been a galley slave asserted that the sun rose out of the sea, far to the east. This all gave rise to further debate about the nature of the sun. A great variety of opinions emerged, not only as to where the sun rose, but also concerning its size, color, and even its shape, until the crowd gathered beneath the tree was in complete uproar.

Ahasuerus, having grasped the subject of the quarrel, was about to leave the spot with a sour smile. He was not going to waste his time waiting for these uneducated people's curious debate to be resolved. There was a blind man who had been listening silently as the others shouted, and he began to speak just as Ahasuerus was about to walk away. The opinion he expressed attracted Ahasuerus's attention:

"The sun does not exist. The sun you are talking about is a complete lie."

Ahasuerus examined him quietly. His clothing was barely better than a beggar's but his face contained a trace of something suggesting that he was a learned man. The people who had been bellowing at one another now paused in their debate and stared at the blind man, dumbfounded by his outrageous utterance. He ignored them all and continued to speak in a voice more incisive than anyone else's.

"I've spent my entire life studying the sun. There was a time when I used to think of the sun in the same way as you, though with far greater knowledge. But I was so intent on learning more about the sun, to discover the truth about it, that I finally lost the sight of both my eyes. I looked up at the sun too often and for too long, and the scorching sunbeams eventually burned my eyes out.

"It was only after losing my sight that I began to doubt the very existence of the sun. Yes: if there is indeed a sun, it cannot be what you now know; it can only be some kind of abstraction bearing that name. For I have realized that the external appearance of things is simply a sensation, temporary and subjective, which our imperfect senses receive at a particular moment and in a particular way, far removed from their true nature."

"Then do these external appearances of things have any objective existence?" Some moments passed before one fellow who had dimly grasped the sense of the blind man's words spoke up with his question. The blind man's reply was yet more incisive.

"They are like rags hung from the structure of a name. Let me give you an example. Concerning the color of the sun, most of us affirm without any doubt that it is white, or red, or something else, and yet this is really only an arbitrary sensation received from our eyes, which are incapable of real precision. Assuming there were a creature whose cornea were like a crystal blackened with soot, it would say that the sun was pure white like the moon in winter, while if it were looking through a cornea of pale amethyst it would say it looked red as blood. Another, with eyes equipped with corneas like well-polished emeralds, would insist it was green, and another, seeing through a cornea cut like a diamond, would say it shone with the five colors of the spectrum. I cannot be sure. There may even be some creatures to whom it would appear merely as a vague brightness, while to others it might not be perceived as light but only as heat—for such creatures the colors we are talking about would not apply, in just the same way as they do not for me, now that I am blind.

"The sun has no color for me. If it has one now, it is either the memory of an impression received back when my eyes still saw, or an abstraction implied by a word. The same could be said of the sun's size or shape or other attributes. We frequently talk about how big the sun is, what it looks like, what its attributes are, and so on, yet in truth that is nothing more than a subjective judgment yielded by our five senses. Suppose that with our supreme capacity of reason we could become free of our imperfect, inconstant, and at time frankly deceptive senses; we would realize that there is nothing more to any entity than a pure abstraction of which the only certain thing is a word—more specifically, its name.

"In fact, it was only after I had lost my sight that I came to realize that. Once I had succeeded in shutting myself off from my five senses by the power of reason, the sun that you are all talking about ceased to exist for me. If anything remains, it is nothing but the pure abstraction attached to the word 'sun.'"

Yet at that very moment the sun was blazing in the sky, bright and hot, a patent reality. Virtually everyone there was uneducated, incapable of understanding precisely what the blind man was saying; but even they could at least grasp the absurdity of it.

"Then what's that up there?" someone sneered, pointing at the sun. "Your eyes aren't the only thing you've lost, it seems." Raucous laughter burst out from the approving crowd.

But Ahasuerus quit the shade of the tree, feeling a sudden somberness. For while he was listening to the blind man's strange sophistry, an unexpected flash of insight entered his mind.

"Why, just as that blind fellow has lost his eyesight, quite clearly so too has my heart. The ten years I have spent traveling to the ends of the earth and encountering such a host of strange gods: wasn't this journey similar in a way to that blind man's endeavor, staring up at the sun far too often and for far too long. Just as the blazing sunlight burned out his eyes, so the doctrines and myths of the countless gods that I encountered have veiled the eyes of my heart. Now I too have reached a point where I doubt the existence of god as anything more than an abstraction produced in the minds of men.

"Yet God exists. The sun in the sky is obviously real, and in the same manner god's providence is penetrating into the infinities of space and time as the sublime light of existence . . ."

With that, a sudden feeling of despair took hold of him. If the last ten years of traveling had simply been a waste of effort, his present attempts to grasp hold of god by logic and knowledge seemed equally likely to be a waste of time and effort.

All those philosophers! Those spiritual masters he had been infatuated with and fascinated by in those years! They had all hoped to achieve something in the name of mankind, had set out to challenge the mysteries and enigmas of the cosmos that have overawed humanity for so long; but how could they help him in his search for god? All they were capable of providing was either a dogmatism detached from reality—like Thales, who gazed up so intently at the stars that he fell into the well beneath his feet—or a series of hypotheses based on a distortion of reality—like Democritus, who is said to have put out his own eyes in order not to be dazzled by the appearances of things. Some clung absurdly to the precision of numbers while at the same time attaching strange superstitions to bodily organs, like Pythagoras; others hurled themselves into volcanic craters seething with molten lava, like Empedocles; some teetered on the brink of a wholly materialistic theory, others floundered in bottomless swamps of doubt.

Although some philosophers earnestly debated the question of god—with Jewish Aristotelians such as Philo of Alexandria and Aristobulus of Paneas daring to graft Hellenistic thinking onto the Hebraic concept of god—what could such an intricately conceptualized god, pallid and smelling of parchment, have to do with living, breathing human beings? Ahasuerus saw these gods as an expression of the solitude and futility of life in a godless world, as well as the excessive confidence people had in their own minds.

At last, Ahasuerus made up his mind: "I must go home. That's enough pointless wandering. Now it's time to turn inward, wait for a new revelation, and encounter god as he truly is. Instead of setting out in search of God, it's time for God to come looking for me. Instead of chasing after God, it's time to welcome his arrival. God will undoubtedly respond to my yearning cry, bring an end to the quest that has occupied one half of my life so far." His Roman friend was sad to see him go. Realizing that he had no choice but to accept their separation, he arranged his sea journey to Tyre as a last favor. They parted one midsummer's day in the thirteenth year of the reign of Tiberius, when Ahasuerus was thirty.

The last portion of the story Sergeant Nam had been reading came to an abrupt end. It was no easier to read than before, but perhaps because he had grown accustomed to the style, he was now able to identify certain characteristics of the text as he read. Compared to the activities of Ahasuerus in Egypt and Babylonia, his time in India was far less developed and the descriptions were much less detailed. And he had the impression that Min Yoseop only had Ahasuerus go to Rome in order to address ancient philosophy.

What rather disappointed Sergeant Nam was the fact that Ahasuerus was heading back home without having encountered any new god. True, he had implied that God was alive within the heart, but having read thus far there seemed to be no guarantee that this would turn out to be a god different from Yahweh. He began to think that it had been in vain, that those hours of reading had merely given him a headache.

Moreover, the mental energy demanded for even a basic comprehension of Min Yoseop's text was such that Sergeant Nam, despite the slender hopes he still retained, was unable to continue reading the remaining section. For a detective always pressed for time, it was no small feat to have read that much in a single sitting. Despite his literary interest having been reawakened by Detective Park's frank confession, he found it impossible to go on reading.

12

The investigation was going around in circles. The police were trying to trace Min Yoseop and Cho Dongpal by every method they could mobilize, but they were unable to find out anything about their lives during the past three years or so. It was incredible that the whereabouts, not of one person but of two, should remain undetectable over such a long period of time—unless, that is, they had crossed over into North Korea together as spies. The crime was finally classified as "unsolved" three months after it had occurred, and the investigation team was disbanded. Spring had come, bringing with it a series of new crimes, and their limited forces could not be tied up indefinitely in a case with no solution in sight. The continuation of the investigation was assigned, almost inevitably, to a team consisting of Detectives Im and Park, headed by Sergeant Nam.

Yet only six days after the affair had been set aside, Sergeant Nam received new information about Min Yoseop—the belated result of the fliers and posters that had been distributed in the neighborhood of the post office in Daegu from which money had last been sent to young men. A report came in that the wife of the owner of a boarding house near the railway station claimed to know Min Yoseop. As soon as he received the news, Sergeant Nam pushed aside what he was doing and hurried to the boarding house. Judging from the landlady's statement and various other indications, it seemed that Min Yoseop had indeed stayed there. But his activity while he was staying there was very unlike what they had traced prior to that.

The biggest difference was that the little group of followers had vanished. According to the landlady, Min Yoseop had stayed almost seven months in her house, entirely on his own. With the exception of a monthly visit to a nearby bathhouse, where he had his hair cut and took a bath, he spent the whole time in his room; during that period, he had not had any visitors or received a single letter.

Apart from his solitude, his personal conduct had also changed. According to Sergeant Nam's previous inquiries, he had always lived somewhere where he could find proper work; but at the boarding house, he seemed to pass his days in a deathlike inactivity. The landlady said he was so immobile and withdrawn that she wondered if he was contemplating suicide, or if he was a spy from the North. But she couldn't report him to the police. Her excuse was that he had regularly paid his rent in advance, and whenever she peeked through a hole in the door he was merely lying there, either on his back staring vacantly up at the ceiling or flat on his stomach, apparently asleep. It wasn't very pleasant to hear his sniffling or what sounded like sobs and incomprehensible muttering that came from his room from time to time, especially late at night . . .

Then, some four months ago, he had left abruptly, like someone pursued, taking a single bag with him, and she had heard nothing from him since.

After hearing the talkative landlady's account, Sergeant Nam asked, "You really mean to say that absolutely no one ever visited him?" He found it hard to believe that Cho Dongpal, whom he had assumed would have accompanied Min Yoseop, had suddenly disappeared. Their separation was not entirely unforeseeable, but according to the impression of Cho Dongpal that Sergeant Nam had formed in his mind, he seemed like someone who would have followed Min Yoseop to the deepest pit of Hell.

"That's right. But there was someone who came after he'd left."

"Who was that?"

"A Mr. Kim. When Mr. Min left, he had left a bundle for him together with a note."

Sergeant Nam, who had assumed it would surely be Cho Dongpal, was disappointed. Suddenly getting a hunch, he took out Cho Dongpal's photo. It was a picture taken during his high school days that he had obtained in Busan.

"It wasn't this fellow, was it?"

The landlady took the picture and examined it for a while before replying.

"Well, it does look quite like him . . . Why, yes, it's him. I recognize those big, bright eyes and that strong chin."

"What did he say when he came?" Sergeant Nam asked, with a voice that quavered despite himself. Her reply was immensely disappointing:

"He looked at the note, rummaged in the bundle Mr. Min had left without saying anything, then staggered out of the house like a zombie."

"Without a word?"

"I asked him what I should do with the rest of Mr. Min's things and he said he would be coming back later to collect them."

"Apart from that, was there anything else odd about him?"

"Yes, there was. The expression on his face made me shudder. Especially right after he read the note . . . I even wonder if Min didn't leave so as to avoid meeting him."

There was no basis for what she suggested, yet it occurred to Sergeant Nam that she might be right. Cho Dongpal had stayed close to Min Yoseop to the very end. But what could have been the reason that had led him to live apart from him? Why had he changed his name to Kim, and where was he now? Why had the two men grown apart? With all these questions going through his head, Sergeant Nam became more and more convinced that there was a direct link between Cho Dongpal and the death of Min Yoseop. As if to reinforce that conviction, the landlady added something else that she had remembered:

"By the way, that fierce looking young man—when I saw him, his head was completely shaved. I suppose that's what made him look even fiercer." Her tone suggested that she was convinced he must be some dreadful criminal.

At her words, Sergeant Nam thought back to Daejeon, and he became even more certain of what he suspected. In Daejeon, the owner of the house where they had been renting a room had told him how a neighbor saw Cho at the police station, dressed as a beggar and trying to pass himself off as someone else. Sergeant Nam hastened to examine the rest of Min Yoseop's belongings. But apart from two bankbooks under false names—for accounts that had once contained a considerable sum of money but were now virtually empty—there was nothing particularly remarkable. Two plain suits, a few sets of cleanly laundered, neatly folded underwear, a miniature transistor radio, a safety razor, as well as a few of the trifling objects a bachelor usually carries about with him. If there was anything odd, it was the fact that there was not a single book to be seen. Even supposing that Cho Dongpal had taken away any notebooks, for Sergeant Nam, who always imagined Min Yoseop as a man of letters, it suggested a big change.

Still, no matter how much he may have changed, it was unrelated to what Sergeant Nam was trying to find out. Nothing that Min Yoseop had left there offered the slightest indication of Cho's present whereabouts. Sergeant Nam had come rushing out here, dropping what he had been doing, but all he had found were the phantoms of Cho Dongpal, Min Yoseop, and their three lost years, which flickered briefly and then vanished again, as if mocking him. The one thing that became clear was that the relations between the two men seemed to have taken a most unexpected turn.

He thought about those three years. "I've managed to find out where they were only a few months ago; soon, I'll surely catch up with Cho Dongpal. I'll find out just how the strange relationship between the two ended—how one of them ended up as a corpse while the other disappeared completely." When he first confirmed that Min Yoseop had been staying in the boarding house, Sergeant Nam's pulse had quickened with a kind of hope; but as he left the

house his shoulders were drooping. He had only rarely felt such de-
jection in his career as a detective.

"How's the novel going?" As he entered the criminal investigations section, Lieutenant Lee questioned him with a sarcastic
smile. He had been watching Sergeant Nam when he had hurriedly
left the office, and now noticed him coming back with a less than
cheerful expression. Sergeant Nam repressed a surge of anger only
with difficulty, then responded in a dry voice:

"Yes. I've just met Cho Dongpal."

Sergeant Nam gave his reply with a straight face, wiping the
sneer from Lieutenant Lee's face, who asked in surprise, "What?
Cho Dongpal? Isn't he the suspect we've been looking for?"

Sergeant Nam's tone did not change as he responded, "That's
right."

"Then you should have brought him in for questioning. Where
is he?"

"How am I supposed to know where someone with two legs
goes running off to?"

This time Sergeant Nam replied in a sarcastic tone, but Lieutenant Lee failed to catch on and raised his voice: "You mean you just
let him go? Didn't you question him? You think you can locate him
any time you want?"

Hearing Lieutenant Lee shouting like that, Sergeant Nam wondered if he hadn't gone too far. But there was no going back.

"And solve an unsolved case? What's the use of solving a case
that's already been shelved as unsolved? First of all, I'd be sorry to
give you that kind of shock."

With that, Lieutenant Lee seemed to realize that Sergeant
Nam was only joking. His face suddenly flushed deep crimson; he
slammed his fist on the desk and stood up, clearly angry.

"Sergeant Nam! What's all this about? Are you making fun of
me?"

"Why, boss, what about you? Even if you had given up all hope,
surely you'd go to check if any new information came in?" Sergeant
Nam replied, determined not to be outdone. His resentment at the
way Lieutenant Lee, from the very start of the investigation, had

mocked the direction he was taking, came bursting out in an uncontrollable fury. It was an acceptable joke but it was the wrong moment to make it, and Lieutenant Lee became furious at Sergeant Nam's insubordination. A few officers who happened to be there intervened, and the head of investigations came in just then, ending the matter; otherwise, it was a quarrel that might have escalated further.

It was perhaps because of the argument with Lieutenant Lee that Sergeant Nam pulled out Min Yoseop's notebooks later that evening from the drawer into which he had thrust them. It was true that he felt the remaining, unread portion of the story to be a tiresome burden, like some homework that had been started then abandoned. But a curious obstinacy made him more determined to continue in that direction, the less confidence Lieutenant Lee showed in it.

Casting aside the memory of the previous day's reading, which had brought no result except a headache, he set about reading as if he was hearing a suspect's statement for the first time. Summoning up all his attention and endurance, as if he were examining a vital piece of material evidence, he set about pursuing the traces of Min Yoseop hidden between the lines of the text.

During the ten years Ahasuerus had been away, his native land of Judea had changed considerably. Mountains and fields were the same as ever, but the romanization that had grown more prevalent since the time of Herod could plainly be felt in the towns. Arenas and theaters modeled on those in Rome had sprung up in every city, as well as temples housing statues of Roman gods. But far graver than any of these things was the way the people themselves had changed.

The people of Judea were weary of waiting for a Messiah to liberate them from Roman oppression, and the discouragement and resignations they felt were causing them to split apart in various ways. The Pharisees had confined themselves within a shell of appearances more hypocritical and exclusive than ever. In contrast, the Sadducees, who had originally been conservative and fundamentalist, had quickly become hellenized, forfeiting their autonomy. Meanwhile, extremists on both sides—Judean Zealots and supporters of Herod—dismayed the populace with their blind patriotism or their shameful collaboration with the conquerors, and sometimes went so far as to defile the blessed land with bloody feuds.

The synagogues with their rabbis and the temple with its priests were likewise caught up in graver tensions than ever before. Just as in their political views, the people of Judea were also in discord in matters concerning the worship of God; their faith, which had originally been united, was now wavering between the crooks of two opposing shepherds.

The Roman domination was merely nominal; the conquerors were lax in their policing of the land. Wearied by the scheming and deceit poisoning relations between different parties, Pilate, the new governor, spent more time in Rome than at his post. Rather than rule over a highly troublesome colony, it was not only more agreeable to attend lavish banquets held at the imperial palace, it was also advantageous for promotion. As a result, the land of Judea had to put up with the oppression and extortion carried out by local magnates and tax collectors in collusion with his subordinates.

Because of all these changes, Ahasuerus's hometown was no longer the welcoming, bountiful village of his memories. As it happened, the day of his return was the day of Purim, and from every house drifted the sound of the *megillah,* the story of Esther, being recited; but there was no trace of the boisterous merrymaking or the gleeful, festive excitement he had known in the old days. He himself was an almost forgotten figure in those streets, and if any recalled him at all, it was usually as the name of someone who had died. His parents were no longer alive. While he was still wandering in the east, his mother had departed this life, heartbroken and grieving at the loss of her son; his father had lived longer, breathing his last, sorrowful breath at about the time when Ahasuerus was boarding the boat that would take him to Rome. All that remained to him was the old family house, virtually a ruin, and distant childhood memories that rose up at every turn.

One would imagine that he would have needed some time to recover from the homesickness that had accumulated in deep layers within his heart over the past ten years; yet apparently Ahasuerus didn't spend much time in the streets of his hometown or in his former home. Less than one month after his return, he followed the example of many other seekers and ascetics of those times, leaving human society behind and going out into the desert. That was in the region known later as Quarantania.

There are many possible explanations as to what led him into the desert. The legend that attempted to portray him as an agent of Satan affirms that he was being called by the evil spirit. If the ghostly voice he apparently heard—while fasting and meditating in his family home, awaiting a new inner awakening—is interpreted as the voice of Satan, then this would be a plausible story. According to another interpretation, Ahasuerus's decision to go into the desert was influenced by the sect of the Essenes, which had gradually attracted more followers thanks to John the Baptist. Rumors about the Teacher of Righteousness, that had stealthily become widespread, might have come to the ears of Ahasuerus and awakened a new interest. Finally, there are claims that he went into the desert because his family home and his old town were not particularly suitable places for receiving a new inner awakening. Upon his return, he had received many visitors: relatives who had assumed he was dead, but now learned he had come back alive, and neighbors who were curious to hear what he had done during his travels. Questions of inheritance and the various mundane annoyances of a settled existence reawakened a carnal interest in material things that had long been absent. These things disturbed his spiritual focus, and if he really hoped for a new revelation through self-immersion, he had no choice but to leave.

All of the above are plausible explanations, or, rather, all three played some role in his decision to go to the desert. Whatever the cause, once he was in the desert he spent his days sustained by a diet of locusts and wild honey, like other hermits and recluses of his time. His first step was to cleanse his soul of the thick layers of worldly dust and the dirt of knowledge that had accumulated over the past ten years. Then, once he judged this self-purification to be more or less complete, he entered a stage of total fasting and meditation, awaiting the call of the true god—a face-to-face encounter with the "Great Spirit" he had not yet found despite all his earnest seeking.

For forty days he was alternately tormented by the desert sun, so hot it seemed it would leave his living body desiccated, and the night winds and dews, so cold they seemed to freeze one's very bones. Then at last, early one morning, he was shaken into wakefulness by a shout like thunder.

"Son of Man! The time has come. Your lengthy and painful supplications have drawn me out of inaction and anonymity. Now the eagle of your wisdom will soar high into the heavens, while the serpent will plunge deep beneath the ground."

Startled, Ahasuerus stared at the owner of this voice; something was standing before him, an indescribable being, veiled in a dazzling cloud that was neither light nor darkness. Meanwhile, the loud voice continued.

"In days gone by you invoked me by a multitude of names, but I made no reply; you bowed down to my many faces, but I did not accept your worship. It was all in preparation for today, so that your soul, weary with thirst, would be able to see me more clearly, hear my voice more distinctly, as dry ground absorbs rain."

Finally regaining his senses, Ahasuerus cautiously asked, "Unknowable One, who indeed are you?"

"I am the beginning and the end, eternity and instant, the perfect and the probable, the absolute and the relative."

The blood circulating in Ahasuerus's body was still of Hebrew origin: hearing such words, he automatically responded, "Are you Yahweh himself?"

"I am he and his negation too."

"I do not understand. How can such a being exist?"

"Son of Man! You are too ensnared by the bad habits of the soul, dividing, comparing, measuring, and weighing. It is all the fault of the poisonous knowledge you have accumulated by chopping up time and dividing space. First empty your mind. Then open wide the eyes and ears of your soul to welcome me."

The Great Spirit then proceeded to speak to Ahasuerus face-to-face, at great length, spending one whole day and one whole night with him. He started with the story of Creation, which had been distorted and falsified, then turned to the origins and ultimate end of the cosmos, and the directions and essence of human destiny. It was a teaching of which only the rough outlines survive, on account of the limits of language and the poor expressive skills of its exponents, members of an ancient esoteric order that had early been considered an enemy of the Christian church and exterminated.

Another deeply significant event also took place in the desert of Quarantania: the first encounter between two worlds that had originally been one but had become irrevocably remote. As the sun was rising, Ahasuerus parted company with the nameless Great Spirit. As he was leaving the desert he came across a young man at the foot of an arid, rocky hill, as deeply immersed in fasting and meditation as he himself had been the day before. He appeared weary and in a weakened state, yet as he sat there, perfectly motionless in the already burning sunlight, a kind of celestial dignity emanated from him. This light that had enveloped him, and then suddenly vanished, was undoubtedly the reflection of a more than human holiness.

Without thinking, Ahasuerus paused in front of the young man. He had no way of knowing that this young man was Jesus, son of Yahweh, who eighteen years previously had been debating with and enraging the teachers in the Temple, while he, likewise still a child, was being led by Thedos on an extensive tour of human misery. An inexplicable feeling of foreboding had brought Ahasuerus to a standstill before him with a sudden shudder of dread.

The young man soon emerged from his prolonged meditation and opened his eyes. His face was framed by flowing side locks and disheveled brown hair, while his newly opened eyes were clearer and bluer than the Sea of Galilee.

After waiting for the young Jesus to look in his direction, Ahasuerus questioned him in a challenging tone, "What are you doing in a place like this?"

Without the slightest hesitation he replied, "I was listening to my father's Word, telling me to save the world."

"Who is he?"

"The God of Abraham and Isaac: Yahweh, the one Lord of all that exists in heaven and earth."

His words took Ahasuerus aback. Due to something the Great Spirit had told him, he had been expecting to meet this man one day—but he had not thought it would happen so soon. Striving to conceal his surprise, Ahasuerus questioned him again, "The moment I saw you, I immediately felt some kind of divine presence. I am inclined to believe what you say. But by what means will you save the world?"

"By every means. I will give them all that they need, all they have prayed and longed for."

"You speak with assurance, but how can you be so confident that what you bring will correspond to that?"

"Because that is the intention of my Father's vast and exalted love."

Jesus replied to Ahasuerus's questions in a voice full of conviction. After a brief, thoughtful pause, Ahasuerus pointed at one of the stones littering the ground before them.

"First, let me ask you something. What people need most of all at present is bread. Can you turn these stones into bread? Can you do something to ensure that they will never again suffer from lack of bread?"

"It is said that man shall not live merely by bread, but rather by the Word of God. For, as was long ago written in the Scriptures, this body, formed of dust and ultimately destined to return to dust, can be nourished with a scrap of bread, but the soul, instilled by my father's breath and destined to live eternally in union with him, can only live by his Word. Do not attempt to reduce the vast depths of my father's love to a simple, material gift."

"Really? Is that really his will? Are the hunger and thirst people have endured for so long still not sufficient? Are starvation and privation to be their bodies' eternal destiny? Their bodies are the clearest proof of their existence; they save their souls from aimless wandering as disembodied ghosts. Individually, there is no escape from the cycles of life and death, but collectively they are united in an unending stream . . ."

"The life of the soul is far greater. No matter how much you exaggerate its value, what is the life of the body, like chaff before the wind, like dew on a blade of grass, compared to the true, everlasting life? Moreover, the promised day is close at hand. Soon those who hunger will be sated, those who thirst will thirst no more. How could their want and the resulting pain endure forever?"

"Aha, you mean that cruel Day of Judgment? You mean the tiny number of 'just' souls that will be happy on that day? On that day of doom, when for each one of them ninety-nine others will be hurled into the fire?"

Ahasuerus's words had begun as a lament but gradually shifted into ridicule. Yet he didn't want this extraordinary encounter to end in a heated debate before it had even begun. There were still a number of questions he wished to pose to this incarnate god.

"Instead of these useless disputes, let me ask you something else. Again I would like to find out if you have indeed brought what they truly long for. I pray you to follow me."

Thus preventing Jesus from making any rebuttal, and without even waiting for his consent, Ahasuerus strode swiftly away.

He led Jesus to a place where one slope of the rocky hill ended on the brink of a precipice. It must have been at least a hundred cubits from the spot where they stood to the ground below.

"If you are truly the Son of God, throw yourself down from here. It is written in the Scriptures, 'For he shall give his angels charge over thee, to keep thee in all thy ways; they shall bear thee up in their hands, lest thou dash thy foot against a stone.' Surely that refers to your power?"

"But it is likewise written, 'Ye shall not tempt the Lord thy God.' What you are bidding me to do is what the acrobats or magicians of this world would do to demonstrate the wiles of evil spirits. Do not try to weigh the will of the one Lord God by shallow human standards."

Once again, Jesus responded without the least hesitation, as if his reply were prepared in advance. As before, Ahasuerus responded to him in a lamenting tone.

"Having heard your reply to my first question, I guessed you would offer a similar answer this time. But alas for human blindness! You will never be able to believe anything without the clear testimony of your five senses, inclined to believe one miracle rather than a hundred sacred words! How many more years of delusion and wandering will you have to spend, groping your way through life, weeping and groaning?"

"Yet what is accomplished by a miracle, like something bought with material wealth, is not true faith or submission. Only a choice that overcomes human unbelief and doubt, one made in the Word and the love of God, that can guide people to the Kingdom of Heaven."

"But that was already difficult for Job and Jonas. Job ceased his lamenting and complaining only after he had heard the voice of the Heavenly Lord in the storm; as for Jonas, didn't he have to visit the stomach of a big fish before he set off for Nineveh? Now you have arrived, the only son of the Heavenly One, and yet people are still obliged to make the choice on their own? You mean to tell me that you still intend to leave that heavy burden of choice to their imperfect judgment and their insufficient knowledge?"

The cool detachment of Jesus's answers was getting Ahasuerus worked up, and he forced himself to be silent once more. After their second exchange his expectations had greatly diminished, but there was still one topic about which he wished to receive confirmation from Jesus's own lips.

Ahasuerus bowed his head briefly in deep thought, then straightened himself and looked directly at Jesus as he began to speak. This time his tone was less that of a question or a challenge, more an earnest attempt at persuasion.

"I understand now what you say about the will of the One who is in heaven. I have a proposition to make. If you truly intend to serve as the Son of Man, this decision will determine the path you take, so think well before you reply. What most people are ardently awaiting is not a spiritual Messiah but a Messiah who is powerful politically and militarily. We could organize and arm the people, then set out to recreate the former glories of David. If we put together my wisdom and your powers, there is nothing that we cannot accomplish.

We must first deliver them from Roman oppression, seize the royal scepter, and take control of the country. If the proclamation of the Word comes afterward, it will not be too late. By following this course of action you will be able to transmit the Word of the One who is in heaven more easily and more powerfully; at the same time, you can expect to see the people put it into practice more confidently. And why should that be all? The human body you were born with can enjoy to the full all the splendors of this world, while your mind savors to the utmost the pleasure of ruling over and commanding others."

"Earthly power can never be anything but an illusion, unless it derives from Him; such splendors can never be anything but sin, unless they are permitted by Him. I have come into this world in order to save it, not to rule over and dominate it; I have come to reduce its sins and sufferings, not to enjoy its pleasures."

"But people were more faithful to the Word in the days of the Kings, who bore swords, than in the days of the Judges, who had no arms. Throughout history, the god most widely believed in has always been the god invoked by the tribe possessing the strongest army. Regarding the splendors and delights of this world, you have never experienced anything of the kind. You have never walked among beautiful women, never been intoxicated by glistening jewels or fragrant wines, the pleasures of resplendent banquets and opulent fare. Whereas in times past I have more than once seen such a world and the people who inhabit it; on occasion I was able to become one of them. At least to my eyes they looked happy. To reject that happiness as vanity and sin is mere self-righteousness on the part of the Word; for definitions of human happiness and unhappiness have always ultimately depended on the viewpoint of the one experiencing them."

Ahasuerus's discourse was meant to counter Jesus's icy rebuff, but to no avail. Totally unshaken, Jesus simply shook his head heavily as he replied:

"What you say seems convincing, but to begin with, the objective measurement of time is missing. If you recall that worldly powers and pleasures are temporary whereas heavenly power and bliss are eternal, you will come to realize the evanescence of this present world."

"But you have also forgotten something. 'Eternal' is hardly different from 'meaningless.' Everything is temporary; eternal happiness, like eternal unhappiness, does not exist. For instance, someone who eats fine white bread and larks' tongues every day cannot appreciate the pleasure of enjoying these delicacies. Such a menu can only yield pleasure for a few days at most, to someone who first tastes that kind of food after living off of dry bread crusts and water. Any more than that, and it becomes nothing more than thoughtless habit or the unfeeling cycle of satiation."

"You say that because you do not have faith in the One, my Father. There is nothing that he cannot do. When the Day he has promised comes, he will fill eternity with a happiness that is renewed at every moment."

"The promised Day? But that is in the distant future, and we have no way of knowing if such a day will ever come. How many people do you think would sacrifice their one and only life here on this earth for such a day? Who would be prepared to give up the immediate joys of the here and now, small though they are, for a day that will not arrive, even if we wait a thousand years? Come with me, let us go down together. I will help you take the scepter of this world into your hand. Even supposing that earthly splendors and pleasures are as you say, it seems to me that you will still need that scepter. I believe that if you have kingly power, you will be able to subject these people to the Word even without bread or miracles. Saving humanity is best done in human ways."

"Not so. The one who knows an object best is he who made it. Since it was my Father who made humanity, he knows human affairs best. It is only right to follow what he has ordained. When he subjected the descendants of David to the power of other nations, he put an end to any faith in scepters and swords."

At this point, Jesus suddenly fell silent and looked intently into Ahasuerus's face. Then, as if acknowledging whatever it was he had seen there, he nodded heavily and addressed him in solemn tones:

"You have tried to tempt me with earthly pleasures, with the vanities of the mind, as well as with the follies of worldly power and pride, but all to no avail. I think I know who you are. Trouble me no more, and be off with you. Follow the wicked path laid down by the wisdom you derive from the teachings of the evil spirit that is now inciting you. I fear the Rod of Wrath may fall on you at any moment, smashing you like a clay vessel."

His eyes seemed to glow with a deep inner fury. Under his gaze, Ahasuerus felt the hopes he had pinned on him crumble completely. He looked at Jesus for a moment, and with a light sigh took a step forward and spoke quietly.

"I sensed what you were like from the very beginning. You really are the perfect embodiment of the Word. You may have borrowed a human body, but your heart is the very Word itself. I'm leaving you now. But do not think that everything will happen as you wish. Now you are shaping lumber to build a palace for God using the same chisel and plane that you once used to build human houses, but I tell you that you cannot build such a palace on this earth. If you are the arrow of self-righteousness aimed at people, I will become their protective shield."

All the disciples whom Jesus told about this meeting would later depict Ahasuerus simply as Satan. Though Jesus presented it as a parable, they took it for the literal truth. Such is the origin of the story of the Temptation in the Desert found near the beginning of more than one Gospel.

13

After this meeting, nothing else about Ahasuerus can be found in the records of the time. His life is left to the legends, which are warped by the malevolence of the Christians, so that the only way to follow the course of his life is to reverse everything they say.

According to these legends, Ahasuerus is supposed to have made a living as a lowly cobbler. It sounds at first like something invented to reduce him to an insignificant social rank, but there may actually be some truth in it. For it is altogether possible that, after his return from the desert, he went to stay with his uncle who was a shoemaker.

His uncle had made no small profit by this business, and during the ten years in which Ahasuerus was traveling, he had prospered more than ever, his business growing until he was now an officially appointed merchant supplying military boots to the Roman army. In addition, while on the surface he was close with Roman officials and the household of Herod, he was secretly a Zealot maintaining links with the Sicarii, which made him indispensable to Ahasuerus. It was the worldly power his uncle wielded, rather than any idea of earning a living, that led Ahasuerus to turn to him at a moment when he was preparing for large-scale future combats. In fact, careful examination of Ahasuerus's later activity reveals signs that he had recourse to his uncle's influence on a number of occasions.

The legends, however, offer no further information. Apart from the claim that he was a cobbler, they say nothing about where he was or what he did during the next three years, during which Jesus pursued his tumultuous preaching journey. But the discovery in recent years of textual fragments from certain heretical sects, which had somehow escaped the Inquisition and the witch trials of the middle ages, make it possible to trace him to some degree. These documents consist of apocryphal scriptures based on oral traditions that were only written down much later.

According to these fragments, Ahasuerus confronted Jesus directly five times over the course of those three years. The perspective and interpretations of those who composed the written texts vary slightly, and the events are scattered across numerous sources; but if the parts on which they agree are brought together and arranged into a coherent narrative, the result is as follows.

After the encounter in the desert, Ahasuerus next met Jesus in Capernaum. It was the occasion of the scene depicted in the gospels from the Marriage at Cana, where Jesus performed his first miracle, turning water into wine.

One day, as Jesus was penetrating deeper into Galilee and proclaiming the Word to wide acclaim, Ahasuerus once again sought Jesus out and tried to warn him.

"Jesus of Nazareth, why have you come again to interfere with us? Do you intend to expel us from the land we have cultivated with tears of sorrow and the sweat of labor? I know who you are. You are the false Son of Man, Son of the Most High and Self-Righteous; you have come to kindle an even greater fire on this already charred land; you have come as heir to one who lays an outdated claim to ownership of our vineyard, which we have been tending on our own; you have come like a proxy for an unjust creditor to demand repayment of a debt of five hundred denarii that we never borrowed.

"I beg you to go back to him now. Go and tell your father: there are no debts for him to collect in this land, there are no rights for him to claim; leaving us alone as we are now would be a greater act of love and blessing to his glory. If out of fear you refuse to do as I say and stay here longer, I'll have my brethren gather stones to hurl at you for your foolishness."

At that, a sudden command unexpectedly issued from Jesus's lips: "Be silent. Vile spirit. Be gone from this man."

Jesus obviously recognized Ahasuerus and understood his words, which were bound to bewilder the onlookers. Instead of engaging in a troublesome quarrel, Jesus designated him as a madman, a person commonly said in those times to be "possessed by spirits." And as the command rang out, an invisible force lifted Ahasuerus's body up and hurled him to the ground. Whereas Ahasuerus was an ordinary son of man, Jesus, son of god, had been invested with superhuman power from the very beginning. The unenlightened people whispered to one another in amazement: "The Word is marvelous indeed. As soon as he gives his command, the impure spirits flee."

Thus Jesus not only closed Ahasuerus's lips by force, he also overawed the simple onlookers. His unenlightened disciples, intent only on increasing Jesus's glory, wrote in the gospels that it had been his second miracle.

The next time Ahasuerus and Jesus met was on the day of the Sermon on the Mount. It is not clear if Ahasuerus had been following him deliberately, hidden in the crowds and observing him, or if he merely happened to get caught up in the crowd following him on that particular occasion. At any event, Ahasuerus emerged from the crowd and went up to Jesus while he was resting after his lengthy sermon.

The other disciples were away preparing the journey back down the hill; only Judas and Thomas were near Jesus, guarding him while he rested. They were keeping off the anxious swarms of people suffering from incurable diseases who believed the inflated rumors and were eager to touch him, just once at least, to say nothing of crackpot debaters, full of vanity at their own knowledge, intent on holding a great debate with Jesus. Seeing Ahasuerus approaching silently, they confronted him.

"Are you sick too? If so, please wait a little while. The master has just begun his prayers."

"I am not sick. Or at least, if I am, it's a disease that your master can do nothing about. I simply came because I want to talk to him."

On hearing him reply in this way, Thomas came, blocked his path and addressed him in stronger tones: "In that case, all the more reason for you to wait. Our master takes no pleasure in hearing people boast of their paltry human knowledge. He would prefer to prepare the Word of God he must proclaim tomorrow, rather than hold a pointless argument with you. You must wait until you have permission."

At that moment, Jesus suddenly opened his eyes, and quietly said, "Send him to me. He's someone I know." As Ahasuerus drew near, Jesus examined him closely and asked, "You've come again? Has the evil spirit still not left you?"

"You know perfectly well that no evil spirit has ever possessed me. If anything is guiding me, it is uniquely the resplendent light of wisdom. Don't treat my justified affirmations as the ravings of someone possessed, as you did at Capernaum. Don't try to elude my sincere questions by any crafty violence this time."

As he spoke, Ahasuerus struggled to blot out the unpleasant memories of their previous meeting. But this time Jesus showed no sign of wishing to avoid him. It seemed that the success he had achieved over the course of his preaching journey had given him greater tolerance.

"What do you want to hear?"

"I want to know if you are still unable to give up your devotion to humanity and this world. Do you still believe that you can bring us back to your holy father by that self-righteous Word and your empty promises of paradise?"

"Indeed I do. Just as I believe in my Father in heaven, so too do I believe that they will come back to us. What makes you think that my teachings are merely self-righteous and my promise an empty one? Haven't the crowds been moved to tears of repentance and filled with an ardent thirst and longing for the coming Kingdom of Heaven?"

At that, Ahasuerus suddenly raised his voice: "That's nothing more than a momentary phenomenon brought about by a combination of their stupidity and despair with your slippery, agile tongue. I am sure that some of them at least must have realized as soon as they turned away that your teachings, stripped of the striking parables and sparkling rhetoric on their surface, contain no truth and no grace.

"You proclaimed the Beatitudes as if you were doing us a favor, but how can they be true blessings? Are they not simply an arbitrary diminution of the unhappiness that weighs so unjustly upon us, bounty that we'll later be forced to give back in shame? Why should people only be able to become truly blessed if they are sorrowful, starving, thirsty, persecuted? You have come to us after thousands of years of waiting; don't you have any blessings for us without those painful conditions attached? If those are the gifts of one who claims to be the God of love and grace, just look how paltry they are. Have you never thought of simply abolishing all the sorrows of this world, so that people would not need this consolation? Can't you make a world in which people do not hunger and thirst for justice, in which there is no lack calling out for satisfaction? Can't you make the world a place where we don't need to be merciful to others because we don't need to receive mercy in return? Can't you give us a world where we don't need to strive for peace, not even to become sons of God in the other world?

"Then you told us to lay up treasures in the kingdom of heaven. You taught us not to worry about our earthly lives—what we eat, what we drink, or how we clothe our bodies—but first to seek the kingdom of God. However, you know nothing of the real misery that the flesh is heir to, although you've come in the borrowed body of a man. When were we ever given a chance to fill our bellies with this world's bread while laying up spiritual treasures in heaven as well? When were we granted an abundance of materials to build houses to keep off this world's wind and rain and also be allowed to build the kingdom of heaven? When did we ever have enough cloth that we could use to protect the body from the cold and then give you glory? Isn't it thanks to your Father's curse that the land has yielded only thorns and thistles, and that we have had to wait decades to find the wood for so much as one good pillar? It might have been different if sufficient bread and abundant supplies had come down to earth together with you. You too must remember how our faith was firmest when manna fell like snow in the desert, how we served the Word most faithfully when it promised us the land of Canaan flowing with milk and honey? But back in the desert of Quarantania, when I requested you to accomplish this feat, you refused. You have been nothing but the proxy of an uncaring father who only stresses filial obligations and rejects his own duties toward his children.

"Still, you have made several hopeful promises today, though you are not very sure. You said: ask and you will receive; seek and you will find; knock and it will be opened. When the children ask for bread, you said, would any father give them a stone? When the children ask for meat, would any father ever give them a serpent? But you must be keenly aware that that is just a huge deception. After we were driven out from the Garden long ago, was there ever a time when we did not ask and seek? So many souls went knocking in tears at heaven's gate, yet how many of them gained entry? In the days of Elijah there were many widows, yet your father sent Elijah to just one of them, in the village of Sarepta near Sidon; and in the days of the prophet Elisha there were many lepers, yet the only one to receive healing was Naaman from Syria. We've grown weary of asking and seeking, of waiting in tears before a door that never opens. And now you're telling us to abandon this land that we have cultivated with such difficulty for these vague promises?

"You also told us to become the light of the world, the salt of the world. You said we should not act in retaliation and should love our enemies. You said that if someone slaps our right cheek, we should offer the left as well; if someone takes our outer garment, we should also give them whatever is underneath; if someone bids us walk one mile, we should go two.

"I ask you sincerely: do you believe we humans can possibly put all those teachings into practice? Do you believe that the creation of humanity was entirely the work of your Father's goodness? I assure you that of all who have ever been born of woman, you are the only one capable of fulfilling those teachings. A tiny number of people may set out to follow you, but not one of them will be able to reach the goal.

"Then for all the rest, for the great majority of humanity, those precepts will merely become an impracticable burden for the soul, a source of guilt and despair from which there is no escape. In you, the Law will be fulfilled, but that will be a self-righteous perfection having nothing to do with humanity in general.

"Once again I say, leave us alone. Before desperation at not being able to put your teachings into practice turns into a furious hail of stones falling on your head. Allow us to enjoy to the full what has been given to us. Grant us freedom from the Word. We won't drown in that confusion and darkness you seem so concerned about, even if they are not merely empty threats. Various worldly advantages as well as what remains of the goodness of your father will regulate our actions, while our wisdom will enable us to maintain a minimum of morality and ethics."

Jesus, who had been listening with close attention, replied in a voice that was quiet but no less passionate than Ahasuerus's: "I understand. That will do. Open your ears that are blocked by wicked wisdom, and hear what I say. You are full of conceit as though you had discovered some great truth, but there is nothing new under the sun. All of these things are nothing but contentions of Satan, repeated countless times by the lips of countless false prophets. They are all part of a ruse inspired by envy toward my one father and of malice toward humanity, nothing more than wordplay intended to negate his great love and his infinite justice, and to stifle humanity's spiritual development. In the end, what do your claims convey apart from a fundamental distrust of human nature? How do they differ from simply saying that people should be left to exist in meaninglessness and blindness, opening the way to Satan and leveling the ground before him?"

"Is that all that leaving the world to humanity means to you? Is that why you have to remain in this world, for that magnificent salvation?"

"Precisely. Until my Father gives permission, until the day the Paradise they have lost is regained."

"You mean you're sending us back to that glittering stud farm? To languish there until that day of salvation so remote no one knows when it will come, and at the price of observing your teachings that are impossible to put into practice? But we're worn out and exhausted. If you were offering it to us immediately, we'd say thanks and take your Paradise; but we're not capable of waiting forever under those harsh conditions. We prefer to keep the land we have cleared and cultivated so arduously and the freedom made more precious by our hardships."

With that, Ahasuerus brought to an end a dispute that he felt there was no point in pursuing any further. Immediately, without giving Jesus time to say anything more, he took his leave.

"I'll leave you now. Farewell. May all you intend to do be for the sake of humanity."

Still, that encounter was not entirely vain from Ahasuerus's point of view. For the dialogue was heard by both Judas, who would later play a role for Ahasuerus, and Thomas, who did not hesitate to express human doubts although he stayed at Jesus's side to the end. The eyes of Judas Iscariot were especially attentive to the scene, switching back and forth apprehensively between the departing Ahasuerus and Jesus who was plunged deep in thought.

The third meeting between Ahasuerus and Jesus occurred on

the day of the miracle of the five loaves and two fish. By that time the ruling class of Judea had begun to be on their guard regarding the advent of Jesus. Herod, who had cut off the head of John the Baptist, was particularly troubled by the rumors that Jesus was John the Baptist come back to life, and was making every effort to find him.

Hearing of this from his disciples, Jesus sensed that his activities had reached a turning point. In preparation for the approaching trials, he wanted to strengthen his own and the disciples' belief and reinforce their resolve; he called them together and addressed them: "Come away to a secluded place and rest with me for a while. The long day will soon begin when there will be no chance of rest."

Thereupon he and the disciples boarded a boat and set out for a remote lakeside village named Bethsaida. They had left as quietly as they possibly could, but a report that Jesus and his followers had left for Bethsaida was spread through the neighboring villages by the few who had seen them go.

When Jesus arrived at his destination, he found a dense crowd of people who had walked from the nearby villages, sitting there waiting. It was a large gathering, more than five thousand adults alone. Jesus considered them with pity as sheep without a shepherd, so he put aside his idea of resting quietly with his disciples, and instead set about teaching again.

As day was drawing to a close, the disciples approached and said: "This is a remote spot and it is already late. You'd better send the people gathered here to the farms and nearby villages to buy food."

Jesus seemed to hesitate for a moment, then spoke slowly: "Give them something to eat yourselves."

"Are you saying we should go and buy two hundred denarii worth of bread to feed them?" The disciples replied, taken aback. Jesus hesitated once again, then spoke solemnly like someone who had finally come to a decision.

"Go and find out how much food they have brought with them."

Hearing that, the disciples went toward the crowd, inquired, and coming back replied: "The only food they have with them is five loaves of bread and two fishes."

"Bring the bread and fish to me and make the people sit down on the grass in groups of fifty."

Once his disciples had done as Jesus directed, he took the bread and fish into his hands, and offered a prayer of thanksgiving.

"Now divide this bread and fish and give it to the people." On completing his prayer, Jesus returned the bread and fish to his disciples and told them what to do. The disciples, who had already seen Jesus's superhuman powers on other occasions, did as he commanded. Something similar to what had happened at the wedding feast in Cana repeated itself. Though they divided the bread and fish time after time, the supply grew no smaller, and soon, after everyone had eaten their fill, twelve basketfuls still remained.

The crowd was filled with admiration and excitement by such an amazing miracle. Going beyond the previous rumors claiming that Jesus was John the Baptist or the prophet Elijah come back to life, they now believed that the long awaited Messiah had finally come. What was strange was the attitude of Jesus. Among all his successes thus far, this was the greatest and most brilliant; yet as he watched the excited crowd his face expressed mixed feelings. He almost looked like he had made some terrible mistake.

"Get into the boat and cross to the other side first. I'll send the people away and then follow you."

With those words, Jesus hurried the disciples into the boat. Left behind on his own to calm the crowd, who were unwilling to disperse, he seemed to betray something of the agitation of a criminal hastily eliminating the traces of a crime.

It was after Jesus had sent, almost driven, the crowd away and had climbed a hill with the intention of praying alone that Ahasuerus appeared before him. Having selected a suitable spot, Jesus was just bringing his hands together when Ahasuerus silently approached and spoke:

"Many thanks. At last you have changed your mind. Today you gave them a miracle and bread together. Now none of them will harbor any doubt as to whether you are the son of Yahweh."

Unlike on previous occasions, his words bore no trace of mockery or provocation. Looking anguished, Jesus shook his head heavily.

"Not so. You have misunderstood. I did not feed those five thousand people in order to show off my power. I had no intention of coercing them by that miracle; I simply made use of my father's power in order to relieve their fatigue and gain more time to proclaim the Word."

"Still, it will have been the miracle that moved them today, far more than any words you spoke. Now they will believe anything you say and follow you wherever you go. If you do not limit yourself to those five thousand but manifest the same marvelous power to everyone in the world, you will be able to turn this land into the Kingdom of Heaven. The goodness of Yahweh will be fulfilled on earth as it is in heaven. Even if that is in fact only a half-truth— nothing more than the fulfillment of his self-righteousness—it will still be considered a form of salvation from a human point of view. No single person will oppose the Word, if only out of fear of your power. Yet you still want to ignore that shortcut and take the long way round?"

"It is not my will but the will of my father in heaven. No matter how long or how rugged the way may be, I shall take the road my Father wishes. I refuse to coerce people's wills by any miracle. My father may be a jealous God, but he has no wish to receive only superficial worship and service in return for the benefits of his amazing power."

At these words, Ahasuerus's tone, which had previously been extremely gentle, began to grow harsh.

"If that is the case, what was it you did just now? I could barely contain my happiness on seeing you manifest your power like that. I thought that our age-old illusions had vanished, that the days of our wanderings were over. Even if it proves ultimately to be nothing more than the fulfillment of an immense self-righteousness, I thought that from a human point of view a sure salvation was being achieved through you. I thought that our hope, communicated to you, was returning with the approval of the One who is in heaven . . . If that is not so, what do you really want? Why did you so rashly show a miracle you will not employ again? Don't you realize that you will only be able to impress them again by an even greater miracle? Don't you see that the result has been to drive yet more people away from the grace of the Word?"

"It was in order to do my father's will more perfectly. My father will be more gracious to souls that are able to choose the truth and justice of the Word without regard to miracles. In the future I may often do as I did today, but when it comes to the basis for their choice I shall always offer only the Word."

Ahasuerus was stunned by what he said. He stared at Jesus for a while with glittering eyes, then sighed as if he had no more energy even to be angry.

"A finely meshed sieve of self-righteousness, indeed! You have already separated out ninety-nine from a hundred as sinners by preaching a love we cannot practice; now you have decided to screen out nine hundred and ninety-nine from a thousand as sinners by your capricious miracle. First you excite us with petty miracles, then you ground salvation uniquely on the righteousness of the Word, determined to punish our guiltless unbelief . . ."

Without any word of farewell, he walked off down the hill as night was falling.

Their fourth meeting took place in the Temple in Jerusalem. It was at the moment when the teachers of the Law and the Pharisees dragged a woman accused of adultery before Jesus. Seeking a pretext to accuse Jesus, they asked him, "Master, this woman was taken in the act of adultery. The Law of Moses condemns a woman guilty of such a crime to die by stoning; what is your opinion?"

Jesus had bent down and was writing something on the ground. Impatient, they kept repeating the question, demanding a reply. Jesus at last stopped writing and answered: "If there is someone without sin among you, let that person be the first to throw a stone at her."

It was a truly ingenious answer. Hearing his words, they began to withdraw one by one, beginning with the eldest, until the woman who had been standing in the middle of the crowd was left there alone. Jesus looked up and asked her, "Where have they all gone? Is there no one who condemns you?"

"No one, Master," the woman replied in a trembling voice.

Jesus quietly said, "I don't condemn you either. Go home, and sin no more."

At those words, the woman quickly disappeared. There is no mention of him in the Gospels but one other person was still there apart from Jesus, and that was Ahasuerus. He had been hidden in the thick of the crowd, and when it had dispersed he had not left the place but had stayed to observe what Jesus did. Now he approached Jesus, who remained bent over, writing on the ground after the woman had gone away.

"Look. You forgave her, but weren't you the only one capable of condemning her? All those who dispersed, they're the real face of the humanity you have to redeem."

When Ahasuerus spoke, Jesus sighed lightly as he replied:

"I am sad, but not in despair. Rather that is all the more reason for having to redeem them."

"How can that be achieved?"

"By my father's great love."

"Will you grant unconditional forgiveness? Will you accept all their wickedness as natural? Will you ask nothing more of them but simply promise salvation and go away?"

"That's not salvation, it's mere neglect. You're asking me to abandon humanity with all its sins and this defiled land?"

"What, really, is sin? Is it not just a needless concept invented by the Word? If goodness does not exist, how can evil exist alone, and how can sin exist in isolation in a place without commandments? Since there is beauty, ugliness stands out; because cleanness exists, it makes filth look worse, doesn't it? If the Word had not placed such emphasis on the one, the other would not have grown so bad. Still, the Word only made nine sinners for every just man; now it will be ninety-nine sinners condemned for each one saved."

"Yet there is nothing that my father's power cannot accomplish. Those ninety-nine will surely repent and come back. I have come above all for them."

"In that case, all the more reason why you should simply go away. They would prefer to keep their lands, painful though this existence may be, rather than set out blindly along the road of re-pentance, troubled by a notion of sin they can't understand and shedding tears they don't feel."

"What then of the purpose of my father who created them? His will of attaining a greater glory by them? Or the submission and praise they are rightly to offer him?"

"God is great in himself, holy and glorious in himself. Why should God wait for their poets to make him great? Will he be any more holy and glorious with their submission and praise? How much can those insignificant beings add to or subtract from him? Moreover, I have heard it said that in all creation only human be-ings are born with an innate purpose, and out of all creatures they receive the most and are permitted the most. In which case they should be able to enjoy all that they are given."

"You mean that in the end not interfering with them is the best way of loving them?"

"No, there is another way."

"And what way is that?"

"I told you already when we met in the desert and at our last meeting too. Comforting them with bread, coercing their wills with miracles and might, and so bringing them back to him. Never giving them a chance to sin again. Withdrawing their painful freedom."

"That again? How is that different from unconditional forgive-ness? And what use is the spirituality and the wisdom they've been given?"

"At least it's preferable to creating a pretext for gruesome pun-ishments."

Jesus, who had shut his eyes and was plunged in deep thought, opened his sparkling eyes and stared at Ahasuerus.

"Now I remember precisely who you are. Your words are identi-cal with those of Satan when he pestered my Father in heaven. You are clearly his son."

"You curse whatever displeases you with that name; I am unfor-tunately a son of man. Unlike you, I have never denied my parents or siblings, have no celestial memories, and no power to make wine out of water. I merely speak as a human being."

But Jesus had shut his eyes again and seemed to be recalling memories of a far distant kingdom, of a time when he had fought Satan in union with God.

"It's no use clinging on to false memories," Ahasuerus said, figuring that he could expect nothing more from Jesus. "The day is done and you are obliged to leave here. Please convey our wishes accurately to Him then. May your Father's blessing be with you . . ." With these parting words, Ahasuerus left the darkening Temple.

Their fifth meeting came immediately after the Last Supper. In those days all Judea was seething with violent opposition to Jesus, far exceeding the brilliant successes that he had enjoyed at first. These movements came from four main factions.

The first were the religious leaders—Pharisees and priests. They scorned his humble origins and abhorred his teachings, which intended to put an end to their prejudices and principles. They resented the scorn and lack of respect he showed for all the things they had been taught were sacred, all their solemn ceremonies and venerable customs. With the self-righteousness of the Word deep in the very marrow of their bones, they saw Jesus as someone tempting the people in collusion with the powers of darkness. In short, Yahweh was wounding himself with his own sword.

Next came the worldly Sadducees and the followers of Herod. For a long time they had shown no interest in the religious movements arising among the lower classes of society. The only thing they cared about was the preservation of the wealth and power they enjoyed. But as time passed and the number of people involved increased, they began to be on their guard. For they feared the reprisals and punishments of Rome if it ever developed into a political insurrection. They had misjudged Jesus, but in fact their sword was to prove the deadliest of all.

Third came various nationalists and patriots, with the party of the Zealots at their head. Many of the underground groups they directed had initially welcomed Jesus with enthusiasm. They had expected that Jesus, at the head of the crowds following him, would save the country that was groaning under the Roman yoke, like many other national heroes of the past. More than that, some of them even nourished glorious dreams of marching to Rome, turning the entire world into a theocracy, and attributing the glory to their one god. By having Simon and Judas infiltrate Jesus's group of disciples, the group hoped to have active links to Jesus if the need arose. Contrary to their expectations, his teachings of love and forgiveness weakened and enervated the crowds who should have been united by hatred and hostility. This was clearly a disappointment, and they expressed their anger before the tribunal of Pilate, choosing to free Barabbas rather than Jesus.

Finally, there was the awakening of certain wise minds, though they were few in number. It was caused by a disappointment that the salvation awaited for thousands of years came with so many unattainable conditions attached; with sorrowful hearts they closed the *Book of Enoch* and banded together in rejection of the salvation that it said was about to come. The shadow of Ahasuerus loomed darkly behind this growing awareness.

A coalition of all these oppositional groups was forming to stop the rise of Jesus. Before a decisive meeting of this group behind the Temple, Ahasuerus decided to make one more visit to Jesus.

He was alone on the Mount of Olives, deep in prayer.

"This will be our last dialogue. I know it's pointless—but I will urge you once more. Won't you go back of your own accord? Won't you go and ask him once again what his will is?"

Emerging from his long prayer, Jesus quietly answered, "I have already asked."

"What is his will?"

"He told me to give them my body and blood; then my soul is to return and sit at his right hand."

"You mean he intends to turn humanity into wicked tenants who killed their master's only son? And therefore lay on their feeble shoulders a heavier burden than that of Adam's fault?"

"He intends to wash their fallen souls in my blood, that of his only son, and summon them back to himself."

"Then there's nothing to be done. But it's you who have called for this blood. Don't hold it against me or any other person."

Ending with those words, Ahasuerus went hurrying back down

the hill; his mind was made up. He had agreed to meet Judas Iscariot, who was to play the main role in the coalition meeting behind the Temple. For a long time now Judas had been keeping him informed.

Judas had not yet arrived at the rendezvous, and Ahasuerus had to wait there for quite some time. At last Judas emerged from the shadows. His face was deathly pale but his eyes were gleaming like ill-omened cat's eyes.

"You're late."

"Yes, a bit."

"Are you shivering? What's happened?"

"It's nothing. I've had a headache and a chill since this afternoon."

"You don't fool me. What is it?"

"No, nothing at all . . ."

"Come on. There's something troubling you."

"You're the same as him; I can't fool either of you. In fact, something did happen today. While we were sharing the evening meal, he unexpectedly announced that one of us was going to betray him. The person sitting beside Peter asked who it was. He replied that it was the one he would give a sop of bread to; he gave it to me and at the same time he whispered: Go and do what you are going to do. Since then I've been feeling ill. He seems to know everything we are planning."

"You've gone weakhearted. What's become of the Judas that you were before? The Judas who used to study the battle lines of Epaminondas, the strategies of Alexander and Caesar; who dreamed of becoming a national hero fit to be heir of the Maccabees; who rushed to join the Zealots swearing on his own blood to save his compatriots from the Roman yoke; who was always more coolheaded and precise than anyone else . . . now talking like a defeated soldier . . ."

"I assure you I've not changed. Nor has anything changed in my disappointment regarding him. At first I thought that he would draw our people together by his immense power. I hoped he would form an alliance with Parthia and drive out the Romans. At present they've made peace with Rome, but the Parthian army is very powerful. Its strong arrows penetrated the armor and shields of Crassus's army; their agile cavalry trampled down the massed infantry of Rome on several occasions. If we rise up strongly united within the country, they will undoubtedly raise a powerful army and cooperate from the outside.

"Yet he has merely divided our people further, creating a new faction, based on servility and nonresistance. His teachings are eroding the explosive power of the lower classes at ever-increasing speed. But he did not blame me, even though he knew I'm going to betray him; he showed not the least disquiet in the face of approaching disaster, and this makes me afraid of him.

"That's the way he always acts. It's been his teaching for a long time. He's wise enough to know that there is no way he can avoid this calamity. It's a cunning form of resignation."

"But I've begun to wonder if he might really be the Messiah."

"Be that as it may, it makes no real difference. You will simply be the instrument to accomplish the plans he and his father have made. Anyway, you are obliged as a human being to keep the promises you have made to other human beings."

"Of course I'll keep my promise. But forget about the thirty pieces of silver. We desperately need operational funds, but for some reason it makes me feel guilty."

"No, you must accept. We're not giving you that silver as the price of his blood, but because you are a human being. Work done on earth must be paid for on earth."

After boosting the hesitant Judas's courage, Ahasuerus accompanied him to the place where Caiaphas, that year's high priest, and a large number of Pharisees were waiting. They had already mobilized several dozen Roman soldiers as well as members of the Temple guard. One elderly Pharisee who had been a close friend of his father recognized Ahasuerus and asked him, "Are you sure that the fellow with you is the right one?"

"Yes, that's Judas Iscariot."

"Are you sure he will keep his promise?"

"He struck his thigh as a sign of his oath; how could he go back on his word?"

Thereupon, Caiaphas the high priest pointed at Judas and gave an order to the person standing beside him: "Pay that man thirty pieces of silver. And give him a cup of wine. He looks pale."

Then drawing near to Judas, he said: "Don't be distressed. It's better that one man should die than that the whole nation should be sacrificed."

Caiaphas's father-in-law, Annas, who was also present, urged Judas on: "Let's go. You only have to indicate the place and which of them he is. Apart from that, there's no need for you to lift so much as a finger."

At last Judas set off in front, guiding the soldiers who were holding torches. At that hour, Jesus was at Gethsemane, on the other side of the Valley of Kidron. All the rest is reported in detail by the Gospels and other texts.

While those astounding events remain in the spotlights of history, the course of Ahasuerus's ensuing life has been consigned to obscure legends and conjecture. The final encounter between him and Jesus has been especially distorted, even in the legends, giving rise to a kind of ghost story circulating among the Jews.

According to that account, on the morning of his execution, as Jesus was on his way to Golgotha carrying his cross, he fell exhausted directly in front of Ahasuerus's house. As it happened, Ahasuerus was at home. He had observed with satisfaction the progress of the previous night's events and was resting, having only returned home after the confirmation of Jesus's sentence of crucifixion. The hubbub of the procession summoned him to the door; Jesus had fallen, with sweat pouring out of his body like raindrops, and as he saw Ahasuerus he raised his head and spoke to him.

"Finally it has come about as you wished. Their salvation is out of my hands now, and lies at the discretion of my Father in heaven. What I desire now is a moment's rest. If this is your house, let me rest here for a while. The human body I've taken finds such punishment hard to bear."

Ahasuerus stared vacantly at Jesus, then shook his head heavily.

"I regret that I cannot allow it. Be on your way quickly. You're the son of god, so ask for rest in god's kingdom. This land belongs to human beings." His voice suddenly became sharp as he continued speaking: "Quickly, now, get away from here quickly. You have not come to forgive humanity's sins but to multiply them. Judging from the miracles you performed in days gone by, it would have been easy for you to avoid all this; isn't this charade of suffering simply intended to be used to plunge a sharper thorn of guilt into human hearts? You want them to commit a sin greater than any they have committed so far, mistreating and killing the son of God, so that they will be obliged later to come running back to you, driven by guilt and fear."

"I cannot say. It is my Father's will alone . . ."

"Your agony will merely reduce them to an even greater desperation and debasement. Who among them will expect to receive a father's forgiveness and blessing after having cruelly slaughtered his son? For crying out loud, don't bequeath them any more painful memories; go your way quickly."

The eyes of Jesus, who had hitherto only taught love and forgiveness, slowly filled with a blazing fury. It was fiercer than when he had driven the money changers from the Temple with a whip or when he had cursed Chorazin. His voice reflected this as he spoke to Ahasuerus: "You reckon that everything will be brought to an end by this, but in fact this is only the beginning. I shall come again. One day I shall fulfill my Father's great love."

"You say you'll come again?"

"Yes, I shall return. If you are doubtful, wait and see. You will undoubtedly witness my Father's glorious victory."

Just then a young girl named Veronica emerged from the crowd and wiped away the sweat covering Jesus's face with a clean cloth. Amazingly, the face of Jesus was imprinted clearly on it. Seeing that, Jesus added quietly and firmly: "That shows that my departure is neither a defeat nor a surrender."

Then he looked tenderly at the owner of the cloth. "Veronica, what you have done for me is recorded in the kingdom of heaven. No matter where you go in this world, God will watch over you."

Then he uttered a rasping sigh, his face full of pain and fatigue. The Roman soldiers, unable to understand Aramaic, concluded that this delay was due to his inability to carry his heavy cross. They laid hold of Simon from Cyrene who was just entering the city at that moment and forced him to carry the cross in his place. The procession set out once again along the road to Golgotha. The only person remaining was Ahasuerus, dumbfounded by Jesus's unexpected announcement of his return and sunk deep in thought.

As a matter of fact, Ahasuerus had often heard Judas mention Jesus's return, but he had merely taken it for a figure of speech. Now he realized that it was their firm expectation, and he could not help feeling dazed, struck by a sudden sense of the great wall of time and space barring his way.

Time and space were innate modes of human perception, the necessary medium for thought and knowledge, but at the same time they were a central means of distinguishing the divine from the human. They were chains binding human life to finiteness, nails by which his body was fixed to one corner of the earth. Unless he broke free of them, he would be helpless to witness a return of Jesus at a time and place he could not know.

In the hours that followed, there occurred the most mysterious incident in Ahasuerus's whole life. As soon as Jesus had left, Ahasuerus locked himself in his room deep in thought—and suddenly, his body was able to transcend those limits of time and space. It was during the time when darkness covered the earth from about noon until three in the afternoon. There is no knowing if that was due to his own strong will or to the power of some great spirit, such as he encountered in the desert. When his family, growing suspicious due to his long silence, forced the lock and opened the door of his room, he was not there. Freed from the restraints of time and space, he had left the room and was observing the last moments of Jesus.

Jesus was breathing his last. Dismas, the brigand crucified at his right, had just completed his repentance. Ahasuerus passed through the crowd and stood before him.

"I have decided to wait for your return."

"The powers of darkness . . . have given you the ability to transcend time and space. I can see that . . . since others cannot perceive you."

His words were squeezed out one by one in agony. Then he gazed desolately at the sky.

"Father, I too would like to remain like that. Returning to life on the third day, I may have power over their eyes and ears for a little while, but what will you do about that man who will walk the earth for thousands of years whispering to people? How can you be sure that when next I come down into this world there will not be another cross waiting for me, that I shall not once more return home in tears? I ask you again, unless it is something I must accept, take this cup from me."

But there was only a pitiless silence and Jesus's last moment came. His body, drenched in blood and sweat, convulsed weakly, and with a grieving cry he gave up the ghost:

"*Eloi, Eloi, lama sabachthani?*"

Some thought he had called on Elijah, but what he really meant was: My God, my God, why have you forsaken me? Words that made him appear human, for almost the only time in his whole life. Far off, Mary of Magdala, Mary the mother of James and Joseph, and Salome were lamenting. Once Ahasuerus was completely sure that Jesus was dead, he left the place and set out on his journey. A journey of lengthy, long-drawn-out waiting, perhaps lasting forever.

In the years that followed, while Christianity — the result of an illicit union of Greek philosophy, the monotheism and ethical code of the Jews, and the mysticism and natural genius for worship of the East — was using the sword of Caesar to expand its authority and gaining control of people's feeble souls by means of pillaged food supplies and petty miracles, the story of Ahasuerus became absurdly distorted. His journey of unending waiting, sad and lonely to human eyes, was explained through the malice of Christians as the result of a curse that Jesus spat out on the morning of his execution. His appearance was reported to be that of a lowly cobbler of those times. Barefooted, wearing a leather apron, with a Roman soldier's sandal that he is stitching and a threaded needle in his hands, he is said to be forever wandering the world, waiting for the dateless return of Jesus.

This time, whether it was because he had grown more accustomed to Min Yoseop's style and method of logical development, or because his mind was more open to his writing, Sergeant Nam was able to finish reading the remaining text with little difficulty. There had been two files left to be read but both were considerably thicker than the previous ones. Reading the last portion, he found himself enjoying it as a novel; he was moved deeply as earlier sections came back to him and he felt he could now understand the themes running through the entire work. He found it strange that, despite the clear anti-Christian argument that flowed through the entire story, the transcendent being that Min Yoseop had tried to present as a substitute was portrayed so vaguely. There was no concrete depiction of the "Great Spirit" that Ahasuerus had encountered in the desert, and his teaching was only depicted as an inversion of the Word. Sergeant Nam was unable to find any reason for this, and he went back to take another look at the section describing the events in the desert; he discovered there that a number of pages had been removed between the part where Ahasuerus goes into the desert and the part when he meets Jesus. He had the impression that Min Yoseop had torn out page after page, dissatisfied with what he had written, then gone on.

Judging from various indications, Min Yoseop had been barely twenty-two or twenty-three when he wrote the story. To invert the existing Word was hard enough; inventing a completely new Word and a new god would have been much more difficult. Maybe this god had only taken full shape in his writing more recently, and—the thought suddenly struck Sergeant Nam—perhaps this new god had something to do with the death of Min Yoseop and the disappearance of Cho Dongpal. But he reminded himself that Min Yoseop had died while staying at a prayer house, and that his path prior to his death had been bringing him back to Christianity; his idea immediately collapsed. It wouldn't make any sense for him to turn back toward Christianity at the very moment he had completed his anti-Christian doctrine. In addition, considering how Cho Dongpal had readily rejected Christianity six years earlier to follow Min Yoseop, it was clear that at that time the doctrine had already been sufficiently formulated to convince him.

Thereupon, Sergeant Nam once again immersed himself in the case with a passion that had almost nothing to do with the professional approach of a detective. In his attempts to trace Cho Dongpal's whereabouts, he would request cooperation in his inquiries without making any distinctions between different administrative sections or ranks. When there was even the vaguest hope that he might turn up somewhere, he made every imaginable effort to have someone waiting for him. He even sent Detective Park to the home in Busan he had not been to for six years; the young detective spent three days keeping watch there before he was pulled out, despite Nam's angry protests. He likewise received a reprimand for telegraphing to the local substations and ordering a general check of all the inns and rooming houses, without any justification. Outwardly, he consistently claimed that he wanted to solve the crime and apprehend the criminal, but in his heart Sergeant Nam was obsessed by the hidden relationship between Min Yoseop and Cho Dongpal and their new doctrine, which he sensed was deeply linked to their separation. It almost seemed as if Sergeant Nam had also been taken in by Min Yoseop's toxic creed.

Still, the results of his investigations were extremely disappointing, considering all the efforts he had made. On the day that his first regular report was due, the only new detail Sergeant Nam was able to add was that he had located one more person who recalled Min Yoseop. It was an elderly spinster who worked at the counter of the city post office; she remembered Min Yoseop's features and his odd personality. When he was sending a money order he would never fill in the name and address of the sender; each time she pointed this out, he would randomly scribble something, and that was why she remembered him.

Yet Sergeant Nam still clung to his hopeless investigation. The passion that made him continue struck him as strange, so that he would smile bitterly whenever he thought about it. It was as if the spirit of the dead Min Yoseop had taken possession of him and was driving him on blindly; as the prospect of solving the crime became less and less probable, Sergeant Nam's tenacity only increased. But within such a large organization, the power of one individual was bound to be limited. What first made Sergeant Nam lose heart and gradually grow weary of the investigation were the simultaneously increasing pressures from above and below, material and immaterial. Whenever Sergeant Nam put in a request for personnel, his superiors would almost invariably shake their heads with expressions of displeasure; and if permission was granted, the officers he dispatched were unhappy with their assignments.

"Where shall I go and wander about today?" When a junior officer, a greenhorn who only seemed to have put on the uniform yesterday, questioned him sarcastically in that way, barely concealing his irritation, it shocked him just as much as when he was scolded by his superiors.

As soon as the picnic season started, an increasing number of crimes in the vicinity of Donggak Temple served to put a brake on Sergeant Nam's obsession. Even with all the newly drafted combat police running around, they still lacked manpower, and it was inevitable that an investigation that had already been classified as unsolved would take a backseat. There were times when Sergeant Nam was so busy in his daily grind that he would completely forget the case of Min Yoseop for days at a time.

So the search for Cho Dongpal slowed to a halt, and as the dates for submitting the next two progress reports went by, there was nothing to be added. Sergeant Nam no longer had time to work on the case, but inwardly he felt an increasing impatience to solve it, the cause of which he could not determine. There were moments when Min Yoseop's dead body loomed up in his mind—early in the morning, when he opened his eyes to find his throat burning from the previous evening's drinking and heard the sound of a far away church bell—and with it he felt a renewed eagerness spurring him on with an intensity it had not previously possessed.

14

It seemed only a few days since he had submitted his previous report, yet the date for the next one was already approaching. Taking advantage of a lull in the picnic season crimes—it was June by now—Sergeant Nam returned to the case. It was partly because he was haunted by a feeling that after twice sending in reports of no progress, there ought to be something new this time; on the other hand, he had also decided to make one last try to solve the case.

Sergeant Nam called in Detectives Im and Park, who, having free time for once, were lounging in the little coffee shop downstairs, and sent them to check out a few of the red-light districts downtown. He wanted them to gather information from the brothel owners or the older prostitutes. In view of what they knew so far, it seemed unlikely they could expect much, but after all both Min Yoseop and Cho Dongpal were young and unmarried.

Detectives Im and Park, who had been cracking idle jokes with the new girl in the shop after getting something cool to drink, left grumbling openly about such preposterous orders. However, Detective Im came back after less than an hour bearing unexpected news: he had found a girl in a nearby brothel who knew Min Yoseop. She was called Yun Hyangsun, and at twenty-seven she was a bit old for the job.

"She said she'd never seen anyone as horny as him in six years as a hooker!" Wiping away the sweat that was pearling on his forehead, Detective Im laughed weakly. His expression was relaxed, unlike when he had left earlier. Sergeant Nam couldn't believe that the words applied to Min Yoseop.

"Not Cho Dongpal, though?"

"She says she's never heard of the guy. She clearly said it was this one, the one with his eyes shut." As he replied, Detective Im pointed at Min Yoseop's photo among the two he was still holding.

"So what else did she say?"

"Nothing much. But you wouldn't really expect him to tell every last detail about himself to a whore he frequents once or twice a month."

"Once or twice a month? That makes him a regular."

"What's so special about visiting a whore regularly? Anyway, the girl seemed like she didn't even know Min Yoseop's name."

Sergeant Nam felt a strange premonition, and at the same time he began to suspect the girl. If she knew Min Yoseop well enough to recognize him in a photo lying dead with his eyes shut, the relationship must have gone beyond that of a whore and a mere passing customer; so if she said she didn't even know his name, she might be concealing what she knew about him. Based on his personal experience, Sergeant Nam would expect a man to reveal at least his name to a girl he met several times, even if she was a hooker.

So Sergeant Nam ignored Detective Im's report and went off to see Yun Hyangsun for himself. Though Detective Im wasn't happy that Sergeant Nam doubted what he said, he considered himself lucky not to have to go back out into the hot streets, and he explained where the girl could be found without further comment.

Under normal circumstances, prowling around a red-light district before lunchtime was something that would have embarrassed him, but today Sergeant Nam felt nothing of the kind. He quickly found the house where Yun Hyangsun worked: the House of Blue Perfume. It was an old building, barely more than a shack, but flashily equipped with glass windows only on the side facing the street, like an old whore's makeup.

Yun Hyangsun was sitting in a slouched posture on the wooden-floored veranda, very scantily dressed—presumably on account of the weather—and she greeted Sergeant Nam with an unwelcoming air. She seemed to recognize what he was at a glance.

"Not another cop! What's up this time, Mr. Detective?"

On seeing the girl sneer provocatively without bothering to bring her wide-splayed legs together, Sergeant Nam was disgusted rather than offended. He also felt the familiar tension that arose whenever he encountered a suspect whose personality grew ever more perverse and crooked with repeated condemnations. He realized he was going to have to take a rough tone with her.

"Is this really the man? The one you say you know?"

"Isn't that what I said?" Perhaps because of the way he spoke, the woman suddenly drew her legs together and the tone of her voice softened.

"When did this fellow start to come around?"

"Well, maybe a year or so ago . . ."

"Recently?"

"About five months ago. I don't know the exact dates."

"Did he come here often?"

"Once or twice a month, perhaps. The other detective asked all this before, and I've already told everything I know, so why keep asking?" She began to whine again, but Sergeant Nam continued to interrogate her as he had seen veteran detectives do, without the least change of expression.

"What did he say he did?"

"He said he earned a living by stealing, but he might just as well have claimed he was the President. It was surely a lie, in any case. How many harebrained idiots do you think come to places like this and spill all the beans about themselves?"

"So you've never once seen this guy?" As Sergeant Nam produced Cho Dongpal's photo he observed her expression closely. It was an exaggerated stare, designed to make her aware she was being watched. That was a trick he had learned from the veterans during his few years in the criminal investigation division; it could sometimes induce people to reveal an expression they had intended to suppress.

"I don't know the bastard. You cops are weird. The other guy asked exactly the same thing just a minute ago . . ."

She denied it stubbornly, but there was a faint uneasiness in her eyes, which looked away the moment they met Sergeant Nam's. The way she denied knowing him without so much as glancing at the photo also suggested that she wasn't telling the whole truth. Yes, there was something . . . sensing that, Sergeant Nam pressed her:

"Stop lying. These two always went about together."

"I'm not lying. I don't know that fellow."

"Listen carefully." Sergeant Nam suddenly lowered his voice to a whisper. Then, adopting an icy expression, he addressed Yun Hyangsun, who was looking even tenser on hearing him change his tone, in a quiet, cutting voice: "I came here after making full inquiries. Don't think you can pull the wool over my eyes. If I catch you out, you won't be doing this business here anymore . . . Miss Park next door says she saw the pair of them coming and going together."

Having noticed her weaken slightly, Sergeant Nam ventured a sly guess. Her reaction was unexpectedly violent. She suddenly began to heap insults on Miss Park, whose name Sergeant Nam had used on the spur of the moment without ever having met her; it gave her an excuse to vent her feelings.

"Did that dirty bitch really say that? That bitch! No loyalty . . ."

"Yes, she told me everything."

"She deserves to be fried in shit. That's why she and I are still here selling cunt, even though we're nearly thirty."

"Spit it out. You know Cho Dongpal well, don't you?"

"Cho Dongpal? I tell you I don't know any Cho Dongpal, Dung-fly, or whatever."

Regaining her confidence, she resumed her denial. Sergeant Nam was puzzled for a moment, then suddenly realized the reason for her change. Previously, when he had met Min Yoseop's landlady, she had said that Cho Dongpal was using the family name Kim. Sergeant Nam guessed that Yun Hyangsun only knew his pseudonym, and she had grown bolder on hearing him use what she reckoned was the wrong name; so he calmly thrust Cho Dongpal's photo before her eyes and spoke in a crushing tone:

"Yes, that's his real name. Sometimes he goes by Kim. Maybe he's passing himself off as a Mr. Kim here too."

"In any case, I don't know him."

"It's not worth going down to the station, fighting till we're blue in the face, then telling the truth, is it? Even if you speak out now, it's not going to hurt the guy . . ."

Seeing her resolve weaken again, Sergeant Nam coaxed her using a gentler voice. She remained silent for a moment. Judging by her unfocused gaze and sudden frown, she seemed to be making up her mind about some difficult problem.

"What the hell's going on, anyway? Why are you looking for Mr. Kim?"

She spoke in a quiet voice, apparently having reached a decision. For the first time since they met, she spoke submissively, but still with a trace of fear somewhere within her.

"So he pretended to be called Kim round here, too?"

"He wasn't pretending; he really was called Kim. Once, when there was a police check, I saw his residence card."

Sergeant Nam finally realized why there were no more traces of Cho Dongpal's whereabouts. He had not simply been using a false name, he had been living as someone completely different and using another residence card for the past several years.

"Kim . . . what was his full name?"

"I can't remember what he was called, though I heard it several times."

Her response disappointed Sergeant Nam considerably, for once he knew the name, Cho Dongpal was as good as found. He made an effort to conceal his feelings and tactfully changed the subject.

"You're sure it's this man?"

"Sure. He always came around here together with that Mr. Min. But what's happened? They're neither of them the kind of people to have the police on their tails."

"The truth is, this Min Yoseop is dead."

"What, him? When?"

"Someone stuck a knife in him. About six months ago."

"And you suspect Mr. Kim of having done it?"

"Not necessarily . . . only he's gone missing for several months past."

A hint of relief showed in her face. Her concern had been for Cho Dongpal; it was clear that she now thought she didn't have to worry about him. Sergeant Nam could sense her strong sympathy for Cho Dongpal.

"In that case, you're wrong to be looking for Mr. Kim. He used to treat Mr. Min like his lord and master. Even in a place like this he always called him 'teacher.' I don't care what you do to me, I swear he didn't kill him."

"We know that too. But for the moment we have to find him first. Only then will we be able to catch the culprit, whoever he is." Yun Hyangsun flinched and stared at Sergeant Nam, as if a thought had just struck her. "You don't mean to arrest him, do you?" Obviously, she was sincerely worried.

Although he felt bad doing so, Sergeant Nam took advantage of this to casually ask, "But why have you been shielding him? Is he your boyfriend?"

"No. It's not like that. It's all on account of Sunja. Sunja, poor girl."

As she spoke, her face grew sad. Anticipating some new information, Sergeant Nam strove to hide his excitement as he asked, "Who's Sunja?"

"She's the girl Mr. Kim's been living with. You won't arrest him, will you? You're not going to make Sunja come back here, are you? Sunja's just a poor kid."

Yun Hyangsun sounded as if she was about to start crying. He had no idea what her relationship with this Sunja was, but Sergeant Nam was surprised that Yun Hyangsun, with the life she had led, could still retain a personal affection sincere enough to bring her to tears.

"We first met ten years ago at Seoul Station. I still remember it. It was early one misty summer morning. I was sick of being poor and sick of the exhausting work I was doing on the farm. I'd caught the train up from the southwest without any clear plan, and I came across this girl standing in front of the station, looking dazed and clutching a scruffy traveling bag, like me. She said she'd run away from an orphanage somewhere in the southeast. We felt a connection right away and became friends. We stayed together from that day until we were separated at the employment agency, ten days later. We had gone there together once we used up all the money we'd brought with us. She got a job in a restaurant while I started working as a housemaid. We kept in touch at first, and would sometimes meet up. But then we both started to move around and it wasn't so easy to meet. We lost touch after less than a year, and for a long time after that I didn't hear anything from her.

"Then, about four years ago, I found her again in Busan, in what was known as the '588 district.' I'd gone from being a housemaid to working in a factory, from the factory to a bar; I cheated and I got cheated; finally, after various ups and downs, I fell into this kind of life and was eventually sold to the place where she was already working. She'd followed a path not very different from mine, and ended up there. How we cried, meeting again like that

... we spent the whole night crying. After that, wherever we went, we were always together, at least until she met Mr. Kim and managed to escape this alley. We might not share the same blood but ... we're sisters. She's my little sister ..."

Overcome with emotion, Yun Hyangsun laid bare the story of her past, half sobbing, half relating, although Sergeant Nam had not asked her to. It wasn't a particularly extraordinary tale, yet Sergeant Nam felt a lump in his throat. But it wasn't the moment for indulging in pointless sentiment.

"When did Cho—I mean Kim, first meet this Sunja?"

"Three years ago. In those days we were in Incheon. Why, you must have heard of it—the Yellow House. She wasn't doing well then; she'd caught some dreadful disease, tuberculosis of the lymphs or something—which usually means certain death to people like us. Our life's always like that, isn't it? The more you save, the more you have to spend, then you're back to square one; how was she going to pay her medical bills when she was sick and unable to work? Her debts were getting bigger, and it seemed like she'd have no choice but to wait helplessly to die. That was when Mr. Kim came along. It seems he'd heard about her on a visit to another girl. To our surprise, he came and took her away the very next day. He paid off all she owed to the madam, then took her to get treatment. And that's not all—he even offered to marry her. But as soon as she was better, she came looking for me! I don't know how she knew I'd moved here ... I asked why she'd come back and not gotten married, and she said it was out of the question, much more than a girl like her deserved."

"What do you mean, deserved?" Sergeant Nam asked casually, trying not to seem to be prying. Finally, after so much difficulty, he had the chance to learn about Cho Dongpal's activities during the last three years. Unaware of Sergeant Nam's hidden intentions, Yun Hyangsun now spoke of Cho Dongpal in tones verging on veneration.

"That Mr. Kim, he's just so great. She says there are over twenty pupils he helps study, and then a whole number of people who are able to eat thanks to him. Once she was better, she spent a month or so helping look after them and she said it made her see that there really is another world. She said they were like people in some edifying children's book. More amazing still is his family background. Apparently he's the only son of immensely rich parents; she said that although he was helping all those people, he never seemed to lack money."

"What did Mr. Min do?"

"According to Sunja, it wasn't clear. She said he just spent the whole day reading or deep in thought and never did anything around the house or for the students. Yet Mr. Kim thought the world of him; she couldn't understand why."

"So is this Sunja living with him nowadays?"

"They came and took her away after she had come back to here. She'd thought she was completely cured but she wasn't. Less than three months after her return, she fell sick again and took to her bed. Then, just as I was beginning to worry that it would turn out like before, they arrive out of nowhere. I don't know if they'd deliberately followed us or not, but they said they'd also moved to this city. A few months after they took Sunja away, a letter arrived. It said she was cured and, persuaded by Mr. Kim's insistence, she married him. And she asked if I never thought of stopping this kind of life and making a new start . . ."

"So why didn't you?"

"I didn't want to be an extra burden. I figured I could go on like this for a few more years, then see what to do once I'd saved up a bit. She wrote one more letter after that, then nothing more . . ."

"What was their address?"

"Gyeongsan. But in her last letter she said that Mr. Kim had left home."

Gyeongsan was a town not very far from Daegu. Overflowing with joy at having finally traced Cho Dongpal, Sergeant Nam hurriedly asked for the exact address.

"Promise me first—you're not going to cause her any trouble?" Before giving him the address, Yun Hyangsun again demanded an assurance. Repressing some vague feelings of bad conscience, Sergeant Nam reassured her with some well-chosen words. Only then did she go inside and bring back an envelope that she showed to Sergeant Nam.

"How did you come to know Min Yoseop?" Sergeant Nam asked, after he had written the address in his notebook. Not that there was anything he had been prevented from learning by their previous conversation, but he asked from a hope that there might still be something new he could learn. Aside from the relationship of Cho Dongpal with Kim Sunja, there might have been something special in her relationship with Min Yoseop.

"What? Well, whenever he came with Mr. Kim, he always ended up in my room."

"Was there anything unusual about him?"

"There were some things. For instance, most people who come here either act awkwardly or try to make excuses, but he didn't at all. How shall I put it? ... He had this cool, calm attitude that was actually somewhat frightening and off-putting. He was also extremely untalkative ..."

"You had said he was really ... horny?"

"Oh ... that was something I made up. Although he was rather special in that way too. After spending one night with him, I would be in no mood for any customers the next day, I was so exhausted. But you couldn't really call it 'horny.' He was just very thoroughgoing in what he did. It was like he was earnestly performing some kind of duty ..."

Despite her profession, she seemed embarrassed to talk about such things in broad daylight. Sergeant Nam's questions were less connected with the investigation than with his personal interest in Min Yoseop; stopping there, he stood up.

"Thanks for everything."

Yun Hyangsun looked at Sergeant Nam with eyes full of worry and suddenly spoke like a woman ten years older: "I just hope it doesn't hurt Sunja ... but once he knows Mr. Min's dead, Mr. Kim won't stay quiet."

Gyeongsan was only about an hour's bus ride from Daegu; by the time Sergeant Nam reached it, the sun was still a hand's breadth above the western horizon. The house where Kim Sunja was living stood at the foot of a hill a little ways outside the main township. The view was good, the air pure; the house they had rented seemed to be well-suited for her convalescence. When Sergeant Nam entered the yard, wiping the sweat from his forehead, a woman in her thirties was sitting on the wooden veranda in the light of the setting sun; she looked at him with an expressionless face. Her pallid complexion and the dark circles around her eyes gave her a sickly appearance; and the way she was sitting there as if trying to absorb every last drop of heat from the setting sun seemed to suggest that she was in poor health.

Because Yun Hyangsun had referred to her as her "younger sister," Sergeant Nam had been thinking of Kim Sunja as someone much younger; he thus casually asked the woman:

"Excuse me. Good evening. Could you tell me if someone called Kim Sunja lives here?"

The woman raised her head and looked at Sergeant Nam. Her expression betrayed neither surprise nor apprehension; it was calm and blank. A low, feeble voice emerged from her thin lips.

"That's me. What is it?"

"Ah. I'm sorry. Yun Hyangsun called you her younger sister . . ."

On hearing Yun Hyangsun's name, she seemed slightly taken aback. Quickly regaining her composure, she spoke:

"She's only one year older than me."

"Ah, I see! Can I ask you a couple of questions? Is your husband, Cho Dongpal, at home now?"

At these words, an expression worthy of the name appeared on the woman's face for the first time. It was not so much one of concern, but rather one suggesting she had heard something unexpected.

"My husband . . . is not Cho Dongpal. His name is . . ."

"Of course. He also uses Kim as his family name." Sergeant Nam interrupted her to show that he knew that much. But she went on without flinching.

"Kim Dong-uk. That's the name on his residence registration and our marriage certificate."

It looked as though Cho Dongpal had not revealed his real name even to her. Filing away the unfamiliar name of Kim Dong-uk firmly into his memory, Sergeant Nam drew Cho Dongpal's picture from his notebook.

"At any rate, that's him, isn't it?"

She examined the photo with a look that, although it seemed relaxed, suggested a strange agitation that could not be expressed by the term "conjugal affection" alone, then nodded quietly as she replied, "The picture looks like him." His immediate impression was that she had not deliberately tried to conceal her husband's name, but Sergeant Nam was not entirely convinced.

"You had no idea your husband's real name was Cho Dongpal?"

"It's the first I've heard of such a thing. But what's happened?"

"Well, I have to see your husband about something. I'll tell him when I see him. Is he inside?"

"No, he hasn't been here for a long time."

"Don't you know where he is?"

"No."

Being man and wife, it was a situation where, there ought to have been some kind of emotion present; yet in replying, her voice showed not the slightest change in its inflection. Sergeant Nam found this slightly suspicious, and he observed her expression closely as he asked:

"Did this ever happen before?"

"Yes. Two months after our marriage he left town with some-one, and only came home a year later."

"Where did he say he had been?"

"He didn't say, but perhaps . . ."

"Perhaps what?—Where had he been?"

"Maybe he'd been in jail. His hair was cut very short and his complexion was bad. After he came home, he stayed in bed for two days straight."

"Didn't you ask him?"

"He seemed not to want to talk about it . . ."

"But still . . . You mean you thought your husband had been in jail and you didn't even ask? Weren't you curious to know why?"

Sergeant Nam asked bluntly. But he was struck by her frozen expression, and didn't even wait for a reply before asking his next question.

"So what about this time?"

"I don't know. Less than a week after coming home, he left again."

"Jail again?"

"Again, I don't know. Last time, there was a letter that came a few days later saying that he would be going somewhere far away, but this time there wasn't even that."

"Then what have you been living on?"

"The first time, his teacher came by once a month and took care of everything."

"His teacher?"

"Yes, my husband's teacher."

"Was his name Min by any chance?"

"That's right. Mr. Min Yoseop."

Sergeant Nam felt himself growing tense.

"In what ways did he take care of things?"

"Mainly by looking after my living expenses. If there were any other problems, he would take care of those too."

"And this time?"

"For some reason he hasn't shown up yet. Luckily there was something left over from what he gave me last time."

"So when was the last time this teacher came here?"

"About six months ago. He came by the day after my husband got back. I think I heard him say he had to go back somewhere."

"Tell me in detail what he said that day."

"They were talking in low voices in the next room, so I couldn't hear exactly. The two of them seemed to be quarreling all night long. I had the impression my husband was urging him not to go back; it was dawn by the time he finally left. That's all I know."

"After that, what did your husband do?"

"He stayed in bed for the whole day. Then, the evening of the next day he went out suddenly, and I've heard nothing of him since then."

"So that was about six months ago. Weren't you worried? You didn't report it."

"I figured he didn't want to tell me where he was."

"So you think it's the same as last time. I should probably tell you I'm from the police."

"I guessed as much. Is he in trouble again?"

"I don't know yet. But Mr. Min is dead."

As he spoke, Sergeant Nam observed her calmly. Again, a clear expression appeared on her face. It was undoubtedly an expression of sorrow and anxiety, but it didn't seem to have any connection to Cho Dongpal.

"How did he die? What about my husband?"

Her voice trembled slightly as she asked, but there was not the least indication that she suspected Cho Dongpal was the assailant.

"It's because we don't know that I've come to see you like this. Min Yoseop was brutally murdered by someone, and we cannot locate your husband. Of course, it's because we've been looking for him under the name of Cho Dongpal, but . . ."

"Then, my husband . . . ?"

A far more pronounced expression came across her face, one that conveyed an outright denial of his insinuations. Feeling immensely discouraged, Sergeant Nam managed to hide his feelings as he continued speaking:

"No one knows. The only thing that's certain is that it must have something to do with Min Yoseop's death. The two of them had established a close relationship and had been working together for six years. Then one is killed and around the same time the other vanishes without trace . . ."

"No. You've got it wrong. If Mr. Min was killed, then you should have started your investigation with the idea that my husband was not safe either. If you suspect my husband at all, you're wrong, utterly wrong."

"And why do you think that?"

"First of all, because my husband respected Mr. Min so deeply he would not so much as step on his shadow. He never forgot even the smallest passing remark he made, and once it was spoken by him, he tried to put it into practice. No matter how bad a mood he was in, if Mr. Min happened to come by, his face would light up immediately. I've felt jealous more than once on seeing that. I can't be sure, of course, but I think my husband would have readily laid down his life for him."

"We know that, to some extent. But there's a saying that love and hate grow deep together. It's not completely unknown for people who were the closest of companions one day to draw knives on each other the next."

"Maybe you're inclined to think like that because I told you they'd quarreled the last time Mr. Min came, but on my husband's part it was more like a desperate appeal than a quarrel. After Mr. Min left, I could hear my husband's muffled sobbing. The next day he stayed in bed all day and looked like he was in bad shape. When he left the house that night, he was staggering like someone seriously ill, so much so that I was really worried."

But that remark alone was enough to reinforce the conviction that was already in Sergeant Nam's mind. He had on several occasions seen cases of one kind of extreme emotion changing instantaneously to another. Strengthened by this, Sergeant Nam decided that he should just try to gather whatever material evidence might be there. He guessed that Kim Sunja would not help much as far as analyzing psychological motivation went.

"I understand. Could I take a look inside the room anyway?"

"He's not here, really. You can ask the landlady."

She spoke in a way that suggested it bothered her, but it did not sound like a straight refusal.

"I do believe you. But there's something I need to find out . . ."

Without waiting for her to lead the way, Sergeant Nam opened the door of the room adjoining the veranda on which she was sitting. The room was far too bare for a young married couple. A few clothes were hanging on the wall, a duvet with a clean cover lay in one corner, and a large aluminum trunk stood at the back. It looked more like a bachelor's room, equipped with the bare minimum needed for daily life.

The trunk, their only piece of furniture, appeared to serve as both dressing table and desk. The top was covered with a small plastic sheet; in one corner stood a round, iron-framed mirror and a few cosmetics; in the other lay a few notebooks and a couple of books.

"Do you go to church?" Sergeant Nam asked, noticing a thick Bible wedged between the other books.

"No."

"What about that book, then?"

"My husband used to consult it."

"Consult?"

"Yes. Before my husband left home the first time, he had been busy writing something, saying he was rewriting the Bible. He often used to refer to it."

Hearing what she said, Sergeant Nam felt his heart begin to race. The fact that Cho Dongpal had been writing was rather unexpected—but he realized that it had to be the part that had been missing from Min Yoseop's text, the part about the new god.

"Is this what your husband wrote?"

Sergeant Nam picked up a plastic-covered notebook lying under the Bible.

"Yes. There was also an old notebook that he used to call the original, but he burned it after he had finished writing this one."

What he had called the original was probably the portion that had been removed from Min Yoseop's text and revised by him later. At first, unsure of what he wanted to write, he must have glossed over the teaching concerning the new god. But why had the completion of it passed into Cho Dongpal's hands?

It was as she had said: the handwriting in the notebook was unfamiliar to Sergeant Nam's eyes, and it had even been elevated to the level of scripture by the grandiose title "The Book of Quarantania." But within the first few lines he could detect Min Yoseop's personal style. Reading on, he found it impossible to discern what was written by Min Yoseop and what had been revised and added by Cho Dongpal.

Sergeant Nam put the notebook aside, resolving to take time to read it carefully, and continued to look for other evidence. But if Cho Dongpal had indeed killed Min Yoseop, it was as if he had used words to accomplish it, for there was nothing else strange in the apartment. Although Min Yoseop had very few possessions, Cho Dongpal seemed to own even less.

"Have you gotten rid of any of your husband's things, or stored them somewhere else?" Sergeant Nam asked, since there was so little belonging to Cho Dongpal in what had been the home they shared as a couple.

Her answer had a boastful ring to it: "He's different from other people. He never wanted to own anything apart from what he had to have. He only ever had a single set of clothing, which he wore in summer and winter alike."

For some reason he felt obliged to believe what she said. Giving up the idea of searching any further, Sergeant Nam rose to his feet, holding the notebook he had set aside just before.

"I'm sorry, but I'm going to have to take this. I assure you I'll bring it back."

At these words, the expression on her face darkened, and she seemed to be reluctant to let him take it. But realizing that she could not refuse if the police wanted it, she soon nodded feebly. She was looking extremely tired. Only then remembering that she wasn't in good health, Sergeant Nam suddenly felt sorry and hurried to leave.

"Don't worry too much about your husband. We're not assuming guilt. But even if he comes back tomorrow, you must contact us without fail. After all, we have to put Mr. Min's soul to rest, don't we?"

15

By the time Sergeant Nam got back to the station, it was well past nine. After he had requested inquiries to be carried out concerning this newly discovered Kim Dong-uk, he left for home, carrying the notebook he had brought from Gyeongsan. He had found out about Cho Dongpal's alter ego and his current situation in considerable detail, but nothing had really become clear; postponing any further investigation until the following day, he intended to examine Cho Dongpal's notebook.

After reaching home and eating a late supper, Sergeant Nam opened the "Book of Quarantania."

In the desert the Great Wisdom
spoke to the Son of Man, saying:

In the beginning was the Great Being, and everything in the universe was one in him. The forms and the substance of all things were one in him, all the concepts and principles surrounding them were also one in him. But that Being was not the original Chaos that your human mythologies are content to start with. How could your shortsighted perspectives reach back to that distant day, how could your little words contain the fullness of that immensity? Whereas volume and size, line and color were all dissolved in the One that was matter prior to form, and varying and opposing concepts and principles mingled in the One that was mind prior to meaning, that was still a totality of living harmony and order, a sublime inaction pregnant with creation and development. To view that as Chaos is merely your mistake in wrongly accepting the sophistry of the One who regards creation as his right.

You are descended from Abraham, so now I will speak using your myths and the name of your god. The Goodness of Yahweh and my Wisdom were a warp and woof comprising that Original Being. We were the first self-aware beings, and we set about shaping ourselves to be the supreme minds of the universe that was to be newly created. By the time it was passed to you, after long ages of grinding and polishing, we were the two spirits that would partially reveal themselves under the names of Justice and Freedom.

The central hypothesis of all your religions that there are two distinct principles that propel the universe is to some extent a reasonable one. You vaguely sensed the existence of our parallel essences from early times. But the connection between us was greatly misconstrued—the most obvious example of this being the way we were only understood as each other's negation: a good god on one side, an evil god on the other.

Initially we were one and we were equal; the principle uniting us was the harmony and order that had enabled the Original Being to stand, not as chaos but as perfection. Just as Goodness cannot be complete without Wisdom, how can Wisdom be complete without Goodness? Sin is simply another name for Goodness without Wisdom; Evil is simply another name for Wisdom without Goodness. You too must have experienced how painful and bitter Justice is without Freedom and likewise Freedom without Justice.

What caused you to envisage the principle connecting the two of us as nothing but disunion and antagonism, hatred and conflict, was probably the discord that arose between us after the act of Creation. This cast a suggestive light onto your spiritual nature, resulting finally in the birth of such a mistaken conclusion.

We undertook the onerous job of the Creation of heaven and earth because we were weary of the loneliness of being the Unique, the unending stillness, and the long inaction. Yet Creation does not signify the right to govern what is created. Creation existed for our sake, certainly—but likewise, we existed for the sake of creation. Creation was our right but also our duty.

The process of Creation was on the whole similar to what your myths record. In the beginning, there was the Word, and everything arose through the Word. Thereby, our duality became embodied in concrete beings, and everything was endowed with an individual name, form, and meaning. However, your interpretation of the myth is mistaken. It is slightly misleading to say that the Word represents the two of us. For prior to the Word came our will, and our being preceded that will. The Word, being nothing but a declaratory act, such as naming or defining, cannot precede being, even if it precedes everything else; and no matter how exalted the Word is, it cannot be anything more than a ceremonial envoy of Creation, unable to attain the endowments of being itself.

However, once the Creation was finished and I had returned to my original silence in a state of contented fatigue, something unexpected occurred. The Word, which should have naturally been brought to an end with the completion of the Creation, remained as the avatar of a single will and began to coerce and shackle every kind of being. The Goodness of Yahweh, once left alone, sent down the Word in a constant flood, subjecting every creature formed in the harmony of our duality to his law alone, intent on confining the essence of their originally distinct being within his arrogant will. The most intolerable aspect of it all was the plight of you humans. Ah, humanity! The very Essence of Creation; most perfect embodiment of our duality in harmony—what blessed beings you were at first. Everything about you was permitted, excused, fulfilled, and perfected. Your creation was the goal of Creation itself, you were perfection emanating from the Original Being. You believe that we fashioned you in imitation of ourselves, but in fact it was by your emanation that we received a likeness.

Yet the Goodness of Yahweh, once left alone, subjected much of what was yours to prohibition, deficiency, and imperfection, and even transformed being itself into his own means. For his Word condemned the half of your nature that was derived from me; his base desire for domination, intent on taking possession of the whole though he only had rights over the half, deprived you of your due reward for obedience, because he wanted you to obey only him. His vainglory, dreaming of absolute domination, made you a standard by which to measure the obedience of all creatures. That was the beginning of our unfortunate self-negation.

I was dumbfounded by the absurd self-righteousness of my Other Half, but hoped at least to avoid the tragedy of a division between us two, who were originally one. What great unhappiness is caused to children by discord between parents! After my cautious remonstrances and admonitions had been ignored, I handed everything over to him, retired to the furthest ends of the universe, and withdrew into a profound self-pity.

That was my first error. That quiet concession convinced him quite baselessly that he had gained a victory, and ultimately gave birth among you to the superstitious belief that he was superior to me. The various myths describing the expulsion of evil gods and dragons that you have heard in your travels through this world are nothing but stories made up to exalt him and diminish me, distorted representations of my relinquishment.

But an even greater error was still to follow. Yielding to a sudden curiosity after having withdrawn into myself, I came back to see this world and you. Alas, if only I had not retained such an imprudent attachment; if my Wisdom had not been blinded by my eagerness to see how you were doing, having been left to his Goodness alone; if I had only foreseen that days like today would come, and not laid claim to a belated right; if I had let things go on forever as they were, the ensuing long-drawn-out agony and distress would not have befallen me . . . but I emerged from retirement and silence, casually thinking that I would just be able to cast a covert glance and then come back.

I flew across great distances of space and alighted on this earth, reaching a spot where I could observe you unseen. But once I had seen the state you had fallen to, my original plan, that I would go right back, was dropped immediately. It was because my worst fears, which had constantly tormented me since I left you, all proved to be correct.

The myth of a lost paradise is widely spread among many peoples, but since your version is closest to the truth, I will follow it. The garden reported to have been a paradise was simply a well-laid-out stud farm; your first parents, reported to have been so happy there, were just a pair of docile animals. Where was the dignity that we had at first intended for them, where was the wisdom and spirituality? Every trace of each glorious attribute that my Wisdom had bestowed on them on the day of creation had vanished in negation and condemnation; all that remained were a habitual submission to the Word of the Self-Righteous One and a vegetable-like vitality.

First I tried to discover what had become of that other half of their original nature, those glorious attributes bestowed by my Wisdom, which seemed now to have been excised. There was no need to seek far, for they were all hidden inside the fruit of a tree in the middle of the garden, which would later be known to you as the tree of the knowledge of good and evil.

The moment I first looked up at that tree, I felt more contempt than rage toward the self-righteousness and vanity of my Other Half. Although he had surrounded it with an iron fence of the strict Word, he had given it a majestic trunk and fresh leaves, and its fruit had a more appetizing appearance and fragrance than anything else in the entire garden. It was through the painful abstinence and obedience of your first parents—overcoming the strong temptation they felt every time they looked at the tree, and repressing the memory of a right to enjoy beauty and know truth that had left its indelible traces upon their nature—that he affirmed and enjoyed his own absolute power.

Even more outrageous were his explanations of the fruit, full of lies and malevolence. Your poor first parents, taken in by what he said and forgetting completely that knowledge had originally been their proudest feature, regarded the fruit only as a vessel of sin and death. The freedom of choice that my Wisdom had given them was enchained by his self-righteous Word, and mistaking their right to regain it for a dangerous temptation, they struggled against it in fear and trembling.

Once I had realized the extent of their plight, I withdrew briefly to a quiet spot and fell into deep thought. Should I simply accept the self-righteousness of my Other Half and you, its victims? Was I going to have to tolerate his tyranny and his unfair impositions upon you? Was I going to silently watch the fall and self-abasement of my Other Half merely to avoid our tragic disunion, even if it was leading us inevitably to a disastrous mutual negation? I simply couldn't let that happen.

As I said before, Creation was both our right and our duty. Creation must always involve a responsibility for beginning and end. Creation which only has misery as its goal cannot be permitted. Embodying the harmony of our sexual duality, you should be able to enjoy the method by which you were originally formed. What was lost must be found; what was bound must be untied—that was what I decided.

Seeking the party that would carry out that decision, I chose the woman rather than the man. That was Eve, Eternal Mother to you. From the start, I noticed that she would often linger near the tree, casting longing glances at the fruit hanging from its branches.

I decided to secretly send the Snake of Wisdom to tell her the whole truth. As you know, this was no cunning act of temptation, but an earnest and innocent way of informing her. My supposition proved correct. Without needing to be coaxed, your Eternal Mother not only magnificently regained all she had lost, she also freed her clumsy and cowardly husband from the self-righteousness of the Word. Undoubtedly some memory of the first day of her creation, like a faint nostalgia lingering in her soul, enabled her to overcome her fear of Yahweh's incoherent wrath.

You have seen in your travels how all the peoples of the world without exception venerate "the Great Mother" or "the Eternal Mother Goddess." You might consider that to be connected with fertility and agricultural yield, but this is not necessarily so. In present days, now that it has become difficult to link women and agriculture in the old sense, people will often be heard speaking of "salvation by the feminine," which may well reflect a belief in a particular spiritual power transmitted only to women since Eve's deed.

My Other Half was furious at losing the symbol of his complete submission of all creatures in a single morning. His wounded self-righteousness and shattered narcissism turned into a violent hatred that fell on the heads of your first parents. Your pitiful age of ignorance was now replaced by your agonizing age of freedom.

On the very same day, your first parents were expelled from the garden, pursued by all kinds of dreadful punishments. The unanticipated realities of birth and death replaced your everlasting life; discords and tensions previously unknown wrecked your mutual happiness. The earth was cursed and brought forth thorns and thistles; you were only able to get food from the remaining parched land by working and sweating. That was the beginning of your days of hard labor and pain; nights of sorrow, solitude, and fear came upon you. In addition, Eve was made to endure the suffering of pregnancy and childbearing.

You will reproach me, but at that moment there was no way even my Wisdom could deal with such wrath. Our disunion had now grown into an irreversible mutual negation; I did not want to see that unique process of creation and development returned to primeval silence and inaction. Furthermore, the sufferings you were to experience served in part as payment for the price of your regained wisdom and freedom. For these things were what your first parents had originally sold to him to gain access to the bliss they enjoyed in the garden.

The only thing I could do was wait until the tears of your grief and the sweat of your labors had pacified his blind wrath. I prayed anxiously that the day would finally come when this world would once again belong to you, when you would return to it to live, love, and enjoy as the beings you were first designed to be.

It was a mistaken hope on my part. Though you had been expelled from the Garden, that did not mean that you had been liberated from his self-righteousness, his perverted attachments, and his groundless self-confidence. Absurdly enough, he was convinced that you would return to him. He believed that one day his Goodness would overwhelm my Wisdom, and that you would choose righteousness without freedom rather than freedom without righteousness.

That was not all. In the Primal Being we had originally been one, and even after we had each come to self-awareness, the principles that bound us together were still harmony and unity; yet in no time at all, he renounced these original principles and gave himself over to violent feelings of antagonism and unilateralism. He considered the restoration of your first parents' full being to be a defeat, and resolved to achieve a redeeming glory by bringing you back to his self-righteousness by way of the freedom that had been bestowed on you. He was so firmly convinced that this would happen that it seemed he was deliberately ignoring my intrusion.

Moreover, as Eve began to give birth and your numbers increased, there arose among you many who encouraged that false belief of his. They were holy priests and mighty princes; among your people they included the numerous patriarchs of the faith, the fervent prophets, the Judges and Kings. Unable to cope with the freedom they had regained after such struggles, or driven by madness, servility, or by earthly needs, they threw themselves back into the arms of the Self-Righteous One. In the name of Goodness they persecuted Wisdom; advocating righteousness, they trampled on freedom, curried favor with Yahweh, and so added to his unfounded self-confidence.

Yet a larger number of you were different. Although you were unable to become complete in any way on account of our discord, most of you harbored hopes of enjoying both sides, incomplete as that was, rather than let yourselves be imprisoned in goodness without wisdom, in righteousness without freedom; you chose to remain in this world as whole beings, fighting against its harsh nature, rather than abandon the half of their being that had been regained with such difficulty and return to his abundant garden. Even in the records of those most faithful to his teaching, there was no one who chose to put an end to his life solely in the hope of rising to the heavenly kingdom.

The first thing to happen on account of this insubordination was the catastrophe of the great flood. He killed all of you who refused to return to him and, not even willing to trust the only survivor Noah, he established the Law. After forty-nine days of deluge had drowned the age of your freedom, the age of the Law began under the covenant of the rainbow. This was an age of the Word organized by a logic more effective to soothe and pacify you, an age that would look forward to and eventually be perfected by the coming of Moses.

But although he could kill every living thing in the world, he could do nothing about my hidden share of Noah's nature. As his descendants grew in number, this part of him, which had shriveled up over the years, returned to life and stood up to the Law that had been forcefully imposed on humanity. Although he repeatedly laid stress on sin—an imagined entity that doesn't even exist—and alternately terrorized you with harrowing calamities in this world and hellfire in the next world, nothing could intimidate you; likewise, you weren't in the least tempted by the abundance and tranquility of the former Paradise, nor by the new form it was given as his heavenly kingdom. It was always the same vicious circle: unintentional sin and indiscriminate punishment.

That is what befell the citizens of those cursed cities, Sodom and Gomorrah, that now lie deep beneath the Dead Sea; the same fate awaited all those other cities and peoples that your Scriptures record. How many children were flogged without knowing why, how many cities and nations were hurled into the fires of destruction simply for not having become a hothouse of saints?

Like many of the world's holy books, your Scriptures say that their deaths were the wages of sin. But from the beginning no such sin ever existed. As I have already stated several times, what is designated as sin is in fact nothing more than one aspect of the being you received in the beginning. In those times, one part of your nature, which had neither color nor name and knew no division between right and wrong, was treated differently merely because it was judged by the Word of the Self-Righteous One to be bad, and because of the fear provoked by his capricious punishments.

Even accepting that such things as sins exist, you have to realize that the cause of many of them lies with the One who also punishes them. Greed is caused by your shortages, resulting from the barren state of the earth that he had covered with thorns and thistles. Cain's envy and hatred began with his favoritism toward Abel. Your lust is a mixture of the penalty of childbirth with your natural fascination with beauty and novelty. Your squabbles are merely an imitation of the way he distinguishes between even the most petty deeds, classifying them into this and that category.

Blasphemy, which he punishes most severely, is even more contradictory. Insofar as you are truly no one's means and your own end, your faith and obedience can only be purchased by grace and love. Is there anything in the world that does not come with a price? What leaf ever shakes when no wind is blowing? Then what do you have to thank and praise him for, when he drives you out with curses and offers you nothing but laws and punishments?

Your people's records boast of many heroes of faith; but in actual fact what they displayed was not faith but a typical form of weakness and servility. Job only submitted to Yahweh's high-handed persuasion due to the fear of suffering something worse than the bitter grief of losing his property, wives, and children, or having his entire body aflame with boils. Likewise, Jonas only set out for Nineveh because he believed that the punishment of Yahweh might be crueler than the persecutions of the Assyrians.

His unfair system of rewards and punishments also encourages and nurtures you in your so-called sins. Let me cite your records once more. How is it that disasters visited you regardless of good or evil, while good fortune brought you smiles without distinction of right and wrong? Why were Esau's mountains a barren land and his sheep prey for wolves while Jacob's flocks prospered and his crops grew in abundance? How can Noah's curse of Canaan be justified? How could Lot's incest with his two daughters be tolerated? Mount Gilboa, why should you have welcomed the bones of good Jonathan, while you, Jerusalem, saw David's illegitimate son enjoy the royal throne although he had shed his brother's blood? Why was the stone that struck Zechariah so sharp, why was the stone that struck Jeremiah so heavy? If Yahweh truly loved a man who practiced goodness and pursued justice, why did he inherit wrath? And if Yahweh truly hated another man who tilled fields of evil and sowed seeds of poison, why was he able to harvest blessings?

Yet many of you suffered and still suffer cruel punishment on account of this unknowable thing called sin. If you are truly guilty of any sin, it is only the sin of not being able to conform to the Word that arrived after your nature was already formed; the sin of not being willing to suffer hunger and thirst and die quietly; the sin of not letting yourselves be killed or robbed helplessly; the sin of not hypocritically pretending to control your physical desires; the sin of not being cunning enough to flatter the Self-Righteous One; and above all, the sin of not being able to submit to every one of his capricious and arrogant choices.

Still I lay in wait. I lingered for thousands and thousands of years, saying nothing, hoping that his blind fury and wrongheaded stubbornness would melt away. I strove to believe that he would one day awaken from his age-old obsession, the two of us would recover our primeval harmony and order, and then you would find happiness.

It was a hopeless expectation. He grew increasingly intractable, and your misery and unhappiness only increased as time went on. At last, unable to listen any longer to your howls of pain and sorrowful laments, I approached him and attempted to compromise.

First, I proposed that we should govern you according to each one's share. My idea was that, if he controlled the aspects of your nature that came from him, and I those that were mine, you would at least be punished for sin according to your responsibilities, if you had to be. That involved the risk of perpetuating our division, but I wanted at least to lessen the floggings you were receiving without knowing why.

Contrary to my expectations, he rejected my proposal outright. Having mistakenly come to consider my long ages of retreat as a recognition of his superiority, he refused even to accept that we could speak on an equal footing. Now going beyond the vanity of being satisfied with only a half, he was enraged at the prospect of losing what he had taken as his.

I found it quite outrageous, but I withdrew in silence. Then after some hesitation I made him a second proposition: that I would renounce my share. I urged him to take away the freedom that had brought you nothing but suffering, and reinstall you in the former garden. It was a bitter renunciation on my part, but the pain I felt at your unhappiness and misery were such that I felt I could not do otherwise. Despite that enormous concession on my part, he once again flatly rejected my proposal. The reason was that he had long harbored hopes of summoning you back into the kingdom of his self-righteousness, but accomplishing this only after depriving you of your freedom would not have satisfied his vanity. He wanted you to choose him instead of me by your own free will. To that end, he had invented the word "repentance" and disseminated it among you, just as he had beautified his acceptance of you with the word "salvation."

After hesitating for a while, he explained that he would respond to my proposal instead with his "Son of Man" about whom he began to drop hints to your people from early on. With this Son of Man, so he said, he would unravel the long-lasting entanglement between us concerning the Creation.

Your fanatical prophets and their interpreters say this and that, but I know who the Son of Man is that he is going to send. He is a persona, another face of the same coin, localized in my Other Half even before the creation of the universe. He will be called "Son of Man" and will be born with a human body, but he will not be the son of a man in the true sense. He is merely an alter ego of my Other Half, an incarnation of his self-righteousness and his Word.

I think I also know what answer the Son of Man will bring from my Other Half. For that reason I have prepared for his arrival by spurring on the madness of Thedos and similar pretenders, hinting at the answer he has to bring and warning of what will happen if he fails, rousing the hearts of the people to think in advance about what true salvation ought to be like. But my main preparation for his arrival has been you: dearly beloved son of my spirit, anointed with the oil of wisdom.

From the moment when, for some reason or other, my Other Half chose a woman of your people, sent down the "Son of Man" and implanted him in her womb, I have had my eye on you. Before you could follow in your father's footsteps and be hardened by the self-righteous Word, I sent Thedos to you; later, once you were grown up, I prodded you to leave the comfort of your father's home and experience directly the pain and misery of people with their bodies of flesh. Finally I called you away from your home and neighbors to roam through every part of the world, where I showed you the two of us under many different names and appearances. Without all those journeys and experiences, you would never have been able to understand and follow what I am telling you now.

And now, at last, the time has come. The Son of Man sent by my Other Half will soon reveal himself to the world. You must visit him first and discover what answer has been sent with him. If you ask him if he has brought bread, miracles, and worldly power, you will soon be able to discover the plan of my Other Half who is in heaven. If he has indeed come with bread, miracles, and worldly power, these things will be used to coerce you to give up your previous painful freedom, enabling you to regain the former garden and attaining at least a semi-salvation.

But if he has not brought those things, which an ominous fore-boding I've had for some time tells me is the case, that means that Yahweh has once again rejected my appeal. It means that he still believes that the wound to his spiritual vanity can only be healed through your painful freedom, and that even longer and more painful years of wandering and delusion await you. This false Son of Man will say that he has come to initiate a new age of love, but in actual fact he will have come merely to render Yahweh's self-righteousness total.

You must first begin by expelling him from this world, that false Son of Man, that living, moving Word of the Self-Righteous. His venomous breath must be prevented from polluting your innocent souls; the leaven of Yahweh must not be allowed to ferment here. You must become the true Son of Man, protecting this world and humanity. The false Son of Man may have come with a hidden power to perform trifling miracles, and he may also have an exceptionally long and slippery tongue. You will have to fight him as an ordinary, powerless son of man, but never forget that this world and its humanity will always be on your side. Engage all your strength, not for the sake of someone higher but for yourself and those like you; employ all your intelligence, not for a kingdom far away in heaven but for this world that you now tread.

The Great Wisdom spoke again to the Son of Man, saying:

Son of Man, I heard your footsteps coming across the desert as you invoked me, full of dread. How pale your face is, and how you stagger! Why, you are already trembling in fear at an unfounded and unbelievable rumor.

But you, anointed by wisdom, have nothing to dread, nothing to fear. Now that the false Son of Man has gone back to where he came from, the earth is delivered into your hands again. Some thieves rolled aside the stone blocking the door of the tomb and ripped off the shroud, then a pack of coyotes dragged away the body, and the story became exaggerated as it passed from mouth to mouth — why let that bother you? If some weak-minded people, misled by all that, see a ghost and go about whispering that he is risen again, what is there for you to be afraid of? The seeds of the Word that he sowed and the blood that drenched his cross may be a burden to you, but I still believe in the immoveable resolve with which you drove him from the world. I feel certain that, thanks to your vigilance, even if he came again he would be driven out in a hail of stones and obliged once more to return in tears to the One who sent him.

In spite of all that, I have come to you now not because your calls were so ardent but because there are still words that I need to speak to you; I want to tell you what awaits you, now that you can pass beyond time and space.

What I have been striving for was the negation of my Other Half, and you were the agent helping me here on earth. I trained you to oppose the Word of the Self-Righteous who had come down to earth in a human body, and now, since I am afraid he will return to the world one day, I have freed you from the chains of time and space.

However, if you believe that all my efforts have been solely aimed at negating my Other Half, you are mistaken. If you thought that I undertook this long and painful fight with the intention of exalting myself alone on the basis of that negation, you would be making an even greater error. And if you thought that I dreamed of taking possession of this world all by myself, that would be more than an error, it would be a blasphemy against our holiness. Just as goodness becomes self-righteousness when it rules on its own, so too wisdom becomes evil when it reigns supreme. If you replace self-righteousness with evil, it is no different from rescuing a man from drowning and then throwing him into a fire.

My negation was for the sake of a greater affirmation; the confrontation within our duality must ultimately be a process designed to arrive at a greater harmony. I began with a recollection of that primal Great One, but my intended goal was to forge our exalted union in the furnace of dialectic. If there is a god that you should believe in and serve, it is the One we two will become at that moment.

The "Two United as One" of that day will not desire your belief or service. We shall be great and perfect in ourself. We shall feel sorry for you if you waste time and wealth in onerous ceremonies and rituals.

There will be no Law or Word coming to you in our name and troubling you. When we formed you, we gave you everything. Do not waste your time striving to know what our will is. Everything is contained within your souls; it will rise up on its own, without you drawing it out.

As you will not have to fear our wrath, so you must not boast of our approval. We will not rebuke or punish your evil, for that too is part of our creation. Nor will we exalt goodness and reward it, since that too derives from us. You must neither add to nor take away so much as a single mustard seed from what we have given. None of your actions have any kind of distinctive coloration, in heaven as on earth.

Even after our distinctions and interventions have come to an end, goodness will continue to be esteemed among you and love and mercy will be encouraged — not because they make us happy but because they are beneficial to you. As ever, evil must be denounced, hatred and quarreling must be restrained — again, not because we dislike them but because they are harmful to you. You must not kill, so that you can avoid being killed. You must not steal, so that you will not be robbed. You must not commit adultery, for then your wives and daughters will remain chaste. Love your neighbors, then your neighbors will love you. Many other rules will remain, but they will not be a continuation of outdated commandments and laws. They will not be imposed downward from above but will be built upward from below as things agreed among yourselves.

I repeat: you were complete when you were made. Instead of having to always clarify it ourselves, we endowed you with goodness; instead of having to always intervene in affairs, we conferred wisdom on you. It was left up to you whether goodness and wisdom were to be enjoyed together as justice and freedom or taken as your own yokes of self-righteousness and evil.

Do not seek us on that day, gazing pointlessly up at the sky. We have established you on earth, so that is where you should seek salvation and forgiveness. Truly I tell you, there is nothing that can oppress you and add to our holiness. There is nothing that can be taken from you that would add to us. There is nothing that could exalt us by humbling you. Our pleasure should not be at the cost of your pain; your sorrow should not be our joy. Whoever serves you best serves us best; all things come from you and end with you.

When Sergeant Nam had finished reading and put the book down, he found himself feeling far more confused than after reading any other part of Min Yoseop's manuscript. Cho Dongpal's clumsy handwriting and half-baked ideas might be partly to blame, but he found it too absurd to call the spirit that spoke those words a god. Even Sergeant Nam, who was unfamiliar with theological debates, could clearly see that the last section was merely unifying for the sake of unifying. He was hugely disappointed that all of Ahasuerus's anti-Christian logic in his attacks on Jesus only resulted in that ill-defined god.

What disappointed Sergeant Nam even more was that the section seemed not to shed any more light on the investigation. He had been convinced that it would contain clues that would show that his own suspicions about Cho Dongpal were not unfounded; yet despite repeated rereadings, he could not find any. Just as he was falling asleep, he recalled the prayer house where Min Yoseop had last stayed and the words of Preacher Hwang; after reflecting on this, he felt he could see where Min Yoseop's and Cho Dongpal's beliefs had parted ways, but that by no means provided a motive for such a grisly murder.

16

By contrast, the riddle of the identity and activities of Kim Dong-uk was easily solved. The next morning Sergeant Nam went to work with a head cloudy from lack of sleep, and arrived at the office to find that a response had already arrived to the inquiry he had submitted the previous evening. Firstly, Kim Dong-uk was an orphan of no fixed abode who had been exempted from military service on grounds of mental deficiency. Yet he had two previous convictions; his first, for theft, had resulted in nine months' imprisonment with two years suspended; the second, for attempted robbery, earned him a year's imprisonment. More surprising still, he was currently serving time for assault in nearby Hwawon prison. Sergeant Nam and Lieutenant Lee, who had examined the report with him, were dumbfounded.

But as the two of them were discussing the surprising report, Detective Kim, who had been listening to their whispers from his place opposite, suddenly broke in: "What if 'mental deficiency' doesn't mean a handicap but someone a bit deranged? What was the fellow's name?"

"Kim Dong-uk."

Sergeant Nam spoke almost unthinkingly. Detective Kim repeated the name to himself a few times, then leapt to his feet, exclaiming: "Then it must be him!"

"Him? Who?" Lieutenant Lee asked, slightly tense.

"Wait a minute. I'll go and check."

Detective Kim went over to the filing cabinet and began to leaf through the old records. Finally he seemed to find what he was looking for: "It's him, there's no doubt about it. Talk about not seeing what's in front of your nose . . ." Pointing to an entry in the files, he spoke in a way that suggested how proud he was of his amazing memory. Sergeant Nam glanced at the date; it was the very day on which Min Yoseop's body had been discovered. The victim of the assault had been a girl — at which Sergeant Nam suddenly recalled the girl in leather boots and the youth with the shaved head. Now he understood why Cho Dongpal's photo had seemed somehow familiar, and why Detective Kim had been able to recall the name — because of the uncommon nature of the incident.

"But — if he got six months, wouldn't yesterday have been the last day?"

Lieutenant Lee spoke after seeming to be calculating something. He was right. The affair might have been classified as a minor offense, but Kim Dong-uk, or Cho Dongpal rather, had been sentenced to six months in prison; he was due to get out that very day.

Sergeant Nam quickly called a car and went speeding toward Gyeongsan with Detective Im. Cho Dongpal had indeed returned home. He was drinking alone, even though it was still broad daylight; he opened the door of his room to them with a calm expression on his face. Sergeant Nam, who had come in fondling the revolver in his pocket just in case, felt somewhat let down. But determined not to give him a breathing space, he asked sharply: "Cho Dongpal?"

"Why call me by the name I hate and have given up?"

"Who's Kim Dong-uk?"

"Isn't he here in front of you?"

There was something sarcastic in Cho Dongpal's voice as he replied to Sergeant Nam without inviting him into his room. Sergeant Nam raised his voice, inwardly growing angry:"Don't play games with me. Who's Kim Dong-uk?"

"Hey, does it really matter that much? Then I'll tell you. He was a wretched guy I met on a building site. He got sick and died; I buried him, then borrowed his identity and residence cards. It's not so difficult to change the photos, you know."

On hearing that, Sergeant Nam understood Cho Dongpal's transformation. Indeed, that kind of change was not at all difficult in the criminal world. Not long before, he had come across someone who had lost his residence card and gained a criminal record without realizing it. But the important questions lay elsewhere.

"You killed him, didn't you? Min Yoseop, I mean." Sergeant Nam accused him abruptly, as if this change of identity was a critical piece of evidence.

"Why? Was he rich enough to be worth killing? Or were we fighting over some beautiful girl?" Cho Dongpal answered in an unshaken voice. Sergeant Nam was suddenly at a loss for what to say. With nothing but a vague hunch to go by, he still couldn't even guess what his motive had been. He must really be a master criminal.

"Don't play innocent. We found out everything before we came."

He tried to make up for his momentary discomfiture by pretending to know more than he did, but Cho Dongpal only laughed, calling his bluff, then boldly invited them inside:

"You think you know, do you? Well, you might as well come inside. Let's talk over a glass of *soju*."

Refusing to let himself be calmed down by his self-assured mood, Sergeant Nam spoke in a harsher tone: "Shut up and come with us. We'll go to the station and talk there."

Cho Dongpal's expression grew menacing.

"What's all this about? You're spoiling the taste of my drink. You think an ex-con has no rights? They can't have issued an arrest warrant on the strength of a report by someone with a head as dumb as yours. Come inside when I ask you to. Let's not make things more difficult than they have to be."

Strangely enough, there was something overpowering in his voice. Sergeant Nam sensed intuitively that it wouldn't work to use force. He could have jumped on Cho Dongpal and dragged him off to the station but, unwilling to risk a desperate resistance, he left Detective Im in the yard and entered the room.

Once Sergeant Nam had entered and sat down, Cho Dongpal addressed someone in a dark corner of the room: "Shut the door, darling. I can't stand the face of that guy sniffing about the yard for no reason with his hair on end. And bring us another bottle."

He had not recognized her, but it was Kim Sunja crouching there like a figure carved in wood. Detective Im, perched on one end of the veranda, glared angrily at Cho Dongpal, but at a sign from Sergeant Nam he restrained himself, pretending not to have heard his malicious words. Cho Dongpal watched vacantly as the woman rose like a shadow and quietly closed the door. Then he addressed Sergeant Nam again.

"Hearing you'd taken away my 'Book of Quarantania,' I thought you must have understood something of what we were up to. But do you really know? Why I killed him, I mean?"

He admitted the suspicions against him as if he were talking of someone else. Sergeant Nam rejoiced inwardly at the confession, but deliberately spoke in a curt, firm voice: "I know everything."

His reply came from a desire not to be too dependent on the other's good will. It seemed to provoke Cho Dongpal, whose tone suddenly became sarcastic again.

"Don't talk nonsense. If I stay silent, the prosecution will have a very hard time making a case against me."

That was certainly true. With no material proof and no clear motive for murder, it would be hard to arrest him, let alone arraign him. The only solution was to get him to tell them everything they needed; but the distinct impression that his had been a crime of conviction, and the strong personality indicated by his prominent nose and upward slanting eyes, suggested that it would be impossible to force anything out of him in the interrogation room.

"It was surely a stupid power struggle. About your doctrines . . ."

Recalling Min Yoseop's notebooks and the "Book of Quarantania" as well as the groups they had led in various towns, Sergeant Nam tried to probe without much confidence. Cho Dongpal laughed sneeringly as if to say it was nonsense.

"Our doctrine? Can there be a doctrine without followers?"

"Then what was that business with those kids you gathered everywhere? And why write that Quarantania Book or whatever it is?"

"Ah, so that's what you're thinking of."

Cho Dongpal smiled contemptuously before continuing.

"You're not so wrong; we started those notes with the idea of making our own scriptures. We even had an ambition of canonizing the rest of Min Yoseop's notebooks and turning them into a proper Bible. But we gave that up long ago. God wills, but it's man who acts. And what really drove me on was the fever of action, so things turned out as they did. And those kids—they weren't our followers. We intended to train a few of them as apostles, but they were mostly just the objects of the belief we were practicing. In reality, right up to the moment when Min Yoseop finally sent them packing, they had no idea they were being brought up and cared for according to any kind of doctrine."

"So why kill him?" Sergeant Nam asked casually, sensing that a strange fever was beginning to invade Cho Dongpal's voice. His question was a step back from his previous claim that he knew everything.

"Now you're speaking frankly. You should have asked earlier." Cho Dongpal broke into a gratified smile as he spoke, emptied his glass in a single gulp, then asked, as if he were the one interrogating Sergeant Nam, "Do you really know what the relationship between him and me was?"

"Of course."

"The same as my father and mother still believe—that Min Yoseop led me astray?"

Sergeant Nam knew that this wasn't the case; but being anxious not to interrupt the flow of words, he replied with what he wanted to hear: "More or less."

"Wrong. Since you've already been investigating, you must know about the high school I attended. In those days, that school was considered one of the ten best in the country. And I was at the top of the class until my second year. I was eighteen when I left home ... and as for Min Yoseop, it was my own decision to follow him. His beliefs and his lonely struggle to practice them were so beautiful and persuasive.

"It was he who tried to get rid of me. When he left our house in the middle of the night like he was running away, it was because of me; in a way, my daring way of putting things into practice had already begun to frighten him."

Cho Dongpal's voice was beginning to tremble, perhaps on account of the drink or his excitement. Sergeant Nam suddenly saw that he was childish and immature for his age.

"Then how did you meet up with him again?"

"I spent two months wandering around looking for him. In those days I couldn't even imagine what it meant to be out there alone; I was pretty desperate. I finally found him on a construction site in Daejeon. Naturally, he tried to persuade me to go back home, but I couldn't go back. He had smashed the idol I had always served and utterly destroyed the faith and system of values I had previously treasured. He had been intending to build a new world on those ruins, but then he suddenly wanted to abandon me ...

"I clung to him desperately. I begged to be allowed to share in that new and splendid world he had created in his heart. He was reluctant, but he finally accepted me."

"When you robbed your parents, was that to get money to go looking for him?"

"You know about that? You mean my parents know too?"

Cho Dongpal seemed to be taken aback for a moment. But he continued on with his own tale, as if any thoughts of his parents were unimportant.

"Sure, I robbed our house, but it wasn't for the money. I needed a special ritual to ensure that my departure would be irreversible.

"It must have been about three days after I first left home. I had been wandering around the wharves in Masan, thinking Min might have gone there. I had walked until it was getting dark without being able to find him; suddenly I longed to go back home. I was madly homesick, so I went back—but just as I entered the alley and could see the lamp in front of our house, I suddenly saw how wretched and weak I was, so attached to the animal-like bonds of blood and the home comforts that they offer. That was what made me decide to rob our house on the spur of the moment. I wanted to make it a place I would never be able to go back to.

"Of course, it was not an easy thing to do. But by calling up memories of a mother who took the meager earnings from out of a whore's hand, and a father who double-crossed his fellow smugglers to get a reward, I was able to treat them as mercilessly as any bandit. I even took the wedding ring mother had worn on her finger for dozens of years; but then, finally, as I was warning them that I would kill them if they informed the police, I found myself getting choked up. If you say they guessed it was me, that must have been the reason . . .

"Of the money I took, I kept just the little I needed, then shared out the rest as I had already decided, to a peddler-woman with three small kids and a husband sick with TB, to shantytown folk feeding a family of six with one measure of flour a day . . ."

"So that was where it started," Sergeant Nam interrupted. "Yet from what I've read there's nothing in your doctrine encouraging you to do that sort of thing . . ." It was something he had been curious about from the start.

Cho Dongpal glanced quickly at him and suddenly raised his voice:

"You've got it wrong. Our god had put everything in our hands. Whatever we could forgive one another for was forgiven by him. But that was not where it started, as you think. If it had not been for Kim Dong-uk's death, we would probably still be relying on our trivial labor and the sympathy of an untrustworthy society."

"Kim Dong-uk's death?"

"That's right. That day I took the dying man on my back and went around to all the hospitals; meanwhile Min Yoseop was making the rounds of the fancy charities, begging for help. But in the end I had no choice but to carry him back to our tent, and Min Yoseop returned empty-handed. They can erect shiny clock towers for everyone to see at the corners of public squares, or fund scholarships that fill a little corner of a newspaper, but they had no money at all for a wretched laborer dying before their very eyes.

"I decided that the time had come for us to act. We realized that even while we were sighing in vain and shedding pointless tears of pity, many other Kim Dong-uks were dying."

Strangely, Cho Dongpal's eyes were losing their brightness, though his voice remained strong. That somehow made him look stupid, helping Sergeant Nam to remain detached from the man's incomprehensible passion.

"Were your two convictions under Kim Dong-uk's name because of that?"

"That's right. I had no bread to satisfy this world's wants, no ability to work miracles, and no power to impose justice. All I could do was transfer the goods of those unfairly possessing too much to people with far too little. Of course, you would call that larceny and robbery."

"But you were caught taking a clock from some small inn and attempting some clumsy burglaries—they weren't exactly big heists, were they?"

"That's your problem, Detective. Those two convictions were occasions when I deliberately bungled things in order to let myself be caught. In my experience, there's no safer hiding place than prison. On a day when I'd pulled off a big job, if I let myself be caught for a petty theft you would leave me right there under your noses while you went running after the wrong suspect. Besides, Kim

Dong-uk was mentally deficient . . . At best, it meant a few months' rest and when I came out it would all be over. Among the unsolved cases in Daejeon, four years back, there should be one where a guy who'd made a fortune by speculating got knifed and robbed of nearly five million Won. With several previous jobs it had become hard for me to stay there any longer, so I deliberately made a big strike; then on the morning of the day following I walked out of the inn where I'd been staying taking a wall clock with me. Then two years ago in Incheon, a young fool who'd become rich buying and selling real estate got robbed, and on the morning of the very next day I vanished into a police station. After handing over the money to Min Yoseop, I went to a neighborhood close to a police station and pretended to be attempting a mugging . . ."

Sergeant Nam felt utterly dazed. There was the brazenness of the confession of course, but more amazing than that was the boldness and ingenuity of the hiding place. It was true that no one would ever imagine that a bandit who had successfully got away with millions of Won thirty minutes earlier would try to take a few thousand from the pocket of a passerby in the street. Especially when the person brought in had been released from military service on grounds of mental deficiency.

Still, it was no mere matter for admiration. Even taking into account the particular characteristics of a crime of conviction, the motives for the crime were too far removed from common sense. In order to test him once more, Sergeant Nam applied sarcasm in place of admiration.

"It's all the same. Whether you stole a few million or a few billion, how many people can you help with that? Are you some kind of belated Hong Gildong or Robin Hood?"

"Because you've been reading Min Yoseop's notebooks, you're talking just like him. I know that if you transform the fundamental structures of society you can help far more people, more effectively, than any belated Hong Gildong. And of course I've heard stories of priests somewhere in Latin America hiding submachine guns under their clerical robes and fighting to bring down structures of oppression and exploitation. But that is as remote and as difficult

as Christian salvation. At this very moment, on every street corner, our neighbors are starving, sick, and dying; where can we find
time for such long-term plans? Better to save one person suffering
before your very eyes now than make plans that might save a million in some unspecified future time. You create an ideology, then
expect to change the world by means of its dissemination, just like
that? That's less realistic than hoping the rich will suddenly wake
up and set about healing the wounds of the world. The betterment
of the world is always delayed because action goes chasing blindly
after philosophy and logic. I, on the other hand, tell them to follow behind and lead the way with action. The beauty of action lies
in achieving something definite, however small . . ."

Cho Dongpal was becoming increasingly excited, as if he had
been waiting for this. Although all that was not without interest,
it was too unrelated to their present business, so Sergeant Nam
turned the conversation in a more practical direction.

"Very interesting. But that will do for now. But tell me: did you
put yourself in prison purposefully again this time? To hide after
having killed Min Yoseop?"

"Now you know."

Unexpectedly, Cho Dongpal assented easily. Yet he was emp-
tying one glass after another, as if unable to subdue his inner confusion. Sergeant Nam was worried that he would get too drunk,
but did not try to stop him, figuring that it would at least keep the
words flowing. In fact, the more he drank, the more animated he
seemed to become.

"So that explains your situation; but what was Min Yoseop doing before he died? I know you and he always kept together."

"He was mainly in charge of the distribution. Occasionally he
helped with the robbing, but unless I judged it was absolutely safe,
I never involved him in what I was doing; when I was arrested, I
never got him involved. You see, that man was not simply the authority serving to justify me, he was the logic and philosophy capable of following behind and interpreting my actions, which were
going on ahead, leading the way. He was also the agent who stayed
outside and cared for people while I was in prison."

"Then why did you kill him?" Trying hard to conceal any appearance of an interrogation, Sergeant Nam finally asked about what puzzled him most. The strain of his dissimulation made his voice tremble awkwardly, but Cho Dongpal replied without paying any particular attention to that.

"Because he had abandoned our god."

"Your god? The one in the Book of Quarantania?"

"Of course. We had already discovered that one god a long time ago. Not being very good at writing, I could only depict him as I did, but that god had been the crystallization of our long quest and the ultimate expression of our minds. I suppose you've read it—a god not involved in notions of good and evil or value judgments; a god that does not impose yokes on the First Being by a belated Word; a god that forgives and approves of everything; a god that does not meddle in life on this earth by means of heaven or hell; a god that does not desire submission and worship, does not demand sacrifices and devotion; a god that trusts our wisdom and reason, making us completely free . . ."

Unlike the sarcastic tone he had adopted earlier, Cho Dongpal's voice had begun to ring with an over-sincere, almost frantic fervor. Noticing this, Sergeant Nam quickly interrupted his flood of words and oriented the conversation back in the direction he wanted.

"Yes, I've read it. But how did Min Yoseop betray that god?"

Cho Dongpal suddenly awoke from his frenzy and opened the new bottle that his wife, approaching like a faint shadow, had placed in front of him. His hand was shaking visibly. Seeing him fill the glass to overflowing, Sergeant Nam was on the verge of stopping him but restrained himself. Apart from an incoherent confession and unreliable circumstantial evidence, he had still not been able to obtain anything solid. Besides, as he thirstily emptied his glass and shut his eyes tightly, as if gathering his thoughts, Cho Dongpal's face radiated a kind of dignity that appeared unchallengeable.

"It was just six months ago. I had completed my second term inside and was duly released. I came looking for him; he had moved here to Daegu. But the twenty kids, who should have been there to welcome me, had all dispersed. Following a note from him, I went to the boarding house where he had gone to live, but he had already left there, leaving behind a long letter.

"Until then, I had no idea that he had gone and shut himself up inside that prayer house. Even if the way he had sent the kids away worried me, at most I assumed that the past had begun to catch up with him, and he had temporarily scattered the group and gone into hiding somewhere. But . . . it wasn't like that. He knew perfectly well when I was due to be released, yet he only turned up three days later, and out of the blue he said we should part ways. He said he had taken the money in the savings account and the key money from the house, given it all to the kids and sent them off for good . . ."

"Why so suddenly?"

"In order to go back to his former god and his church. Back into that religion of women and slaves, that self-righteous Word and that masochistic fervor . . . He said he had grown lonely and afraid. He was tired of our god who never smiled or grew angry, who was never happy or sad, who never rebuked or praised; he came to think that actions disengaged from any notion of good or evil—evil without punishment, and good without reward—were all equally hollow."

Cho Dongpal reached for the bottle of liquor and brought it up to his lips, drinking several gulps with his eyes closed. Although anyone would find Cho Dongpal's behavior odd, Sergeant Nam was so taken with his story that he simply stared at him blankly and waited for him to go on.

"He also said that whether we were pursuing the theological eradication of the individual, or developing a theology of revolution, or even joining hands with Marxism, we should always remain 'in God'—that no matter how irrational it might seem, ultimately we had to leave salvation and forgiveness to heaven. Then he concluded that, while we had labored to construct our new god as if we had received some kind of sacred calling, our half-baked knowledge and vague notions were actually only leading us to reproduce the crudest form of atheism—and that what we had believed so surely to be a god had been at most the God of Reason, who had appeared like a kind of madness during the Century of Revolutions and then vanished in derision, if it was not merely the deification of a vulgar, rough kind of ethics. After all that, he was going back to the foot of the cross in a shameful, exaggerated repentance.

"But I could not follow him. Since he had made it himself, he could destroy it himself, whereas I had received it from him and could not destroy it. Regarding practice too, he had always vacillated on the threshold between hesitation and doubt, so that going back would be easy for him; while I, on the other hand, had fallen in far too deep and had no way to turn back. Rather than confront him with hopeless arguments, I tried to hold him back in the name of the long years I had spent with him. On my knees I begged him not to go back to Yahweh, I entreated him with tears. But in the end it was to no avail.

"After he left that night, I did not sleep a wink. I felt that the world had suddenly become an empty, lonely place. Then as dawn broke, I heard a great roar, as if the world I had trusted in all that time had collapsed. He himself had been that world. Ever since I set out to follow him, my life had found its meaning in him; all my actions had found their justification by him. Then in a moment everything crumbled. A bottomless abyss opened up beneath my feet. There was nothing left but the wretchedness of Sancho Panza watching Don Quixote emerge from his illusions.

"I tried my hardest to forget him. I resolved to stand on my own two feet, to think for myself, to go groping along my path without him. I even fostered an ambition of going beyond him and perfecting our notion of holiness. But there was one thing I could not forgive. That was the sign of our defeat, he himself kneeling in front of the cross shedding humiliating tears of repentance at the very hour when I would be engaged in my painful struggle. With him there like that, it was as if I would never be able to begin anything on my own again. It seemed that I and my new god would only be safe if he were eliminated. So, after hours of detailed planning, I went to find him at the prayer house he was staying in . . ."

Cho Dongpal once again paused and raised the bottle to his lips. For some time, the sound of Detective Im's impatient throat clearings outside the door had been reminding him to hurry up. At last Sergeant Nam began to realize that his behavior was much too relaxed for a detective confronting a murder suspect, yet he continued to stare at Cho Dongpal, seized by a strange feeling. Perhaps the interest and curiosity accumulated over the course of the past few months had overwhelmed his sense of professional duty. For his part, Cho Dongpal seemed to have completely forgotten the very existence of Sergeant Nam; taking the bottle from his lips, he began to chatter again. He gave the impression of someone pursued.

"It was still dark, very early in the morning, when I climbed the hill behind the prayer house, unobserved by anyone. I was familiar with his habit of going for a stroll at dawn, so I selected a lonely wooded path that he seemed likely to take, and waited. I had been standing there shivering for about an hour when he appeared, as if I had summoned him. I don't know if he had been praying all night, or if he hadn't been able to sleep on account of me, but his hair looked disheveled in the dim light and his face was haggard. I lured him into the woods, and pleaded with him there one last time. Once more I fell to my knees, joined my hands and begged . . ."

Seemingly out of breath, Cho Dongpal stopped talking, but this time he didn't drink. He clenched his teeth as if suppressing pain and spoke with difficulty.

"It was no use. Instead he urged me to return with him to the foot of the cross. He wanted us to make a new beginning there. When I realized there was no way I could make him change his mind, I pulled out the knife. But, still . . ."

Cho Dongpal was suddenly seized by a convulsion that interrupted his story. He seemed to try to gather his strength to overcome it, and then, as if finding that useless, raised the bottle to his lips with a shaking hand. He was breathing in harsh gasps. Sensing now that something was seriously wrong, Sergeant Nam snatched the bottle from his hand.

"You've drunk too much. No more."

Cho Dongpal resisted briefly, then gave up, and began talking again.

"He showed no special alarm, and did not try to escape. I might be wrong, but I thought I could see a slight smile on his lips. His eyes seemed to have filled with a kind of mysterious light . . . then, blinded by a sudden hatred, I lunged at his breast with my knife . . ."

At that moment Cho Dongpal curved in on himself, unable to finish what he was saying, and fell forward. His teeth were clenched so hard that the veins of his neck stood out strongly; he was clearly suffering some kind of intense pain. Surprised, Sergeant Nam helped him sit up and questioned him urgently, "What's wrong? What's the matter?"

But Cho Dongpal made no reply. Clutching his stomach as if suffering from spasms, he squirmed violently. Kim Sunja, who until then had been sitting there like a still life observing her husband, threw herself facedown on the floor and began to sob quietly. Hearing Sergeant Nam's urgent cry, Detective Im wrenched open the door and rushed in. His face was tense and he had even pulled out his revolver.

"It's not the drink. Get the car, quickly. I'll carry him down." Sergeant Nam barked the order as he pulled Cho Dongpal onto his back. Detective Im glared at him angrily, then hurried out.

"It's very late. This man took a fatal dose of poison several hours ago. Seeing the way that alcohol helped delay the effect, I suppose it may have been methanol. I'll do what I can, but it will be difficult. Retinal edema has already set in." The middle-aged doctor shook his head as he spoke.

Cho Dongpal regained consciousness just once before he died. Like the sudden flare of an expiring candle, he spoke in a tone clearer than ever before:

"Don't think that I've fallen defeated like him. What's summoning me now is Min Yoseop's blood, not any kind of despair about our god. What will remain alive forever is our god, before this hour and after this hour; even if nobody is able to sense it, his solitary holiness will always be shining above your heads . . ."

About the Author

YI MUN-YOL was born in Seoul in 1948 and is the author of numerous books, including *Hail to the Emperor!*, *Our Twisted Hero*, and the novella *Saehagok*, which won the New Spring Literary Contest sponsored by *Dong-a-Ilbo*. He is among South Korea's most celebrated writers, and is currently a chair professor at Hankuk University of Foreign Studies in Seoul.

About the Translator

Born in England in 1942, BROTHER ANTHONY has lived in Korea since 1980. He is currently an emeritus professor of Sogang University and chair-professor of Dankook University. He has published over 30 volumes of translations, including Yi Mun-yol's *The Poet*.